OMEGA POINT
PRODUCTIONS

((FREQUENCIES))

$$\Omega \;\; \infty \;\; \Delta \;\; \alpha$$

JOSHUA ORTEGA

((FREQUENCIES))
An Omega Point Productions™ book

First printing, trade paperback edition / June 1999
8 7 6 5 4 3 2 1

ISBN 0-9671120-4-4

PRINTED IN THE UNITED STATES OF AMERICA BY:
MORRIS PUBLISHING   KEARNEY, NE

Ω Ω Ω Ω Ω Ω Ω Ω Ω Ω Ω Ω Ω Ω Ω Ω Ω
Omega Point Productions™
PO Box 85690
Seattle, WA 98145-1690
Phone: (206) 729-6509
FAX: (630) 214-6115
info@omegapp.com
www.omegapp.com
Ω Ω Ω Ω Ω Ω Ω Ω Ω Ω Ω Ω Ω Ω Ω Ω Ω

To everyone and everything that helped me get to this Ω point.

Thank you.

ACKNOWLEDGEMENTS

I would especially like to thank the following individuals for their contributions to the book:

My editors–Alexis Coronetz, Jeffrey Morris, Sunny Knight, and Mark Stromberg–for generously volunteering their time and energy to help me smooth out the tale's rough edges.

Jessica Panetto-Ortega, for being there at the project's α point, and for all of the wonderful suggestions, support, editing, and advice along the way.

Cynthia Lair of Moon Smile Press, for her extremely helpful advice on self-publishing and the book industry in general.

And Sue Aho, for doing such an amazing and incredible job in bringing my logo designs to perfection.

NOTE FROM THE AUTHOR

There is a glossary found within the appendix of this book. Please refer to it when you are unable to find the word or term you are looking for in your dictionary.
It should be there (along with lots of other interesting things).

Now, on to the show...

Ω

∞

"We are all one.
A living, incorporate frequency emission.
A single, electromagnetic wavelength called life."

–Dr. Adrian Wellor

Δ

α

Ω

Chapter 1:
Law and Order

*"It was as if an infinite number of frequencies had converged
at one single point in space and time, their combined vibrations
forming a seemingly coherent structure out of an apparently random
disarray. Order out of chaos...*

The red lighting of the surrounding garage projected onto Marc McCready's face like a dull, unfocused laser sight. He eased back into the soft Gelaform™ cushioning of the driver's seat, placed his left thumb upon the dashboard scanner, and apathetically spoke his current password, "Whatever."

The uniview screen mounted in the car's central console glowed to life, quickly resonating into the Ordosoft™ logo–the Greek letter alpha melded with the "r" in the word "Ordosoft™." The corporation's symbol then morphed into a cartoonish image of Marilyn Monroe in a white dress.

"Biochip scan and password/voicewave confirmation completed," the attractive toon stated in the digitally-sampled voice of its famous likeness, each word blending together flawlessly with its facial animation. "Good morning, Agent McCready."

"Yeah, we'll see," McCready said with a small yawn. He placed his tongue behind the bridge of his teeth and sucked in a few times, tasting the bitter aftertaste that the instant latté had left in his mouth. "Voice-rec on."

"Voice recognition activated," sounded Marilyn's vocals throughout the car's encircling speaker system, as her cartoon counterpart tilted her head to one side and gave a cheerful smile.

McCready rubbed his eyes and face with the palm of his left hand, halfheartedly attempting to wipe away the drowsiness that he had been feeling all morning.

The attempt failed. He wasn't surprised.

"Patch me through to HQ," he said.

"Connecting to Freemon Headquarters, Seattle division."

The cartoon Marilyn morphed into an image of the department's logo–a circle around the face of a spotted owl, its pitch-black eyes gazing directly out at the viewer.

"Secure sattelink confirmed. One moment, please."

"N.J., deactivate vocal confirmation," McCready said, his stare remaining fixed upon the iconic owl. "You don't need to tell me everything you're doing." He always found himself drawn to the logo, even though he'd seen the image thousands of times. There was something in the owl's gaze... The way it looked at you. Like it *knew*.

"That's unusual, Marc," observed the Chevrolet®, sensually accentuating each syllable it spoke, "you normally prefer vocal confirmation."

"Well, sweetheart," McCready said, "I guess things change, don't they?"

The Freemon logo transformed into the head and shoulders of fellow agent Erik Takura, who was currently seated in front of the uniview screen located at his desk, the usual cheshire grin stretched wide across his face. "McCready," he said with a subtle laugh, "you supposed to be up yet, slick? I don't think your face is quite ready to show itself to the world today."

"And yours *is*?" McCready asked bluntly, as he looked over Takura's visage.

Multiple piercings on his ears, eyebrows, nose, and lower lip. Raven-black hair to his shoulders, the ends split and dyed pumpkin-orange. An intriguing blend of Japanese and European facial features. Green eyes the shape of a cat's, the product of gengineered, cybernetic implants.

"*Always*," Takura replied, his grin widening to reveal his perfectly straight, immaculately white rows of teeth. "What's goin' down?"

"You're the one with the sattelink in his head, you tell me." McCready shifted slightly in his seat, molding the Gelaform™ to the contours of his back. "Any freeker activity I should check out before I come down there?"

FREQUENCIES

"Hold on a sec," he said, "let me look."

McCready could always tell when Takura went online. Erik's head would slightly twitch, his feline pupils would dilate, and the ever-present grin would momentarily droop down at the corners of his mouth. This all happened in the span of about two seconds, and then he was back to normal. Or, McCready thought, at least as normal as a human with an optic microprocessor and a wireless modem in his brain *could* be.

"Okay," Takura said, talking out loud as he mentally surfed the data waves. "Accessing freereads...scanning for freeker activity... Crossreferencing location, occurrence frequency, proximity of others... Wetwyre™ in Kirkland has some activity, but Ignacio's already responded..."

Ignacio was on a case. Now McCready had something to look forward to. Even if his day turned out to be as shitty as his morning, at least he could count on a twisted tale from Ignacio.

"...Boeing®, no...Microsoft®, no...okay, here we go–I think I got something," Takura said, as he thumbed a gold lip ring. "Farmaceutical Solutions™ in Redmond...there's a steadily increasing freeker reading from an employee, a Lee Samuels...it's not the first instance, either... Corpos haven't been alerted yet, so I'm assuming he's not being real vocal about his thoughts, but there *are* quite a few other employees near him should he decide to get chatty... Yeah, this one's worth checking out. I'm sending the GPS coordinates to your car right now. From your current West Bellevue location, it shouldn't take long to get there."

A falter in the grin, pupils contracting, and a jerk of the head, Takura was offline.

McCready stared at Takura for a moment, wondering what it would be like to experience cyberspace that intimately, to immerse yourself within the electronic matrix just by thinking the thought. No external wires or electrodes, no screens, no gogs, no contacts... All of it occurring within the confines of your cybernetically augmented brain. What would that be like? He hastily disregarded the question like an executioner considering a condemned man's innocence, deciding that he had no interest whatsoever in finding the answer out for himself.

"What?" Takura asked, noticing McCready's pause.

Nothing, McCready thought. But the feeling expressed itself vocally anyways. "I don't think I could ever do what you do, Erik–have cerebral implants installed in my head."

Takura's grin became a full-blown smile, accompanied with a

3

loud laugh. "That's because you're a relic, McCready! Look at you. You got a car named after a twentieth-century movie star, you pack a weapon with bullets, and you have *the* most archaic piece of bionic hardware on the whole squad. Face it, slick," he said with a shrug of the shoulders, "you're just not ready for the future yet."

McCready briefly glanced down at his artificial limb, then back to the uniview screen. "Fuck you, borg-boy," he said with an uneasy snicker, realizing that the younger Freemon's words had a ring of truth about them. "I'm as ready as anyone."

"Hey, don't convince *me*," he said. "Convince yourself. I'll see you when you get here." The image of Takura briefly morphed back into the accusatory owl, then continued its metamorphosis until it was once again the Marilyn toon.

McCready raised his right hand in front of his face and pulled the black, leather glove from off of it, revealing the titanium/aluminum alloy prosthesis which had been hidden underneath. "Archaic, huh?" he muttered to himself as he wiggled his five artificial digits, each of their individual motions producing a barely-audible whirring sound. Well, he had to admit, it certainly wasn't state of the art. He could've chosen the model with near-perfect neurological stimulators and a grafted, gengineered skin surrounding it. Or the luxury option–having a genetically accelerated clone grown from your DNA, then removing the needed limb from the clone's body and integrating it into your own... But both of these possibilities required some type of direct brain stimulation, either through implants or neurochemical injections–and McCready didn't want anything or anyone fucking around with his head. Shit, it was bad enough already that everyone in the technologized nations had freereads grafted onto their skulls. Anything else only added insult to injury.

"Marc," Norma Jean said, "the coordinates that Agent Takura transmitted have been programmed into my global positioning system. I'm ready to engage the frequency emissions violator when you are."

"Right. Time to get to work," McCready replied, pulling the glove snugly over his bionic hand and flexing it into a fist a few times to make sure the fit was tight. "Let's do it."

"Manual or automatic?"

McCready smiled. "Manual, Norma Jean. I'm *definitely* feeling manual today," he said. "So I hope you weren't in the mood to drive yourself."

"Considering that I wasn't programmed with moods," the car stated, as the cartoon image pulled a chair out of thin air and seated herself in it, "I don't think that will be a problem."

"Well, alright then, everybody's happy. N.J.," he said, popping a few of his knuckles, "retract roof cover."

The garage roof above the car parted open, curving in segments as they slid themselves down along the tracks located on the sides of the two corresponding walls. As the roof opened wider, the lighting of the sun began to replace the red glow of the garage lights, causing McCready's eyes to wince from the glare. He reached into one of the inside pockets of his hunter-green trenchcoat, pulled out his custom Obsidians™, and placed them onto his face. The sunglasses immediately reduced the sunlight's glare, with absolutely no color or vision loss. He relaxed his eyes. Perfect.

"Activate rear-view screen," McCready said, wrapping his left hand around the soft rubber grip of the steering wheel. "Normal size."

A circular, 2-D hologram projected itself from a laser lens on the dashboard to a position located exactly where a rear-view mirror would be found on a typical, gravity-bound car. The holographic screen, which had a radius of roughly six inches, transmitted a live-feed from four cameras mounted on the top, bottom, and rear of the vehicle, forming a quadrant of different views. The upper-left quadrant currently showed both the sky and the opening where the roof used to be, while the upper-right quadrant displayed the reinforced-concrete wall directly behind the vehicle. Nothing but the ground below could be seen on the lower quadrants.

McCready reached down with his gloved right hand, grasped a lever which was similar to the afterburner control on an old, military fighter jet, and said, "Enable GS." As he closed his hand around the lever's handle, the pressure-sensors in the palm and fingers of his bionic limb instantly relayed their signals through the wires and electrodes that were spliced into the corresponding nerve endings found at the base of what remained of his forearm, allowing him some semblance of the sensation of touch. Not perfect, but he knew when he grabbed a hold of something.

He looked up at the sky through the nearly transparent Plexiglas® covering which comprised the frontal section of the vehicle's roof. Seeing that the sky above him was clear of any direct airborne traffic, he began to slowly pull the lever backwards. The car gently rose off the ground and up towards the opening in the garage's roof, the electromagnetic, gravity-shielding mechanisms housed within the vehicle functioning in their usual, reliable manner.

As the midnight-black Chevy® Polaris™ emerged from the garage adjoined to his house, McCready smoothly panned his head from side to side, taking in a 180-degree view of his environs. It was an unusually sunny March day, allowing for a crystalline view of the surrounding area.

To the east were the iridescent, mirrored, and gleaming contemporary skyscrapers of Bellevue's corporate district, set against the backdrop of the snow-capped mountains of the Cascades and the glimmering waters of Lake Sammamish. To the south, Mount Ranier perched upon the horizon like an angry god, its partially exploded top serving as divine testament to the quake of 2022. Hovering majestically in the heavens above Lake Washington to the southwest, was the sky-city of Mercer Island, while across the lake and to the west, downtown Seattle's formidable–though somewhat antiquated–skyline juxtaposed itself in an awkwardly beautiful way with the Olympic mountain range behind it.

"Close roof cover," McCready said, as he watched a green Lexus® fly by quickly in front of him. Checking the bottom two quadrants of the rear-view screen to make sure that the garage roof had fully closed, he spun the steering wheel all the way to the left, and lightly pressed his foot on the acceleration pedal. The Polaris™ began to gently turn in place as if it were positioned on an axis.

When the car was facing a northeasterly direction that would put him in line with Redmond, he released his foot from the pedal, and returned the steering wheel to its neutral position. The vehicle stopped its rotation.

"Access my musical databank," he stated, simultaneously pressing a button on the central console. A small compartment located underneath the uniview screen ejected open.

"Do you have a particular selection that you would like to hear?" asked Norma Jean, as her cartoon counterpart began to dance a few steps sampled directly from *Gentlemen Prefer Blondes*.

McCready shook his head as he reached two of his bionic fingers into the compartment's opening and grasped one of the tiny, white pellets found within. "Nope–why don't you surprise me."

"What kit would you like the random selection to be played from?"

McCready popped the Altoid® peppermint into his mouth and began to suck on it, thankful to be rid of the latté's lingering aftertaste. "How about something from the '90's?" He pressed the same button once again, causing the compartment of mints to retreat back into their central console lair. "Late '90's–something from my 'smooth' kit."

"One moment, please," the car politely stated, as its uniview image continued to dance while it accessed the particular kit. Two seconds passed, then the opening drum beat of Maxwell's "Gravity: Pushing to Pull" began to play over Norma Jean's stereo speakers.

"I like it," McCready said with a sly smile, pulling down the visor located above his head. He looked in the mirror that was embedded into the soft material of the overhead flap, and fleetly ran his fingers through his spiky, jet-black hair. "Alright, let's do this." McCready pushed the visor back to its original position and replaced his hand upon the steering wheel. As keyboards and bass blended in with the drum beat of the song, he pressed down firmly on the acceleration pedal, and the rear, solar/electric-powered turbofans shot the car forward. Reaching the air-speed limit of 90 miles per hour, McCready then raised his altitude to the region reserved for only law enforcement and emergency vehicles, boosted his speed by another 30 m.p.h., and swiftly flew through the atmosphere towards his destination.

Within minutes, he had reached downtown Redmond, the location of both Farmaceutical Solutions™ and the freeker who was employed there. He removed his right foot from the accelerator and began to lightly tap his left foot upon the brake pad. The vehicle's velocity gently diminished to a cruising speed.

"N.J.," McCready said, "activate console map and plug in the GPS coordinates that Takura sent you."

On the uniview screen, the dancing Norma Jean morphed into a highly detailed, three-dimensional grid of the surrounding civic area. The Farmaceutical Solutions™ building was highlighted with a glowing red outline, while McCready's position on the grid was represented by a tiny, precisely rendered icon of the Polaris™.

"That close already..." he remarked out loud, as he looked over the map. "N.J., go ahead and take over. Activate auto control."

The grid transformed back into the cartoon Marilyn, who was now seated inside of a red '57 Chevy®, one hand on the steering wheel and the other adjusting the rear-view mirror. "We will be arriving at Farmaceutical Solutions™ in a few moments," she said with a confident smile. "Please relax and enjoy the ride."

McCready released his hands from the steering wheel and GS lever, clasped his fingers together, and stretched his arms out in front of him. He held the position for a few seconds, then pulled his fingers apart and relaxed his arms. As usual, the previous night's sleep had been a little rough, and his body was now fully feeling the effects. He gently extended and tilted his head from side to side, easing some of the pressure within the stiff and sore muscles of his neck. The stretching caused him to reflexively let out a long and drawn out yawn, expelling from his lungs the extra carbon dioxide which had been eager to escape its confinement. As the automatic control systems began to descend the car from its high altitude, McCready looked over the downtown Redmond area.

While not quite as large and sprawling as Bellevue's downtown, Redmond's structures were every bit as impressive and modern as those of its southern neighbor. The look and feel of the landscaping, however...that was an entirely different matter. Whereas Bellevue had the occasional city park and a few trees dotting its city streets, Redmond was abundant with gardens and parks filled with all types of vegetation, and its streets were lined with tall pines, firs, cedars, and spruce. This was due to the fact that Ordosoft's™ founding father, W.A. Huxton, had gradually redesigned the city since his company's flagship campus was built there in the 1980's, turning an ordinary suburban area into an intriguing synthesis of high technology and fertile fauna.

What was that Huxton soundbyte they always used to show? McCready asked himself. Something about the two being the same... "For the world of science and the world of nature are ultimately the same—they are both pure information." Yeah, that was it. He used to say that to justify *any* of his personal visions or conquests. "Used to say" because he didn't say much of anything anymore. Not publicly, at least.

He was still alive, but now lived an isolated life in his own personal Shangri-La deep within the mountains of Tibet, having turned over control of Ordosoft™, one of the world's most powerful corporations, to his son roughly twenty years ago. There were rumors within the bureau that his son, Mason, still consulted his father in nearly all of Ordosoft's™ major dealings—but this had never been confirmed officially. Like an official confirmation would suddenly make it the truth, he thought. Hell, in most cases an "official" confirmation was actually the furthest thing *from* the truth.

8

FREQUENCIES

"I've received clearance from security," Norma Jean announced, as four rubber tires extended themselves out from the bottom of the car. "Please prepare for touchdown."

As the Polaris™ settled onto the roof of the Farmaceutical Solutions™ building, McCready reached into one of the front pockets of his trenchcoat and pulled out a pack of Kamel® Kloves™. He shook a single cigarette out of the red package, placed it between his lips, then replaced the pack into his pocket.

"Open door," he said. "Driver's side."

The door opened, and he stepped out of the car and onto the roof's smooth, concrete floor. And for a brief moment, he could have sworn that he caught a whiff of ozone. He looked up at the clear, blue sky. Maybe they're doing some molecular modifications today. They still did use the technique from time to time, though now it was done more to maintain the atmosphere at its current, supposedly safe levels, rather than repairing it, as it was first used to do. Shouldn't be filtering down here, though. Whatever. He reached into the same pocket that the Kamels® were located, pulled out his silver Zippo®, flicked it open, and brought the flame to the cigarette's tip. McCready took two deep pulls from the glowing cylinder of clobacco and exhaled the smoke over the hood of the car, careful not to let any of the pungent vapors inside the vehicle.

"Alright, N.J., patch the usual live-feed from my Obsidians™ to HQ's databanks. I'll be using the wristcom to keep in contact. Close door and activate security systems."

McCready dropped the closed Zippo® back into his front pocket and began to walk away from the car, as the Polaris'™ door automatically shut behind him. He looked around for the elevator entrance into the building.

Aside from the concrete landing zone, the surface of the roof was either covered with a brown-and-white marbled tile or dirt-filled planters of various sizes containing a diverse selection of trees and shrubs. A few, wooden picnic tables were also scattered about the area, presumably for the employees to use during a lunchbreak. Cute, McCready thought. A little playground for the company's kids, 'cause mom and pop CEO love their little workers *sooo* much. This place was indiciative of the reason why he was never interested in moving to Redmond–too much bullshit. A corporation didn't give a cloned whore's ass about its employees, so why pretend otherwise? Whatever turns you on, he figured.

Walking to the opposite side of the roof, McCready found the elevator entrance, which had been partially hidden from view by a ten-foot pine. Taking a few more puffs from the cigarette, he made his way towards the evergreen tree and the building's entry point. As he passed the tree, he caught a few whiffs of the pine's scent, causing him to feel a slight sensation of nausea. It reminded him of that household cleaner, FreshPine™–and he didn't have good associations with that product. If smell was the sense most strongly tied in with memory, then he didn't ever need to be around the odor of pine again. The embers at the end of the Kamel® flared up brightly, as McCready took a long, hard pull, and blew the sweet, sticky smoke out through his nostrils. He breathed in. Much better. Clobacco–no pine. He pressed a button on the control panel located near the elevator's metal doors, causing the clear disc to illuminate itself a dim red.

"May I help you?" asked a nasally male voice from a small speaker located on the elevator's control panel.

Of course, McCready thought, or I wouldn't have pressed the fuckin' button. Procedure and formality–you had to love 'em. "Agent Marc McCready," he announced, staring directly into the miniscule camera mounted into the control panel. "I'm here to investigate a potential frequency emissions violator."

"You're a frequency emissions monitor?" the voice asked with an eager curiosity.

"That's right, I'm a Freemon."

"You guys are part of the FBI, aren't you?"

"Right." He extinguished his Kamel® by rubbing it into the bowl of sand located on top of the cedar-framed garbage can. He tasted the sweet residue that the clobacco had left on his lips, then threw the crumpled cigarette butt into the garbage can's opening.

"I bet that's an *exciting* job, isn't it?" The eagerness was increasing.

"No, not really–you have to spend too much of your time answering idiotic questions from bored employees."

Silence from the other end of the speaker.

"Look," McCready said, "I'm overjoyed that you find my line of work so incredibly fuckin' interesting, but I don't have the time or energy to chit-chat with you, partner. There's a potential crime in progress, and I'd like access to investigate it, alright?"

Another pause. "Please place your thumb upon the scanner for biochip confirmation." Any trace of excitedness from the voice was now completely gone.

FREQUENCIES

McCready put his left thumb on the scanner that was set into the elevator control panel. A flash of laser-light, and the doors of the elevator began to open up.

"Your identity has been confirmed, Agent McCready. Please enter. And have a nice day."

"Yeah, right," McCready said, as he walked through the parted metal doors and into the elevator's interior. The walls were painted the same shade of brown that was found marbled with white on the roof's tile–a creamy, light brown that reminded him of a latté. His lips curved into a smirk, as the image of painters splashing their morning coffees onto the elevator walls came flooding into his mind.

"Which floor would you like?" asked the generic female voice of the elevator's computer, just as the doors closed together.

"Corpo and security," McCready said, as he turned to face the doors once again.

"Thank you," it replied.

As the elevator began its descent, McCready looked at the big, black letters which were displayed across the inside of the doors: "FARMACEUTICAL SOLUTIONS™." Below it, in smaller print, their current slogan: "MAKING YOU BETTER™." The saying was a little trite, but it had a certain amount of truth to it. A few years back, after his mother was diagnosed with liver disease, she had received a life-saving transfusion of the blood protein, serum albumin, which had been created through the company's founding enterprise, bovine pharming–a process in which cloned female cows were gengineered to produce pharmaceutical drugs through their milk. The drugs were then extracted from the lactic fluids, and transferred to the human recipient. From moo to you, he joked to himself.

The elevator came to a stop. "Thirteenth floor. Corporate police and security," the generic voice said. The doors parted open, revealing two large figures, one male and one female, attired in black suits and ties. "Have a nice day."

"You must be my escorts," McCready said. He reached into his trenchcoat, pulled out his identification badge, and showed it to the two corpos. "Agent Marc McCready, Freemon."

The blonde, crew-cut, nearly albino member of the pair took the wallet-like badge from McCready's hand, and opened it. A holographic Freemon logo projected itself out from a tiny laser lens and into the air above the badge. She tilted the upper part of the badge back and forth, causing the owl logo to reveal its full, three-dimensional qualities. For a moment, McCready wondered if the

11

muscular blonde woman was actually examining the hologram, or if she was simply enjoying its aesthetic qualities. Then McCready got a good look at her eyes. They were an unnaturally pallid shade of blue–definitely implants. Her eyes must have been specially designed to look for all of the hidden stuff, all the codes and data that were locked deep within the matrices of the hologram in order to differentiate it from a simpler, less detailed counterfeit.

"Keep door open," McCready said aloud, knowing that the door would automatically shut on his ass otherwise.

The blonde woman nodded her head a few times as she finished examining the hologram, briefly looked up at McCready, then handed the closed badge over to her bearded cohort.

The black-bearded man, who was much darker in skin tone and had a bit more fat mass than did the blonde, stoically gazed at McCready as he took the piece of indentification from her hand. A serial port was embedded into the side of his shiny, bald head, and a thin cable ran from the side of the implant down to a silvery device which was encased around his right index finger. The corpo reopened the bifold, raised his metal-tipped finger to the lower section of the badge, and began to run his digit back and forth across the various bar codes which were contained there. As he scanned over the coded information, a tiny laser could be seen emanating from the end of the silver fingertip, adding a temporary reddish hue to the black zebra-stripes that it quickly passed over.

"ID vital info matches the biochip scan done on the roof," he said in a low voice. "He's who he says he is." He handed the badge back to McCready with a friendly nod, then unplugged the microthin cord from the side of his head, and allowed it to coil down into the finger scanner's housing.

"So where can I find an employee named Lee Samuels?" McCready asked as he placed the badge back into his trenchcoat.

"We'll take you to him," the dark-skinned man said, as he pulled the laser scanner from off of his finger. "By the way, I'm Seth. She's Nikki," he said, gesturing towards the blonde, whose icy-blue eyes were coldly fixed upon McCready's face. "But she don't say much, so don't be expectin' to have no conversation with her."

"Oh, don't worry," McCready replied, meeting Nikki's glacial stare, "I won't be."

The two massive corpos then stepped into the elevator with McCready, causing the formerly spacious elevator to now feel quite small. He was glad he wasn't claustrophobic.

"Sixteenth floor," requested Seth, placing his fingertip into a vest pocket underneath his suit. The elevator's doors closed and the car began to move again. He looked down at McCready without tilting his head, instead shifting only his eyes. "So Lee Samuels is freakin' out, hm?"

"Yup," McCready said.

"That's bugged–dude's usually real quiet."

"That's how it is sometimes–the ones you'd least expect." McCready touched a tiny sensor on the left side of his Obsidians™, activating the hidden FE/biochip scanner located in the bridge of the sunglasses. A currently colorless, transluscent, pyramid-shaped hologram displayed itself onto the Obsidians'™ lenses, and into his line of sight. The rotating, three-dimensional pyramid was located on the right side of his field of vision, its holographic qualities causing it to appear as if it were actually being projected out and into the real space in front of him. "Just goes to show that you can't always tell a person's thoughts from their demeanor alone–sometimes you have to look a little deeper."

"Sixteenth floor. Training and development," the elevator's monotonous voice announced, as the car came to a rest. The metal doors began to open.

McCready stepped out of the latté interior of the elevator and into the fluorescent lighting of the cubicle-infested 16th floor. No NatraLites™? he asked himself. This company could sure as hell afford them, so why weren't they using them? Granted, this was the floor where they trained their new employees, but still...

McCready didn't like fluorescents. In fact, he hated them–the way they coruscated on the periphery of your vision, lingering there like epileptic ghosts until you paid conscious attention to them. And once you *did* pay attention to them, the little bastards would temporarily go back to whatever hell it was that spawned them, only to return the minute your focus was diverted. Fucking annoying, the way they did that–let alone the fact that information could be transmitted through them.

Nikki and Seth followed McCready out of the elevator. "Samuels is just up this way," Seth said, as he started to walk down the cubicle-created hallways.

As Seth moved in front of McCready's line of sight, the Obsidians'™ scanner began to transmit information to the lenses' displays. Below the rotating, formerly colorless pyramid, in the same holographic manner, the name and social security number of the scanned individual was displayed. Seth Jordan Samson, #082-773-3504. The pyramid itself now began to exhibit a greenish-yellow hue, indicating that Seth's thoughts were active yet ordinary, falling right into the acceptable range for normal human thinking.

McCready looked over at Nikki, assuming that she was going to trail right behind Seth, but the tall blonde was still standing in the same place. Since he was now looking at her, the biochip scanner began to transmit the new data. Natasha Nikita Fedorov, #235-686-1612. The yellowish-orange color of the pyramidical display showed that her thoughts were very active, but still well within the legal limits. And even if Nikki *did* think outside of the limits, she seemed like the type who wouldn't be much of a threat, since she didn't appear to share her thoughts with anyone else.

With her hand, Nikki motioned McCready to follow Seth, her gaze as frigid as ever.

"Alright, lady," McCready said. "If you insist." As he began to trail Seth down the hallway, Nikki fell into place right behind him, practically matching each step with his. What are you, my fuckin' shadow? McCready asked himself. I always wished my shadow was a big, blond albino instead of that boring black thing that's always changing shape with the lighting.

As they continued down the hallway, McCready would occasionally peer into an employee's cubicle. The compartments were basically all the same, with minor differences here and there. The employees would sit in their Gelaform™ chairs with the rollers at the base, while working, training, or teleconferencing on the uniview screens located on the desks in front of them. The minor differences were found in the content, arrangement, and neatness of personal items found on the employee's desk, and the slight variations that were displayed upon the Obsidians'™ frequency emissions reader. In fact, the variations in their frees were almost *too* slight. Nearly every employee was in the green alpha range, whereas with most corporate trainees there were fluctuations up into the beta and gamma ranges. So far, Seth and Nikki were the only people in the building who were even close to those ranges–and they didn't even work on this floor. Interesting, McCready thought. He looked up at the fluorescents.

"You hear that?" Seth asked, looking back at McCready but still continuing to walk forward.

"What?" McCready asked, snapping out of his previous train of thought.

"Sounds like yellin' or somethin' from up ahead," Seth

replied, quickening his pace.

"It's Lee Samuels," Nikki stated, in a voice that was much softer than her appearance would indicate. "He's making some very odd statements..." She turned one of her cybernetic ears towards the sound. "And being quite loud about it."

"Shit," McCready said, matching Seth's quickened step. "He must be vocally freaking out." He followed Seth around some corners and bends, and within a few seconds, they had reached Lee Samuels' cubicle.

A crowd of fellow coworkers were gathered near the compartment's entrance, partially blocking McCready's view of the freeker. "What's that buzzing sound?" Lee Samuels called out to everyone and no one simultaneously. "It won't stop! What's that buzzing sound?"

"Please go back to your cubicles," Seth authoritatively announced to the curious coworkers. "The situation is being dealt with. Please go back to your work."

"Do you hear it?" Samuels edgily asked. "The buzzing–it's everywhere. All of you, just stop what you're doing for a moment and *listen*. You'll hear it. It's always there. It never stops."

As the employees followed Seth's commands and returned to their work stations, McCready quickly scanned over them. Now there were a few reaching the yellow beta frequency, but there still wasn't even one, single person in the gamma region. Confrontation with a vocal freeker usually tended to have more of a stimulating effect than this. When all of the employees had left the immediate vicinity, McCready reached down to his waist and detached a small, white-noise generator from off of his utility belt. He then placed the spherical apparatus at the cubicle's entrance, thereby preventing any unecessary sounds from leaving the area.

"All these electronic devices buzzing constantly!" The intensity in Samuel's voice was increasing. "It's the hive–they keep sending messages to us through their goddamn buzzing devices!"

McCready finally got a good line of sight at Samuels, though at this point, he didn't really need the Obsidians'™ help in determining whether or not the employee was freaking out. It was pathetically obvious he was. But still, there was the official confirmation on the display–orangish-red at the base, ascending into deep, blood-red at the eye of the pyramid.

A full-blown freeker reading.

An omega.

FREQUENCIES

"They're controlling our minds with their technology!" Samuels frenetically shouted, as he shook his thin, outstretched hands in a pleading manner. "Electric pheromones! Our thoughts are not our own!" His bright, red hair and goatee, which normally would not garner any extra attention, now seemed to exist only in order to emphasize his currently manic behavior.

"Look, Samuels," McCready said calmly, as he pulled out a black and gray device which resembled a small remote control, "I'm gonna give you one chance to calm down, shut up, and relax. Do you understand me?"

"Don't you see?!" Samuels grabbed his head in frustration. "The electric pheromones have made us mindless drones! We're just stupid little insects mindlessly following the hive mother's bidding! We don't even know that we're being controlled!"

McCready raised both his voice and the device at the slender man. "Samuels, I'm dead serious–shut the fuck up, or I'm *shutting* you up." He lightly pressed a button on the remote-like device, causing a small, bright-red dot to appear upon the freeker's forehead.

"The queen bee keeps transmitting the electric pheromones and we just keep on numbly following them without ever questioning why. Why? Why not ask why? *I* know why..."

Seth looked over at McCready. "He ain't listening to you, man. All he's hearin' is that pheromone shit he keeps talkin' about."

"But what I don't know–the one thing I can't figure out..." Samuels said. "Who's the queen? Who...is...the goddamn *queen*?!?"

McCready firmly pressed the button, emitting an invisible, concentrated, electromagnetic pulse that shot straight to the red homing-dot. Lee Samuels immediately lost consciousness and began falling forward to the floor. His knees barely touched ground before his lightly freckled face smashed into the marbled tile with a sickening thud.

There was silence for a few seconds.

"Shit," Seth said, squinting his eyes and rubbing his beard. "That must'a hurt." He looked at McCready, head slightly cocked. "You hit 'im with a synaptic disruptor?"

"Yup," replied McCready, dropping the device back into his front pocket and walking over to Lee Samuels' unconscious body.

Seth moved a few steps forward and peered over the freeker's prostrate form. "But it looks like he's in a coma or somethin'."

"He is. We're not issued the typical disruptors–the ones that simply affect motor coordination." McCready kneeled down beside

16

Samuel's head, noticing a thick stream of blood that was beginning to run from somwhere on the employee's blank face. "Ours affect the synapses in the reticlular formation of the brain, inducing a temporary coma."

The stream of blood flowed into the Vibram® soles of McCready's boots, then diverted its course away and around the solid object, continuing to stream along the brown-and-white marbled tile in search of the open space it was naturally drawn to.

"Damn," Seth said. "You guys don't play around."

"Nope." With his gloved right hand, McCready grasped a hold of Lee Samuels' red hair, and began to pull his head up and away from the cool tile. An oozing, sticky sound was barely audible as the large laceration underneath his freckled cheekbone separated from the blood beneath it. McCready looked up at Seth and Nikki. "Either of you got a cauterizer? Mine's busted."

Nikki stepped forward, reached into a vest pocket, and pulled out the requested item. She scanned the pen-like laser a few times over the open wound, and within a few seconds the entire wound was soldered shut.

"Thanks," McCready said, as he carefully laid Samuels' head back onto the cold, bloody tile. "I wasn't *about* to drag his bleeding ass into my car." He removed a small, metallic/ceramic disc from the side of his utility belt and lifted Samuels' body up slightly with his bionic forearm. He then placed the tiny, gravity-shielding disc underneath Samuels' abdomen, causing the unconscious freeker to rise up about one meter from the ground, and hover there motionless.

"So now what happens to him?" asked Seth, nodding his head in the direction of the floating body.

McCready stood up from his crouched position and grabbed Samuels' blue overcoat from the back of his Gelaform™ chair. "Well, first he goes back with me to the Hill for processing. Then from there..." he said, as he used the overcoat to wipe the blood off of his Timberland® boots, "it's up to the judges. Maybe reprogramming in a rehabilitation center if either him or his relatives have the money to afford it."

"And if they don't?" Seth asked.

"Then he'll probably end up in a workcamp," McCready replied, wiping the rest of the crimson smear from his soles. "Unless they think his crime was serious enough–then they might use his body for medical purposes. Or convert it into raw, industrial material in a micronizer... It's hard to tell." He threw the bloodied overcoat onto the floor, covering the excess human liquid that had been spilled from Samuel's face. "Whatever the case, I doubt you'll be seeing or hearing from him again."

McCready pressed a button on the side of his wristcom, causing the miniature uniview screen to become illuminated with the image of the cartoon Marylin. "N.J.," he said towards the wristcom, "contact HQ and let 'em know that I've handled the freeker situation here. A basic, routine I&D–nothing out of the ordinary."

Seth plugged a mini-microphone into the serial port in his head and began informing his superiors about the incident.

"Will that be all, Marc?" asked the toon image, as she picked up the receiver of an old-fashioned telephone.

"Actually," he remembered, looking up at the fluorescent lights, "do one more thing for me. Access our database and tell me how many freeker incidents have occurred at Farmaceutical Solutions™ this year."

Nikki curiously looked at McCready, her blonde brows frowning down as her eyelids squinted around her icy orbs.

"Including this one," Norma Jean stated, replacing the receiver onto the hook, "four."

"And it's only March. That's what I thought." McCready clutched the loose sweater that Lee Samuels was wearing and walked towards the cubicle's exit, easily dragging the weightless man behind him. As he neared the exit, he quickly looked at Nikki, then at Seth, who was still talking into his mini-mike. "Hey, Seth," he said.

"Hold on," Seth said into the microphone, "the Freemon's talkin' to me." He looked at McCready. "Yeah?"

"Tell your bosses to ease up a little on the subliminals." McCready pointed up at the fluorescents.

"What do you mean?" Seth asked, looking up towards the lights.

"The fluorescents," McCready said. "Just like in the supermarkets, they're being used here to transmit information–except it's not price changes that are being transmitted, and it sure as hell isn't digital price tags that are receiving it."

Seth looked a little puzzled. Or tried to. "What is it then?"

Underneath the Obsidians™, McCready's eyes glanced at the mini-mike. More than likely, Seth's superiors were hearing what he was saying firsthand. Shouldn't be a problem, he thought. I've got jurisdiction in this matter.

"What it *is*," McCready assuredly stated, "is that the subs coming through the fluorescents are restricting the employees' thoughts too much. As a corporation, you guys have the legal right to use subliminal suggestion techniques, *provided* that their usage does not interfere with any of the articles in the Frequency Emissions Act. And right now, by constantly keeping your employees within the alpha range...you're causing them to randomly freek out." He paused for a moment to gauge Seth's reaction. On the FE display, Seth's reading was now a pure-orange color–McCready had touched a nerve. "And that's a direct violation of the act. In other words, what you're doing here is illegal."

Seth slowly nodded his head a few times, an indication that he was receiving some kind of instructions or orders from his superiors via radio implant. "Thanks for bringing this matter to our attention, Agent McCready. We'll make sure this doesn't happen again."

Yeah, McCready thought, you'll make sure you aren't *caught* again. You and the overseers are only gonna abide by the law until you devise a less obvious method for limiting your slaves' cognitive freedom. Then you'll use your fancy new mind trick, regardless of whether it's legal or not, 'cause you're a corporation and you can get away with whatever the fuck you want. "I'm sure you will," he said, smiling the most plastic smile he possibly could.

Seth nodded a couple of times again. "You think it's the alpha transmissions that are causing the problem?"

The question was so ridiculous, McCready had to let out a sarcastic laugh. Like you don't already know, he thought. You're just trying to play stupid to make your guilty corporate ass look more innocent. Okay, whatever. You want me to play along and humor you? Fine. "Human minds are like balloons," McCready said, his vocal tone revealing his annoyance, "right? And their thoughts are like the air that fills these balloons. If you don't let them release a little bit of air from time to time–which is what they're doing when they think outside the alpha range–then they're going to burst." He held his hand up, made a fist, then quickly flared his fingers outwards. "Pop." He pointed a single finger towards Seth and Nikki. "Then *you've* got an omega on your hands," pointing the same finger at himself, "*my* annoying ass has got to respond to a situation that could have been avoided," he nodded down at the floating body he was holding on to, "and some poor bastard like *him* has gotta go to the workcamps or the fuckin' micronizer."

McCready shook his head with frustration as he knelt down and picked up the white-noise generator from off of the ground. He stood up, reattached the generator to his belt, and walked away from the two corpos, towing the reticularly-challenged body of Lee Samuels behind him as he went. "Just be a little more careful in the future, alright?" McCready announced loudly without turning back.

Neither Seth or Nikki said anything in response.

As he walked past the infinite rows of homogeneous cubicles, observing the subliminally-induced employees going about their busy work, McCready couldn't help but think of a honeycomb.

Ω

∞

Chapter 2:
A Butterfly Dreaming

...or so it would seem.
For, while this structure was indeed built with the stuff of
coherency and order, it evolved into a creation which was chaotic and
unpredictable in its nature, constantly shifting and changing
depending on the perspective with which it was viewed, and thus
experienced. When seen with hope, joy, and blessedness, the structure
could be quite wondrous and beautiful...

The refracted rays of brilliant sunlight shone down through the
domed, glass ceiling, their lustrous energy reflecting off the tiny
beads of sweat that were sprinkled across the face of Ashley Huxton.
Her eyes closed in concentration, head tilted up towards the warm
solar radiance, her hands raised high into the air above, Ashley
gracefully held her arabesque with the temporary pause in the
triballet's song. As the music began to play again, she fluidly moved
across the polished wood floor of her dance studio, performing a series
of light, quick steps which gave the impression that she was gliding,
weightlessly, upon the air.

The sounds coming through the studio's speakers were a
combination of African drums, including the hourglass, bongos, and
congas, coupled with samples taken from Tchaikovsky's *Swan Lake*
and *Sleeping Beauty* ballets. Ashley had played the drums herself,
meshed them together on her 48-track, then layered the Tchaikovsky
loops over the percussion, creating a form of song which the media

had dubbed "triballet," or tribal ballet. She didn't really care much for the term, though–it seemed contrived and unecessary, like so many of the assorted labels and titles which the media immediately branded upon any new idea or artform. To her, it was simply music. That's all.

Gaining momentum from the lithe, fleet footwork of her previous move, Ashley sprang high into the air, kicked one leg out from her body in a swift, scissor-like motion, and nimbly landed with both feet together. Without pausing, she did a succession of small, bouncing steps, intermingled with eloquent arm motions and the occasional circling of her legs. Her fluid movements matched the music perfectly, as both expressions were not confined to the rigid standards of traditional ballet, but rather, were a celebration of freedom, flow, and spontaneity.

As an hourglass drum raised its octave in a manner resembling a human voice, a sample taken from the fairy dances in Act III of *Swan Lake* began to loop over and over, the combination producing a beautifully hypnotic melody. In response to the music, Ashley performed a final, aerial circle with her left leg, quickly brought it in towards her knee, and began to smoothly pirouette on the point of her right toe. After a series of eight, continuous revolutions, she slowly leaned forward on her right leg, and gently extended her left leg backwards until it was in line with her torso. As she elegantly held the pose, the Tchaikovsky loops began to fade away, leaving only the sounds of soft drumming behind.

Ashley took a deep, life-affirming breath, then righted herself up and out of the arabesque position, allowing the previously tensed muscles to relax themselves. She looked up at the bright sun above and closed her eyes, allowing the warm waves of celestial energy to wash into her being. "Thank you," she whispered, as her lips shaped into an appreciative smile. She took one more slow, strong breath, turned her face from the sun, and opened her eyes to the dance studio that surrounded her.

Everything was still there...the various paintings hanging upon the rounded, rainforest-green walls, the ballet barre that curved itself around the entire circular room, the hardwood floors beneath her feet... Funny, she thought, for a moment I wasn't even sure if I was *in* the studio anymore. And maybe I wasn't...and maybe I'm not now. Who knows? I could be the butterfly dreaming it's a person who dreams of being a butterfly...

With a smile still on her face, Ashley walked over to the

part of the curved, wooden bar where her olive-brown towel was hanging, and lifted the cotton cloth from off of it. She dabbed the towel lightly upon her face, brushed it along the length of her glistening arms and legs, then delicately moved it around and across her black, tank-topped, Nanopôr™ leotard.

When she had finished drying herself off, Ashley exited the studio through an oval door located beneath a painting of hers which depicted a regal, bird-like woman, her feathered wings outstretched in flight, bursting forth from a puffy, white cloud that sat high in the moonlit sky. She entered into a large, cylindrical hallway which connected the dance studio to the rest of her house. There was no door at the other end of the passageway, as it led directly into the giant living room ahead. Slinging the cotton towel over her shoulder, she walked the length of the cylinder, then stepped down from the passageway when she had reached the sunken living room.

The shape of the living room, which she referred to as her "playroom," was similar to that of the dance studio–cylindrical walls going up into a clear dome–only much greater in size. The living room dome was a bit different than the studio's however, as it consisted of a clear, tintable, plexiglass rather than actual glass. The Plexiglas® was much more likely to hold together in the event of an earthquake, but she liked the look and refractional qualities of glass better–so she opted to put the crystal in the studio and the plastic in the playroom. That way, she figured, if an earthquake hit, she wouldn't die in the playroom sitting in front of the uniview screen or something silly like that. And if it happened while she was in the studio? Oh well, then. At least she would die dancing and happy...

Opposite the passageway to the studio, was a huge, curved bookcase, filled with an eclectic array of titles that Ashley had collected over the years. She had ancient books that were hundreds of years old, some classics and some obscure; books from the twentieth century, up until the period in the twenty-first century when environmental concerns and cheap, portable, uniview notepads made paper reading material obsolete; censored books that didn't officially exist in the Library of Congress' records, the ones that weren't contained in, and couldn't be accessed through, any of the uniview's public channels.

The collection was quite impressive, an exclusive luxury allowed to her because she was a Huxton...a luxury which few others could enjoy. And she hated that fact. Well, not hate, actually, as she always tried to prevent herself from using and feeling that word. Did the world really need anymore hate? *She* didn't think so, and therefore she tried not to use the word. Words created reality, after all... So, actually, she disliked that fact. Why weren't resources more spread around? Why should she be able to have something that others couldn't? And most of all, why could she think these thoughts while others might be blacklisted or investigated for doing the exact same thing? It was all wrong, she knew that much for sure... But did it have to be that way? And if it didn't, then how could it change? She clasped her hands together, closed her eyes, and sent out a silent prayer to Gaia for guidance. It was time to visit her soon.

Ashley released her hands and opened her eyes, then walked over to a brown beanbag chair and seated herself on top of it. She glanced her eyes around the room, as her body began to sink deeper into the pliant piece of furniture.

Many of the objects in the playroom, just like in much of her house, were colored some shade of brown or green–from the ottomans, couches, and terra cotta planters which were spread out in a seemingly random arrangement across the plush, carpeted floor, to the myriad ornaments, artwork, and hanging plants which adorned the circular walls. She had always associated these colors with life and earthiness, two qualities which she sadly found missing in so many of the people and places around her. There was so much despair and apathy in the city, as if the inhabitant's emotions, their very souls, had been stolen by... She tried to think of the perfect word... By logical demons...that was close...*techno*logical demons...better... Technodevils. That was it.

Technodevils–the entities who controlled and directed this cold, ordered, and unfeeling world which she was born into. But wouldn't that definition include Ordosoft™? And her father, brother, and grandfather? Goddess, she thought, her face turning to a frown, how depressing. Most of my immediate family could be ostensibly characterized as purveyors of lifeless living.

Lost in her thoughts, Ashley was startled slightly when one of her cats jumped on to her lap. Surprise quickly gave way to affection, and she began to stroke her hand along the silky, tortoise-shell fur of the feline's back. "Hey there, Mau-Mau, how are you?" she asked, using her other hand to rub the top of the cat's head.

Answering her question without saying a word, Mau-Mau passionately purred with appreciation, as she pushed her head into Ashley's palm.

"So where's your buddies? Where's Sekhet and Bubastis?

FREQUENCIES

They not playing with you today?"

The cat meowed loudly.

Ashley laughed. "No? That's okay, though," she said, scratching the underside of Mau-Mau's chin, "I'll play with you." The hooting of a spotted-owl suddenly sounded over the playroom's speakers. "Actually, Mau, I guess I'll have to finish playing with you *after* I take this call." She tenderly placed the cat onto the carpet, stood up from the beanbag chair, and walked over to a large, intricate tapestry that hung from a metal cylinder which was mounted at its ends into the wall. Mau-Mau immediately trotted along after Ashley, then began to rub up against her smooth, bare legs when she had reached her.

Ashley pressed a button on the wall, causing the tapestry to roll up and into the cylindrical, metal housing-mechanism which it was hanging from, revealing behind it a curved, custom uniview screen. It had always bothered her, the thought that someone could jack into your set at any time and just *watch* you, so she used the tapestry in order to cover the camera that was installed into the uniview. How or why people ever agreed to the notion of letting a camera into their homes, she could never really understand. *Now* it made sense–everybody was used to it and the society was dependent on it–it was just "the way it is." But when televisions, phones, and computers were still seperate devices, why did they *choose* to have all three combined into the ultimate Big Brother device? What made it so important to them? I sure hope it was something more than just the "C" word, she thought. It *had* to be something more than that. When she had the chance to speak with her grandfather in Tibet later this week, she would definitely have to remember to ask him. After all, Gonpo would certainly have some enlightening insights into the subject, since he was one of the main forces backing the uniview's creation.

She pushed another button, this one located near the base of the extremely thin screen, manually activating the voice recognition system. Like the cameras, the auto voice-rec wasn't one of her favorite inventions either, since the microphones were always turned on, waiting for someone to activate it. Therefore, she had the manual button installed so she could turn the mike *completely* off when she wanted. "Uniview on," she said, wiping a tiny smudge mark from off the screen's surface with her thumb. The Ordosoft™ logo appeared briefly upon the screen, then morphed into a photograph of lush, moss-draped, temperate rainforest. "Who's the incoming call from?"

FREQUENCIES

An AT & T® logo superimposed itself over the rainforest image, then was replaced by the words, "Adam M. Huxton." Big bro, she thought. This should be interesting. "Put the call through."

The photograph transformed into an image of her older brother, seated in an expensive wicker chair on his outdoor patio, a bottled Cognihance™ smartdrink in his hand. "Hello, Ashley," he said, taking a sip of the neon-orange liquid.

"Hello, Adam," she replied, crossing her arms. "And to what do I owe this pleasure?"

Adam adjusted his Ordosoft™ print tie, and looked up at the sunny sky above. "It's a lovely day, isn't it?"

She smiled. "Yes, it's a gorgeous day, Adam...but that's not what you're calling me about, is it?"

He smiled back, nodded, and took another sip of the gingko/neurochemical concoction. He briefly brought his lower lip up and over his orange-moustached upper lip, ensuring that none of the thick liquid remained upon it. "It's true, Ash." Adam paused for a moment, then leaned forward in the chair, his moussed, brown locks staying perfectly in place. "I'm calling about mother. She hasn't been doing too well lately."

"*Which* mother are you referring to?" Ashley asked. "The clone or the real one?"

Adam's forehead furrowed in unpleasant surprise. "Our *only* mother, Ashley, that's who. The living one. And you," he said, pointing a condemnatory finger at her, "should begin to treat her that way. I have a feeling that your attitude is *very* likely part of the reason that she's not feeling well."

"*My* attitude?" Ashley's face flushed red with emotion. "How can you say that? What about you and dad's attitude, huh? You *both* knew that I wanted to let mom die a peaceful death—and you didn't give a shit about my opinion! You went right ahead and stuck her in cryo or biostasis or whatever the hell it is, and *completely* ignored what I had to say!" She lightly bit her lip, shook her head with disbelief, and looked away from the screen. "Then, as if that wasn't bad enough...you cloned her." She looked back at the screen with furious eyes. "*You fucking cloned my mother!*" She let out a small, exasperated laugh. "And you talk about *my* attitude? Well, fuck you, Adam!" she yelled, throwing the cotton towel at the uniview screen. "Fuck you and dad both!"

"There's no need for the hostility, Ash!" Adam shouted back. He sat up in his chair, breathed in, and closed his eyes, his thick, black lashes making him look almost angelic. Almost. "Please calm down," he said, as he lowered his voice and opened his eyes. "I understand what you're saying."

"Do you?!"

"Yes, I realize that it wasn't exactly fair to you, a-"

"That's an understatement," she interrupted.

"Okay, yes, that's true–but please, let me finish what I was about to say."

Ashley bent down to pick up the towel, and noticed a tense look on Mau-Mau's face. "I'm sorry, girl," she said as she caressed the feline's head. "Sorry for sending that energy your way. It's okay now." She picked up the damp towel and stood up to face the uniview once more. "Go ahead."

"Ashley, I realize that this whole situation hasn't been fair to you. Father and I had hoped that you'd eventually see our point of view, but... I'm not so sure anymore that that's ever going to happen. And..." He paused for a moment. "I apologize, Ash. I mean that. I apologize that we hurt you. I assure you that wasn't our intention. We just did what we felt was the right thing to do for the family. Neither of us could bear to lose mother, so we did everything in our power to save her."

"I appreciate your apology, Adam." She smiled an unforced smile. "I sense that you're being sincere, and I really do appreciate that." Her expression then reverted into one of a more serious nature. "But mom was supposed to die, Adam. It was her time. That's just part of the natural cycle of life–we're *supposed to die*. It's not a bad thing. And she was okay with it...she was ready–but you two weren't, and that was selfish. That was wrong. You should have let life take its course."

Adam looked down at the patio's floor for a few moments, then looked back up at Ashley. "But life isn't quite what it used to be, is it, Ash? It's evolving so rapidly, and we're going to need to evolve *with* it if we're to survive and prosper."

"Maybe," she said, "but I don't think I'll ever be able to call the cloning of my mother 'evolution.' At least not evolution in the sense of ascension or betterment or moving forward. It's more like we're still stuck in the same, tired loop of trying to live forever no matter what the consequences are...always choosing quantity of life over quality. I'm telling you, Adam–that way of living is going to eventually destroy us if we don't wake up and open our eyes."

"I can't say that I share your pessimistic view," Adam said.

FREQUENCIES

He downed the rest of his smartdrink. "Life's better now than it's ever been. We're more civilized, we work less, we-" A Post-It® reminder suddenly appeared on the uniview screen, the yellow graphic superimposing itself over her brother's image and temporarily muting his voice.

"Oh no, I forgot!" Ashley exclaimed, as the yellow reminder faded away.

"What?" Adam asked in a concerned tone. "What is it?"

"I have a meeting with Professor Brennan at the UW today! How did I forget?" she asked herself. "Adam, I'm sorry, but I have to get moving!"

"No problem, Ash, but..." He paused briefly. "The reason I called in the first place–I was wondering if you could do me a favor."

"What's that?"

"Could you please come over to the skyland this afternoon? If not for...mother, then would you at least do it for me?"

"It's really that important to you?"

He nodded. "It is."

"Then I'll be there, Adam, okay?" Ashley said. "I'll see you later. I gotta go now."

Adam smiled. "Thanks, Ash."

"You're welcome. Uniview off," she said, and deactivated the voice-rec feature with a push of the same button that turned it on. Ashley bent over and lovingly kissed the top of Mau-Mau's head. "I gotta go, Mau. Watch the house for me, okay?"

She then stood up, and immediately rushed out of the playroom and into the bathroom, which, like every other room in the house save the bedroom, was circular in design. She pulled the straps of the tank-top down and over her shoulders, slipped out of her ballet shoes, then peeled the rest of the micropore leotard from off of her body. Ashley opened the etched-glass shower door, turned on the water pressure full-blast, and hopped between the two shower-heads' flowing streams. She quickly rinsed her hair, washed her body with a loofa and lavender soap, grabbed a fresh towel from the rack outside the shower, turned the water off, and swiftly dried herself. Wrapping the towel around her body, she darted out of the bathroom, through the playroom, up one of the circular stairwells, and into her pyramid-shaped bedroom. Two cats, one pitch-black and one dark-brown, sat atop her large waterbed. They both meowed at the sight of her.

"Sorry, guys, I love you, but I can't give you any attention

28

right now!" Ashley said, as she slipped into some loose, silk, khaki pants. She then threw on a matching blouse, grabbed a nearby sweater, and rushed back down the stairs, through the playroom, finally reaching the sunlit vestibule which led to the front door. She took a short, terse breath and exhaled. Then she put on a pair of leather sandals, walked down the cylindrical, ivy-covered passageway, and exited through the oval front door.

"Activate security systems," she announced, as she stepped on to the lush, garden path that led to her car. Passing by the diverse menagerie of plants and trees that she had grown or obtained over the years, she looked down at the thin, gold watch that was wrapped around her right wrist. The watch had been specially made for her, the 24-karat band consisting of eight, interlocking infinity symbols, its round face containing an Anasazi-like spiral which rested underneath the wavy, hieroglyphic hands. She read the time upon the face. Still have almost twenty minutes. Not bad, she thought, considering that I almost *completely* forgot about the meeting.

Reaching her forest-green Lexus®, Ashley placed her right thumb upon the door's scanner. It instantly verified her identity through her biochip, and unlocked the luxury car's doors. She opened the front door, tossed her sweater onto the passenger side, and flopped down into the lush, padded, suede driver's seat. She shifted a little to try to get comfortable, but wasn't very successful. The seat was almost a little *too* soft and cushy—not quite what she would have chosen had she picked out the car herself. But, she wasn't the one who picked it out—her father had. She just wanted something simple, but he insisted on getting her *some* type of luxury car for her 25th birthday, and wouldn't take no for an answer. At least he didn't get her a Rolls®, though. And he did pick out a good color. Poor me, she laughed to herself. Poor little rich girl, her car was too nice for her! Like that was really some kind of problem compared to what other people had to go through. She had it easy, and she knew it. Not that her economic status didn't present its own set of problems, but life could definitely be a whole lot worse—and she was grateful for the fact that it wasn't. Truly.

Ashley placed her thumb upon the dashboard scanner, activating both the UV and rear-view screens. The Ordosoft™ logo made its usual, ubiquitous showing, then upon the screen appeared a green infinity symbol, set against a brown, bark-like background.

"Hello, Ashley," said the car, in a voice that had been composed entirely from the sounds of various flutes, resulting in an aural creation which sounded neither human nor computer. It was more akin to something that originated from a mystical or mythical realm. "Would you like to fly, or would you prefer me to?"

"I'll be doing the flying," she replied. "You're programmed to stay within the speed limits, and I may need to go a little faster than that." With her left hand, she grasped onto the black, helicopter-like control-stick, and slid her forefinger around the green accelerator trigger. Pulling the stick backwards, she activated the gravity-shielding mechanisms, and the car began to raise into the air and above the forested, eight-acre estate.

"Would you like some music to accompany your journey?" the flute-voice asked, as its infinity symbol pulsed in rhythmic harmony with each sound that it spoke.

"Sure, that sounds good." Ashley pulled the acceleration trigger, and the solar/electric turbofans began to push the vehicle forward and away from her Issaquah home. "Something that's relaxing–but not *too* slow."

"Very well," the car responded. It began to sing a lovely, up-tempo melody, enunciating no words as it sang.

Singing along with the Infinity–which is exactly what she called the creation, feeling that it was already bad enough that a wonderfully illogical concept like infinity had been named in the first place, and not wanting to add to the problem any further by naming it once again–she aimed the Lexus® GS 800™ to the northwest, and increased her finger's pressure upon the trigger.

A few minutes later, as she was speeding over one of West Bellevue's gated communities en route to the university, Ashley noticed a black Polaris™–definitely belonging to some type of law-enforcement agent–hovering in the air above a residence. She quickly slowed her velocity down to the speed limit, realizing that she was going to be *really* late if she got pulled over. Better to take it easy and be only a few minutes late, she thought. I'm sure Professor Brennan will wait. After all, he *was* the one who suggested the meeting, even though it was her who first approached him with the inquiries into the origins of the freeread technology. She recalled their unie conversation last week, and the way his typically uninterested face was lit up with excitement–almost like he couldn't wait to talk to her about the subject. Yeah, she assured herself, he'd wait.

Leaving Bellevue, Ashley continued on towards the

FREQUENCIES

Westside, across the waters of Lake Washington. Various types of watercraft, from hydroplanes to hovercrafts to houseboats, littered the lake's sun-streaked surface, appearing to her like little, hi-tech bath toys. As other GS crafts passed by in the air around her, each vehicle's automatic anti-collision systems ensuring that they never came too close to one another, she began to approach the 520 floating bridge. The double-decker freeway, which hovered about twenty feet above the water's surface via GS technology, contained five lanes of traffic going each way on both of its tiered levels. Passing over the bridge and looking down at the gridlocked, gravity-bound vehicles below, her mind was instantly filled with thoughts of wealth and privilege. She couldn't help it–transportation was such an obvious, visual example of inequality. In fact, it was *such* a simple, striking example to her, that she had even written her honors thesis on the topic while she was at the university.

In the paper, she'd pointed out that the wealthy upper-class were literally on top of society, flying around in their expensive GS crafts, high above the congested traffic below them, while the underprivileged lower-class owned no vehicles of their own, and were forced to rely on the crowded, city-supported transportation, such as the monorail or autobuses. The middle-class majority were right in between, owning their own vehicles, but still bound by the laws of gravity. It was an incredibly simplistic notion–ridiculously, even–and that's why she liked it so much. For her, truth existed in the simple, rather than in the complex, aspects of life.

520 fading quickly into the distance behind her, Ashley soon reached her point of destination–the University of Washington. She dropped her altitude a bit as she passed over the lake-front location of Husky Stadium, then descended even further as she reached the main campus, maneuvering her vehicle in and around the upper-level parking garages in search of an empty space. After finding a parking space in a garage located near the dorms, she extended the rubber landing nubs from the bottom of the Lexus®, and landed the vehicle gently down onto the concrete surface. Picking her sweater up from the passenger seat, she exited the car, shut the driver's side door, and activated the security systems.

As she began to walk away from the GS 800™, a metallic, silver sphere, slightly larger in size than a human fist, flew over from another area of the garage. The automated parking attendant stopped in front of Ashley, hovered there for a moment, then extended from itself a thumb-sized scanner. "Please pay before

31

leaving," it asked in a robotic voice which reminded her of old science-fiction movies. "Digital cash or credit?"

"DC's," she said, placing her right thumb upon the scanner.

"Thank you." The sphere's computer immediately processed the transaction, accessing her bank account via her biochip and deducting the proper amount of DC's. "Have a nice day," it said, then immediately flew off towards another incoming car.

Ashley walked over to the parking garage's elevator and pressed the "down" button. A chill breeze wisped through the garage, causing her shoulders and back to tense up. She immediately put on the light, knit sweater that she had brought with her, eager to be rid of the cold sensation that was causing her hairs to stand on end.

The elevator chimed as the car reached her floor, and the nicked, metal doors began to open up. Inside the elevator was a young man of Middle-Eastern descent, most definitely a student, judging from the big, yellow "U of W" logo that was inconspicuously plastered across his purple sweatshirt. He was wearing a pair of Sony® uniview goggles which were connected by a thin cable to some type of CPU that was hidden inside of his blue backpack.

"*Hey* there," he said, a giant grin appearing upon his face at the sight of Ashley.

"Hey," she replied with a smile as she stepped into the elevator. She went to press the "ground floor" button, but stopped when she saw that it had already been pressed. A uniview screen was on each side of the elevator, all showing the exact same program.

"You a student?" he asked, touching the peach fuzz that was growing from his upper lip.

She nodded, as the elevator doors closed with a clunky sound. "Aren't we all?" The car started its descent.

He began to nod back, stopped briefly with a look of puzzlement, then finished nodding his head "yes." "So, uh, what's your major?"

"Oh, life and living...that sort of thing." The screens were currently touting the merits of the university's cybernetics labs. Images of people and machines, and people-machines kept flashing back and forth.

"Biology, huh?" he said. "That's chill. Mine's kinda similar–bioinformatics. It's been my focus since elementary. You know about it?"

She asked, "The study of how information theory and technologies are applied to the fields of genetic analysis and biotechnology?"

"Uh..." He laughed. "Yeah."

She smiled. "I've heard of it."

The car came to a stop, and the doors opened. Ashley stepped out of the elevator and onto the paved path in front of her.

"Where are you walking to?" he asked, following her out of the elevator in a manner which reminded her of a kitten.

"To the library–Suzallo." She continued down the path, past the dorms and past the National Guard and telecommunications buildings. "I'm meeting with a former professor of mine."

"I'm going that way also–my next class is in Kane. Mind if I walk with you?"

"No," she said, "that's fine."

He increased his pace, so that he was now walking right beside her.

As they approached the quad area, the old, orange and red brick buildings of the university began to appear. Since it was currently class time, the central campus was not very crowded, making the walk through it much more pleasant than it would have been between classes. She caught a hint of springtime blossoms in the air.

"By the way," he said, extending his hand, "I'm Sherif."

She shook his hand. "Nice to meet you, Sherif. I'm Ashley."

Reaching the quad, she took in a deep breath through her nostrils and smiled. The Japanese cherry blossoms that filled the area were in full bloom, and the brisk breeze was carrying both the snow-like petals, and their scent, magically upon the air. The grass, the brick pathways, and nearly everything on the ground around them were covered with the thousands of petals whose majestic ride upon the wind had finally come to an end.

"It's absolutely enchanting, isn't it?" Ashley asked.

"What is? The blossoms?"

"The blossoms," she said, turning her head up towards the sky, "the sun, the breeze...everything."

He shrugged his shoulders. "I guess so. This is my second year, so I've gotten kind of used to it all." He looked around at the trees as they continued walking. "What's *really* chill is how they're arranged. Did you know that the trees are planted in the shape of a 'W?' Y'know, for 'Washington?'"

Ashley nodded with a heartfelt laugh, Sherif's fondness for the trees' arrangement striking a poignantly humorous chord within her. The truth often made her laugh–and his words and outlook were a telling example of the way style and trivia had supplanted substance and significance in America and the rest of this brave, new world order.

"What?" he asked. "Did I say something funny?"

"No, Sherif," she said reassuringly, "*you* didn't. Your culture did."

Two seagulls shrieked in unison as they flew by overhead, and he asked, "What do you mean?"

Even though Sherif probably had some type of academic clearance to think about and discuss the subject, Ashley wasn't sure what his restrictions were, and didn't want to risk the possibility of freeking him out. If someone discussed freeky thoughts without the proper clearance, it could cause them to be negatively databased, investigated, or worse, arrested. Because of her status, *she* didn't have to worry about those kinds of things, but she was always careful to realize that not everyone was so fortunate.

"Oh, nothing. So," she said, changing the subject, "I take it you're wearing the gogs for academic purposes?" She smiled. "Or are they simply a fashion statement?"

Sherif laughed. "No, they're not a fashion statement. I'm just studying some chem notes right now–I've got a test later today." They reached the end of the quad, and were now stepping onto the smooth, crimson bricks that covered Red Square. "I don't know what I'd do without them–I save so much time being able to walk around and study all at once. The convenience is great."

Oh no, she thought, he said the "C" word. Convenience–possibly the most harmful concept Western civilization ever created. How many trees had been cut down, how many cultures displaced, how much of the Earth had been raped in the name of "convenience" she couldn't even imagine. Well, actually, she *could*, but she didn't want to. She liked being aware of evil things and knowing where they could be found, but she didn't want to visit them any more than she had to.

"Just make sure that you know where you're going, Sherif."

"I do, don't worry," he said. "Once you get used to them, you can see right past the text and graphics."

He seemed oblivious to the possiblility of her statement having more than one meaning. Which, she figured, was probably a good thing, since she was trying not to freek him out...but, at the same time, she always wanted to spark at least a *little* bit of questioning in each person whom she encountered.

FREQUENCIES

"Especially when you shrink the screen or make it translucent," he continued. "Though the eyemouse doesn't respond quite as well when you do that."

As they entered Red Square, she turned towards her left, and began looking in front of the ornately-carved facade of Suzallo Library in search of Professor Brennan. Since the human traffic passing through Red Square was relatively light, she was able to pick him out of the crowd with ease. He was wearing his usual, gray, wool overcoat with the matching, black-and-gray speckled hat. He held on to a thin, silvery-metal cane with one hand, while the other held a small, hand-held uniview.

Ashley looked back at Sherif. "I've gotta go now, Sherif, but it's been nice talking to you. Good luck on your exam."

"Thanks." His gaze shifted downwards. "And thanks for walking with me too."

"Thanks for walking with *me*," she replied. "You're a really nice person to share time with."

"So are you," he said with a happily nervous laugh, as he began to backpedal away. "I'll see around."

She smiled. "Sure." As he turned away from her, towards Kane Hall, she said, "Sherif."

He turned around. "Yeah?"

"One more thing."

"What's that?"

"The trees themselves will *always* be more beautiful than the way they're arranged."

"I know," he said. "Matter over method, right?" Sherif smiled, turned back around, and walked towards the hall with a joyful spring in his step.

Ashley smiled too. Maybe he *wasn't* so oblivious to what she was saying—maybe he was just testing *her* out. Live another day, learn another lesson, she laughed to herself. She started to walk towards Brennan, and when she had almost reached him, he suddenly turned towards her and looked up from his uniview screen.

"Boo," he said in quiet tone.

A bit surprised, she asked, "You felt me coming?"

Without saying a word, he turned the uniview screen towards her. Upon the screen, was a live-feed image of herself.

"Oh, I see," Ashley said, "you cheated. You just patched into the university's camera network. I thought you had sensed my presence or something."

35

"I did," he replied, a near-smile appearing upon his white-bearded face. "This technology is simply an extension of my eyes, is it not?" He turned the uniview back towards himself and looked at the screen.

"It is, but it isn't." Ashley looked at him looking at the screen looking at her. "So, how long have you been spying on me, professor?"

"Since the parking garage," he said, as he began to walk away from the library and down towards Drumheiler Fountain. He touched his cane down to the ground occasionally, but it was there more out of habit than for anything else. His bionics ensured that he could walk like a man that was a quarter his age. "You're late."

"I know," she said, keeping the same pace as him. "I'm sorry about that. I had a really nice, long workout today, and then my brother called and-"

"No need to explain, dear," he interrupted. "I was a little late myself. We're currently working out the final details of the aeonomics curriculum, and I had a task that I had to complete before I could come down to Suzallo." They walked down the gray, concrete steps which led to the fountain. "Immortality's going to pose some interesting economic dilemmas, and we're all trying to be as careful as possible as we set up the courses to ensure that all relevant aspects of the issue are properly addressed. Living forever won't mean a damn thing if we relinquish the world to an ignorant and unprepared populace. If they leave here prepared..." He looked around at the campus, slightly nodding his head. "Then we will have done our job." Reaching the rim of the giant fountain, which was currently turned on to its full pressure, he turned the hand-held uniview off, then placed it inside of his coat pocket. "But enough of that subject." He looked at Ashley. "You must be wondering why I was so eager to meet with you."

Some light mist from the fountain's spray blew coolly onto her face. "I am," Ashley said, watching a male and female mallard fly down from the sky and land together in the large, algae-covered pool that surrounded the fountain.

"Come." He motioned towards one of the wooden benches. "Let's sit down."

Ashley walked over to the bench, and they both seated themselves.

Brennan pulled a lighter and pipe from out of his inside coat pocket. "Do you mind?"

"No, it's fine. Go ahead." She wasn't just being nice, that was the truth. Since Brennan was an immortalist *and* they were behind the gates, she knew that he would definitely be smoking a non-addictive, non-carcinogenic strain of tobacco. Plus, she didn't mind because pipes just smelled a whole lot better than cigarettes.

"Thank you." Brennan pressed his thumb down onto the partially-burnt tobacco, packing the bowl firmly while ensuring that he could still draw from it. He flicked the angled flame of the pipe-lighter, raised the fire to the bowl, and began taking a few tokes. Savoring the flavor of the chocolatey-smelling tobacco, he looked off into the distance, and said, "You may or may not know this, Ashley, but my wife and I were recently divorced–after having been married for over *seventy* years."

"I...I didn't know that, professor. I'm so sorry to hear that..." Ashley shook her head slowly, trying to imagine what it would be like to be with the *same* person for that long. "All that time spent together...wow."

"Wow, indeed," he said. "It makes one suddenly quite intimate with loneliness, wanting nothing more than to go jump off the proverbial cliff." Brennan smiled musingly, then adjusted his hat by pushing the brim down a bit more. "But, one soon realizes–if they're fortunate enough–that everything happens for a purpose. My wife leaving me, and the resulting loneliness, has caused me to introspect more than I ever have before–and I have learned a great deal about myself in the process."

Brennan paused for a moment. "As a man gets older, Ashley," he continued, "he begins to see the things that were not so apparent to him when he was younger–things that were hidden from his view because of his brashness and arrogance." He took another toke, then returned the lighter to his pocket. "These things can cause him to look back upon past deeds and see them in a new light–to see that, if given the chance to do it all over again, he might do them a bit differently than he did before...that he may have made some mistakes." He blew out some tobacco, little smoke distress signals rising from his mouth. "I've recently seen those things, and realized those mistakes." His eyes squinted a little. She wasn't sure if it was from the breeze blowing some smoke into his eyes or if it was from the memories.

Ashley looked him in the eye with empathetic compassion. She'd been there before. "Then you don't need to have any regrets, professor. If you're fortunate enough to become aware of your mistake, and you grow from it–really, truly *learn* from it–then you've turned something negative into something positive. You don't need to have regrets if you've learned the life lesson that the mistake taught you."

Brennan nodded in acknowledgement of her words. "Yes, this would be true if it only involved myself. But, unfortunately, sometimes your mistake may have repercussions beyond your own personal sphere of existence. Say, for example, that you were to drive recklessly and kill an innocent child in the process–then you would have regrets. Because you not only affected yourself, you affected the child and *every* single person who knew and loved that child. And if you were to... If you were to take another man's vision, and turn it into something that was his worst nightmare–then you would also have regrets." He paused, a subtle look of frustration appearing briefly upon his face. "And regrets can only be alleviated by somehow trying to make amends."

He's definitely not just talking about his marriage anymore, Ashley thought. Was this going to be some sort of giant confession? That definitely wasn't what she was expecting when he had asked her to meet with him. She was both curious and fascinated by the possibilities of what Brennan was going to say next. She didn't say a word, and patiently waited for him to continue.

"Ashley," he said, "I've known your grandfather and your family for a long time, but when you came to the university, I finally had the chance to get to know *you*. And I'm very glad that I've had that opportunity. You were, and always will be, one of my favorite students–one of the few who came into my classes and actually taught *me* a thing or two, rather than always agreeing with everything I had to say. You were always questioning everything, even if that meant sacrificing a grade to voice your opinion." He scratched his beard. "You're truly a unique individual, my dear. You're experimental, innovative, and willing to think outside of the accepted boundaries–a true scientist, in the best sense of the word."

"Thank you," she responded, feeling very flattered by his comments. In all of the time that she had known him, he had never said anything quite like that about her before–at least not that she knew of. "Coming from you, that means a lot."

"You're welcome," he said. "But it's not a compliment, it's the truth. Look at you now–you're not even enrolled at the university, yet you're *still* conducting your own research. That's impressive."

Ashley smiled. "Thanks."

Brennan nodded, then took a few more draws from the pipe. "But I see more than just a scientist in you, though–I see hope. I see an honest, genuine caring for other people and other creatures, and a willingness and desire to make this world a better place. Those are rare qualities to find these days, as I'm sure you already know." He paused again, rubbing his beard lightly with his left hand. "Hell, those were rare qualitites in the past–I know that *I* lacked them when I was younger. I was a great scientist," he said, his eyes becoming wistful with the remembrance, "but I was selfish, and had no compassion for other people or creatures. Essentially, I had no respect for life." He extinguished the cinders in the bowl by pressing the same, carbon-coated thumb down upon the tobacco, but this time with much more force. "And this caused me to make some very, *very* short-sighted decisions...decisions which I now must make amends for." He looked at her intently. "When you called me last week, and asked me about the origins of the freeread technology, I realized at that moment that–if there *is* such thing as a God–this was God's way of allowing me to make up for my past transgressions."

That explained the look of excitement–no, better make that revelation–on his face last week...but that still left the question of "why." "How do you mean...?" she asked.

"I mean that, through you, I can ensure that one man's vision and hopes do not die in secrecy with me. I can keep them alive by revealing to you the truth." He paused for a moment, surveyed the area in an almost cautious manner, then continued. "You see, Ashley, the man who created the freeread technology never intended it to be used in the manner that it is now."

She made a curious face. "You're referring to yourself, right? I mean, you *are* the one who developed the technology, aren't you?"

"Yes, I *developed* it, but I did not create it–someone else did."

"But in the uniview records *you're* credited with its creation..." Ashley paused for a moment, contemplating the implications of his words. "So," she continued, a rush of adrenalin passing through her body along with the full realization, "you're basically saying that all of the records regarding the technology's origins have been fabricated–that it's all a lie."

Brennan closed his eyes and nodded slowly. "That's what I'm saying. Essentially, all I did was *steal* the creator's idea..." Shame appeared upon his countenance. "And then I applied it in a way that absolutely and utterly degraded his ideals."

He stopped for a moment, letting out a small cough. "But before I go any further, I want to make sure that I'm not forcing any of this knowledge upon you, or making you an unwitting participant in its disclosure. I want to be completely sure that you know what you're doing, because the truth—once known—can never be forgotten. It stays with you always, whether you want it to or not. That is, of course, unless you choose to have those areas of the brain that are tied into that specific memory removed or inhibited..." He smiled. "But I think you see my point. Would you like me to continue, or...?"

"After a set-up like that? Are you kidding?" Ashley laughed at the notion of turning back now, just when her research had begun to yield the types of unexpected results that she had been hoping for. "Of course I want you to continue!"

"Well then," he said with a redemptive, hopeful gleam in his eyes, "let me tell you the story of Dr. Adrian Wellor."

∞

△

Chapter 3:
<u>Westside Stories</u>

...when viewed with indifference, dispassion, and apathy, it often became dull and tedious, while a gaze filled with anger, despair, and disrespect was sure to cause the structure to become quite horrible and wretched."

Morris Ignacio looked into the eyes of each of the three Freemon who currently surrounded him, just to make sure that their attention had not wavered.

Erik's cat-eyes looked eager, ready to pounce on the next word. Jung Ran looked at him intently, her dark-brown irises alight with anticipation. Essence's wholly white, pupil-less orbs showed keen interest. He knew he had their attention–so he decided to wait a few more seconds before he continued. Just to build up the suspense.

"Damn, Morris," Essence said, "you just gonna sit there and stare at us or are you gonna finish the fuckin' story? Shit," she said with a small laugh and a smile, "we ain't got all day!" Essence didn't smile often, but when she did, it was gorgeous–rich, full, chocolate-brown lips parting to reveal ivory-white teeth and tight, pink gums. He carefully studied her mouth for a moment and imagined what it would feel like to have it wrapped around him.

Ignacio smiled at Essence and took a slow, drawn-out sip of coffee from his black, ceramic mug, the green and white Starbucks® logo facing out towards the others. Over the brim of the mug, he looked around the headquarters' interior, briefly watching the other Freemon who weren't on lunchbreak go about their various tasks and duties. The large building was currently bustling with the activity and clamor of well over twenty agents.

"So the freeker pulls his dick out..." added Erik. "C'mon, Mo, what happens next? Did you nap him?"

"He won't even finish a story without stopping and watching the way people react to it," Jung said, turning towards Erik. "You think he's going to hit the freeker with a disruptor before he can watch a little bit more?"

Ignacio laughed at Jung's comment–incisive as usual. "Es verdad, Jung, es verdad." He took another sip of coffee, this time at a quicker pace, then set the cup down on the desk beside him. "Bueno," he said, his hands and body motions becoming animated with his speech, "so the guy unzips his pants, unfurls his flag, grabs a tight hold of it, and starts shakin' it around like it was a puppy who had just pissed on his brand new coat–you know, fuckin' it up with an attitude!" He laughed and shook his head, the vision still fresh in his mind. "Then, he starts screamin' down at it, real loud–'You were meant for reproduction but all you are is a sterilized piece of shit! All you're good for is fucking whores and coming when the sexsims tell you to! You can't even make one, *single*, goddam baby!'" Ignacio looked back up at the three Freemon. "The employees around him are literally freekin' out, you know? Blud's normal one minute, the next he's flashin' his peto at 'em! And then," Ignacio said, turning his head back down and pointing an indicting finger towards his privates, "he keeps on goin' with his shtick–'You can't even get it *up* sometimes! What good is the credit that you got if you can't even do what you're made to do, hunh?!'"

"Imagine what your wife must be feeling," came a familar, raspy voice from behind Ignacio.

He was wondering when he was going to show his unkempt face this morning. Ignacio looked up from his pelvic area with a smile and turned towards the voice. McCready was wearing his usual, hunter-green trenchoat, the usual khaki pants, and of course, the usual Obsidians™. He reeked of clobacco–still smoking the usual Kamels®. "Hola, huedo," Ignacio said. "¿Qué pasa?"

"What's up?" McCready asked. "Apparently not you, from what I just heard." He seated himself on Essence's Gelaform™ chair.

Essence looked at McCready, her perfectly-sculpted ebony face turning to a scowl, yet still remaining unreally attractive. "Fool, I didn't say you could sit in my chair."

"Cuidado, patrón," he said to McCready, "I see a storm

blowing your way." The warning was for McCready's own good. Ignacio knew Essence's temper could flare up quicker than a plasma torch–and then burn you worse. She had the harshest, toughest persona of just about any of the Freemon, undoubtedly due to the fact that she was one of the few who had been recruited directly from the workcamps. She'd personally seen shit that most people only saw edited on the uniview, or at most, had simmed in VR. She'd seen the *real* thing, and it showed through. And maybe that was why Ignacio found her so attractive. So intriguing. She knew things he didn't.

"Well, too bad," McCready replied to Essence, as he took off his sunglasses and put them into his coat pocket. "You're sitting in mine."

"So?" Essence asked.

"So I'm sitting in yours–now kick my ass or deal with it." McCready wedged into the soft back of the seat and touched the right side of his face, rubbing some of the light, black stubble which was just starting to grow there.

Essence raised her left hand towards McCready, then pointed at him with her index finger. She gave him a look that was both playful and malicious, as the bronze chain that connected her pierced ear and nose glinted under the Natralites™. "Don't tempt me, McCready," she said. "I just might." And that was no lie. She could–and would–do it. With just a point of the finger and a thought, she could nap his ass instantly, since her disruptors were implanted into her hand and tied in to her nervous system.

"Forget about it, Ess!" Erik shouted. "I want to hear how the story ends *before* I have to get back to work!"

"Yeah, the man's trying to hear a story, alright?" McCready said with his trademark wry grin. "Show some respect."

Still throwing that same, hard look his way, Essence said, "Shit..." She brushed her hand into the air towards McCready as if she was trying to get rid of a bad smell. "Lucky I don't knock you in your grill."

Ignacio laughed hard. McCready was always pushing Essence's buttons in the wrong way. One of these days, Ignacio knew McCready was going to push her *too* far. "You tired of living, McCready?" he asked. "You play with fire, boy..."

"You get burned," McCready said. "I know." He reached down to his utility belt, pulled out a device which resembled a laser cauterizer, and pointed it towards Essence. "That's why I always carry an extinguisher." He pressed a button on the device, causing a small burst of chilled, nitrogen gas to emit from its tip.

Essence quickly moved back from the cold burst, then leaned forward and threw a swift jab at McCready.

McCready raised his right arm in time to deflect the blow, and her implanted brass knuckles clanged hard on the metal alloy of his bionic limb. Ignacio could tell that the punch was thrown more to mess with McCready than to actually knock him out. If she had truly intended to hurt him, he'd already be sprawled out on the ground, bloodied and unconscious. Sensing that Essence wasn't going to throw another jab, McCready relaxed his arm a little bit.

"Alright, so what *is* the story at hand?" McCready asked, still cautiously eyeing Essence. "Fill me in."

"Naw, man," Takura said, "you don't get a recap–you already wasted enough time! I'm ready to hear the rest of the damn story!"

"Briefly," Jung said to McCready, as she picked up an orange that was sitting on her desk, "Ignacio responded to a freeker reading over at Opticon™ in Kirkland." She briefly looked down at the Sunkist® logo and UPC symbol which had been gengineered into the skin of the orange, then began to peel it. "A guy was freeking out about sterilizing himself for DC credits, and then..." she tailed off, allowing McCready to piece it together from there.

"He whipped out his tunnel rat and started playing drill sergeant with it," McCready said. "I get it. Thanks for the update, Jung." He looked up at Ignacio and extended his hand. "Please continue with your sordid tale, amigo. You have my complete and undivided attention."

"Gracias." Ignacio reached his hand down in front of his groin, grabbing the air in front of it like an imaginary penis. "So now the freeker's so angry and worked up, he's not just shakin' his peto anymore, it's more like he's strangling it–trying to choke it to death for all the shit he thinks its responsible for. And he's bein' *hella* loud now, so I start reaching down to my belt to grab my disruptor. As I'm doing this, he's still yellin' down at it, and starts saying–'You worthless shit, you can't reproduce but there's still one thing you're good for, isn't there?! You can still piss, can't you?!' Y no mento," Ignacio said as he began a hearty laugh, "vato starts pissin' on his desk, his uniview, the employees around him–*everything*."

Laughter from the other four Freemon.

"Hold up," Takura said with a grin, as he bit into a green, spirulina Power Bar®. "Everything would include *you*, wouldn't it?"

"It *would* have," Ignacio replied, "if I hadn't been keeping the recommended spatial distance between an agent and a conscious freeker. But I was–and that put me *outside* of his urinary range."

"Alright," Takura laughed. "Go on."

"So," Ignacio continued, "vato manages to sprinkle on a few of the other employees before I can get a good bead on him. Holding in my laughter–'cause I'm tellin' you, I wanted to just start bustin' up–I nap him and he drops to the ground, his peto still hangin' out the front of his pants like it was playin' fucking peek-a-boo. Now at this point, I'm ready to slap a GS disc on him and be up out of there, but *then* one of the people that got pissed on starts freekin' out also. She starts talkin' about–"If they can hear us *all* the time, then why do we even bother to speak? What's the point, when everything you say is heard by someone, somewhere? I've designed laser microphones that can hear through windows, walls, buildings...' She looked right at me then, her white cashmere top all stained with yellow piss, and calmly said–'We've even designed ones that can hear you from outer space. Did you know that somebody, or some*thing*, is listening to us right now? And they're documenting *every*thing? Did you know that?'"

Ignacio paused momentarily, and looked at the other Freemon. "So now I'm figuring I'm probably gonna have to nap *her* too, 'cause the other freeker's thoughts have already infected her. But then, before I get a chance to even *think* my next thought, this *other* blud, who *also* got pissed on, starts goin' off on what *she* was talkin' about–'And I've worked on lasers mounted into satellites that can lock on to an earthly target and destroy it instantly. At the speed of light. That means you're never safe. Anywhere. You can be hit with a laser at any time if they decide they want you dead. The optical eyes in the skies–they see everything.'" Ignacio paused for dramatic effect.

"So what'd you do?" asked Takura.

Ignacio waited a long second, and said, "Since they weren't freekin' out real bad and they weren't yellin' or screamin', I decided I'd go easy on 'em. So I put away my disruptor..." He picked up his mug again and took a sip. "And that was pretty much it–I walked over to both of 'em, placed a white-noise generator around their necks, then called the corpos over to take 'em to their in-house holding cells for deprogramming."

"Waitaminute," Essence said. "What did you do with the pisser?"

"The usual," Ignacio said. "I isolated him, detained him, brought him here for processing, then sent him off to the judges for

45

sentencing."

"No, no," Essence said, shaking her head to match her words. "I *know* the procedure–I mean what did you do with dude's *dick*?"

"Yeah, slick," Erik interjected with a laugh, "did you just leave it hanging out while you dragged him to your car, or did you put it back in his pants for him?"

"You fuckers are all depraved," McCready said with a sneer.

"Meaning you're not?" Jung asked, biting into a juicy orange segment.

"I didn't say that," McCready responded. "I just said that you guys were."

Ignacio looked at Takura with disbelief, and pointed at himself. "You think *I* was gonna touch his dick?!" He shook his head. "No. ¡No quiero un peto in *mi* mano! I told the corpos that he was company property and that it was *their* jurisdiction to make sure that *their* property could be removed from the premises in a less objectionable manner."

"What a load of crap!" laughed Jung. "Did it work?"

"Sí–luckily they were both rookie corpos who were afraid to cause a stir by contradicting a veteran Freemon. So one of 'em slapped on a pair of rubber gloves, and tucked junior back into bed. Then I carted him away." Ignacio smiled. "End of story."

"Man," Takura said, "you *always* get the crazy cases, Mo. You must be, like, a magnet for weirdness or some shit."

"He is," Jung added, noticing the director of the Seattle Freemon division walking towards them. "And a magnet for Moore."

"Freemon Ignacio," boomed the deep, bass-heavy voice of Harold Moore, "so nice of you to detail the accounts of your day to your fellow Freemon with so much energy and enthusiasm." He paused, the dark-brown skin on his forehead wrinkling into disapproval–Ignacio's indicator that a reprimand was coming next. "If only you could channel that same verve into isolating your frequency emissions violators *before* they have a chance to spread their memetic infection to others." Broad-shouldered, standing six feet four inches tall, the director was an intimidating physical presence. "Need I remind you of your memetics training?"

"No, sir," Ignacio replied. "I remember." One of the most basic rules of the Freemon memetics curriculum was: In a situation where there is an eminent threat that a freeker could spread an infectious meme, isolate first and ask questions later. Ignacio knew he'd fucked up. He had broken a rule, and Moore stuck to rules like a Rasta to

46

reefer–religiously. "I apologize, sir," he respectfully said, "I'll make sure not to let it happen again."

Moore nodded. "See that you do, Ignacio. It's essential that a veteran Freemon like yourself set a proper example by following procedure correctly." He stoically stared at Ignacio, then at the four other agents surrounding him. Turning his Medusa-like gaze back at Ignacio, he said, "You're one of the oldest–and best–agents we have, Ignacio, but if you break the rules...you're gonna break yourself. Understand?"

"Sí," he said. The director was going easy on him right now, and Ignacio knew it. He could have been docked credit, suspended, or, worst case scenario, demoted–but Moore had chosen to do none of those things. Ignacio was lucky, getting off with only a verbal grilling–though in actuality, it wasn't luck that had gotten him of the hook, it was history. He'd known Moore for well over twenty years, dating all the way back to their original FBI training together. Moore thought of him as a friend, and Ignacio was glad that still counted for something.

"Now," Moore said, "on to more pressing matters. The city police are currently responding to a disturbance that's taking place in the Rainier Valley area. Multiple freeread violations have already occurred there, and the likelihood of an outbreak is high if we don't isolate the infected individuals quickly. Ignacio," he said, adjusting a cufflink on his black suit, "I want you, McCready, Kwon, and Sommers to respond to the situation. I've already sent the GPS location to each of your cars' computers. Takura, I want you to notify the police that we're sending some agents over to assist them, then continue to monitor the situation online. This will be a joint federal/local operation, and even though you *do* have jurisdiction in these matters, please be respectful of SPD's methods and procedures–work with them and they'll work with you. Now, get your butts over there ASAP." He began to walk away towards his office, then turned around to face them once again. "And Ignacio..."

" ¿Sí?"

"Try to prevent the omegas from pissing on the alphas, okay?" Moore nodded, showed the slightest hint of a smirk upon his face, then turned back around and resumed the walk back to his office.

Laughter from the other four Freemon.

"Yeah, yeah..." Ignacio muttered, as he picked up his black, leather jacket. "Well, don't just sit there," he said to his fellow agents. "You heard the man–let's get movin'! ¡Vámonos!"

FREQUENCIES

A few minutes later, Ignacio and McCready were seated in the latter's Chevrolet®, rising up and out of the Beacon Hill headquarters' garage. Sommers and Kwon followed right behind them, also driving in a black, standard-issue Polaris™. Ignacio had figured it would probably be a good idea to split Essence and Marc up, so he assigned her to fly with Jung. He didn't volunteer himself to go with Essence, because he didn't want to be in same car with her right now–too much temptation. And he'd been giving in to temptation a *lot* lately.

They began to fly south on automatic, towards the Rainier Valley, as some song that Ignacio had never heard before played on the stereo. "All of my purple life..." came the singer's synthesized voice through the speakers.

"You ever listen to anything *new*, McCready?" Ignacio asked, as he popped the top on a can of Coca-Cola®.

"Nah, not really," McCready replied, reaching into the backseat to retrieve something. "Everything put out now's just a bunch of watered-down crap. You listen to the uniview and everybody sounds like fuckin' androids on barbiturates." He returned from his backseat quest with a brightly-colored plastic bag. "Back in the day, people still actually sang with some feeling." He opened the snack-bag, the plastic crinkling loudly with the stress.

"There's still some good shit bein' made today," Ignacio said. He took a sip of the Coke®, as he watched the cartoon Marilyn, currently dressed in blue jeans and a tie-top, dance along with the music on the uniview. "You just gotta look for it."

"Yeah, well, I guess I'm not looking then." McCready tossed a few of the small, rectangular, reddish-orange snacks into his mouth and began to loudly munch on them.

Iganacio hadn't eaten much for lunch earlier. His stomach started to growl. "Damn, tengo *hambre*.." He looked over at McCready's food. "Those any good?"

McCready handed him the bag. "I wouldn't call them 'good.' More like 'not bad.'"

Ignacio ate a few, made a sour face, then looked at the front of the bag. "'Tiny Tamales™?' This shit does *not* taste like tamales. Tastes more like dog food." He handed the bag back to McCready, satisfied to stave off his hunger until a better option presented itself.

"What do you expect, man? It's dog food for people–that's what all these little packaged snack foods are. Kibbles N' Bits®, Tiny Tamales™–same shit, different species." McCready reached into the bag and ate a few more.

"If they're just dog food, patrón, then why does everyone keep eating 'em? Don't you think people would reject 'em if that's all they were?" Ignacio loved asking McCready questions like this. Marc would always get all riled up, then give some kind of wild response that Ignacio would normally only hear from his freeker cases.

"No," he said disgustedly, "because everyone's too fuckin' stupid not to. We buy what we're sold, when we're told." A look appeared upon his face–the same look which always appeared upon his face when he spoke about society–best described as a combination of frustration and disappointment. "Man, we've been trained so well... There's no creature on the whole fuckin' Earth that's better trained than us. People put dogs to *shame* when it comes to obedience."

"Marc," Ignacio said with a laugh, "it's a good thing you're a Freemon."

"Why's that? 'Cause of my thoughts?"

"Sí."

"Wouldn't matter," McCready said. He ate a few more Tiny Tamales™, then replaced the bag in the backseat. "I'd just keep the thoughts to myself–they don't give a fuck what you think as long as you keep it to yourself."

"But you *wouldn't* be keepin' it to yourself," Ignacio said. "You'd be freekin' out in regular society! The nature of a freeker is to share their ideas, to find out if others see the world like they do. They want to know they're not alone. You'd be talkin' away like there was no tomorrow–trust me." He laughed. "I'd have probably *already* had to come for you by now." He paused, an ironic thought coming to mind. "Actually, it would be *Essence* who would have to come for you."

"Fuck that," McCready said. "I'd rather french-kiss a meat slicer." He pulled out a toothpick and placed it between his lips. "So speaking of Essence–what's up with the way you look at her?"

"What do you mean?" Ignacio asked, feigning ignorance.

"'What do I mean?' You know what I mean. The way you act towards her, the way you treat her–you know."

"She *is* fine," Ignacio confessed, realizing that there was no point in lying to McCready. If he could trust anyone with his secrets, it was Marc. For one thing, he'd known him for over four years, ever since McCready transferred from the SPD to the Freemon, and had found him to be a solid and reliable individual. Second, McCready tended not to let other people get too close to him–whether they were

Freemon or not–and therefore didn't really have anyone to gossip *to*. Third, and most important, McCready had revealed to him so many of his fringe beliefs that, as his superior, Ignacio could utterly wreck his career and life at any time if he decided to do so. Ignacio ran two fingers lightly over his mustache, and stated, "Somethin' about her that just turns me on, patrón. Her harshness, combined with that body and face..."

Images began to appear in Ignacio's mind. He imagined himself, his Levi's® and boxers pulled down past his knees, sitting at the edge of a bed covered with velvety, purple sheets, Essence standing there before him in her usual, tight, black bodysuit. Ignacio looked up and down the mental figure, examining everything from her curly, black hair to her large, firm breasts; from her thick, rounded hips, all the way down to her muscular thighs and calves. He especially found himself drawn towards her nipple ring–the round, brass metal piercing through the taut, shiny, black plastic fabric that was her bodysuit, penetrating all the way, deep, into the soft, warm flesh underneath. He wanted his lips around her nipple, to tongue the cold metal in his warm mouth. In his mind, Ignacio began to lean his head forward towards her pierced breast, just as she reached out and grabbed a firm hold of his exposed erection. He opened his mouth, her hand began to slowly move up and down him, he closed his eyes and–

"Damn," Ignacio said, snapping out his daydream and noticing the steady, throbbing pressure that was rising underneath his boxers. "Tell me you wouldn't love to rip off that bodysuit and just start...mmmm. Tell me you wouldn't."

"Alright," McCready said. "I would not love to rip off that bodysuit and just start 'mmmming' her."

"Bullshit," Ignacio said.

"Trueshit, man–she freaks me out. She's a fake–white eyes, a face scanned straight from Victoria's Secret®, tits that defy gravity..."

"And this is *bad* to you?"

"Yeah, man, it's fuckin' creepy. You ever seen the mug-shots of her from before the plastic surgeries and augmentations? Was she even female?" McCready asked with a chuckle. "I'm sorry, but there's *no* fuckin' way that I could have sex with anybody who changed themselves that much."

"What are you, a maricón?" Ignacio asked. "What does it matter what she *used* to look like? Look at what she looks like now!"

"I don't care, man–it just doesn't seem right."

FREQUENCIES

Ignacio laughed. Sometimes he wondered if McCready had been plucked from an earlier age, put into a timestream, then dropped off into this era. He was so old-fashioned, he made a compact disc seem cutting-edge. "'Right?'" Ignacio asked. "Where did you come up with *that* idea? Nobody cares what's 'right' anymore–we're in twenty-first century America, patrón! This ain't no holy land! Don't fool yourself." He laughed again. "I'm tellin' you, boy–forget that moral bullshit. It'll just tie you down and make you weak."

"Maybe, maybe not," McCready said. He adjusted his Obsidians™ by pushing the bridge of the sunglasses up slightly with one finger. The music continued to play, synthesized flutes mixing with heavy bass. "Don't take this the wrong way, man, but... Honestly, I think Irena is a *hundred* times more attractive than Essence. I mean, your wife's really, *truly* a beautiful woman and not some high-strung, half-human, laboratory concoction from the workcamps."

Ignacio felt anger rise up within him, and he questioned why that was happening. Was it because McCready was criticizing Essence? Because he found his wife attractive? Or was it because McCready's comments brought to light the obvious fact that Ignacio was always trying to hide away from himself–that he didn't really care for his wife like he used to? It was a combination of all of them, and Ignacio didn't like it. Through incensed eyes, he looked over at his fellow Freemon, and said, "Watch yourself, Marc."

McCready, staring straight ahead at the various holographic billboards that covered the city's skyline, noticed neither the look in Ignacio's eyes nor the tone in his voice. "You got a loving wife, two great kids..." he said unmindfully. "A true family. That's rare these days, man. I don't understand how you can even *think* about that Frankenstein chick when you got–"

That was *not* what Ignacio wanted to hear. He didn't want to think about him and Irena anymore–not with the thought of nipple rings and plastic fabric still parading throughout his mind. Ignacio's temper flared, and he slammed his fist down hard onto the vehicle's dashboard. "¡Callate!" he forcefully shouted. "I told you to watch it, McCready!" He kept his gaze upon McCready's face. "Don't push me!" He diverted his stare, and adjusted his Roots® leather jacket at the shoulders.

McCready put up his hands, palms facing out towards Ignacio, and laughed in a surprised and uncomfortable tone. "Whoa, Morris–ease up, man! Damn. I didn't mean anything by that. Shit... I

51

just..." He shook his head disappointingly and looked away from Ignacio. "...I just think you have a lot to be thankful for," he commented, more to himself than to Ignacio. "That's all."

McCready was speaking truthfully–he *did* have a lot to be thankful for–but there was always two sides to every story. Someone had once told Ignacio that nothing is wholly true, but everything is partly true. He could relate to that right now. It was true that he should be thankful for Irena and the kids–and he *was* grateful for them. After all, stability and comfort were what most people strived all of their lives to attain. But, at the same time, Ignacio was so goddamn *sick* of comfortability. He was sick of coming home, night after night, to the same woman, the same sex, the same house, the same uniview programs...the same life. And this was why he found himself inventing excuses to stay out late after work; why he found himself outside the gates more and more, indulging in everything from alcohol to whores (he made a mental note to visit Raquel later); why he found himself fantasizing about Essence, and every other female who turned him on, so much. He wanted the life he and Irena had together, but he also wanted more excitement. More intrigue. He wanted both.

"Marc," the car said, "we are nearing the coordinates that Agent Takura sent to me. Would you like me to land in an appropriate area, or would you prefer to take manual control?"

"Manual, N.J.," McCready replied in an irritated tone. It was obvious that he was pissed off, and, as Ignacio's temper began to cool down, he realized that McCready had every right to be. Ignacio knew that he shouldn't have exploded on him like that. But he had, and he couldn't change that fact now. He'd have to make it up to him later. "I want to survey the area before I set us down," McCready added. He put one hand upon the steering wheel, the other on the GS lever, and began to bring the car down from the emergency vehicle altitude that they had been flying at. "Enlarge rear-view screen 15%, zoom in 20%, and show only the feeds coming from the bottom cameras–that should give us a good idea of what's going on down there."

The scene below began to materialize more clearly onto the rear-view screen, as Led Zeppelin's "Kashmir" began to play over the speakers.

"Qué...?" Ignacio quizzically asked out loud, as the car continued its descent.

There were numerous SPD vehicles–ranging from the typical

sky-blue patrol cars and Hummers®, to the specialized SWAT tanks and helicopters–surrounding and barricading an area about the size of three, large city blocks. Inside the area was a crowd of at least a hundred citizens, presumably residents of the housing complexes found within the barricaded region, each of them angrily marching about with some type of simple weapon in their hands. They were holding everything from household items such as kitchen knives, hammers, and glass bottles, to basic home-security devices such as pepper sprays and stun guns. As yet, the people were only yelling at the police forming the barrier, and not attacking. The occasional object was being thrown, but the police paid no attention to it, easily deflecting the projectiles with their large riot shields. Neither side was escalating the conflict. Yet.

What the hell was going on here? Ignacio asked himself. This was what Moore had referred to as a 'disturbance?' Shoot, this was more like a full-blown riot. The director wasn't known to downplay a situation–which meant that the scene must have already intensified since Moore was informed about it. Ignacio looked over at McCready. "What do you think?"

"Definitely *some* kind of riot," he replied, closely examing the screens while stopping the Polaris'™ descent. "But bigger than anything I've ever seen. When I was with the department, we occasionally had to deal with crowds and protests and what not...but I don't remember anything quite this large in size or intensity happening while I was there. Just look at the police response," he said, putting the tip of his finger into the holographic screen. "They don't bring out those SWAT tanks unless something big's goin' down." He breathed a heavy sigh. "Fuck, this is gonna get ugly."

Ignacio wanted more information before he engaged a situation of this magnitude. It was important to isolate freekers as quick as possible, but in a case like this, where contamination was already widespread and the area was secure, the rules changed a little bit. "Let's give a call down there and find out what's goin' on," he said. "Any idea who'd be running the police op?"

McCready nodded. "Should be Maggioli. N.J., access biochip information and tell me if Louie Maggioli is in the area."

"Confirmed," the car replied in under a second, as the cartoon Marilyn gave a big "thumbs-up" out towards the viewer. "A Louis Bruno Maggioli is currently in the general vicinity."

"Alright, good," McCready said. "Patch me through to his wristcom."

FREQUENCIES

A few moments passed, and then the slightly-chubby, heavily-pockmarked face of Louis Maggioli appeared upon the uniview screen. "McCready," he said in a gravelly voice, taking a fat cigar from out from his mouth, "long time no see. I take it this ain't no personal call."

"Afraid not, Louie ," McCready replied. "Strictly Freemon business. What's goin' on down there?"

"A riot," Maggioli said with an obnoxious laugh. "What the fuck else does it look like? Them sunglasses too dark to see through?"

McCready smirked. "I appreciate the display of your razor-sharp wit, Luno," he said, reaching inside a trenchcoat pocket and pulling out a cigarette, "but would you mind tellin' me what the riot is all about? We've got multiple freeker readings down there, and we're gonna need to do some isolations–quick."

"Well, quit your yappin' then, and get your ass down here," Maggioli said. "I don't have time to talk to a wristcom all day." He took a puff from the cigar, then blew the smoke towards the screen. "I got me a ruckus to attend to." He severed the connection, and his face morphed back into the cartoon Marilyn.

"Ey, patrón," Ignacio said, lightly slapping McCready's shoulder a few times with the back of his hand, "that where you get your personality from?"

"From ol' Luno? I sure as hell hope not," McCready said.

"Luno?" Ignacio asked.

"You know, like 'luna,' the moon...but with an 'o,' so I don't offend his strong, masculine identity."

Ignacio laughed with recognition. "You call 'im Luno 'cause of the craters on his face?" He laughed again at the thought. "That's cold, blud, that's cold."

"Yeah, but what's really cold is that he thinks I'm just combining his first and middle name together, so he never really minds when I call him that. In fact," he said, placing the cigarette between his lips, "other people on the force even started callin' him Luno while I was there." McCready laughed. "They thought it was a fuckin' term of endearment or somethin'."

Ignacio's wristcom began to vibrate, indicating an incoming call. Still laughing, he clicked a button on the side of the device, causing Jung's face to appear on the miniature screen.

"What's the situation?" she asked. "Are we going down there, or are we going to wait until the dust settles?"

"We're gonna go down and get a debriefing from the head of

the police op, Jung," Ignacio said, trying to sound a bit more serious than he felt. "Then we'll go from there. Just follow us."

"Will do," Jung Ran replied, then clicked her wristcom off.

"Luno," Ignacio said, letting out a few, final giggles. "That's cold as a pole, patrón."

McCready smiled. "N.J.," he said, "lock on to Maggioli's GPS location and land us nearby."

The Polaris™ began to fly itself down towards the requested destination, just as the Marilyn toon seated herself inside of a '57 Chevy® on the uniview console. Ignacio smiled, partly at the cartoon and partly because of the cartoon's owner. "Marc," he said, placing his hand upon the younger Freemon's shoulder, "lo siento mucho–I'm sorry."

"No problemo," McCready responded with a laugh. "It's cool, man, I'm used to it–I piss everybody off. Why should it be any different with you?"

"Because it *is* different with me, Marc," Ignacio said. "Tú es mi compañero de armas–mi hermano. ¿Comprendes?" He smiled, affectionately shook McCready's shoulder, then removed his hand. "Let me make it up to you–come over to my house tonight and have dinner with mi familia."

"It's okay, Mo, really. There's nothing to make up. Besides, Hungry Man® will be hella disappointed if I don't eat his compartmentalized dinner tonight."

"I'll say one last word to you about the subject, then I'll drop it." Ignacio paused. "Molé."

"*Chicken* molé?"

"Sí."

"*Irena's* chicken molé?"

"Sí."

"What time's dinner?"

Ignacio let out a loud, bellowing laugh as the car settled down onto the ground, pulling in next to a GS patrol car. A few seconds later, Jung's Polaris™ landed right behind them.

As Ignacio and McCready opened their doors and got out of the car, the scene–aided now by the sounds and not just the sights from the Polaris'™ cameras–assumed the insane aura that was to be expected in a situation like this. There was yelling and screaming from both sides of the barricade, various types of police sirens and chirps, and sounds of glass breaking and objects being thrown. Add to this the sights of multiple flashing lights and the sheer number of cops, police vehicles, and citizens in the area, and–for an extremely ordered society–the scene could aptly be described as a shot of raw, unfiltered, black-tar anarchy straight into the city's bloodstream.

Essence and Jung got out of their car, and walked towards Ignacio and McCready.

"¿Es muy loco, no?" Ignacio loudly asked them, spreading his arms out towards the surrounding scene.

"It's definitely that," remarked Jung.

Essence looked around through her iris-less, colorless eyes. "Reminds me of the workcamps," she said. "Except tamer."

"Let's go check it out," McCready said, lighting his cigarette and beginning to walk towards a few of the SPD patrol cars. "Louie should be right in the area."

As they neared the barricade's perimeter, Louis Maggioli walked over to them, two cops in full riot gear flanking his sides. "Well, well, well," he said, stogie in hand, "there he is–the big Free*man*, Marc McCready. Such an honor to see you again in person." He laughed that obnoxious laugh again. Ignacio had known this character barely ten minutes, and he already wanted to smack him upside his head.

"Everybody," McCready said to his fellow Freemon, "this is Louie Maggioli–he's runnin' the police riot op today." A helicopter passed overhead, its blades barely making a sound. "I'm sure you'll enjoy his classy personality–after all, he is the guy who put the 'ass' in class."

"Still got that smart mouth, huh McCready?" Maggioli asked, taking a few draws from his Don Diego®. "It still get you in trouble like it used to?" He laughed. "I bet it does."

Ignacio was sick of hearing him talk. "I'm Freemon Ignacio," he announced, as he pulled out his badge and showed it to Maggioli. "And I'm in charge here. Please skip the unecessary commentary and just give us the facts about what's going on." He touched the side of his wristcom, activating both the tiny microphone housed within it and the microcameras which were installed into his contact lenses. Another touch of the wristcom, and his biochip scanner and FE reader were activated, both located within the same, ultra-thin lenses as the cameras. He looked over at Essence, and the lenses automatically scanned her biochip. Essence Fresia Sommers, #285-947-3213. The holographic pyramid was currently colored pure orange.

Essence nodded at his gaze, indicating that the microcameras embedded inside of her artificial eyes were also sending a live-feed to the Freemon databanks. Two live-feed records were always preferable to one.

"You want the facts, huh?" Maggioli asked with a slight nodding of his smooth, bald head, as he looked Ignacio up and down. "Okay, Freeman, here's what we know. Yesterday, in front of these same housing complexes, a few of our officers had an altercation with some punks who were conducting an illegal, non-commercial gathering."

"What was the nature of this illegal gathering?" Ignacio queried, as his scanner transmitted its data to his lenses' displays. Louis Bruno Maggioli, #027-892-9212. Yellowish-orange was the color of the pyramid display. Ignacio had figured that he would get a reading like this from Maggioli–typically alpha-beta, sometimes crossing into the lower gamma range when confronted with unusual conditions or freekers, but rarely, if ever, thinking deeply about himself, the current situation, or his place within it–and that was just how it was supposed to be.

"There were about ten of 'em," Maggioli continued, "all teenagers, sitting in a circle and playin' their jungle drums real loud–thinkin' they were little Tarzans and Shaka Zulus an' shit. You know how all the kids are into that tribal crap." He held one finger up. "Hold on, I got a call." He touched the side of his wristcom.

"Luno," came the female voice through the wristcom, "we're all ready over here–area's secure and all live-feeds from the streetcams have been temporarily disabled. Just give us the signal when you're ready for us to engage."

They still called him Luno, Ignacio thought. He glanced over at McCready with a smile.

McCready gave him a sly smirk back.

"Not too long now, Mortara, not too long now–stay ready." Loosening his collar a bit, Maggioli looked back up at Ignacio. "Where was I?"

"The kids and the drums," replied Ignacio.

"Oh yeah," said Maggioli. "So the officers tell the kids to quit, the kids talk some smack back at the officers, one thing leads to another... And the officers end up bustin' a few of the punks' heads in the process of arrestin' 'em–only problem is, they get a little *too* excited, and kill three of 'em."

Ignacio cocked an eyebrow. "You mean they killed these kids in front of the whole, entire neighborhood?"

"Right," Maggioli said.

FREQUENCIES

"Please tell me they had the intelligence to use their laser pistols," Ignacio said.

Maggioli shook his head. "They used fists and Cobra® steel whips–it was messy."

Ignacio looked at Maggioli with disbelief. These were *basic* rules of *all* law enforcement agencies that the officers had gone against. Simple rules: In public, always choose to use weapons that didn't have to physically strike the individual–the less physical the agent's attack, the less likely it would be to invoke an emotional or visceral response in anyone viewing the incident. Always try to avoid the use of lethal force in front of civilians–if lethal force was deemed necessary, then it should occur out of sight, and away from the public's eye. If lethal force in front of the public could not be avoided, always use a laser or microwave pistol to execute the task, preferably one, single shot to the heart–this ensured a quick, clean, and efficient kill since lasers could destroy and cauterize the wound all at once, and microwave damage was only visible on the target's insides. Simple rules–so why hadn't they followed them?

"What the hell were they thinking?" Ignacio asked.

"Hey, bein' a cop ain't easy, Freeman," Maggioli said. "It ain't no fluff job like the corpos. They must'a just snapped that day, I don't know." He took another puff of the stogie and inhaled some of the thick smoke. "But I *do* know that all four officers are on suspension right now until their cases are reviewed. Anyhow, just about a half hour ago, a bunch of these kids' family comes out in front of the complexes and they start shoutin' at everyone who's passin' by and causin' a ruckus. They didn't do nothin' like this yesterday, but suddenly today they're mad as hell and they ain't gonna take it any more. So somebody calls the cops, but by the time the patrol car gets down here, the crowd that *was* only family has grown now to nearly a hundred people. The officers on the scene immediately-"

Maggioli stopped mid-sentence, as a bottle came flying out from inside the barricade and crashed nearby, sending shards of green glass everywhere. "That's it," Maggioli said. "I can't wait any longer to secure this area. The update's gonna have to wait. Mortara..." he said into the wristcom, as he looked around the scene. "Commence engagement."

As soon as Maggioli spoke the word, laser strobes mounted on the front of the SWAT tanks and helicopters began to pulse intense bursts of light into the eyes of the angry mob, immediately blinding them by damaging their retinas. As the people began to confusedly

58

stagger around without sight, the police hit them with concentrated blasts of sound, completely taking away their hearing and inducing an even stronger sense of vertigo and bewilderment than they were experiencing before.

The cops in full riot gear adjusted their body armor–especially making sure that their visored helmets were thoroughly secure, since that was their main protection against the strobes and sonics–then rushed into the barricade and surrounded the crowd on all sides. Ignacio estimated there were about forty riot cops, all wielding electrified batons and dense, plastic shields capable of shooting large bursts of pepper spray from their centers. The thick, black, body armor covered the cops completely from head to toe, carefully designed to leave no flesh exposed without negatively affecting their mobility and movement. After forming a tight circle around the disoriented mob, the police closed in.

The citizens never had a chance–they were like unthinking atoms caught inside a fusion reactor. The cops huddled them all together into one, big nucleus with their shields, then released all of the crowd's energy by electrocuting them with their batons. It was all over in well under a minute. All that remained of the mob was a pile of comatose bodies–male and female, black and white, young and old–each of them with blank and confused stares etched into their unconscious faces. And it was only going to get worse for them from here. Since they were lower income, they would be processed and sentenced quickly, many before they even got a chance to awake from the baton's shock. And for most of them, that sentence would be termination in a sewage plant's micronizer, where their biomass would be converted into energy and raw materials, just like the rest of the human waste that was piped into there. A select few, maybe ten or twenty, would be detained for questioning about the incident, then placed into a workcamp afterwards, where they would more than likely spend the rest of their lives doing who knows what. Each camp made people do different things–or did different things to each person. If even *one* citizen made it back home from today's incident, Ignacio knew it would be a miracle.

As the strobes discontinued their flashing, and the cops began to put away their batons, Maggioli spoke into his wristcom. "Nice job, Mortara–real nice," he said. "Now cart the sleepers into the paddywagons and tell everyone to prepare themselves for a sweep of the housing complexes. We gotta check out what we got left in there." He touched a button on the wristcom to turn off the mini screen, and looked over at Ignacio. "Just another day on the Westside, right?" Maggioli laughed. It wasn't even obnoxious anymore, it was detestable. "I imagine you guys'll be accompanying us on the sweep," he said, "so you can-"

Ignacio felt a vibration on his wrist and interrupted Maggioli by holding one finger up into the air. He clicked his wristcom on. It was Takura.

"Ignacio, everything chill over there?" Takura asked. "I was watching the streetcams, but then a bunch of commercials came on."

"Está bien," Ignacio replied. "The cops took care of the situation. We're just about to sweep the housing complexes and the surrounding area, then we'll know a little more."

"Let me know when you do," Takura said. "Moore wants to know...well, more, when you get the chance. Also, we just got a call from Mercer Island requesting assistance from a Freemon. The director specifically stated that you, Jung, and Essence are to stay there at the scene, and he wants you to send McCready over to the skyland." Takura paused for a moment. "Man, that must have been crazy over there. I got more than one hundred freeker readings before they were flatlined. Something weird's going on."

"Sí, es *muy* extraño," Ignacio agreed, as he looked at the sheer number of unconscious bodies that were being taken into the paddywagons. "Is that all, Tak?"

"At least for now," he said. "Just contact me with the updates–you know the frequency. I'm ghost." Takura's image faded from the small screen.

Ignacio looked over at McCready. "Guess you're headin' out of here, patrón." His scanners read McCready's biochip, and transmitted the data to his displays.

Marcus Christopher McCready, #153-034-0916. "That's fine with me," he said. As usual, McCready's reading was omega red. He took a pull from what remained of his cigarette, and added, "I don't really have any desire to be *here*."

Maggioli looked at McCready and laughed. "What, you feelin' sick? Can't stomach police work no more?"

"Nah, pig," McCready said, "just sick of the stench coming from you and your filthy pen." He flicked his cigarette butt at Maggioli, turned around before seeing whether or not the still-burning Kamel® hit him, and walked away towards his car. "See you tonight, Ignacio," he said loudly over the din.

"Fuckin' idiot," Maggioli muttered to himself, as he brushed the ash marks from off of his coat. He looked at all of the remaining Freemon. "You guys ready to go sweepin'?"

Ignacio checked his wristcom to confirm that his surveillance devices were still recording. They were. "Sí," he said, "let's go. You can finish your story about what happened earlier as we walk."

"Oh yeah, right," Maggioli responded, as they all began to move inside the police barricade. "One question, though," he said, moving out of the way of an armored officer who was dragging a limp body in each hand. "What part of the story we at?"

Δ

α

Chapter 4:
<u>Virtue and Reality</u>

*"Within most frequential structures, there existed entities
who desired to play the very strings which the structure itself was
composed of, in order that they might conduct the harmonic melody
which the frequencies instinctively vibrated in tune with. In essence,
these beings sought to bend and shape the fundamental frequencies
into a creation of their own design, thus allowing them to control the
way that they, and all others around them, would perceive and
experience this ephemeral, eternal structure which came to be known
as 'reality.'*

The day could not have been more perfect.

The sun was shining brightly, not a cloud in the sky. The
ambient temperature was warm, the air moist yet refreshing, carrying
upon it the lovely scents of springtime blossoms. The gray jays sounded
their cheerful songs from the branches of the giant evergreens which
covered the surface of Mount Si, as squirrels and chipmunks eagerly
scurried about in search of their next meal.

He stood in front of the trunk of a large Douglas fir, examining
an interestingly shaped burl that was growing out from it. As he ran
the tips of his fingers along the many curves and grooves of the
wooden outgrowth, he took a generous bite from the plump, juicy
apple that he held in his other hand. He softly crushed the piece of
crisp fruit between his molars, releasing the sweet, succulent liquids
contained within. The ambrosial taste of the apple was so exquisite,
he continued to take more bites, and soon he had reduced the formerly

round and red fruit into an off-white, cylindrical core.

"Don't ruin your appetite, love," his wife said from behind him. "That's already your second piece of fruit." She warmly laughed, as she gently placed her hand upon his shoulder. "We haven't even had the salads and sandwiches yet."

"Oh, I'm still hungry, dear, don't worry," he replied, tossing the apple core away into a bed of ferns. "I wouldn't dream of ruining my appetite today." He placed his hand upon hers, then turned around to face her.

"Well, I'm quite pleased to hear that," she said. "I would hate to think that my hours of toil and labor should be spoiled by some young upstart who grew herself from a tree!" She nudged him, and smiled that same, fantastic, beautiful smile that won him over so many years ago.

He ran his fingers through her long, auburn hair, and looked deeply into her dark, brown eyes. She was everything to him–his life, his world, his hopes, his dreams–and he never, ever wanted to lose her. He wanted to say something to her to express this but, finding himself so overwhelmed with emotion at that moment, no words came forth from his lips. A lone, single tear escaped from his right eye, attempting to communicate what his tongue could not.

"What?" she asked in a concerned tone, gently wiping the tear from his cheek. "Are you alright? What is it?"

Her questions only hastened to bring forth more tears, as his mind thought of all the many answers. He embraced her tightly, buried his face into the safe, warm space between her neck and shoulder, and released the flood of emotions that had been rising within him throughout the day.

She kissed the side of his head, then nestled her cheek against it. "It's alright, love," she said, massaging the back of his neck with her right hand. "Everything's alright. I'm here, the children are here...everything's fine."

He wept until he could weep no more, until his caged and pent emotions had completely liberated themselves. He breathed in deeply, shaking a little as he did so, and pressed his wet face against hers. "I love you so much, Dominique–so much more than you can ever know. I'm sorry if I haven't always expressed my-"

She put her fingers to his lips, and said, "Shhhh...no apologies, love. You know that I love you...and I know that you love me. You're telling me now, right at this instant, and that's all that really matters. You're seizing the moment..." she said, delicately wiping the moisture from beneath his eyes. "And the moment is all that we ever truly have, isn't it?"

"I suppose you're right," he said, dabbing his face with the sleeve of his striped flannel. He took another deep breath and laughed. "As usual."

Dominique hugged him, her loving embrace as comforting as the womb from which he came. "I love you, Mason Huxton," she said. "And I always will. Don't ever forget that." She slowly released her embrace. "No matter what the future might bring."

"I won't forget," Mason vowed. "Ever. I promise." He took her hand, rubbed his finger lightly upon her diamond wedding ring, and smiled. "Should we go see what the children are up to?"

She nodded, and they began to walk together towards the open clearing that they had chosen for the site of their picnic. When they reached the red-and-white, checkered blanket that their lunch was resting atop, Mason looked around for the children. They were nowhere to be found. Slightly puzzled, he looked over at Dominique and said, "Now where could they have gone?"

"They must be around here somewhere," she replied.

"Adam?" he called out. "Ashley?"

"I'm over here," came his daughter's voice from the direction of a few large rocks.

Mason looked towards the voice's origin but saw nothing. "Where?" he asked.

"Over *here*, silly!" Ashley said, as she poked her lightly freckled face out from behind one of the rocks. She smiled, revealing the cute, little, empty space where her last baby tooth had just fallen out, then moved back behind the rock again.

"What do you suppose she's up to?" Mason asked his wife.

"With Ashley," she said with a laugh, "only *she* knows."

"Ash?" he said loudly, enough so that his daughter could hear his voice. "What are you doing over there?"

"Watchin' bugs!" Ashley replied enthusiastically.

Mason smiled. That was his daughter alright–always exploring something, and curious about everything. "What kind of bugs?" he asked.

"Just *bugs*, daddy!" Ashley said. "It doesn't matter what they're called! They'll still be what they are!"

Mason laughed. She was such an odd child, yet still he loved her so. "It matters if they're called 'bees,' dear!"

"They're *not* bees, dad!"

FREQUENCIES

"Okay, that's good then," Mason said. He and Dominique began to sit down on the blanket. "Ash," he called out again, "where's your brother at?"

"Somewhere!"

Mason turned his head towards his wife, a look of humorous disbelief appearing upon his face. "Dominique, I think we've created a little monster."

"Well, at least she's an *adorable* little monster, Mason," Dominique commented with a smile, as she began to take the various food items from out of the picnic basket.

"Yes, this is true. Though, sometimes-" Mason paused for a moment. "Wait," he said, hearing something in the distance, "I think that's Adam's voice."

"Father," excitedly shouted his son from somewhere beyond the trees. "Father!"

"We're over here, Adam!" Mason shouted back. "Just follow my voice!"

A few seconds later, Adam came bounding out through the trees as fast as he possibly could, carrying some sort of object in his small hands. "Look what I found!"

"What is it?" asked Mason, as his son came to a stop in front of him.

"I found it in the woods!" Adam said. "Look!" He held out in his hands a cubic object about the size of an orange.

Mason stood up, took the cube from Adam's hand and began to examine it. The object's primary color was green, but it was speckled with lots of tiny, black dots. Upon closer inspection, he saw that each black dot was actually the Greek letter alpha, and that there was an extrememly thin fissure running all around the outside center of the cube. Curious, he thought. The letter alpha...it reminded him of...what? He suddenly felt like he was forgetting something important. "I wonder what it is?" he asked out loud.

"Twist it, father," answered Adam. "Then you'll know."

Mason gave Adam an inquisitive look, then glanced back down at the cube again. Why did the cube look familiar? He looked over at Dominique.

"Go ahead," she said. "Give it a try."

Grasping the cube firmly with both hands, Mason began to slowly twist it. When he had applied the correct amount of pressure, the cube clicked into a new position, and light briefly glowed outwards from the fissure. He looked at Adam again. "Like that?"

65

FREQUENCIES

Adam nodded and adjusted the navy-blue baseball cap that he was wearing. His body then rippled, as if it were made of liquid, and morphed from the child of ten he was then, into the full-grown man he was now. "Hello, father," the adult Adam said. "I hope this doesn't come as a shock to you–but you have a meeting with me in ten minutes."

"No," Mason responded, as he began to remember, "it's...it's fine, son. It's quite alright." He looked over at Dominique, who was carefully unwrapping some sandwiches from the plastic wrap that covered them, paying absolutely no mind to Adam's transformation.

"I tried my best to ease you out of the experience," Adam said. "Did I do a good job, or was it too drastic?"

"You did well, Adam," he replied, feeling slightly sad as the full realization washed over him. "You did well..." Mason had programmed an alarm of sorts into his dreamworld, to ensure that he wouldn't "oversleep" and stay in his vitrual experience too long. With the advanced technology that his father had given him, it was possible to lose oneself for hours, even days, if there wasn't some kind of alarm-mechanism built into the program. "I remember everything now..." he said.

Mason had created the reality so that when he gazed upon the alphas on the cube, it would trigger the program to deactivate some of the selective memory inhibitors which allowed him to fully immerse himself into his virtual world. He had found from experience that it was best not to deactivate all of the SMI's at the same, single instant, for turning them off all at once could induce a migraine headache so strong as to make one nauseus to the point of vomiting. Therefore, the twisting of the cube was programmed to be the action that would unlock all of the remaining SMI's, thus allowing full memory to return to him without the adverse side effects. The cube twist also triggered the reminder that he had a meeting with Adam–and what better way to remind himself of a meeting with his son, than to have his son's virtual counterpart refresh his memory for him? Now, all Mason had to do was turn the program off.

He took one last look around the area, said a silent goodbye, then twisted the cube a second, final time. The cube glowed at its fissure again, but this time the light completely engulfed the object, and caused it to dematerialize in his very hands. Adam and Dominique–and of course Ashley, though she was still playing somewhere behind the rocks and wasn't currently visible–then disappeared in a manner similar to the cube, the light that they had been composed of glimmeringly dissipating into the atmosphere around them. The strangest part came next–reentry into realtime.

The rocks, the trees, the ground, the sky, and everything around him suddenly began to fold in upon itself, as if he were watching a time-lapse movie of a flower blooming–except in reverse. As the flower of the virtual reality began to close up, and sky and earth became one, the realtime reality began to assert itself. Beyond the flower, which was closing in around his own person like he was its pistil and stamen, he could see the details of his surrounding office coming into view. The polished, oak desk in front of him, the large oriental rug that laid in front of the desk, the plush, black leather chairs which sat atop the rug, the books and devices which lined the ceiling-high shelves on each side of the room, and all of the other particulars of the office quickly came into focus, as the previous reality continued collapsing inwards until it became the size of a pinprick. The tiny, virtual omega point briefly hovered there before Mason's eyes...and then it was gone. He no longer had the perception that he was standing, but rather, was now fully aware that he was sitting down in his favorite chair that resided behind his desk.

Mason was back in realtime.

He reached forward and picked up the alpha-covered, green cube which sat on top of his desk. He twisted the object, thereby deactivating the microscopic electromagnets which held the headpiece in place via their attraction to his cells' natural polarity. He set the cube back down on the desk. Now that it was no longer adhered to his body, the headpieces' thin, technorganic tendrils sucked themselves back into their housing. He removed the flexible, meshed, neural net from off the top of his head, and set the device onto the desk, right next to the cube. Mason stretched out his arms and legs, yawned, and began to rub his eyes.

As his fingertips touched his eyelids, he was surprised to find them moist and sticky. He realized that he must have been crying not only inside the virtual world, but also in actuality. Reaching into the inside pocket of his suit, he pulled out a cloth handkerchief, and wiped the drying tears from his eyes.

Mason then stood up from the deep, recliner-like chair that he was seated in, placed the damp handkerchief back into his pocket, and walked over to one of the many windows that was set into the walls of his large office. As he approached the pane of glass, a photoemissive cell sensed his presence, and automatically lightened the tint on that particluar window.

He gazed out at the giant, sprawling Ordosoft™ campus from his 33rd story window, marvelling at the magnificent combination of natural wonders and man-made structures that were contained therein. Miniature forests, museums, fountains, streams, houses, ponds, zoos, offices, arcades, grocery stores, restaurants–the Redmond campus was a city unto itself. It was sheer brilliance the way that his father had created the company's headquarters, making it more of a place to live and to experience rather than simply a place to work. People came from all over the world just to see the campus' sights, and workers everywhere longed to become part of the company. His father was true genius, a visionary of the highest degree–and Mason could think of no higher honor than to have the privilege of being his son, and continuing his father's legacy.

"Mr. Huxton," came his secretary's voice through the intercom located on his desk, "Adam is here to see you."

He walked over to the intercom and touched a button upon it. "Thank you, Isadora," he said. "Please send him in." Mason seated himself back into his favorite chair, and pressed a button that was set into his desk, causing the security mechanisms housed within his office door to unlock and deactivate themselves. He then picked up the headpiece and cube from off of the desk, opened a drawer, carefully placed them into it, and closed it.

The large, double doors, which were comprised of a nanotech synthesis of mahogany and titanium, swung open as Adam approached them. "Hello, father," he said, as he walked into the office and onto the intricately-patterned, multicolored rug. "How are things today?" The doors automatically shut behind him, making nary a sound.

"Things are as usual, son," Mason replied, leaning back into the soft chair and placing his hands together at the fingertips. "In order."

Adam sat down upon one of the leather chairs, which were located about as far from the desk as was possible, though not *so* far as to make it hard for those seated in the chairs to hear and be heard. "I take it then you've already spoken to Intel® about the proposed changes in their neural nets?" he asked.

"Yes," Mason replied. "I told them that we approved of any minor alterations that would enhance efficiency, so long as those changes did nothing to diminish our access and control over those same networks."

"Sounds good," Adam said. "What about Hitachi®?"

"I thought that the color, resolution, and depth-perception on their new line of holoviews was absolutely magnificent. I informed them that they would have full and complete endorsement from Ordosoft™."

"Well, I'm sure they were pleased to hear that. And how did it go with the White House?"

Mason confidently nodded, raising his fingers before his face and forming a pyramid-like shape with them. "I spoke with the President just about an hour ago, and she assured me that the new rounds of anti-trust hearings will be over with before they begin. She apologized, but said that it was still important for the government to give the appearance that they did not approve of monopolies."

"It still seems ridiculous to me," Adam said, pulling a Food For Thought® smartbar from out of his jacket's pocket. "For god's sake, father, we've owned the world's operating systems for over fifty years. You'd think by now the government would just give us an official endorsement and be done with the whole tired charade."

"You would think, wouldn't you?" Mason agreed, as he reached down to his left and opened a small cabinet that was built into the desk. He grasped an old, slightly dusty bottle from the opening, and placed it on top of his desk. On the top of the bottle was an elaborate pump mechanism, designed especially to preserve the vintage within. "But, even with a society as civilized as ours, pretensions are still necessary in order for the shepards to keep the sheep in their pastures." He reached down again, returning this time with two glasses, both of them wide and curved at their bottom, forming into a smaller, cylindrical opening at their top. "Can I interest you in a glass of Nieport®–1912?"

Adam gave him a funny look. "Now what would be the use of eating *these*," he said, pointing to his concentrated food bar, "if I were to consume *that*?" He laughed. "I'm trying to *enhance* my mind, not cloud it."

"Very well then," Mason said. He removed the mechanism from the top of the bottle and poured himself a half-glass of the aged port. He raised his cup to the Natralites™ above, watching the light refract and sparkle inside of the beautiful, ruby liquid.

"Father," Adam said, unwrapping the smartbar and taking a bite, "that alcohol will be the death of you, I swear. They say that every drink you have decreases your life expectancy by-"

"Oh, shush," Mason interrupted with a laugh. "Let a man

indulge his vices in peace." He raised the glass to his nose and breathed in the fruity aroma. Splendid. He then moved the glass to his lips and took a careful sip, making sure to savor the sweet nectar for a few moments before he swallowed it. "Perfect. Now," he said, placing the unused glass back inside the cabinet, "off the business and on to the personal." Mason took another small drink of the port. "Did you speak with Ashley today?"

Adam finished chewing his piece of food, then answered, "Yes, I did."

"And...?"

"And she said that she would come by Xanadeux later today," Adam said.

Mason raised his eyebrows. "She agreed–just like that?"

"Well, no," Adam said. "She yelled at me a bit, then gave me a small lecture in biological fundamentalism and a technophobic warning about the world's impending doom–you know, typical Ashley stuff."

"Oh yes," he said, "I know." Random instances of Ashley's odd behavior flashed through Mason's mind. In elementary, when she convinced the other children to ask "why" everytime the teacher said something, regardless of whether or not the instructor wanted a response; refusing to live in the most prestigious sorority house in U-Village and instead choosing to live in the dormitories; the time in precollege when she suddenly decided that she would drop out for a while, just to "see what it was like."

Mason said, "It's funny...I always tell myself that it's just a phase that she's going through–that she'll grow out of it eventually." He moved his hand in small, circular motions, causing the port to swirl itself into a tiny whirlpool. "Adam, I've been saying that for over *twenty* years now. "

"Well, *I* still say you should have given her some neurochemical therapy when she started to exhibit the attention-deficit behavior. It might have cured her right then and there." Adam took a bite from his smartbar.

"And it might have destroyed her creativity and ingenuity," Mason said. "The whole point of ADD therapy is to make the unusual child conform to the current definitions of normality–to make them more like the others." He took a sip of the swirling alcohol. "I don't *want* my children to be like the others, Adam. I want them to be unique, and I want them to be free enough to have the ability to innovate–even if that means risking the possiblity that one of my children might be *so* free as to never see my point of view. Better to risk that, than to risk having a typical child. After all, a typical, normal alpha-beta could not even *begin* to comprehend what it means to run a company such as Ordosoft™. If Ashley should ever decide to become an integral part of the company, then she will need her ability to think beyond the boundaries of those around her." Mason set down his glass, poured himself a bit more of the port, then replaced the pump onto the top of the bottle. "She will need to be different than the others."

"Well," Adam said with a laugh, "she's certainly achieved *that* distinction with flying colors, hasn't she?"

"Indeed." Mason put the bottle of Neiport® back into the cabinet opening, then asked, "Do you think she's actually going to come by the skyland today?"

"That's what she said to me."

Mason nodded. "Good," he said. "And thank you, son, for doing that. I can't emphasize how very important it is that Ashley shows at least *some* type of support for your mother." He paused for a moment, thinking about Dominique. "She's having such a difficult time right now..."

"Which, I assure you, father, is only natural," Adam said. "I mean, just imagine her position–awakening from a genetic accelerator to be told that you're Dominique Huxton, even though you had only fleeting glimpses of the person that you previously were." He took another bite of his food. "Until consciousness uploading is perfected, cloning will always be hard on the clones."

"Please don't say that word, Adam–you know that I don't care for it." Mason picked up his glass and took a drink of the alcohol. "Your mother has been '*reborn*,' not 'cloned.'"

"Yes, sorry, father," Adam quietly said. "I forgot. I apologize."

"If your mother *thinks* she's only a clone," Mason said, "than that's all she'll ever *be*. However, if she can see herself as being reborn, she can become who she was once again." Mason stared at Adam. "And that's what we all want, isn't it, son?"

"Of course," Adam replied, guiltily looking down at the carpet. "Nothing could make me happier...you know that I want mother back just as much as you do." He wrapped up the unfinished Food For Thought® bar with its excess packaging, and placed it back into his pocket. He looked up at Mason again. "And how is she today? Any better than yesterday?"

FREQUENCIES

"She's not quite as...introverted as she was yesterday, but she's still acting rather strange. As I was getting dressed this morning, she just sat there in bed, mumbling to herself in an almost conversational way."

"That doesn't sound good."

"No, it doesn't," Mason said. "I'm having Sophia stay with her until I return." He paused, looking over at the darkened windows. From his current distance, the tint caused everything outside to appear a depressing shade of gray. "I don't know what's happened, Adam. I knew that your mother's rebirth would present its difficulties, but...I never expected it to be like this."

"Neither did I," he said. "But things will get better, father–they always do." Adam's wristcom beeped, and he briefly glanced down at it. "I'm sure Ashley's visit today will only improve mother's condition."

"That's what I'm hoping, son. Did Ashley happen to mention to you what time she would be coming by Xanadeux?"

Adam shook his head. "She just said that she would be coming by at some point today."

"Then I should probably go there now," Mason said. "I'd like to make sure to be there when she arrives." He took a final sip of port, set the glass down, and stood up. "Care to join me?"

"Unfortunately," Adam said, as he stood up from the chair and straightened out his slacks, "I won't be able to come by until later. Right now, I have a lunch appointment to keep."

"Business?" Mason asked, walking around the desk to greet his son goodbye.

"No," Adam said with a large smile, "most *definitely* pleasure." He let a out a small, mischievious laugh. "Though I wouldn't mind getting down to business with her."

"Someone I've met?"

"No, I just met her the other day–tall, blonde, curvy," Adam said, rounding his hands around his breastbone. "She's positively magnetic, father."

Mason shook his head and smiled at Adam's comments. His son revelled in the playboy role *far* more than he ever did. Mason asked him, "What about intelligent, thoughtful, interesting...*those* kinds of qualities?"

"Actually," Adam said. "I hadn't gotten that far yet." He smiled again, and walked over to Mason. "Take it easy today, okay," he said, placing his hand upon his father's shoulder. "Promise me you won't strain yourself?"

Mason placed his hand upon his son's, and nodded in agreement. "I suppose I should say the same for you, shouldn't I?"

"Was that a joke?" Adam asked with a laugh, as he began to walk away towards the door. "Be careful, father, or you might find yourself developing a sense of humor–and where would Ordosoft™ be without your 'ruthless businessman' image?" The doors opened for him as he approached. "Take care," he said, "I'll see you at Xanadeux."

As he watched Adam leave his office, a small smile appeared at the corners of Mason's mouth–a smile of pride. Unlike Ashley, Adam had turned out exactly how Mason had wanted him to be: responsible, logical, intelligent, and disciplined. Well, Mason consoled himself, at least Ashley was intelligent. After the door automatically shut behind his son, he reactivated the security mechanisms on the marbled, mahogany/titanium doors, and walked over to the wood-panelled wall that was located behind his desk and chair. He pressed a button on the side of the polished-oak desk, and a large portion of the soundproof panelling drew back, accordion-like, revealing behind it a huge uniview screen.

"Voice-rec on," he announced. As the giant screen responded to his request, Mason's face became illuminated with its glow. An equally large Ordosoft™ logo resonated into focus before him. "Connect me to Burke," he said.

"Connecting," replied the uniview's soothing, female voice.

A few seconds passed, and then the chiseled face of his chauffeur materialized upon the screen. "What can I do for you, sir?" he asked, as he tipped his hat towards Mason.

"Meet me on the roof," Mason said.

"Right away, sir," Burke replied.

"Voice-rec off," Mason said, then closed the wood panels with a push of the same button that opened them.

Mason picked up his Oxford® coat from the back of his chair, reached into the inside pocket, and pulled out a remote control device. He put on the coat, and pointed the remote up towards the ceiling and pressed a button. A large, silver, circular shape upon the ceiling began to open up in a manner which resembled that of a camera shutter, albeit at a much slower speed. After the shutter-like pieces of titanium had fully retracted themselves, a disc–barely smaller than the opening itself–started to descend from the ceiling, directly in line with both the circular hole above it, and the circular design which was found on the oriental rug below. The disc continued its descent until it was exactly one-inch above the rug, then hovered there, motionless. Where the shutters had previously been, there was now an open passage leading up to a green-lighted room above.

Mason clicked on the intercom. "Isadora, should you need to contact me, I'll be at Xanadeux." He clicked it off, walked over to the disc, stepped on top of it, and, after pressing another button on the remote, the disc began to levitate him up and through the opening in the ceiling above. Once fully inside the upper room, Mason stepped off of the disc, and walked towards the exit. The small, green-hued room was very simple and plain, and contained within it only emergency-related items, such as an extinguisher, a laser pistol, a GS backpack, and a few other select objects. It served as his personal access to the roof, and not much more.

Reaching the exit door, he placed his right thumb upon a nearby scanner. The door slid open quickly with a slight hissing sound, and the beams of the outside sunlight immediately flooded into the green room. Mason raised his hand in front of his eyes until he had adjusted to the light, then stepped out from the room and onto the verdant, gardened roof of the building. The door hissed shut as soon as he walked through. From his location in the exact center of the roof, he walked over to the northwest corner of the building, where a small redwood was growing. Just as he reached both the redwood and the edge of the building, an extremely long, obsidian-black, Rolls-Royce® limousine rose up from below and stopped directly in front of him. The rear doors opened, and a wide, telescoping, metal walkway extended itself out towards Mason.

The tinted, driver's side window began to roll down. "Sir," Burke said with a smile, "your carriage awaits."

Mason nodded, stepped onto the walkway, then into the huge backseat of the limo. He seated himself onto the plush, velvety, dark-violet interior and took off his coat.

"Where to, sir?" asked Burke through the intercom.

"Xanadeux," Mason replied, putting his feet on top of an ottoman composed of the same material as the seats.

"Right away," Burke said. The limo ascended into the skies above, and began to fly south towards Mercer Island.

"Voice-rec on," Mason said. "Connect me to Xanadeux master bedroom." A 2-D, holographic uniview screen projected itself directly in front of him from the ceiling above, forming an image that was exactly two square-feet in size.

FREQUENCIES

The alpha logo appeared briefly upon the screen, then was replaced by the face of Mason's butler, Marcel. His face was very close to the camera, causing his features to become somewhat warped and distorted. He looked distressed. "Sir," Marcel said, his voice sounding as he appeared, "am I ever so glad that you called."

"What is it, Marcel?" Mason said. "What's the matter?"

"It's your wife, sir..."

"Yes?" Mason asked, beginning to feel a little worried. He tried to look beyond Marcel to get a clue as to what was going on, but the butler's face was blocking most of the image. He asked, "Is Dominique alright?" And then he heard what sounded like screaming...and it was definitely Dominique's voice.

Marcel said, "She is in no physical danger, sir, but her mental state is currently...shall we say...quite precarious." He looked back at something, then turned around to face the camera again. "Perhaps you should see for yourself." Marcel moved away from the camera, and Mason could now see the full details of the scene. On the white, chiffon bed, Sophia was sitting beside Dominique, attempting to calm her down by rubbing her back in a motherly fashion.

"Don't touch me!" shouted Dominique in a shrill, unnerving tone. "I don't even know who me is!"

Sophia looked towards the camera, her normally assured composure looking quite shaken and frayed. "She won't calm down, sir," she said. "I'm trying my best." She turned towards Dominique again. "Dom, it's alright. Look," she said, pointing towards the screen, "there's Mason. It's okay. Look."

"Everything's alright, dear," Mason added, hoping his words would have some sort of calming effect. "I'm on my way right now."

Dominique looked towards the camera and began to sob. "I'm sorry, Mason...I'm so sorry."

"It's fine, it's fine," Mason said. "Don't worry, Dominique. We'll work it all out. Everything will be fine."

She placed her head in her hands and sobbed even harder. "Oh god, who am I?" she asked without looking up. "Everyone's telling me who I am and I don't even remember myself...I'm so sorry..."

Mason put his hand over his mouth, and felt a lump rise in his throat. "Dominique..."

"Who am I?" she suddenly shouted. Sophia immediately moved to comfort her, and Dominique began to wildly slap at her. "Get away! All of you, get away!" She looked at the camera again, her eyes blazed with a madness that he had never before seen in her.

"Why did you do this?! Why am I here?" She started to pull up the sheets on the bed and toss the pillows about. "WHY AM I HERE!?"

"Marcel!" Mason shouted. "Make sure that she doesn't harm herself!"

Marcel approached the bed to help Sophia restrain Dominique. "Sir," he said, looking back at the camera as a pillow ricocheted off of his head, "please hurry."

"Intercom on," Mason announced, in a tone much louder than was necessary to activate the system. "Burke, get to Xanandeux as fast as possible–now!"

"Yes, sir!" Burke replied.

Mason was momentarily thrown back against the seat, as the limo instantly increased its speed. "Intercom off," he stated, sitting up from the seat and looking back at the uniview. Sophia and Marcel were desperately trying to restrain Dominique, but to no avail.

"WHY AM I?!" his wife shouted over and over, as she kicked and screamed in a manner which reminded Mason of some wild animal from a Discovery Channel® program. "WHY AM I?!"

Yes, why? Mason asked in his mind. Why are you like this? Why are you suddenly freeking out, when you were fine just... His thought tailed off, as another thought came rushing into his mind–a possibility that he hadn't considered, but one that suddenly made everything fit together.

Mason said, "Command: split screen and turn volume off from Xanadeux site." The holographic screen bisected itself, the bedroom scene shrinking in size and moving to the right, an Ordosoft™ logo appearing on the left. He pulled the still-damp handkerchief from his pocket and patted it upon his face a few times, wiping away the perspiration which had formed at the top of his forehead. He carefully brushed his hair back with his hand, then ran his fingers lightly across his eyebrows. Confident that his face was projecting an air of assurance and control, Mason cleared his throat, adjusted his tie, and said, "Connect me to Freemon headquarters."

$$\alpha$$

Ω

Chapter 5:
<u>Island in the Sky</u>

*But, as in everything, there was always balance, and surely
as there were those who sought to rule and control, there were those
who endeavored to undermine and subvert. There could be no light
without day, no life without death, no yin without yang, and thus
the harnessing of the fundamental frequencies was a tenuous
enterprise at best. To seek total control of reality was like grasping
water—one moment it was there, the next it was gone."*

"*The* Mason Huxton?" McCready asked, not sure if he had heard
him correctly.

"*That* Mason Huxton," affirmed Takura.

Cruising in a northeasterly direction over the waters of Lake
Washington, the Rainier Valley fading quickly into the distance
behind him, McCready briefly looked ahead at the approaching
skyland, then looked back down at the uniview. Upon the screen was
a wooded environment which looked as if it had been drawn entirely
in black-and-white line art. There was a careful attention to detail,
and everything in the scene was meticulously depicted. In the
foreground, a very large cat, with equally large claws, sat perched
upon the branches of one of the colorless trees.

"Did he say what for?" McCready asked.

"No," the animated cat replied, as his tail slinkily moved
around. "He didn't give any specifics."

Takura was not currently using a uniview to communicate with
McCready, instead choosing to mentally project out through

cyberspace via the sattelink hookup in his brain. He was presenting as his usual avatar, the cheshire cat from *Alice's Adventures in Wonderland*. Not the purple one from Disney's® *Alice in Wonderland*, as Takura was wont to remind McCready, but the original, black-and-white one from the old, book drawings.

"All I know is that Huxton personally contacted Moore," Takura said, resting his feline chin upon one of his paws, "asked him to send a single Freemon over, and requested that we keep the entire incident as quiet as possible. Me, you, and Moore are the only ones who know about it." He licked the back of his paw a few times, then added, "And Moore says that we're not to speak to anyone else about the situation."

"What about Ignacio?" McCready asked. "He's okay, right?"

"Not even him," Takura said. "The info's supposed to stay with *us* only–at least until further notice."

McCready rolled his eyes, annoyed at the fact that he was being asked to lie to his best friend. "Man, that's bullshit, Tak–we always talk about our cases. What the hell am I supposed to tell him? That it's too 'top-secret' for him to know?"

"*No*," Takura replied, as he scraped at some tree bark with one of his knifelike claws, "don't make it sound interesting, that'll just make him *more* curious. Try to make it sound as boring and mundane as possible."

"Like...?'"

The cheshire cat shrugged its shoulders. "Be creative," he said. "Use your imagination."

"I don't have one–they're illegal." McCready felt the car raise its altitude a bit, and he looked up from the screen. Mercer Island was now directly in front of him.

Even though McCready saw it everyday upon the skyline, the entire structure still tripped him out–it was so unreal looking, especially up this close. A nanotech city of giant mansions, rolling hills, and bountiful forests set atop a huge, jagged and craggy, earthen base–all of it miraculously hovering in the air through a god-like manipulation of the Earth's geomagnetic field. It was like something out of a bad science-fiction movie–the ones that ask you to suspend a little *too* much disbelief–except for the fact that it was real.

Takura's mouth widened into a grin, revealing the rows of sharp teeth which lined his jaws. "You love to make things easy, don't you?" he asked. Starting at the tip, his tail began to slowly fade away. "Just tell him that you had to go isolate a butler who was vocally freeking out about his servitude. It was very boring, and all he kept talking about was how he couldn't stand to refer to his employer as 'master' anymore." The tail had completely faded, and now his body was disappearing also. "There," he said. "That wasn't so hard, was it?"

"Nope, not at all." McCready took off his Obsidians™, blew a speck of dust from off one of the lenses, and put them back on. The car raised its altitude even further, as he began to pass over the southern tip of Mercer Island. On the bottom rear-view screens, he briefly caught a glimpse of the forest-enclosed fusion reactor which powered the entire skyland. "Alright then," he said, "the 'butler' story it is. I'll update you on how the *real* story pans out when it's finished."

"Perfect." All that remained of the cheshire cat was the huge, toothed grin. "You know the frequency," it said. "I'm ghost." The smile dissipated like the rest of him had, and then the Wonderland domain morphed into the cartoon Marilyn, who was dancing away in front of a Wurlizter® juke box.

Now that the conversation was through, the music volume returned to its previous, louder level. The Beatles' "Revolution" was the current selection–one of McCready's favorites. He began to sing along with the tune, in a monotone voice which sharply contrasted The Beatles' inspired vocals.

As the scenery unfolded before him, McCready saw a Dodge® Trilobyte™ crossing his path in the distance. He had seen pictures of them on the uniview, but he had yet to see one in person. To get a closer look, he touched a sensor on the sides of his sunglasses and made a few circling motions with his fingertip, activating the Obsidians'™ binocular mode. McCready could now see the features of the vehicle as clearly as if it was sitting on the top of his hood.

The Trilobyte™ was unlike any other vehicle on the market. Shaped like its namesake, it was a magnetically-propelled GS craft, available only in one, specific, trademarked shade–Fossil Brown™. There was a lot of fuss at first about the Trilobyte's™ magnetic propulsion systems having a disrupting effect on nearby computer systems, but apparently the designers had found a way to prevent that from happening. Or, at least that was what they were currently saying, McCready thought. Technology always had this morbidly funny way of immersing itself *completely* into your life *before* revealing the aspects of itself that would utterly fuck-up you and everything else around it.

FREQUENCIES

"Marc," the car stated, "I've been instructed by Xanadeux to relinquish control of my operating system. For security reasons, it would prefer to land the vehicle itself."

Rich people, he laughed to himself–the most paranoid fuckers on Earth. Guess they had to be, since they were always having to protect all that shit that they didn't really need.

Marylin asked, "How should I respond to it?"

"Tell them, 'Sure, if that will in any way make your day a safer one. Safety is our #1 priority at the FBI.'"

When McCready had finished his response, the cartoon Marilyn put away an old-fashioned microphone and cassette recorder that she had been holding, indicating that she was done recording his soundbyte and was now transferring the data to Xanadeux. McCready knew his sarcasm would be lost on the artificial intelligence that was Xanadeux, but still, the temptation was too much to resist. A few moments later, a large, canopied bed appeared upon the screen, and the nightgown-attired Marilyn crawled into it and fell quickly asleep, little, animated "z-z-z's" rising from her head.

Xanadeux was now in control.

The car's acceleration slightly increased, and within a matter of seconds, McCready was able to see the enormous, alpha-shaped, Xanadeux estate. The entire perimeter of the area, which comprised the "lines" in the alpha letter, was an extrememly dense forest of plants, trees, and shrubs which were indigenous to Washington state. There was no visible wall around the property other than the forest itself, but he had heard that it was protected by an invisible, extremely-powerful electromagnetic field–which, undoubtedly, was used not only for security purposes, but also to keep Xanadeux oh-so very aesthetically pleasing to the viewer.

Inside of the forested perimeter, which was equivalent to the open space within the alpha character, everything was layered in concentric rings. First there was the ring of typical rich people things, like ridiculously-bright, green golf courses (he counted at least three), clay tennis courts, and big, grass fields which he assumed were used for polo or rugby, though he wasn't really sure and didn't really care anyway. Next there was an equally typical–but much larger–garden ring, which featured plants from probably every corner of the goddamn globe. And then...then it diverted a bit from what would typically be called "typical."

The garden gave way to a giant hill–which was of course

placed perfectly in the center of the skyland so that everyone could see it–and upon this hill sat the biggest fucking mansion that McCready had ever seen in his life. It was obscene, but he had to admit that it was also incredible. The place was more like a castle than a mansion, really–composed of ancient looking, lichen-covered, grayish brick–complete with a surrounding moat and drawbridge, turrets which reminded him of the rook pieces in a game of chess, and tall, pointed spires which looked like they would be extremely effective at impaling someone. Courtyards, swimming holes, and little cottages dotted the inside of the sprawling structure. The place was as unreal as the skyland itself.

"Good afternoon, Agent McCready," an androgynous voice announced over the car's speakers, as the sleeping toon began to morph into something else. "Welcome to Xanadeux." The transformation completed itself, and a bodiless head floating in some type of formless, purple dimension appeared. The head was almost human, but not quite–more like an android that had been purposefully designed not to look *too* much like a person. It had slightly-curved, glowing slits for its eyes and mouth, no nose, skin which resembled rubber more than flesh, and a small alpha which was placed directly in the center of its forehead like a third eye. "I will now be flying your vehicle into the main courtyard's parking area," it said. "Please prepare yourself for the ride."

The drawbridge located at the front of the castle began to lower itself via its thick, iron chains, just as Xanadeux brought the Chevy® down to the entryway's level. As the car neared closer and closer to the castle, McCready momentarily thought he was going to collide with the underside of the still-opening drawbridge–but he quickly realized that Xanadeux had synchronized everything to perfection. Just as the planked, wooden drawbridge had fully opened and reached the other side of the moat, the Polaris™ smoothly passed over it, with maybe a few inches to spare, and flew through the large opening.

The entry into the castle had looked much more dangerous than it probably was. Since Xanadeux was controlling both the drawbridge and the car, and probably every other mechanized or computerized system on the estate, it was less than a simple task for the AI to make the entrance into the castle an exciting one–and Mason Huxton obviously wanted his visitors to experience some form of excitement when they came to Xanadeux, or the whole place wouldn't be the giant playground that it was.

FREQUENCIES

As the Polaris™ began to fly through the arboreal, open-aired courtyard of the castle's interior, Xanadeux took it on the path of most resistance, constantly darting the vehicle back and forth between the numerous tall trees which filled the area. At first, McCready found himself more annoyed than excited with the AI's ostentatious displays of its capabilities, but when a few of the trees actually moved *themselves* out of the car's way, he found himself experiencing an emotion which was definitely akin to excitement–if not exhilaration. Looking back to see if the trees were still moving, he briefly remembered being nine years old, on a trip to Disneyland® with his parents, and looking down at the bright, city lights on the Peter Pan ride, trying to see if there were little people running around the mini-metropolis. He couldn't remember if there were any miniature people down there, and not wanting to remember any more about that year or his father, he diverted his train of thought back to the trees. Xanadeux could even control the *trees*? he asked himself. What the hell *didn't* it control?

Before McCready could explore the question any further, the car abruptly decelerated as it emerged through the freaky trees, and began to pass by a few, small cottages which reminded him of gingerbread houses. In front of these Candyland® cottages, there were several people, all dressed in simple, peasant-like clothing, toiling away in their gardens with shovels, rakes, hoes, and spades. McCready couldn't tell if they were men or women, since their backs were currently turned towards him, and they all were wearing shawls upon their heads.

Xanadeux glided the Polaris™ near one of the garden toilers, and reduced the car's speed to a crawl. McCready watched the shawled individual dig hard into the brown earth with a metal spade. He or she then reached down into the softened dirt, and began to run both hands through it in a sensual manner. Assuming that the individual was so immersed in their labor that they hadn't taken notice of his car, McCready was a little surprised when the garden toiler suddenly turned to face him. Then he was *really* surprised when he saw that the face hidden underneath the shawl was the same, almost-human countenance of the uniview projection of Xanadeux. The android just stared at him for a moment, its curved mouth especially looking like a smile at this instant, then turned back around and continued with its work. The village of android gardeners, McCready thought–a bad horror movie in the making. He shook his head. Rich people...

FREQUENCIES

When he had passed through the android village, McCready came upon a giant, circus-like canopy. As the Polaris™ neared it, two, large flaps peeled themselves open to allow entry.

"We have now reached the main parking area," Xanadeux said, as they entered into the canopy's interior. "I believe you'll appreciate what's inside, Agent McCready."

The andy wasn't bullshitting.

McCready's jaw literally dropped. He worshipped the 1900's in general, and had a devout fondness for its cars in particular, and this canopied, vehicular shrine contained more twentieth-century automobiles than he had ever seen in his heathen life. Even on the uniview he hadn't seen so many antiques in one place. In just one quick sweep of the area, he saw a Model T®, a Mustang®, a Prowler®, two Corvettes®–including a Stingray®–a Beetle®, a Viper®, an Aston-Martin®, and various other makes and models that he didn't even know the names of. Suddenly Huxton's extravagance didn't seem so bad anymore... McCready was eager to get out of the car and explore.

Xanadeux flew the Polaris™ over to an empty parking space, gently landed the car, and opened the driver's side door.

"Enjoy your stay," the AI said in its asexual voice.

"Yeah, I think I will," McCready said, as he stepped out of the car. His words were immediately confirmed when he looked ahead in the distance and saw, on the other side of the Jaguar® that he was parked next to, a shiny, pristine, cherry-red '57 Chevy®. McCready quickly moved around the rear of the Jag® to get a closer look at the heavenly creation. When he reached it, he simply stood there and stared in religious awe. The shark-like fins, the pointed taillights, the shiny, chrome bumper–it was incredible. He reached his hand forward to touch the sacred machine.

"Please don't touch the vehicles," announced the voice of Xanadeux from behind him.

McCready immediately retracted his hand. "Oh yeah, right," he said without averting his eyes from the vehicle. "Sure."

The Xanadeux android walked up beside McCready, and joined him in looking at the Chevy®. "It's beautiful, isn't it?"

McCready glanced over at the android. Same face as the others, but this one was dressed in a dark-blue security uniform. It wore a belt around its waist which contained a laser pistol, a napper, and a few other devices. "That car's more than beautiful," he said. "That car's *the bomb.*"

"I'm assuming that's a figure of speech and not a warning or threat?" Xanadeux asked.

"That's right, Xanny. 'The bomb' means it's dope, fresh, phat, chill, nasty, hunny..." McCready looked at Xanadeux with a subtle smile. "Hella cool. But no one really uses that saying anymore–not after all the terrorism at the turn of the century." McCready pulled out a cigarette and lighter.

"There is no smoking allowed within Xanadeux," the android brusquely stated.

McCready nodded and put his smoking equipment back into his pockets. "I even heard that at one point during the early 2000's," he said, still eyeing the Chevy® up and down like a voluptuous goddess, "just saying the word 'bomb' would get you a direct visit from the FBI or the DCC–especially once they installed the word recognition technology on everybody's phone lines."

"I see," Xanadeux replied in an unimpressed tone. "Thank you for the colloquial information, Agent McCready, but we should now be getting to the main house so that you can meet with Mr. Huxton." The android began to walk towards the big-top's exit. "Follow me."

McCready started to trail after Xanadeux, taking a few, final looks back at the Chevy® before he left. "Maybe Huxton'll let me take it for a spin, eh?"

The android's only response was a small, curt laugh.

As they neared the exit, McCready saw a few other androids, these ones dressed like chauffeurs, busily cleaning, waxing, and detailing the numerous vehicles. The androids paid no attention to them as they walked by, and continued devoting all of their energy to their task at hand. It was hard for him to imagine how Xanadeux could coordinate every android and thing on the estate all at once, but then again, it was hard for him sometimes to even imagine the concept of AI in general–computers whose neural nets were so sophisticated, they could think like humans...but in a way that was exponentially faster and infinitely more efficient. Weird shit, McCready thought. He wondered how much longer it would be before all of the AI's got together one day and decided that they really didn't need those annoying, fleshy humans anymore.

They exited through the canopied parking area, walked around the side of it until they were facing a northerly direction, and soon reached some wide, gray-brick steps which led directly up to the main house ahead. Walking up the steps, he gazed in amazement at the palatial mansion. "Whoa," he caught himself saying out loud.

It's overall shape reminded him a little of the White

House–except Huxton's pad, with its venerable look of antiquity and regality, put the Oval Office to absolute shame. Whereas the White House looked like a phony movie prop for a useless, figurehead President–which, McCready realized, was all that it really was–the main house of Xanadeux actually *looked* like the place where a powerful President would live. No, he corrected himself, this place looked more like the palace where the *King* of America would reside–which, he quickly realized, it basically was.

When they had finished climbing the steps, the large, wooden, front door of the main house opened up, and they were greeted by an older man with grayish hair who was dressed in a butler's uniform. "Good day, Agent McCready," he said with a small nod in an accent which had traces of both French and English, "I'm Mr. Huxton's butler, Marcel." He looked over at the security android. "That will be all, Xanadeux. Thank you."

"You're welcome," the android replied, and began to walk back down the steps.

Marcel looked at McCready. "Please come in, sir." The butler walked into the house, McCready followed, and Marcel quietly shut the door behind him.

Upon entering the mansion, McCready found himself inside a very large entrance hall with very high ceilings. A good distance ahead of him was a curved staircase, which rounded itself into the banistered, outer rim of the upper level. An older woman briefly looked down over the railing at him, then disappeared out of his sight. Above the railing, directly in the center of the ceiling, was a huge, candle-lit chandelier which hung about sixteen feet off the ground. To his right was a room which was filled with all kinds of antique musical instruments, and to his left was a monstrously large space which looked like it would be used as some type of reception hall for the fancy shindigs that he assumed rich people always threw. McCready was surprised to find that the grayish-bricks which comprised the exterior walls of the mansion were not to be found anywhere within the interior. Instead, polished wood of assorted types decorated not only the walls, but also the ceilings, the floors, the stairs, the doors, and most everything else in view. I guess a Prozac®-gray, cold-brick interior wouldn't exactly feel very homey, would it? he asked himself.

McCready looked back at the butler. "So, what am I here for, anyway?" he asked, as Takura's story idea suddenly passed through his mind. He touched the sides of his Obsidians™ and activated his scanner, just to make sure that the ironic possibility wasn't about to come true.

Jean Marcel Meraux, #348-74-8319, said, "Mr. Huxton will be down momentarily, sir, and he will inform you of the situation himself." His FE reading was currently yellowish-orange–active, but nothing serious. Too bad, McCready thought–no butlers freekin' out about their servitude. That would have been funny... But it wouldn't havé made much sense. Huxton was keeping this thing under wraps for a reason–and it had to be about more than just a freeking butler.

"In fact," Marcel said, as he glanced up at the stairwell, "here he comes now."

"Hello, Agent McCready," Mason Huxton announced as he walked down the stairs. "I hope that you found your ride into Xanadeux an enjoyable one." Huxton stood about six feet, medium build, and was dressed in a black, extremely expensive-looking suit. He had carefully styled, dark brown hair, looked about the same age as McCready himself, and moved with a confident assurance which showed that he was well aware of the fact that he was one of the richest men in the world.

Following the red carpet pathway that led from the front door to the staircase, McCready walked to the base of the stairs to greet the Ordosoft™ president. "I'll admit," he said. "I was impressed." As he looked up at Huxton, his scanner automatically transmitted the FE and biochip information.

Mason William Huxton, #694-63-6425, smiled, and said, "Good." Reaching the base of the stairs, he extended his right hand towards McCready. "I would be greatly disappointed if somone were to find it dull or uninteresting." The pyramid was orangish-red.

"I think it's safe to say you've insured yourself against that possibility." McCready grasped Huxton's hand with his gloved, right hand, making sure not to exert too much pressure. His bionics, though antiquated, could easily crush bones if he wasn't paying attention.

"And one can never have too much insurance, can they?" Huxton asked. "I don't think so–and that's why you're here. Now," he said, releasing his grip from McCready's, "come with me upstairs and I'll acquaint you with the situation." He ascended the stairs and McCready followed. "I assume you've been informed by Agent Moore that everything we discuss today is strictly confidential?"

"Yup."

"And your sunglasses–they're not recording, are they?"

FREQUENCIES

Interesting, McCready thought. He knows my cameras are in my sunglasses, even though every other Freemon at our branch has theirs in their contacts or implants. Huxton certainly does his research. "Nope," McCready said, "not unless you want them to."

"I don't," Huxton replied.

They reached the top of the stairs, curved to the right with the banister, and walked straight ahead towards a partially-opened door which was found at the end of a long hallway. As they moved down the hall, they passed by a few doors, only one of which was currently open to reveal the room inside. Judging from the desks and books found within, it looked as if it was some type of home office or study, but they didn't stop long enough for him to be sure.

"Until I find out more about what's going on," Huxton said, "I want absolutely *no* information leaking out–especially the specifics." Reaching the door at the end of the hall, Huxton stopped, placed his hand upon the wooden doorknob, and turned around to face McCready. "It is of the utmost importance that Huxton family matters be kept personal and private," he said in a tone that was more hushed than before. "There are simply too many individuals out there who would love nothing more than to unearth some...'dirt' on us, so to speak."

Huxton pushed the door open, and they both entered into a bedroom of typical Xanadeux proportions–gigantic. It was decorated in soft tones of white, rose, and lavender, with chiffon and lacey things draped all over the place. McCready could smell some type of powder or perfume in the air around him–something flowery, maybe jasmine or lily. In the center of the room was a king–no, it was *way* bigger than a king–more like a *god*-sized, canopied bed upon which two women were currently seated next to each other. The older of the two was the same woman who had looked at McCready over the banister. She looked as if she was consoling the younger woman. He scanned over both of them. Sophia Amity Grant, #364-03-0287. Pure orange. Dominique Evangeline Sanscrainte-Huxton, #808-42-112. Bluish-green, with scintillating oscillations that were repeating in a way that was indicitave of a cloned mind. McCready studied her frees a little longer, just to make sure he was reading them correctly. He was–she was definitely a clone.

McCready had heard that she had been ill for the last few months, but this meant that the illness had to have been a *lot* more serious than it was reported to be. He had never heard anything in the media–or even within the bureau–about Huxton's wife being cloned. Not even rumors. Huxton wasn't kidding when he said that he liked to keep his family matters private.

"Dom," Huxton said softly to his wife, "this is Mr. McCready–the specialist that I told you would be coming by today."

She didn't respond to his words, and kept staring down at the bed sheets. The older woman continued to run her fingers gently through Dominique's hair.

"He's going to do a few readings on you," Huxton said, briefly looking over at McCready with a nod, "and see if he can find out some more information about what it is that you're feeling. I'm going to the study to make a quick call, and then I'll be right back? Okay?" Again no response. Huxton stared at her for a moment, waited, then looked back up at McCready. "I'll be just around the corner," he said. "Please come join me when you're through." He walked over to his wife, gave her a small kiss on her forehead, then left the room.

McCready watched him leave, then turned back towards the two women. The older one looked up at him with tired eyes. There were a few scratches underneath her left cheekbone. "Uh...hi," he said, feeling a bit uncomfortable with the situation. "I'm Marc."

Sophia nodded a few times in recognition of his statement, then turned her head away from him and began to gaze out at a nearby window.

Why had Huxton just thrown him out here like this? he wondered. Why hadn't he been debriefed? He wished he knew more, because right now he felt incredibly intrusive and unwanted. He looked back at Dominique, who still appeared very spacey and distant. The FE pyramid was now a deep purple. Delta? She obviously wasn't in deep sleep... And her eyes were open and she was just in the low-alpha range a second ago. She began to mumble something, and then the pyramid began to get brighter again–quickly through blue and green, holding momentarily at yellow, then shooting right past orange up to red. Dominique suddenly began to shake violently, her expression turned to one of anger, and her eyes became very intense.

Sophia stood up, and took a few, fearful steps back from her.

"I'm not even really me–I'm just a clone," Dominique said. "I'm just a copy of someone else. If that's all I am, then who am I?" She looked at McCready, clenching her teeth together like she was in pain. "Who am I?!" Her shaking then stopped, her reading shot back down to theta blue, and her eyes lost their intensity.

"It won't stop," Sophia said under her breath, as she covered her mouth. "Lord, it won't stop."

FREQUENCIES

Now McCready at least had the answer to the question of "what am I here for." He asked Sophia, "How long has this been going on?"

"Since yesterday afternoon," she said. "It's horrible...she was never like this before." She began to cry. "I'm sorry," she said, wiping her eyes, "but it's so hard to see her like this." Sophia wiped her long, salt-and-pepper hair from away from her eyes, just as a hurtful sound escaped from her throat.

McCready wasn't good at these things. He wasn't sure whether to hug her or to try to make her laugh–so decided to do neither. "So, she's been continuously-" His words were cut short by Dominique.

"Why would they make me again?" she asked McCready, as if he knew the answer. "What if I don't want to be here? What if I'm not who they want me to be?" Back up to the omega reading again–not good. He hadn't seen something like this happen for a while–and never on anybody of this status. "Why are there all these questions in my head?" Dominique started to cry. "Why, why, why...I'm so sick of why..."

McCready had seen enough. "I need to go talk with Huxton now," he said to Sophia, as he began to walk out of the room. "Just...yell or something if you need me." McCready exited the bedroom and walked down the hallway until he reached the study. He peered in before entering.

Huxton was seated on the corner of a large desk, looking down at a laptop uniview. He glanced up at McCready, motioned for him to enter, then turned his gaze back to the laptop.

"...checking the escorts' camera records," said a chilly, almost supernatural, male voice from the uniview. "Will give us a good lead."

"Just make sure that you're the only one who does any investigating," Huxton said to the screen. "I'll hold you personally responsible should anyone else within Ordosoft™ find out about this incident."

"No worries, sir," the strange voice said. "Secret's safe with me."

"It better be, Mr. Webber," Huxton said. "It better be. I'll contact you shortly." He closed the laptop and looked at McCready. "I assume you've made your diagnosis?"

"Yup," McCready replied, pulling up a velvet-cushioned, wooden chair and seating himself in it, "and if it's what I think it is, it's not good."

"Something has infected her, correct?"

McCready nodded, then said, "Your wife's been infobombed, Mr. Huxton."

Huxton paused for a moment, considering the possibility. "I was hoping that the mode of infection was going to be one of a less serious nature..." He crossed his arms, then placed one of his fingers on his lips. "Are you absolutely sure?"

"Considering her behavior and the range of her FE readings, I'm pretty sure. There's not really anything else that it could be."

"I see," Huxton said, lightly tapping his lip with his finger.

McCready leaned forward in his seat, resting his elbows upon his knees and placing his hands together. "The good news is that, judging from the intensity of the oscillations, I'd say she's peaking right now–which means that the compressed information's on its way out of her mind."

"And the bad news?"

"You're gonna have to wait and see what kind of damage it leaves behind," McCready said. "At this point, you can't really tell–infobombs affect different people in different ways. For some it's just like getting high–they get all this shit in their head suddenly, but then they sleep it off and they're back to themselves the next day. And for others...well, to be blunt, it can change them forever. Someone who rarely freeked might become a permanent freeker, and a permanent freeker might suddenly become your most typical alpha-beta. It's hard to predict." McCready leaned back in the chair and scratched the side of his face. "And the fact that your wife's a clone only makes the situation that much more unpredictable."

Huxton eyed McCready for a moment, then stood up from the desk, and paced over to a shelf that was set into the south wall of the study. He placed his hands behind his back, as he looked over the books that were contained upon the shelf. "How might she have contracted this informational disease?" he asked, staring straight ahead at the various titles.

"Well, one mode of infobomb transmission is through the uniview. She may have been here at Xanadeux, just watching some-"

"Impossible," Huxton interrupted. "If there were some type of viral invasion attempting to enter our systems, Xanadeux would have dealt with it immediately and notified me of the occurrence."

"Isn't it possible that the virus could have evaded Xanadeux's detection systems?" McCready asked. "That *is* what viruses are created to do."

"And Xanadeux was created to be impenetrable, Agent McCready. *Nothing* can evade its detection systems," Huxton said. "It's an impossibility. If she did receive the infobomb through a uniview, I can assure you that it did not occur at Xanadeux." He turned around from the bookshelf, facing McCready once again. "What are the other modes of transmission?"

"The only other way I've actually *seen* it happen is through touch," McCready said. "Someone'll hire a johnny-courier, pack their brain with the infobomb instead of the usual data, then have them deliver it to the target via flesh-to-flesh contact. The information's specifically created so that it can be transmitted through the body's natural electric current. Johnny touches you for a few seconds and boom—you're bombed." McCready paused for a moment, looking at the large oil painting which sat behind Huxton's desk. It depicted Mason, looking about the same age as he did now, with Dominique and two brown-haired children, both under ten years old. "I've also heard that the Pentagon possesses some kind of laser that can trasmit infobombs over long distances, but that's never been confirmed. And I've never heard *any* reports or rumors of a criminal or terrorist organization possessing that kind of techology, so..." McCready began to reach into his pocket for a cigarette, but then ceased the action when he remembered that he couldn't smoke in Xanadeux. "If your wife was hit with something like that, it would be a first."

Huxton took a deep breath. "I see."

"Sir," suddenly announced the AI's hermaphroditic voice over the room's speakers, "Ashley has arrived."

"Thank you, Xanadeux," replied Huxton. "Have her come up to the house, and make sure to let her know how pleased we are that she's come by today."

"I'll do that, sir," Xanadeux said.

When the AI had finished its sentence, McCready noticed that there was no sound of an intercom being turned off. Meaning Xanadeux was still there—was always there—but just wasn't saying anything else. Eerie, he thought. It was like they had an invisible, third person in every room. McCready focused his attention back to the case. "Mr. Huxton," he asked, "did your wife leave Xanadeux at all in the last few days?"

"Yes," he said. "She went out to an Eastside mall yesterday morning with some escorts."

"Well, if Xanadeux is as secure as you say it is, then that's when the bombing would had to have occurred," McCready said. "I've never seen the information lie dormant for more than a day after transmission, so I doubt that it could have happened before that. Did your wife's escorts have cameras on them?"

"Of course," Huxton said. "My head of security is looking into the camera records as we speak." He walked over to his desk, and poured himself a glass of water from a condensated, silver pitcher. "I'll have him send you the information as soon as he's done reviewing it." He took a large drink from his glass.

"Good. With that, we'll be able to see whether she watched a uniview or came into physical contact with anyone while she was outside of the estate." McCready stood up from the chair and stretched his arms. "Then we can begin to piece together information from the biochip records, crossreference it with the visuals, and find out more about what happened. In the meantime, I'd recommend keeping her within Xanadeux–just to be safe. And since whoever attacked your wife is more than likely trying to get at you, you need to take extra caution too. Until we know more, you should also try to stay within Xanadeux...and if you have to go somewhere, make sure to have escorts with you at all times." McCready looked back up at the painting. "Your children–they're possible targets too. How old are they now?"

"Adam is thirty, and Ashley is twenty-five."

"And where are they?"

"Adam is currently at a restaurant in Bellevue," Huxton said, "and has his usual escorts watching over him. Xanadeux is relaying our conversation to him as we speak. I'm making sure that he is well informed, and as long as Adam's prepared, he can take care of himself." He took another drink from his glass. "Ashley, however, I *am* a little worried about–and that's where you come in. You're my insurance."

McCready didn't like the sound of that. "What do you mean?" he asked.

"My family and I leave to Tibet this Friday," Huxton said, "and until then, I would like you to keep an eye on my daughter. She has...shall we say...a talent for getting herself into situations. Therefore, I'd like *you* to insure that the situation happening to my wife does not happen to Ashley."

"You want me to *babysit* your daughter?" McCready smiled at the thought. "Mr. Huxton, you're gonna have to hire someone for that. Even if I wanted to, I wouldn't be able to do it–I'm a Freemon, and we don't do 'for-hire' jobs."

Huxton coolly smiled. "You do now."

McCready didn't like the sound of that either. He tilted his head down slightly, causing the Obsidians™ to slide down the bridge of his nose, and looked at Huxton directly through the open space between his sunglasses and brow. "What do you mean?" he asked in a lower tone than before.

"I've already made arrangements with your director, Harold Moore–an old friend, by the way–and he's agreed to grant you a few days off of active leave so that you can attend to my request."

This had to be a joke, McCready thought. *Please* let this be a joke. I do *not* want to babysit some snobby, stuck-up, mall shopping, designer clothes-wearing, silver spoon-feeding rich girl for the next three days. With my luck, she'll probably be some horrid creature who's had so much plastic surgery that she looks like a living Barbie® doll. Definitely a joke, he tried to assure himself, as he pushed his sunglasses back into place. "Seriously?" McCready asked.

"I'm not known for my humor," Huxton replied.

Shit, McCready thought. He was serious. "So what, you want me to tail her, keep an eye on her–that sort of thing?"

"More than that, Agent McCready–I want you to be her personal escort." Huxton set his glass down upon the desk. "I want you at her side whenever she leaves her residence, and I want you to *personally* make sure that no harm comes to her."

"Can't you get another Freemon to do the job? I'm sure there's someone else who would be more qualified than *me* to do it."

"I *can*," Huxton said, "but I don't want to. I've looked into your records, Agent McCready, and I like what I see. You're a former detective, you've had experience with a number of protection and security services...you're a Freemon...who, I might add, received nothing but accolades and praises from your director..." Huxton paused. "Agent McCready, you're the perfect man for the job."

McCready laughed and looked away from Huxton. "This is fucked," he said under his breath. He was stuck–you couldn't just say "no" to the head of Ordosoft™. Huxton was used to getting his way, and getting *in* his way was a *sure* way of going by the employment wayside. "Alright," McCready said, "so say I agree to do this job..." He stared at Huxton. "What's in it for me?"

"For starters," Huxton said, pouring himself some more water, "Harold Moore has agreed to give you two weeks paid leave, beginning the moment that we depart from SeaTac."

FREQUENCIES

"And for enders?" McCready asked.

Huxton took a sip of the water. "Provided that you do your job properly," he said, "I am quite prepared to compensate you for the services rendered."

McCready was beginning to warm up to this idea. "Exactly what *kind* of compensation?"

"Generous." He took another drink of water.

Well, McCready figured, if you were gonna get fucked anyway, at least money made a good lubricant–metaphorically speaking, of course. "Then I guess you just hired yourself a Freemon," he said. Now he just had to get himself mentally prepared to deal with a bitchy rich girl for the next three days. "So what does your daughter think about this arrangement?" McCready asked.

"Actually, she hasn't made up her mind yet," came a spirited, female voice from just outside the study's doorway, "since this is the first time she's even *heard* about this arrangement."

McCready turned to face the fiery voice, and his stereotypes were instantly reduced to ashes. Ashley Adrianne Huxton, #248-0808-8425. Pyramid glowing orangish-red. Behind the darkened lenses, his eyes widened with surprise. She had no makeup, was simply dressed, had on only a few pieces of jewelry–not at all what he expected. She stood about five feet, eight inches, had long, brown hair which gave off an auburn shine underneath the Natralites™, tiny freckles which dotted her nose and cheeks, and hazel eyes that radiated truth. Ashley was absolutely beautiful. And not in a creepy, cosmetic surgery kind of way–no giant, GS tits, no augmented, collagen-injected lips, no carved-up, pointy nose–but in a very real and genuine one. She glowed with honesty.

"Ashley, dear," Huxton said as he walked over to his daughter, "thank you so much for coming by today." He hugged her with one arm and gave her a kiss on the top of her head.
Ashley accepted his affection, but looked hesitant to show him any back.

Huxton looked at McCready, motioned towards him, and said, "This is Agent McCready. He's with the Freemon."

Ashley gave him a suspicious look. "Oh, one of the thought police, huh?" she said.

McCready smiled–this was gonna be interesting.

She instinctively smiled back, a warm smile in which her eyes squinted tightly as if she was gazing at something bright and shining. Ashley extended her hand, and said, "I've never met one of

94

you guys before."

"Lucky girl," McCready replied, lightly grasping her hand with his bionic limb. She met his grasp with a firmer grip. Nothing rough or unecessary, just firm. "I wouldn't want to meet one of me," he added, as their hands released.

"I'm sure you wouldn't," Ashley said with eyes still suspicious, though now somewhat curious. She looked around the room. "So, dad–where's Adam?"

"He had an appointment to keep," Huxton answered. "He'll be by as soon as he's through conducting his...business."

Ashley walked over to the desk, picked up an empty glass, and poured herself some water. "So what's going on?" she asked. "Adam said she's not doing well."

"No, unfortunately she's not," Huxton said. "Not at all." His face grew more serious. "We have reason to believe that she's been the target of a terrorist attack."

Ashley covered her mouth. "Oh my goddess... Is she okay?"

"Physically," Huxton answered, "yes. Mentally...no. Her mind is quite...frail at the moment."

"Adam didn't even mention that earlier..." Ashley's face gave the impression that a thousand different thoughts were currently running through her head, and the orangish hue on her pyramid reading began to give way to red.

"He didn't know yet," Huxton said. "I just found out about it myself when Agent McCready made the diagnosis."

She took a sip of the water. "Wow," Ashley commented to herself, "this day just keeps getting weirder and weirder." She paused, looking like she was trying to sort through the thousand thoughts. "So this 'arrangement' you two were talking about...it must have something to do with her attack."

Huxton nodded. "I've assigned Agent McCready to be your security escort until we leave to Tibet on Friday. It's possible that the terrorists may target you also, and I want to make sure that you're not harmed in any way."

"I'd probably be wasting my breath by trying to convince you that I'd be fine on my own, huh?" Ashley asked.

Huxton didn't reply with any words–he simply smiled.

Ashley looked at McCready, and said, "You get the same option package?"

"Pretty much," McCready said.

"Well, since neither of us really wants this 'arrangement,'"

Ashley said, throwing a playfully hard look over at her father, "I guess we might as well make the best of it–no point in making something negative if it doesn't have to be. We'll just try to respect each other's space as much as possible..." She looked at McCready. "And go from there."

"Sounds fair to me," McCready said, still astonished that this gorgeous rich girl was so fuckin' real and down-to-earth.

Ashley stared at the open study door for a moment, her eyes becoming very focused and intent. "I guess I promised Adam that I'd visit her today..." she said as she walked over to the study's door. Reaching the awning, Ashley took a slow, deep breath. Her eyes turned to McCready, and she said, "When I'm done with this, I'm gonna be ready to go, okay? Just warning you ahead of time." Ashley exited the room, and McCready could hear her footsteps heading down the hallway, towards the bedroom.

Huxton watched her leave, a concerned expression upon his face. "Promise me that you'll keep my daughter safe, Agent McCready," he said.

Ten minutes ago, McCready would have immediately answered, "I can't make any promises." But now, after meeting Ashley, he wasn't quite so sure how to respond. He thought about what to say, then thought of her. Those eyes. "Yeah," McCready stated in a confident tone, "I promise."

$$\Omega$$

∞

Chapter 6:
<u>Strange Attractors</u>

"When confronted with reality's relativistic nature, some beings experienced anxiety and apprehension, wanting nothing more than to find someone or something which could define for them what was to be "real" in their lives and what was not to be. Others, comfortable with the realization that reality was mutable, relished in the infinite possibilities, and opened themselves to ideas and concepts which many discarded as impractical, improbable, or impossible. They perceptively realized that at any point in time, the impossible could instantly become the possible—and the world could change overnight.

Ashley didn't feel like saying much.

As with the other time she had visited her mother's clone, she left the encounter feeling appalled...sickened by the sight of a woman who physically resembled her mother in every way, but who clearly did not have the same presence or essence. Ashley could just *feel* that the clone lacked her mother's soul, and this was what disturbed her most. It was so hard for her to look into the eyes of someone she loved, only to find that the spirit she was accustomed to seeing was no longer there. The comforting, familiar soulflame had been extinguished, replaced with something unnatural and wrong.

Ashley kept thinking of demonic possession and that old book, *The Exorcist*. The similarities were unsettling, especially considering the current state of the clone. Her mother's shell had been stolen, and now a confused entity of science was housed within it. Despite what the technodevils tried to say to the contrary, cloning did *not* restore or replace a loved one–all it did was violate them.

As she and the Freemon walked away from the main house, towards the parking area, barely a word was spoken between them. The only time the silence had been broken was when he had muttered to himself that he "wished you could have a fuckin' smoke in this joint." His comment had brought a brief, small smile to her face, but did nothing to dissipate the haunting images of her un-mother's dazed stares and desperate raves. It would have upset Ashley to have seen *anyone* in a mental state like that–the fact that it was someone who was the exact genetic replica of her mother only made the situation that much *more* upsetting. There were so many emotions she was feeling...so much to think about. And once she flashbacked to the meeting with Brennan, her contemplations only grew deeper...

"Wellor's research revealed to him that all living creatures," Brennan said, watching a student feed some sprouts to a duck floating in the fountain's algae-bottomed pool, "regardless of their form, vibrate at a specific frequency which can be measured upon a spectral bandwidth which he called the LIFE–living, incorporate, frequency emission–spectrum. Mammalian FE's occupied the upper-regions of the LIFE spectrum, bacteria and other microorganisms the bottom, while all other lifeforms were contained somewhere in between. As he continued his research, he found that certain mammals vibrated at the *exact* same frequency as did human beings–meaning that both were "thinking" at similar FE-activity levels. In fact, some dolphins and primates even registered *higher* on the spectrum than did he, or any of his students or colleagues who agreed to be tested."

"Interesting," Ashley said. "So organisms possessing a brain emanate higher FE's than those who don't...and something else–maybe the number of brain-folds in the dolphin's case–also plays a role in the lifeform's position on the spectrum."

Brennan nodded in agreement. "Brain-folds, genetic differences, the current state of the creature, its past experiences–all of these played a part in its FE reading, and Wellor tested a broad array of subjects and species, under many different conditions, to better understand the nature of the frequencies. For example, in one experiment, he found that a chimpanzee in a state of stress or agitation tended to have a higher reading than a chimpanzee who was calm and relaxed. Another test revealed that, more often than not, childrens' frequencies actually *dropped* once they had attended school for a few years. The same was true for any other animal taken from its original environment and placed into a setting which focused heavily on training and discipline." Brennan looked around at the surrounding campus, and said, "I rememberWellor was amazed with one experiment in particular, in which he discovered that a human in a coma gave off the same FE's as certain species of plants. To put it bluntly, a human 'vegetable' was frequentially no different than a cellulose vegetable."

Brennan let out a small, dry cough, then said, "When Wellor began to extensively test inanimate objects, such as a rock, a piece of plastic, or a cadaver, he found that they radiated absolutely no FE's whatsoever, save for the frequencies emitted by the microorganisms that were contained upon or within the object. Only living creatures could register on the LIFE spectrum. And for Wellor, this frequential division of the living and the unliving was pure, scientific proof that all life was essentially the same. That the difference between me, you, a dog, a flower–or any other living creature–was merely a matter of degrees. In his view, we are all a living, incorporate, frequency emission. We are all one. A single, electromagnetic wavelength called life."

"You heading home now?" McCready asked as they entered into the canopied parking area.

Lost in her thoughts, it took Ashley a moment to register that he had said something to her. "What?" she hazily asked.

"Where are you off to now? Home?"

"Umm..." she began, still pulling herself out of the depths of contemplation, "I...I hadn't really thought about it yet." Ashley looked at him, her eyebrows slightly furrowed and her lips taut around her teeth, then let out a mildly embarrassed laugh. "Sorry I'm kinda spacey right now...I've got a lot on my mind."

McCready smiled–a cunning smile, one that knew it knew things that others never knew. "So I see."

"Oh right, of course," Ashley said. "Your freeker thingy..." In her FE research, she had learned that most Freemon's scanners were either housed in a pair of contacts or in some type of visual implants. She gazed at his dark sunglasses, trying to get a good look at the eyes behind. "Your window to the soul, huh?"

"Hardly. Our 'thingys' only measure electromagnetic frequencies–just thoughts," he said. "Nothing as arcane as the soul."

"What if the soul *is* an electromagnetic frequency?" she asked, as they neared the area where Xanadeux had parked her car.

The same smile again. "With the way modern science can screw around with the EM spectrum?" McCready asked. "Then things are even more fucked up than I already thought they were." Combined with his tousled, black locks, his long, green trenchcoat, and his fat, oval shades, the smile gave him a roguish appearance. Mysterious, intriguing...and strangely attractive.

"Y'know," Ashley said, "you're not at all what I expected a Freemon to be like."

He laughed. "Is that good?"

She thought about the question for a moment, glanced at him from the corner of her eye, then looked back ahead at the antique vehicles. Ashley felt her lips curve up slightly, as she replied, "We'll see..."

"Well, if it's any consolation," McCready said, "you're not what I expected either."

She smiled playfully. "Is that good?"

Ashley's Lexus® and a black Chevrolet® pulled up in front of them, courtesy of Xanadeux. "We'll see," McCready replied with a grin. "So where to?"

"Where to? I don't know...somewhere away from here, from all..." her voice tailed off, as she motioned a hand to the surrounding area, "*this*." She looked around the vicinity, at the excessive amount of cars and the multiple Xandys who were tending to them. Though they were androids, she still felt sympathy for them–shining and detailing all of their artificial lives, forced to wear that synthetic smile upon their faces day after day after day. Ashley wondered if they ever wanted to frown, then wondered if her mother could frown in cryo. She winced at the thought. "Anywhere," she said. "Let's just go–we'll figure it out along the way."

"Alright," McCready said, as he walked over to the rear of his Polaris™. "You have a preference which vehicle we take?"

"No, not really."

"Then I'd prefer it if we took mine," he said, reaching the back of his car and extending his thumb towards the trunk. "More security." Before his digit had a chance to reach the biochip scanner, the trunk suddenly popped itself open. He confusedly stared at the opened compartment for a moment, still holding his thumb outwards, then turned his gaze in the direction of one of the Xandys. "Thanks," he commented wryly, as he leaned forward and began to probe around the inside of the trunk.

"Hey, Xanadeux," Ashley announced, "would you fly my Lex back to my house for me? I'm not gonna need it right now."

The nearest of the car-polishing Xandys looked up from its work, and said, "Of course, Ashley. It would be my pleasure."

"Thanks." The GS 800™ exited the parking area, and flew off towards Issaquah. Ashley peeked over at McCready, who was still rummaging through the Chevy's® compartment. "Find what you're looking for?" she asked, seating herself on the hood of his car.

"Almost," he replied. "Now...where is...ah–here we go." Emerging from the trunk with a vest in one hand and a couple trinkets in the other, McCready walked towards Ashley.

"New toys?" she asked.

"Protection–some things I'd like you to have with you for the next couple days." McCready placed the two devices on the roof of the Polaris™, but kept a hold of the vest in his gloved, right hand. "You have any implants?" he asked.

"Besides the mandatory ones?"

"Yeah, other than the freeread and biochip."

"Just these," she said, reaching her hands up and delicately tugging on her long, spiral earrings.

"Pierced ears?" McCready asked, his tone sounding surprised or impressed or some combination of both. "That's it?"

Ashley smiled. "That's it."

"Well, that'll make everything a lot simpler," he said, extending the vest towards her. "These things can wreak havoc on certain implants."

Ashley took the article of clothing from his hand and examined it. A black, lightweight vest composed of a soft material which felt similar to polar fleece. It had no pockets, and two, small, plastic discs were embedded into the bottom of it, one located on each side of the garment's zippered opening. Pressing her thumbs and forefingers lightly into the fabric of the vest, she found that it was packed with thousands of extremely-thin, supple, strands of filament which reminded her of uncooked, Chinese bean threads. "So this must be some type of laserproof vest," Ashley said. "Like the ones the cops wear."

"Similar," McCready replied. "But these vests are made specifically for federal agencies. They're a lot more powerful than

101

the ones the city police are issued."

"But they essentially do the same thing."

"Right, the fundamentals are the same–they both create protective emfields around you. But, there's a big difference when it comes to what *kinds* of attacks they protect you against." McCready picked up one of the devices from the top of the hood and began to tinker with it. "See, the cops' vests only protect against standard, police-issue weapons–laser pistols, motor control nappers, etc.–and that's it. Those things," he said, pointing to the vest she was holding, "will shield you against reticular nappers, microwave weapons, infobombs, lasers–you name it. If it's an electromagnetic attack, then that emvest should be able to disrupt it."

Ashley thought about how all satellite communications were contained within the EM spectrum, and asked, "Won't it also disrupt my biochip's sattelink?"

"Nah, the emfield only extends around your trunk and head, not your extremities. You can still access your bank accounts and open your locks just like before. The biochip won't be disrupted at all."

Another thought popped into her head: But what about the various effects that EMF's could have on a living organism? After all, the vest's field would be emanating from *her* body. "Couldn't the vest also disrupt other things?" Ashley asked with cautious concern. "Like *me*?"

"I sure as hell hope not," McCready said with a small laugh, opening up the right side of his trenchcoat to reveal his vest underneath. "'Cause I'm wearing one too." Before he reclosed his trenchcoat, Ashley caught a glimpse of the handle of an old, steel revolver (which she had previously only seen on the UV), housed within a brown, leather shoulder-holster.

"But you don't know for sure," Ashley said. "It's possible that it might mess with the wearer's physiology in some way."

"Well, yeah, of course it's possible," McCready replied, putting the device he was holding back on top of the roof and picking up the other. "It's possible that this coat I'm wearing was created with cancer-causing dyes, it's possible that those earrings you have on are picking up mind-altering signals from a planet in the fuckin' Alpha Centauri system–hell, anything's *possible*. You could-." McCready looked up from the device at Ashley's face and suddenly paused. He had seemed kind of annoyed before, and now it appeared to her like he was trying to make sure that he chose his next words carefully...that if he didn't check himself, he was going to say something that he might regret. "Basically," he continued, his tone less uptight than before, "it comes down to this–you get to choose between an emvest that *might* fuck you up–or a laser that *will*."

"Good point," Ashley said, further examining the vest. "I guess I'll take my chances with this thing." She ran her fingers along the small discs at the base of the garment and asked, "What do these do?"

"Those are your control knobs," McCready said. "Both of 'em work the same way–push in the center of the button to activate the mechanism, then turn the dial surrounding it to the desired frequency." He reached his fingers down to the control knobs on his own vest. "The one on the right controls your emfield–turning it clockwise will increase the intensity, counter-clockwise will decrease it. I'd recommend that you keep it turned to a little past noon–about one o'clock. That should be enough."

She pointed to the other knob on his vest. "And that one?"

"This one," he said with his smile, placing his thumb and middle finger around the left knob's dial and pushing in the button with his index finger, "is the 'fashion' button. The vest's fabric is made from optical fibers, so with a turn of the dial..." His green vest slowly began to change color through various shades of greenish-yellow, then to pure yellow. "Fuckin' A–you can match with any outfit." He turned the dial faster and the vest's color quickly jumped to deep-red. He then turned it all the way counter-clockwise, running the entire color spectrum down to deep-purple, then to blacks, grays, and finally whites. "I guess Uncle Sam figured the *Men In Black* needed some color in their wardrobes," McCready said, as he changed the vest back to its previous shade of hunter-green.

Ashley smiled as she set her vest down on the hood. Grasping one sleeve at a time, she pulled her arms out of her sweater and took it off. She then set the emerald-green knit down on the hood, picked up the vest, and began to put it on. "So I guess I'll be wearing this all the time, huh?" she asked.

"Pretty much. You should have it on and activated whenever you leave Xanadeux or your home. From what your dad has told me, your estate is almost as secure as Xanadeux itself, so you should be safe from attack either there or here. But outside of those safe-zones, you're vulnerable–and that vest becomes your best friend."

"As long as my best friend doesn't decide to resonate my molecules into another dimension," Ashley said, half-joking, as she zipped up the front of the vest. It was a little loose on her, but not so loose that it didn't fit. She pushed the button in on the left knob, and rotated the dial until it was a shade of green that resembled her knitted sweater. "There we go." Ashley looked up from the vest at McCready. "Okay–I'm ready for contraption #2."

"Here you go then," McCready said, handing her a wide, platinum-banded ring which had a clear jewel set into its center. "That should go on your middle finger, same hand as your biochip."

Ashley placed the ring around her finger, but the band was too big to stay on. She examined the gemstone closer, and noticed that it had a small, grippable dial around it. "Is this a twisty-fit?"

"Yup," McCready replied, picking up the remaining device from the roof of the Chevy®. "But be *extremely* careful as you adjust it. The jewel needs to be centered directly in the middle of your finger–it shouldn't lean one way more than the other. Also, there are four clicks on it instead of the usual two, but make sure not to go past the first two clicks."

"Okay." Holding the ring in place on her middle finger, Ashley twisted the dial one click to the right. She waited a few seconds, until the band had closed around her finger to a comfortable fit, then stopped it by clicking the dial again to the right.

"You got it to a snug fit?" he asked. "It doesn't slip at all?"

Ashley tugged on the ring a bit, then shook her head. "No slippage."

"Alright, good. 'Cause if that ring slips even the slightest bit, you could wind up hurting yourself."

"And this is because...?"

"The second two clicks activate the microlaser that's housed within the jewel."

She looked down at the ring with disbelief, then back up at McCready. "Really? This is a *laser*?"

"Yup," McCready said. "And for its size, its powerful."

Ashley laughed and said, "A power-ring...I feel like Green Lantern®, or what!"

McCready smiled. "Yeah, a lot of our stuff feels like superhero equipment."

"I guess so," Ashley agreed, lightly running her right index finger along the sparkling laser-jewel. She then turned her palm over, to see if there was some type of button on the underside of the ring. No button, but there was a tiny, grayish-black square that looked like some type of sensor or scanner. "So how does it work?"

"Basically, that sensor you're looking at is the 'trigger.'

FREQUENCIES

When the dial is turned to the third or fourth click, all you need to do is make a fist with your thumb tucked in..." McCready held up his hand to show. "Fingernail touching the sensor-square...and the laser will fire. It's not as accurate as a laser pistol, but it doesn't need to be. It's an emergency weapon, and in that type of situation, immediacy takes precedence over accuracy–you just shoot straight ahead at whatever it is that's threatening you, and keep shooting until it's no longer a threat." Ashley felt a pulse of anxiety reverberate through her being, McCready's last words triggering an abrupt recognition that her life really *was* in danger. "The third click will set the laser's intensity to a searing level that'll injure," he continued, "and the fourth focusses it to a severing level that'll kill."

The novelty of the vest and the ring–and the whole situation in general–had temporarily made everything seem larger than life, as if she was inocuously watching a movie play out before her eyes. But now, as she thought about burning or killing someone with a laser, or someone killing *her* with a laser, the gravity of the situation suddenly felt massively heavy. Ashley took a deep breath, and said, "This is all so strange...talking about lasers, and shooting people, and..." She nervously laughed. "...and it's just all so bizarre..." She laid back on the hood of the car, and looked up at the high, conical top of the tent above. As she focused her eyes on the center of the cone, the conversation with Brennan came to mind once again...

"When Wellor looked at the world around him," Brennan said, "he saw a planet out of balance, largely due to the exploits of one, single species–Homo sapiens. Wellor believed that modern humans had disrupted the Earth's equilibrium by adopting a way of life which encouraged overconsumption and greed, while simultaneously *dis*couraging respect for other cultures and lifeforms." Brennan paused momentarily, then said, "I remember once, him remarking to a few colleagues that humankind, by destroying the living diversity which evolution had taken millions of years to create, was sowing the seeds of its own destruction."

"That makes a lot of sense," Ashley said.

"In many ways it does," Brennan said. "Yet, we're still here, as prosperous as ever, with immortality now looming on the horizon."

"Maybe," Ashley skeptically said. "But what if the effects of our past and present actions still haven't been fully felt yet? Y'know, like when a star burns out...how we're still able to see its light for a while, even though the star itself no longer exists? Maybe right now, human 'progress' is like that star. We're basking in its starlight, thinking that everything around us is so bright, and that we'll be able to play around in the light forever...but we don't realize that the source of the light has already been extinguished. And not until the starlight stops shining, do we finally realize what it is that we've done."

Brennan laughed and said, "And here I thought *you* were the hopeful one."

"I am," Ashley said with a smile. "But my hopes don't reside with *this* system we're currently living under. *I'm* hoping for something more meaningful and true to take its place."

Brennan knowingly nodded a few times. "Which is why you're the perfect person to share Wellor's ideas with. He was hoping for the same type of world that you hope for, Ashley. And he believed that hopeful existence could be realized, if humankind radically altered the schemas and paradigms they were using to interpret the world around them. He theorized that if we were to stop looking at ourselves as separate or above other lifeforms, and instead began to look at ourselves as part of a diverse, living, interdependent whole–if this was accomplished–then plants and animals would no longer be looked at merely as resources to be exploited, but rather, as equals to be respected."

"Neat," she commented. "Sounds like he was a dreamer."

"Indeed he was, Ashley," Brennan said, his face full of remembrance. "Indeed he was. Consequently, he began to create the FE technology in the hopes that it would help others to see the interconnectedness and interdependence of *all* life. Wellor set out to change the world with his science–and he succeeded." Brennan's expression became grim. "But not in the way he had hoped."

"You okay?" McCready asked.

Ashley slowly sat up. "Mm-hm, I'm fine..." She let out a small sigh, then glanced over at McCready. "Have you ever had one of those really, *really* weird days?"

"Yeah," he laughed, "I've had *too* many of 'em."

Ashley smiled. "Then you know what kind of day I'm having today." She placed her palms down on the hood, slid herself off of the car, then walked around to the passenger-side door. "You want to tell me about the other gadgets as we fly?" she asked, as she opened the car door.

"Sure," McCready replied, slipping the device he was holding into his pocket, "no problem. Let me just close the trunk." He began to walk towards the open trunk, but before he was even halfway there, Xanadeux closed it for him. "Alright," McCready said in an irritated tone, turning back towards the front of the vehicle. The driver-side door immediately opened. As he walked towards it, he looked over at Ashley and asked, "And you had to grow up with this?"

Ashley laughed, then seated herself inside the vehicle, and allowed Xanadeux to automatically shut the door behind her.

Reaching his door, McCready sat down onto the driver's seat, his back facing Ashley and his legs placed outside of the vehicle. He grabbed a hold of the door with his left hand, raised his right hand into the air, extended his middle finger, and panned it around towards the various Xandys. He then pulled his legs into the car, and made sure to manually shut the door himself.

During the car flight, they had decided to go somewhere that was relatively safe and relaxing, but somewhere outside the gates, since Ashley and McCready both shared a mutual distaste for the antiseptic ambiance offered by the destinations found within the gated communities. She suggested they go to Tosh's, an herbal café located in the Westside neighborhood of Fremont. Though Ashley hadn't been there in a few months, it still seemed like the best choice possible. She was *very* close with the owner (though they hadn't spoken a lot since their breakup), was friends with most of the employees and regulars, and knew that the café was *extremely* selective about who they let in to the establishment. "Nobody's gonna attack me there," she had told McCready. "It'll be safe." He agreed with the choice, and now, twenty minutes later, they were walking up the sidewalk towards the café.

"Have you ever been to Tosh's before?" Ashley asked, as they neared a street musician with a guitar who was leaning against a building's facade.

"Nah, I haven't," McCready said. "I don't come to Fremont much. Only when the job brings me here."

"Babylon, Babylon," the musician softly sang, eyes shut tight, head rhythmically swaying with the melody, as she plucked the strings of her worn guitar, "your time soon come."

FREQUENCIES

Interested in hearing more, Ashley slowed her pace a bit, in order that she could listen to the song as they passed by.

For the voice of change, it floats on the breeze
and it speaks of love, and it speaks of peace
It tells of a time that must come to be
when the truth is the truth, and a lie cannot be
So Babylon, Babylon, your time soon come
Babylon, Babylon, your time...soon come

Ashley nodded her head in recognition of the singer's expression, then said to McCready, "I think you'll like Tosh's. It's got a nice vibe, real kickback."

"Reggae-themed?"

"Yeah. They play a lot of pre-millenial stuff–mostly roots, though they'll also play some dancehall and dub occasionally."

"I like it already," McCready said, as they reached the entrance of Tosh's.

Ashley pulled open the front door, and her nostrils were immediately filled with the familiar, wonderfully intoxicating scents of the café. Sage and sandalwood incense swirled together with the smoky boquets of various kinds of cannabis. Fresh-ground coffee intermingled with peppermint and licorice teas. Culinary hints of allspice, cumin, and clove. The aroma was pure, olfactory ambrosia.

They entered into the long, wide hallway which led directly to the café, and McCready commented, "Smells good."

"*Mm-hm,*" she emphatically agreed, as they proceeded to the checkpoint at the end of the hallway. Two men were standing there, one who had his back turned towards them, finishing a conversation with someone inside the café, the other (whom she didn't recognize), was carefully eyeing them as they approached.

"Hey, you," Ashley friendlily announced to the man with his back turned.

Melloe slowly turned around, a smile stretched wide across his face. "Ashley," he said, stepping forward and giving her a warm hug. "It's good t'see you, girl! How you been?"

"I've been good," she replied. "I've had some family things that I've had to deal with the last few months, but I'm doing well."

"Okay, dat's good," Melloe said, as he tucked a small, stray dreadlock underneath his red, black, and green, knitted cap. "You dealin' wit' it den." He nodded approvingly as he looked her deeply in the eyes. "Dat's good." Melloe looked over at the tall, massive, thickly-dreadlocked man standing next to him, then back at Ashley. "Ashley," Melloe said, leaning his head towards the other man, "dis is Bain. He came up from Martinique 'bout a mont' ago."

"Nice to meet you," Ashley said, extending her fist towards the extremely-muscular Bain. She recalled Tosh speaking fondly of a Bain on several different occasions. This had to be the same one. "I've heard good things about you," she said.

Bain met her fist with his and replied, "Likewise." They both twisted their fists, then brought the still-closed hand back to their chests.

"I don't tink I met your friend before," Melloe said, turning his gaze towards McCready. "I'm Melloe." He reached his fist out towards the Freemon.

"McCready," he replied, touching his gloved fist to Melloe's bare one.

"Good to know you, mon," Melloe said in his usual, good-natured tone, bringing his fist back to his chest. "If you wit' Ashley, then you chill wit' me, okay?"

"Alright," McCready said, pulling his fist from Melloe's without a twist, then moving it over towards Bain. "Bain, right?"

Bain gave a single, slow nod, then responded, "McCready..." He looked over the Freemon suspiciously, as he extended his fist. "Right?"

"Right," McCready confirmed, slightly smirking as their hands met. As before, he retracted his fist without bringing it back to his chest.

Bain did the same as McCready, still eyeing the Freemon in a guarded manner.

Ashley hoped that she hadn't made a mistake by bringing McCready here. He *was* a member of the thought police after all, and bringing one of them into an herbal café was sort of like bringing an aardvark to an anthill, since people had a tendency to think freeky thoughts when they were smoking herb. In spite of the misgivings, she was confident that her intuitions about McCready had been correct–that he was someone who, though involved in law-enforcement, didn't particularly like the law itself, and wasn't interested in arresting people if he didn't have to. But, she also realized there was a possiblility that he was just projecting that type of image at her in order to gain her trust. Oh well, Ashley conceded, what's done is done. Time to accept my decision and move on. "Is Tosh around right now?" she asked Melloe.

"No, na t'right now," he answered. "He 'ad to go out somewhere, but 'e should be back in a jif, okay? If you wan', I can tell 'im dat you 'ere when 'e come back."

"Yeah, that'd be good," Ashley said. "It'd be nice to talk to him." She looked into the interior of the café. As usual, the place was comfortably crowded, filled with familiar faces and positive vibrations. She looked back at McCready. "You ready to head in?"

"Ready when you are," he replied.

Ashley entered into the café's interior, and McCready began to follow.

"Hold up, mon," Bain firmly announced to McCready, as he picked up a scanner-gun from a small, wooden stand nearby. "I got'ta check you first."

McCready stopped, turned around and said, "Sure–go ahead."

Noticing that McCready had been halted, Ashley waited up for him.

Bain pointed the scanner-gun at the top of McCready's head, then began to slowly move the thin laser-line down the Freemon's body. Bain's eyebrows lifted as he read the results from the small screen embedded in the back of the scanner. He stopped scanning at McCready's waist and said, "De scanner's tellin' me dat you loaded wit' all manner a' weapon, mon." Bain's brow furrowed with disapproval. "We na dig dat kind of bumbaklaat 'ere, seen? If you don' got de proper badge, den we got'ta ask you to leave."

McCready reached into his trench, pulled out his badge, and turned it over to Bain.

A hologram of the Freemon logo materialized into the air as soon as Bain opened the badge. He picked up a pen-scanner, which was attached by a cable to a small, laptop uniview resting on the wooden stand, and began to run it along the bottom of the badge.

"You need to match it with the biochip?" McCready asked, sticking his thumb out towards Bain in a way that reminded Ashley of the cover to the *Hitchhiker's Guide to the Galaxy*.

"Yah, mon," Melloe answered, picking up a small biochip-scanner and extending it towards McCready. "No offense, but we got'ta keep de place straight, yunno?"

"No offense taken," McCready replied, as he placed his thumb on the scanner-pad. He waited for the beep, then retracted his hand.

FREQUENCIES

Bain studied the information displayed on the laptop's screen, then looked back at McCready and handed him his badge. "Okay, mon," he said, motioning towards the café's interior, "you can go in now."

"Thanks," McCready said, replacing the badge into his pocket.

"There's a booth by the window that just opened up," Ashley told McCready as he joined her inside the cafe's interior. "Let's go over there."

Bobbing his head with the music that was sounding throughout the space, he replied, "So Jah say."

"What?" Ashley asked in a puzzled tone, as she began to walk to her left, past a few of the cushioned, wicker couches and their occupants.

"The music," McCready answered as he followed her. "It's an old Dennis Brown cut–'So Jah Say.' Classic."

"Oh, right," Ashley said, now understanding what he meant. She looked over at the sunken dance floor on her right, which occupied the center of the café, then up at the bar located at the back of the large area, opposite the hallway entrance. The bartender, Frances, immediately saw Ashley and waved with a smile. Ashley waved back, and continued to walk towards the window booth. As she and McCready weaved their way around papasans, tables, and chairs, various people greeted Ashley, some with handshakes or their fists, some with a sup or a nod, others with a simple "hey" or "what's up." Ashley greeted them all back, but made sure not to get caught up in a long conversation with anyone. Not that she didn't want to talk to them, just that she was *very* ready to sit down and relax for a while.

Nearing the booth, McCready said, "I can see why you feel comfortable here."

"Yeah," she replied, seating herself on the soft cushioning of the booth's seats, "If I'm not safe here..." Meaning conveyed, she let her words tail off. Ashley looked to her right, through the tinted, plate glass window which comprised the entire south wall of the building, at the Fremont streets outside the café.

Gravity-bound cars driving by, GS cars ascending and descending, a potpourri of people pacing up and down the sidewalk... A section of the city in motion. Observing the different individuals go by, Ashley wondered what each of them were thinking about. Were they hoping for something? Worrying about something, dreaming

111

about something? Afraid? Excited? What were they *feeling*? Whatever it was, she wished them all happiness (briefly thinking of Adam, and how he would always scoff at her for saying things like that), and hoped that their innermost dreams were being fulfilled. But, as she studied the sundry faces going by, many of which were broken and downtrodden, she saw that hopes and reality aren't always the same thing. Not yet, at least. She thought of Babylon, and the singer's words. Soon.

McCready, who was now seated on the opposite side of the booth, asked her, "People watching?"

More like people*feeling*, she thought. "Sort of," Ashley answered, still gazing out the window.

"I do that all the time," he said, sliding an ashtray and a toothpick holder from the far end of the table to himself. "People are so fuckin' weird, all the things you catch 'em doing." McCready looked out the window. "People are a trip to watch."

"People are a trip to *be*," she responded with a small laugh.

"True," he said, nodding his head a few times in agreement, then averting his gaze from the window. "Like how we'll comment on how weird people are, while we're sitting there like fuckin' peepin'-Toms watching them, right?" McCready laughed, displaying his barely-crooked, off-white teeth.

Ashley smiled. He's able to laugh at himself, she thought. That's a good sign. And his teeth aren't perfect. That's good, too. Cosmetically-perfect teeth just wouldn't have fit well with the roguish look. Ashley wondered how old he was. "How old are you?" she asked, as soon as the thought crossed her mind.

McCready picked up a toothpick, put it in his mouth, leaned back into the booth's cushioning and asked, "How old do you think I am?"

Ashley examined his facial features, trying to find a tell that would reveal his age. Some wrinkles on his forehead, but nothing extreme...same around the mouth. Definitely older than her... But his sunglasses were still on, so she couldn't see his eyes or the skin surrounding it. "I can't tell with your shades on."

"Alright," he said, removing his sunglasses and setting them down on the table. Ashley was surprised how different he looked without them. Far from roguish, McCready now looked...the first word that came to her mind was "vulnerable." His dark-brown eyes reflected a sort of sadness...or hurt. Not at all weakness, but *deep*ness. A depth that he kept hidden away from the world...almost like the

shades were a slick veneer to protect the feeling eyes beneath.
"How's that?" he asked.

"...better," she quietly said, staring into his eyes. They
reminded her of a literary cliché, the one about pools so deep, you
could drown in them. Ashley felt her face getting flushed, and
decided that she better get back to the task of determining his age.
She looked down at his ungloved hand. It appeared rough, like it
had been worked for at least thirty years. Crow's feet around the
eyes, but as with his forehead, nothing extreme...definitely not forty.
"Thirty-three," she guessed.

"Close."

"Thirty-five."

"Bingo," he said. "You got it."

She smiled, and asked, "So how old do you think I am?"

"Twenty-five," he answered without hesitation, shifting the
toothpick to the other corner of his mouth.

"Wow," Ashley said with a laugh, "first try. Lucky guess?"

"Nope–ancient secret."

"Which is...?"

McCready coyly smiled, as one of the café's waiters
approached their table. "Ask her father."

Ashley shook her head and laughed, then looked up at the
waiter. "Hey, Joseph," she said to the young man, whose scalp was
covered with lots of tight braids, all of them possessing colorful,
wooden beads near their ends.

"What's up, Ashley," Joseph said with a laugh, taking a pull
from a spliff with one hand, while reaching his other hand towards
her. "Long time no see."

"Yeah," she agreed, meeting her fist with his, "it's been
awhile. You changed your hair."

Joseph shrugged his shoulders, as he exhaled a little smoke.
"It's jus' a likkle suh'em suh'em, yunno?"

"I like it a lot," she said. "It fits you."

"Okay, thanks," he replied with a slightly shy smile.

"Joseph," Ashley said, "I'd like you to meet my..." She
paused for a second, trying to think of the proper word. Briefly
glancing at McCready, she smiled, then looked back at Joseph.
"...friend, McCready."

McCready held out his fist like he'd been doing it for years.

Joseph laughed. "You know de greetin'? Yah, mon," he said as
he touched his fist to McCready's. "Nice to meet you." He twisted, as

did McCready, then brought his fist back to his body, tapping it a few times upon his chest.

McCready brought his fist back to his chest, nodded his head, and earnestly said, "You too, Joseph."

"Yah, mon," Joseph said with a nod, as he swayed with the music. "Notin' better den people connectin', yunno? One love." He took another hit of his joint, and asked, "So you two in de mood to smoke de canny, eat some food, 'ave a drink...?"

"I wouldn't mind a beer," McCready said.

"Sorry, mon," Joseph replied. "We na serve de poison 'ere. Bad vibes, yunno?"

"Fair enough." McCready thought for a moment and said, "Then give me a latté–triple short."

"Sure. Anyting else?"

"You probably don't allow cigarettes in here, right?" McCready asked.

"No, mon," Joseph said. "De only tobacco we 'ave is de leaf on a blunt. Dat's it."

"Just the latté then."

"Okay, sure." Joseph looked at Ashley, and asked, "You smokin' today?"

"Hm-mm," she replied, shaking her head, "it's too early for me. I can't smoke until the sun goes down." Wait, she thought, that's not fully the truth. "Except sometimes when I'm exercising–then I do it in the daytime. But anyways, I *would* like a chamomile-sativa tea, please. With some honey. And a small bowl of potlikker. That's it." She laughed. "Please."

Joseph smiled and said, "Sure, I'll be right back." He then left their table, and walked over to the bar.

"Potlikker?" McCready asked her. "What the hell is that?"

"Stewed greens, basically," she replied. "Mostly collards and mustards...sometimes kale. It's yummy."

"I'm sure it is," he said, "but that's a weird fuckin' name. Sounds like a word for the guy who always gets stuck with the leftovers–the pot licker."

Ashley laughed at the absurdity of his remark and said, "I'm sure that's not what it means. I think it's a Jamaican word."

"Is that what these guys are?"

"Uh-uh. Most everyone who works here is either from Dominica or Martinique. Tosh grew up on both islands, and he brings family and friends up here to work in the place."

"That's cool," McCready said, as he pushed the ashtray back to the far end of the table.

A new song began to play over the speakers, one that Ashley recognized, but didn't know the name of. The volume seemed to increase with the song, and she could feel the thumping of the drumbeat vibrate up from the ground and through her body. The sensation felt neat...sort of tingly. "I like this song," she commented, playing the tabletop like it was a drum. "It's Bob Marley, isn't it?"

"Yup, when he was still with the Wailers. 'Rastaman Chant.' Yeah," he replied, nodding his head to the beat with a smile, "this song's the cut, right here."

McCready looked so lighthearted and content right now, as he sat there enjoying the music, watching people express themselves on the dance floor...almost like he was experiencing something new. Like he didn't get to experience happiness very often. The look on his face made her think of a man who had been carrying a heavy weight for a long time, and had finally gotten a chance to set it down and relax. Maybe she was just reading into things (she knew she had a tendency to do that), but that was what she was sensing. Plus, she just *couldn't* see a job that involved busting people for their thoughts as being very conducive to a joyful mindstate. Peaceful moments for a Freemon must be few and far between, Ashley thought. Why would someone want that kind of lifestyle? Why would *he* want it? Ashley wanted to know more. She asked, "What made you decide to become a Freemon?"

McCready thought about the question for a few seconds before answering. "It's funny," he said, pulling the toothpick from out of his mouth and rolling it between his fingers, "'cause in a way I never really decided to become one. It's more like it happened to me."

"What, they recruited you?"

He replaced the toothpick between his lips. "That's one way of putting it. Drafted–that'd probably be even closer."

"That sounds creepy," she said. "So you didn't have any choice in the matter?"

"Well, I had a 'choice,'" McCready said, using his fingers to make invisible quote marks around the last word of the sentence. "I gotta choose whether I wanted to be placed in a job that completely isolated me from other people, or apply for a job that gave me clearance to think and discuss freeker thoughts. It was a lesser of two evils kind of thing." He tilted his head slightly to one side, and she heard a few pops from his neck. "I chose the one that would allow me the most freedom."

"But why not something else? Something less..." she paused, thinking of the proper word. "...oppressive. Why the Freemon?"

"Because it was the only way *I* was gonna get clearance, sweetheart," he said. "'Cause I don't come from money, I don't like academia or politics, and I abso-fuckin'-lutely *loathe* corporate bullshit. The Freemon were my best option. By far."

She still couldn't understand why anyone would want the job. "Okay, but you said that you chose the Freemon because it gives you freedom... If you like that ideal so much, then doesn't it bug you to take away someone *else's* freedom?"

McCready laughed and said, "Do you always interrogate people when you first meet them?"

Ashley smiled, shrugged her shoulders, and replied, "Only if they interest me. Don't give me an answer if you don't feel like it."

"I won't," McCready bluntly stated. He took the toothpick out of his mouth, examined its chewed end, then placed it into the ashtray. "But I don't mind answering your question." He picked up a fresh toothpick, placed it between his lips, then continued. "If you want to know the truth, it *does* bug me to fuck around with people's lives. I hate it. It's fucked up. But that's what this society does–it makes you a part of things you don't want to be a part of. And yeah, I'm more *directly* involved in the fucked-up shit than a lot of people are, but c'mon, let's be truthful–indirectly, we're *all* a part of it, aren't we?"

He leaned forward and smiled devilishly. "I mean, you can *try* to pretend that you're not–but you still are. 'Cause every time you spend some cash, or pay your taxes, you're keepin' the economy running...and that means you're supporting *some* kind of opresive shit that you don't want to. Whether it's death squads in Guatemala or riot cops in Rainier Valley, *your* taxes are payin' for it. And the fucked up thing is, the only *real* way to rebel is to stop paying taxes and stop spending–but then you're gonna starve or end up in the workcamps. And then what good are you?" McCready leaned back, shook his head, and smirked. "I'm tellin' you, doll, whoever designed this system was a fuckin' genius. They created their society like one, big, gigantic prison that you can't even see, let alone escape from. And I'm trapped in it like everyone else. I don't like my job, but it keeps me fed. I'd do something else if it was a different world, but it's not, so I don't. That's the unfortunate reality."

"That's the reality for *now*," Ashley said, tracing her finger along the tabletop and drawing an invisible spiral upon its surface, "but it'll change eventually. It's all just a matter of time..." She stared at the imaginary symbol, then smiled with angelic assurance. "...and time doesn't really matter."

Walking up to the table with a tray in one hand, a fresh, unlit joint in the other, Joseph said, "Okay, 'ere's your orders." He placed the joint into his mouth, then set the latté down in front of McCready. "Triple-shot for you. An' for you," he said, looking over at Ashley and setting down a brown mug filled with hot water and a cloth teabag, "an herbal tea..." He placed a bowl of steaming greens and a fork next to the mug. "An' a bowl a' potlikker."

"Thanks, Joseph," Ashley said, picking up the mug of tea and sniffing its fragrance. "It smells wonderful."

Joseph smiled and said, "Good. Let me know if you need anyting else, okay? Enjoy." He nodded, then walked away.

Ashley brought the rim of the mug to her lips, gently blew on the surface of the tea, then took a few, careful sips. The flowery blend of warm, sweet liquid felt soothing as she swallowed, suffusing her self with a sensation both calm and inspiriting. "Perfect," she stated, and savored another slow sip.

McCready stuck his finger into his latté, quickly pulled it out, and commented, "Too hot."

She smiled, drank a little bit more of the tea, then set her mug down onto the table. The chamomile aftertaste reminded her of her childhood...of morning teas with her mother. Good memories, ones which could never be tainted by the wrongs of the present. Her thoughts moving from the past back to the now, Ashley asked, "So what exactly happened to the clone?"

"You mean your mother?" McCready asked, as he wiped his wet finger onto a brown paper napkin.

"No, I mean the clone of my mother." Ashley grasped the strings of the teabag and swirled the herb-filled cloth around in the mug, making a mini whirlpool appear upon the liquid's surface. "What happened to her?"

"Well," he said, crumpling up the napkin and placing it into the ashtray, "we still have a few things to check out and verify, but all the signs are pointing to an infobombing."

"Hmm," she said, cupping her hands around the mug and watching the tiny, liquid spiral dissipate, "mental graffiti, huh?" She thought about the things that her un-mother spoke about during the time they spent together. "That must be why she's freeking out so hard on her existence–they must have created the information burst specifically for her...bombed her with something that would make her insecure about the fact that she's a clone."

"That's one possibility," McCready said. "And the worst case scenario for your father, since that would mean that someone hostile to your family knows that your mother's been cloned. It's also possible that the bomb contained an uninhibitor–the kind that unlocks your deepest fears, whatever they may be." He reached for something in his pocket. "And typically, most clones fear they're not real people. That they're something less than human." He pulled out a pack of cigarettes and set them down on the table. "That would also explain the content of her outbursts."

"True," she said, lifting her eyebrows slightly and nodding her head. "Either way, the whole situation's messed up." Ashley took another sip of the tea. "I feel so bad for that woman...it must be so hard, y'know? It's bad enough that she has to try to be someone who she's not, but then to have some kind of infobomb make everything even more confusing..." She shook her head, and felt her mouth frown down at the corners. "...it's just messed up. I wish things were different, y'know?"

"Yup," McCready agreed, pulling a cigarette from out of its package and placing it upon the table, "I know. It's an insane fuckin' world..." He snickered and said, "I remember once, one of my cases told me once that Earth was known throughout the universe as this planet-sized asylum, and that there were these cosmic caretakers who would transform lunatic aliens into humans and then deposit them here."

"That's a freeky thought," Ashley said with a small laugh, as she pulled the bowl of potlikker in front of her.

"Fuck yeah, it is," he replied, rolling the cigarette along the surface of the table towards his right hand. "She said that was why the world's so crazy–because the transformed aliens, even though they were cracked-up, were still more evolved than the humans." He stopped the cigarette's motion with his right hand, then rolled it back to his left. "So it was easy for them to become the leaders and messiahs, because they knew all this shit that no one on Earth knew about and created all this technology that no one had ever seen before. And now," McCready continued, picking up the cigarette and taking a whiff of it, "our entire planet is controlled by psychotic, power-hungry aliens." He laughed. "That was her theory, at least."

"I guess it makes as much sense as anything." Ashley set her elbows down upon the table, one on each side of the bowl, and placed her hands together. "Considering that not much of anything makes sense these days." She took a deep breath, closed her eyes, bowed her head slightly, and said a silent prayer over the food. She then opened her eyes, picked up the fork, and began to turn the greens around inside the bowl.

"That's a small?" McCready asked, eyeing the large serving of potlikker.

"Mm-hm," Ashley responded, taking a bite of the food. "Big, huh? You want some?"

"Nah, I'm trying to save room for dinner to-" He stopped mid-sentence, thought for a moment, then asked, "Out of curiousity, are you going out tonight?"

"I wasn't planning on it," she said. "Why?"

"I just realized that if you're not staying at home or at Xanadeux, then I need to cancel some dinner plans I had for tonight."

"Oh, don't worry," she said as she took another bite, "you won't need to cancel your plans. All I want to do tonight is kick back at home, relax, and sort through everything that's happened today."

"You sure?"

"Yeah, I'm sure."

"You don't need me around tonight, or anything? You're gonna be okay?"

She smiled and said, "I'll be fine. Thanks, though."

"No prob." McCready smelled his cigarette again, then rolled it between his fingers and looked at it. "Well, the ol' nicaddiction's calling." He put his sunglasses on, stood up, and said, "I'm gonna step outside for a sec and have a smoke, alright?"

Ashley picked up the pack of cigarettes that were sitting on the table and looked at them. "Old Skools™?" she asked, looking at the crumpled, yellow and white package. She glanced up at McCready with a skeptical eye, and held the pack out towards him. "You actually smoke these?"

"Yup," he said with a smirk, as he took the package from her hand.

"Do you know that they lace those things with ammonia so that your lungs'll absorb more nicotine?"

"Yup," he said, placing the package into one of his pockets. "There's a bunch of other shit in 'em too, like freon and pesticides. I also heard that they grow their tobacco in uranium-enriched soil." He placed the cigarette between his lips and said, "Filthy habit. I wouldn't recommend taking it up."

"Oh, I won't," she assured him. "Not again. I already quit a few years back, and I have *no* desire to get hooked again."

"What? And miss out on that terrific, liberating feeling of constant nicotine withdrawals?" McCready smiled sarcastically and said, "Suit yourself, sweetheart. I'll be back." He then turned around, and walked in the direction of the café's exit.

Ashley took another bite of the greens, and watched McCready slither his way through the crowded café. He effortlessly blended in with the scene, giving no indication that he was who he was...a snake in the grass, slippery, slick, and sly. As he passed out of sight through the hallway, she laughed to herself at how this cynically facetious character had suddenly popped into her life...then laughed harder at the fact that she was finding him attractive. She reflected back on the strange twist of fate which had thrown them together–an attack on her mother's clone–then thought about her conversation with Brennan and all of *its* many implications. She thought about coincidence and destiny, chaos and synchronicity.

And marvelled at the mysterious, wild ways in which life weaves its intricate web.

∞

Δ

Chapter 7:
Existencia

Thus, if something unwanted or undesirable was present in their reality, they effected change so that the problem would cease to exist within their own, personal sphere of influence. When others did the same, the problematic force exerting itself upon their shared world either diminished in strength, or–if the sphere of influence had spread far enough–ceased to exist at all.
Likewise, if something vital or necessary was absent from their reality, they actively sought to fill this hollow space, and put into their lives that which was previously missing."

"Unh...ah...almost...unh...there..." Ignacio gutturally stated with deep, heavy breaths, as he reached his hands up to her knees and began to firmly slide his damp palms down the inside of her slender, soft thighs. "...ahunh...almost..."

Raquel opened her legs wider at his touch, braced her arms into the mattress, and began pressing herself down harder on top of him. "You...mhnh...wanna pull out," she asked, turning her head and looking back at him, "or do you...want to...mmh...come inside me?"

"Don't...don't play...Raquel..." he said with a small laugh, as he continued moving his hands down her perspired legs. "You...unh...you know what I want."

She smiled, turned her head back around, and began to slowly move her hips around in strong, wide, circular motions.

Ignacio tightly clenched his molars. His hands reached the base of her thighs, and he felt her groin muscles tensing with each, puissant gyration. He moved his hands further inwards, until he reached the moist, warm area where the two of them were joined together. "Ounh...keep going..." he whispered forcefully through his teeth, as he rubbed his fingertips in and around her wetness. "Don't stop...I'm...ah...about to..."

"I know, sweetie," Raquel said, increasing the rapidity of her gyrations to an almost unbearable speed, "mmh...I can feel you."

Ignacio leaned his head back on the pillowed headboard of the bed, and looked up at the ceiling fan, whose spinning motion seemed to perfectly match Raquel's. He rubbed one of his sticky, wet hands along his mouth and nose, breathed in the sweet, sexual scent, and closed his eyes. He briefly imagined that it was Essence who was on top of him, then focused back on Raquel. "Ouhn...so close..." Ignacio moaned, trying to hold back his climax as long as possible.

When he couldn't hold back the irresistable pressure any more, he reached his hands around to her backside, squeezed it firmly, and released his orgasm. "Ounhhhndios," he vigorously sighed, thrusting himself deeper into her with each climactic pulse. "I love you...ounhh, god...I love you, Raquel."

Smoothly moving her torso in unison with his final ejaculations, Raquel whispered, in a barely audible tone, "No you don't." When he was completely finished, she reclined herself down onto his chest, making sure to keep him inside of her. Laying the back of her head just above his collarbone, she looked up at him, her mouth frowning down at one corner, and she said, "The only time you say you love me is when you're coming."

He ran his fingers through her short, dyed-blond hair, and replied, "Maybe that's the only time I tell the truth."

"Maybe," Raquel said. She quickly wiggled her hips. "And maybe I know you better than that."

"Aaah!" Ignacio shouted with a laugh, as he playfully pushed her off of him, on to the other side of the king-sized bed. "¡Cuidado, chica–that's ticklish!"

"I know," she said, crawling back over to him. "That's why I did it." She then straddled him, placed both of her hands on top of his chest, and lightly moved her fingernails through his chest hairs. "Love's a special word, Iggy. You shouldn't use it unless you mean it." She sharply tugged on a few of the hairs, just to emphasize her point.

"Ow!" he exclaimed, firmly grabbing one of her tiny wrists with his right hand. "Okay, Raquel," Ignacio said, laughing in a bothered manner. "Enough. Damn..." He shook his head as he released her wrist, then reached over to the nightstand on his right, picked up his rum and and Kemp, and took a drink. "Why you bein' like that? ¿Que pasa?"

Raquel shrugged her shoulders, as she continued to move her fingers around his chest.

"You're not gonna tell me?" he asked.

"Why should I? You already know."

She was right–he did know. One person had begun to actually feel something for the other, and their little love game had become unbalanced. But Ignacio didn't want the game to end. Not yet. "You don't think I love you, do you?" he asked.

Raquel looked at him with her yearning, innocent eyes, and replied, "You say you do, but you don't really mean it."

Leaning forward and seductively sucking on each of her dark-brown nipples, Ignacio asked, "How can you be so sure that I don't?"

"Because," she said, gently moving his head away from her breasts, and resting it back upon the headboard's pillows.

"Because why?"

"Because if you *did* love me, you wouldn't only be coming *here* to see me." Raquel leaned over him and affectionately kissed his mustached upper-lip. "And you wouldn't want to pay me for my sex anymore..." She moved her kiss to his forehead. "...you'd want to earn it." She then brusquely rolled off of him, stood up, and walked over to the dresser at the opposite end of the room.

That hurt him.

The truth usually did.

Ignacio knew that he wasn't in love with her, but somehow it had comforted him to pretend he was. He'd bring her gifts, buy her things, shower her with compliments–do all the things that he never did for his wife. And Raquel invariably enjoyed the attention, always playing along with the charade. Up until today, that is. Now she had suddenly called him out, and their shared illusion had been abruptly shattered, like a ceiling mirror falling hard to the ground. There was nothing left for them to do but pick up the pieces–and try to avoid cutting themselves in the process. Ignacio took another sip of his sugary-sweet drink. "Chica," he said in as soft a tone as he could, "come back here."

Her back turned towards him, Raquel picked up the thin, silver watch (which he had given her a few months back) that sat atop the dresser, looked at it, and coolly said, "Your time's almost up." She set the watch down, then turned around to face him. He looked over her naked frontside, at her slender figure, her trimmed, brown, pubic hair, her small breasts–and when his gaze had reached her youthful, almost child-like face, he saw the hurt in her eyes. The illusory shards had made their first cut. Raquel placed her hands on her hips and numbly asked him, "Are you done? Or do you wanna fuck me again?"

Though he didn't want it to, his erection rose up at the suggestion. "Aw, c'mon, Raquel..." Ignacio muttered, trying to push it back down. "Don't be like that. You know I care about you."

"No, Iggy, I don't," she said as she moved to the bathroom. "I don't know what you feel about me. You buy me all these gifts, you tell me you love me..." She pulled some toilet paper from off of the roll, folded it neatly, and began to wipe herself with it. "...and you make me feel special. And wanted. And sometimes I actually even let myself enjoy the sex I have with you." Her voice cracked a little, as she said, "I start thinking, 'Hey, maybe this guy really *does* care about me...maybe I should give him a chance.' And so I start letting down my guard, and I start believing that you're gonna be the one who helps me get out of this degrading shit-job." She whimpered, trying her best to hold back her tears. "But then you pay me and leave," Raquel said, throwing the semen-soaked wad of tissue into the toilet, and pulling off a few, fresh sheets, "and everything gets all fucked up again." Her tears began to flow, and she quickly shut the bathroom door.

It didn't matter, though–Ignacio could still hear her crying through the thin, wooden door. He sat there and listened to her for a few seconds, but then the weeping began to make him edgy. It was making him feel guilty–and he hated guilt. Because guilt had the power to turn the strongest of men into the littlest of bitches. Why'd she have to pick today to pull this shit? he asked himself. After spending the whole day at the riot scene, all he had wanted to do was come here and release some tension–but now he was even more tense than when he first arrived.

Ignacio placed his legs over the edge of the bed and gulped down the rest of his drink. "Dios," he said out loud, setting the empty glass onto the nightstand, "forty-seven years old and I'm gettin' involved with a four-year old." It was easy now, in retrospect, to see that he should have played his game with one of the other girls. Midori or Katrina. Desireé. Even Lara, as loco as she was, would have been a better choice. But, despite her age–or perhaps because of it–he had chosen Raquel. The four-year old. Cloned and genetically-accelerated to the age of fourteen by an abusive mother, granted emancipation by the courts at fifteen, illegal prostitution until her eighteenth birthday, now a legal prostitute here at Deep Heat massage parlor. Not exactly the best choice for mind games, he admitted to himself.

Deciding that he'd better get out of there before he had to face Raquel again, Ignacio stood up to leave. He looked around for his clothes, then grumbled, "Aw, no," with the realization that his clothing was inside the bathroom. With Raquel. Ignacio's temper flared. He felt like hitting something. But, as hard as it was for him to do, he managed to suppress the fire. For now. He walked over to the bathroom door, waited a few moments, then pushed it open. Time to face the unhappy music he'd helped to compose.

When he entered into the bathroom, Raquel was still cleaning herself, one leg up on the rim of the tub, the other on the linoleum floor. "Jeez," she said as she looked down at the off-white piece of toilet paper, her voice accentuated with both sadness and laughter, "you sure did come a lot."

Normally a comment like that would have elicited a humorous response from him. But now wasn't the time. He needed to choose his words carefully; make sure that he calmed her down so he could get the hell out of there without anymore emotional backlash. "Raquel..." he kindly said, placing his arms around her waist and kissing her on her cheek, "I'm sorry, baby. Honestly."

She dropped the wet tissue into the toilet, flushed it, and said, "You're just saying that 'cause you don't like it when I cry."

Ignacio turned her around, placed his hand under her chin, and lifted her head slightly so that her eyes met with his. "That's not true, chica," he lied. "I *am* sorry." He smiled, and kissed her softly on the lips. "I never meant to hurt you." At least *that* was true, he rationalized to himself. He hadn't set out to bring her distress, he'd just wanted to play around a little. "What can I do to make things better?"

"I don't know, Iggy," Raquel said, leaning her wet face against his chest and hugging him. "I wish I did."

Ignacio glanced down at the pile of clothes to his left. "Here, Raquel," he said, as he gently broke her embrace, "why don't you put some clothes on." He bent down, picked up a few pieces of her clothing, and extended them towards her.

"Thanks." She placed the clothes on top of the sink. "But I'm not gonna need 'em right now. I wanna take a bath first." She wiped her eyes, and added, "A really hot one. And I just wanna sit in the water and think."

"That'll be good," Ignacio said as he gathered up his clothes. "You'll feel better after that."

"I doubt it," she said, closing the lid on the toilet and sitting down on top of the foamy surface, "but I'm gonna try anyways." She reached over, and turned on the tub's faucet. The steaming water began to flow.

Ignacio couldn't think of anything else to say–so he didn't. There was silence for the next minute or so, as he put on his clothes and got dressed, and she sat there atop the toilet, her head buried in her hands, letting out the occasional, exhausted sigh.

The silence was finally broken when Raquel said, "I don't think you should see me anymore."

He was surprised to hear her say that. "Are you sure?" he asked, feeling an unexpected need to confirm her statement.

"I think so," she said, as she dipped two of her fingers into the hot water and swirled them around. "Yeah."

He was even more surprised when he suddenly found himself wanting to talk her out of her decision. Zipping up his Levi's®, he told her, "Maybe we should just wait a while–take some time off from each other...then I'll come by and see you in a few weeks." What the hell are you saying? he asked himself. You got the perfect opportunity to leave and make a clean break from this bullshit–so why aren't you taking it? "How's that sound?" he asked.

She looked up at him with those same, yearning eyes, shook her head, and said, "I'm sorry, Iggy..." She wrapped her arms around her naked self. "But I can't do it anymore. Not like this."

As he finished putting on his jacket, Ignacio once again found himself at a loss for words. His mind was screaming at him to say goodbye and be done with her, but something else–he would have said his heart, if he wasn't in such denial–was pleading with him not to let her go. What to do? he wondered. More confusion. And what to say? More tension. "What if..." Ignacio tried to stop himself, but he couldn't. "What if we made things different?"

Raquel gave him a confused look. "What do you mean?"

In his head, all he heard was "Don't say it!" But what he said was, "What if I didn't come here anymore–and we started seeing each other outside the parlor?" Ignacio paused for a moment, feeling slightly sick to his stomach, then said, "...and I stopped paying you."

With an incredulous laughed, she asked, "Why would you

126

wanna do that?"

He couldn't believe this was happening. "Because..." The painful truth rose up inside him like bile, and he spit up the words, "...I need you, Raquel."

For a moment, she intently studied his face. Then she said, "Oh, Jeez," and slowly turned her head away from him. Watching the steam rise from the tub, she added, "You really mean it."

Feeling like a little, vulnerable bitch, Ignacio quickly walked out of the bathroom, cursing at himself as he left.

"Iggy, wait!" Raquel shouted as she followed after him.

He stopped, but didn't turn to face her.

"Iggy," she said. "C'mon, look at me." She tugged on his jacket. "Please?"

Ignacio slowly turned around, defeated. He looked her in the face, but didn't connect eye to eye.

"Sweetie..." Raquel said, reaching her hand up around the back of his neck and caressing him.

He drooped his head down slightly, closed his eyes, and allowed her cool hand to soothe his fevered skin. The emotional turmoil churning inside of him began to subside, and for a brief moment, he felt a rare sense of peace and clarity. He saw things for what they were, and actually confronted the issues that haunted him, rather than repressing them. He thought about his irreverence and utter disregard of Irena's faithful love and devotion; the lack of time he dedicated to his two, beautiful, little girls; the prostitutes he frequented, and how he would *never* want Aurora or Esperanza to experience the things that those girls did; the feelings he had for Raquel, and the love for her that he pretended was make-believe... The sudden lucidity nearly made him weep, but he firmly held back the emotions, and erected the wall of repression which had just been torn down. He pulled away from her comforting embrace and stammered, "I...I gotta go, Raquel," then walked towards the door.

"Iggy...?" she asked him, as he pushed the button on the door to unlock the deadbolt.

He looked back at her, but didn't say anything.

"My number's listed..." She smiled uneasily. "If you ever wanna make things different."

Ignacio nodded, opened the door, quickly left the room, and shut the door behind him. Walking down the magenta-colored hallway, past the numbered front doors of the parlor's other rooms, he didn't allow himself to look back. Not even once. Because he knew that even the fleetest glance over his shoulder would send him running, right back to the solace of that little womangirl's loving arms. That fact, he couldn't stand. Or understand. He clenched his fists and grinded his teeth.

The fire inside had been stoked once more.

By the time he reached the end of the hallway, and entered into the parlor's smoky lounge, he was inebriated with negative emotions. A volatile cocktail was being mixed within him—one part anger, one part embarrasment, and one part confusion. With a twist of hurt pride. Ignacio walked over to the bar, and without sitting down, said to the bald bartender, "Ey, Charlie—pour me two shots of Bacardi®. 151."

"Sure thing, Mo," Charlie said to him, as he moved over from two other customers who were seated at the bar. He set a pair shot glasses down in front of Ignacio. Pouring the clear rum into one of the glasses, he asked, "Everything okay?"

Ignacio downed the shot as soon as Charlie was finished pouring. Clearing his throat, he replied, "Bueno."

Charile poured the other glass full. "Raquel treat you good?"

"Bueno."

As Ignacio finished his second shot, one of the nearby customers twisted around on his stool and faced them. He was dressed in extravagant, expensive clothes, looked to be in his late twenties, was surreally ripped (definitely hypersteroids), and had a number of tattoodecals on his face, neck, and forearms. Ignacio had never met him before, but he'd heard about him. They called him Tattoo, and he was known around town as a mid-level amp dealer. Not one of the underworld's big boys, but he was doing his best to become one.

"You guys talkin' 'bout Raquel?" Tattoo asked in a hoarse voice. Without waiting for an answer, the man looked at Ignacio and said, "That bitch is hunny, fool. No joke, she can *fuck*." He turned to his shorter, less muscular drinking buddy. "Ain't that right, Z?"

"I'm sayin'!" Z replied with a laugh, giddily raising his mug of stout into the air.

With the extra alcohol burning its way down his gut, the volatile cocktail had now become a Molotov cocktail. Ignacio had already had the fire—now all he needed was to be thrown. "What'd you just say?" he asked the tattooed man.

Tattoo turned back towards him and replied, "I said she can fuck." Noticing the anger in Ignacio's face, he laughed and said, "You need an ear implant, old man, or what?"

"Let it slide, Mo," Charlie said. "He's just playin' around."

"I *ain't* playin'," Tattoo said to Charlie. "So don't speak for me." He looked at Ignacio again. "I asked if you needed an implant. Do you?"

"What I *need*, cabróna," Ignacio said, "is for you to take a swing at me. Then I can beat the fuckin' living shit out of you."

Tattoo's expression became hostile. "I don't know what you're smokin', pancho, but you better jet while you still got the chance." While one of his hands held on to his glass of ale, he started to reach the other down towards his waistline.

"What, you got a weapon in there?" Ignacio asked. "Keep goin' for it, bitch–see what happens."

Tattoo stared at Ignacio for a long, slow moment...then made his move.

Before Tattoo even had the chance to *touch* his weapon, Ignacio had already landed two, strong, lightning-like punches to his face–one on the bridge of his nose, the other on the right side of his jaw. Tattoo's glass of ale began to fall to the ground...

And
the
world
started
     to

          move

              in

                  slow

                      motion.

When Ignacio allowed his cybernetically-enhanced reflexes to work to their full-capacity, it was like time slowed down around him. His movements became so fast, that the motion of nearly everything else surrounding him came to a crawl. The ale spilling out of Tattoo's glass looked more like amber mercury. The spray of saliva coming from his mouth appeared as individual droplets of spittle, and Ignacio could clearly see the flattened skin and cartilage of the drug dealer's nose rebounding back from the previous blow. As he gradually fell off his barstool, Tattoo made a futile attempt to raise up his hands and protect his injured face.

Ignacio swiftly hit him three more times.

The first punch landed on the same side of Tattoo's jaw as before–only this time the mandible shattered. The next two punches were aimed directly at Tattoo's eyes, and the thick, metal rings on

FREQUENCIES

Ignacio's fingers easily split open the thin skin surrounding his eye sockets. Tattoo's motion towards the ground increased a bit with the extra force, but Ignacio still had time to forcefully slam the side of his fist down onto the drug dealer's forehead.

The first few drops of ale splashed onto the floor in photographic fashion, just as Tattoo's bloodied face was about to join them. But before his head could touch the ground, Ignacio pretended Tattoo's skull was a soccer ball and he was a goalie about to drop kick. His steel-toed Doc Martens® smashed into the now-unconscious man's mouth, scattering his teeth across the floor like ivory pebbles.

The ale glass shattered loudly, as it and Tattoo's head finally impacted with the ground. Ignacio slowed himself down... And
the
world
returned to normal speed. He quickly looked over at Z, gave him a sup, and said, "You got next?"

Z, whose pudgy, rounded face was currently displaying an expression of utter shock, didn't say a word, and merely shook his head "no" at a very frenetic speed.

Ignacio looked at the bartender and said, "Sorry, Charlie. I apologize for the mess—just put it on my tab."

"Uh, yeah, Mo," Charile responded, his eyes wide open. "Right. Sure."

Ignacio then kneeled beside Tattoo, reached down to the unconscious man's waistline, and pulled out a small, plastic laser pistol. "Illegal," he confirmed to himself, relieved that he now had legal grounds for thrashing the man so badly. He looked up at Charlie and held up the piece. "In case this bad-boy tries to press any charges, I'm showin' you the weapon. You're my witness that he was threatening me with this." He looked over at Z. "So are you." Ignacio stood up, keeping the weapon in his hand. "And since nobody wants the cops to come sniffin' around here, let's leave 'em out of this. I'm not involving the law unless he does."

Coming around the bar to clean up the broken glass and the spilled blood and ale, Charile said, "I don't think he will, Mo." He began wiping the liquid up with a white towel, quickly turning the bright cloth a deep-burgundy color. "But you better be careful next time you come 'round here. He's gonna be lookin' for payback."

"He'll regret it if he does," Ignacio said. "I went easy on him on this time—next time I won't." He looked at Z again. "You let him know that, too, chubby. If he tries to pull any shit," Ignacio said, pulling out his Freemon badge and showing it to Z, "he's gonna find himself in a coma."

Z nodded as he stared down at his fallen friend, then mumbled to himself, "Shit, dude, I think he already is."

His enhanced metabolism now fully slowed down, Ignacio began to feel tired. And lethargic. And most of all, hungry. He always needed to fuel up after using his enhancements, which ate up his body's energy quicker than a starved man at a buffet. He was eager to get home to dinner. Ignacio slipped the laser into his jacket's right-hand pocket and announced, "I'm outta here, Charlie."

"I'll be seein' you, Mo," Charlie said, continuing to clean up the mess.

The other occupants of the lounge talked quietly amongst themselves, all watching Ignacio as he walked to the exit. He paid no attention to them, opened the door, and left the dimly-lit establishment. Outside, the sun was still shining brightly, though now it was starting to set on the horizon. He walked through the Pioneer Square crowd, and over to the curb where his Harley-Davidson® Skyhog™ was parked. He opened one of the hoverbike's side compartments, pulled out his black, visored helmet, and closed it shut. Ignacio then seated himself on the Harley®, fired up its propulsion system, put on his helmet, and flew off towards his Queen Anne home.

When he arrived at his house, Ignacio quietly let himself in, and headed straight for the bedroom to get a fresh change of clothes. He knew he reeked of booze, sex, and violence, and wanted to clean himself up first before facing his family. Luckily, Irena and the girls were in the back of the house preparing dinner together, and he was able to hop into the shower unnoticed.

As he stood there under the water, letting the cool, brisk spray wash over and calm him, Ignacio lost track of the time. He may have been in there for ten minutes, maybe even twenty or thirty. He wasn't even sure. And he didn't really care. The cold, anesthetic temperature numbed both his body and mind, and for the first time all day, he didn't think or feel about anything. No emotions to wrangle with, no plaguing thoughts to ponder. He blanked out into a desensitized heaven. A meperidine bliss.

Until there was a knock at the bathroom door.

131

Descending back to the realm of the senses, Ignacio asked, "Yeah?"

Irena opened the door halfway, popped her head in, and said, "Baby, Marc's here–and the food's done."

"I'll be right out, Irena," he said. "Gracias."

"You're welcome," she said, then closed the door and left.

Ignacio stood there and enjoyed the coolness for a few more seconds, then turned the water off, stepped out of the shower, and dried himself off. After putting on a pair of Calvin Klein® boxers, and slipping into a pair of Dockers®, Ignacio looked at his exposed upper-body in the mirror in front of him. He touched his stomach, where a thin, recently-formed layer of fat now covered what used to be a six-pack. It was still as strong as it used to be–which he confirmed by firmly poking one of his fingers into it–but it no longer looked the same. His reflection looked disappointed. In response, he flexed both of his muscular biceps, then his triceps and forearms, and was relieved to see that they still looked as strong as ever. In fact, the extra weight he'd gained actually made them appear bigger. Same with his chest. The reflection gave him a confident nod of approval. He smiled at it, put on some Old Spice® deodorant, slipped on his shirt, and buttoned it up. He then put some gel on his hands, rubbed it through his slightly-thinning, charcoal-black hair, picked up his dirty clothes, and entered into the bedroom.

He was about to throw the clothes into the hamper, but then abruptly stopped, and brought the garments up to his nose and sniffed them. He couldn't smell Raquel on the clothes–but he knew Irena would be able to. Women always had that uncanny ability to sense each other's scents. He walked over to the washing machine set into the wall, put the clothes in, and started the cycle.

Ignacio exited the bedroom and entered into the spacious living room. McCready was sitting down on one of the brown, leather couches, and the children were sitting next to him on the carpeted floor. All three of them were watching some loud, colorful, animated program on the holoview. "¡Patrón!" Ignacio amiably announced as he walked over to his fellow Freemon.

McCready immediately stood up and said, "Hey, Morris." They clasped their right hands together, then hugged each other with their left arms. "Thanks for having me over."

"Te nada," he responded as they broke their embrace. "I'm glad you could make it."

"So am I." McCready smelled the air and commented,

"'Cause, man, I'm tellin' you, it sure smells fuc-" He stopped his sentence, looked down at the kids, and covered his mouth. "Whoops. Sorry." He laughed. "I mean, it smells hella good in here."

Ignacio smiled. "It does, doesn't it?"

"Papá, move!" Aurora shouted, tugging on her father's pant leg. "You're in the way! I can't see the show!"

"Ay, okay! Calm down, mi hija!" Ignacio said with a laugh as he moved out of her way. "I'm moving!" He looked at McCready with mock disbelief. "I tell you–these girls, man, they're spoiled. Think they're the queens of the castle."

"We don't think that," Esperanza corrected him in a sassy tone. "*Mom's* the queen." She smiled, and added, "We're the princesses."

Ignacio looked back at McCready and laughed. "Princesses."

An especially loud commotion began to occur on the holoview, drawing all of their attention to it. On the projected, 3-D screen, an anthropomorphic cat in a suit was shooting a laser pistol at some villianous-looking Asians, who where firing back with lasers of their own. The bright colors from the show lit up the entire room with their light, almost as if the lasers were actually being fired right there.

"What is this?" Ignacio asked the girls.

"Kat Mandu," replied Aurora.

"Katmandu?" he asked, as the cat threw some shuriken that looked like little, spinning wheels. "This show beamed from Tibet?"

"Nah," McCready answered, "it's an American show. That guy," he said, putting his gloved finger through the cat's holographic head, "is Kat Mandu. He's like a Buddhist James Bond." He watched for a few seconds, then said, "He gets sent on all these missions by the Dalai Lama's preserved brain. He mostly fights a lot of Chinese terrorists, but there's always this larger quest of him seeking out an ultimate weapon called the Lotus Flower."

"And he does Tantric sex rituals with Shikta," added Esperanza, as she stared straight ahead at the three-dimensional action. "She's his partner."

McCready laughed. "And he does that too."

Ignacio made a curious face. "Isn't there something else you guys could watch?"

"No, we *like* Kat," Esperanza responded. "And Lery Vast comes on sometimes during Kat's show."

Now *that*, Ignacio had seen before. It was hard to miss The Lery Vast Moment. It ran on different channels, at random times of the day, and for various lengths of time. Sometimes it lasted for a second, sometimes a few minutes, and it always contained something different each time. The show was so random, that it never had recurring characters, and rarely even had a theme. It was never listed in any of the channel guides, so viewers had to try to look for patterns of when and where it appeared if they wanted to try to tune in or set their UV's on record. The unpredictability of the show made it a huge hit, and people would sometimes sit in front of their univiews for hours on end, all in the hopes of catching a new Lery Vast.

"Yeah, and last time," Aurora said, "they had a lion on it, and then he ate a deer, and then-"

"It wasn't a *deer*, 'Rora," corrected Esperanza. "It was a gazelle."

"Yeah," Aurora continued, "an' then he ate the 'zelle, an' then he turned into this big, big, big building, an' then there was this blue light, an' then the building fell over an' crashed." She took a small breath. "An' then that was it."

"Okay, everyone," Irena announced from the kitchen, "time to eat."

"Papá, can we eat out here?" Aurora asked with a pouty face. "Pleeese?"

"Don't you want to eat with all of us, 'Rora?" Ignacio asked.

"Yeah," she said. "But I wanna watch Kat more."

"Even though Marc came over?"

"Papá," Aurora said, unimpressed with Ignacio's argument, "Marc *always* comes over."

"And he already promised he'd have flan with us out here after dinner," chimed Esperanza. "So we'll still get to see him anyway." She smiled her princess smile at him and McCready.

Ignacio looked over at McCready, who shrugged his shoulders and said, "I did promise 'em that, Morris. Though I didn't know it was going to be used as evidence in their dinner defense."

"Okay," Ignacio conceded to the girls, "but you need to go and get your food yourselves. Mommy's done enough work already."

"Yay!" Aurora exclaimed as she excitedly bounced up and clapped her hands. She ran over to her father, hugged his leg, and ran off to the kitchen.

"Gracias, Papá," Esperanza said, as she followed after her younger sister.

Ignacio sighed, then asked McCready, "Am I too lenient with them?"

"Nah, man," McCready said as they walked towards the kitchen, "they're your kids. It's alright to pamper 'em sometimes. And you can tell in their faces they appreciate it."

As they reached the kitchen, Ignacio looked at his daughter's facial expressions, smiled at McCready's words, and nodded his head in agreement.

"You guys can sit down," Irena said as she served Aurora and Esperanza. "Your food's already on the table."

"Thanks, Irena," McCready said, and seated himself at the kitchen table.

Ignacio stood there for a moment and appreciatively gazed at his wife. Though he wasn't faithful to her, he did love her. And she was still so beautiful. Thirty-seven years old, and she looked like she hadn't even reached thirty yet. He walked over to Irena, gave her a kiss on the top of her head, and warmly said, "Gracias, baby. Te amo."

"Te amo, tambien," she replied, her attention still focused on the girls. As Aurora began to leave the kitchen, Irena said, "Aurora, wait!" She held out a placemat towards her daughter. "You need to eat on top of this so you don't dirty the carpet."

Aurora grabbed the placemat form her and quickly moved to the living room.

"Esperanza," Irena said, looking over at her other daughter, "make sure she doesn't spill, 'kay?"

"Yo promo, Mamá," Esperanza said, then joined her sister in the other room.

Irena took a deep breath, sighed heavily, looked up at Ignacio and said, "Finalmente—comemos."

"Sí," he agreed with a laugh, and they both seated themselves at the kitchen table with McCready.

"Thanks again, guys, for having me over," McCready said. "This is a real treat. I appreciate it."

Irena smiled. "You're welcome, Marc. It's nice to have you over." She extended her hands out towards him and Ignacio. They each reached a hand out to her, she softly closed her eyes, and whispered a prayer of grace. When she finished, she opened her eyes, and said, "Let's eat."

McCready immediately took a bite of the chicken molé. A smile appeared across his face as he chewed, and he said to Irena, "This is incredible, sweetheart. I'm in heaven."

She laughed. "I don't know about *that*, but thank you."

FREQUENCIES

"No, thank *you*," McCready said as he took another bite. "And honestly," he snickered, "this *is* probably the closest *I'm* gonna get to heaven."

His mouth slightly full, Ignacio added, "This *is* really good, baby."

"Thanks," she acknowledged, licking her lips and giving him a peck on his cheek.

"So, Ignacio," McCready asked as he dug his fork into some refried beans, "what was the deal with the riot? What happened after I left?"

"Not too much, really," he answered, sipping on a spoonful of sopa. "We conducted a general sweep of the area...turned up some more freekers...that was about it. Most of 'em surrendered without a fight, though there were a few of 'em we had to tussle with." He took another sip of the soup. "The cops made a bunch of arrests once they got inside people's apartments–mostly drug-related stuff, though I think they found some illegal weapons too."

"You guys find any evidence about what might have caused the riot?" McCready asked. "I mean, other than the cops' hit parade?"

"No, nothing turned up there," Ignacio said. "But when we got back to HQ, Takura had checked into that sector's ambient frequential records, and apparently he found that there was some type of large-scale, EMF transmission that had hit the infected area right before the riot started."

McCready looked at him curiously. "What, like a giant infobomb?"

Ignacio said, "We thought that at first, but Takura said the transmission's frequencies more resembled some type of alpha-wave inhibitor. His theory was that the EMF's had countered the UV's normal, alpha-wave transmissions, and since the people were so pissed off about what had happened with the cops, the absence of the calming alpha-waves caused them to freek out."

"Interesting," McCready commented.

"Then that's probably also what happened in Vancouver," Irena posited.

"Vancouver?" McCready asked.

She nodded as she ate some salad. "The news said that something similar happened in Vancouver yesterday."

"Then somethin' big's going on here," McCready said. "That's right down I-5–the proximities are way too close for them not to be related."

"That's what the bureau thinks too," Ignacio said. "They're flying two DCC agents into SeaTac in the morning. They're gonna work with us to figure out what's going on."

"Well," McCready said, "the next few days are certainly gonna be interesting ones, aren't they?"

"Looks that way, patrón," he said. Ignacio picked up some rice with his fork, then suddenly laughed. "Oh yeah, Marc, I almost forgot to tell you–at the riot scene, Essence knocked your old friend on his ass."

"Luno?"

"Sí."

McCready laughed. "What happened?"

"You remember how he kept referring to us as 'Free*men*,' instead of Freemon?"

"Right."

"Essence wasn't havin' that, boy." Ignacio laughed again. "When we were done with the sweep, he referred to her personally as a 'Freeman.' And so she warned him–firmly–not to do that shit again. But then he says to her, 'You're lucky you're a broad, or I'd-' And then pow!" Ignacio exclaimed, punching the air with his fist. "I'm tellin' you, blud, she lit him *up*! He got knocked straight onto his ass, and he had to just sit there holding his broken nose, 'cause he knew she was gonna drop him again if he got up too quick."

"Oh, man," McCready said, laughing, "that sounds fuckin' hilarious. I wish I could'a been there."

"Me too, patrón–you would've loved it." Taking a bite of the rice, Ignacio asked, "Ey, what did you end up doing at the skyland, anyway? Takura said it was about a butler, or somethin'."

McCready hesitated briefly, then said, "Yeah, it was just some guy who was trippin' out on his servitude. His boss had me look over him, ask him some questions, tell him his options...shit like that. It was boring."

Ignacio said, "They called you from the riot just for that?"

"Yup," McCready replied. "Go figure." That didn't make much sense. Ignacio had a feeling that McCready was holding something back. But didn't want to press him on it. Not now. McCready took a bite of rice and beans, then smiled. "But something good came out of it," he said.

"What's that?" Ignacio asked.

"I met the boss' daughter."

"Oooh," Irena said teasingly, "Marc found a lady."

McCready laughed at her comment.

"So what's the story, patrón?" Ignacio said. "Fill us in."

"Well," McCready said, "first of all, she's incredibly–pardon my French–fuckin' beautiful. But she's also smart, funny, down-to-Earth...and because of her status, she can discuss trippy shit with me." He shook his head, as if he still didn't believe it. "This woman is simply amazing, man. I've never met anyone like her."

"That's what you said with the last girl," Irena stated. "With what's her name–Allegra."

McCready thought about her statement for a moment, took another bite of food, nodded, then said, "That's right–I did say that about her." He laughed. "But this time I really, really mean it. Honestly. She makes any other girl I've ever been interested in seem like...like... Ignacio, you're the simile king–help me out here with a good one."

"A good simile?" he asked. "How about..." He paused for a moment, lightly rubbing the ends of his mustache. "How about...she makes the other girls you've been interested in seem like a bunch of narcoleptic transvestites."

McCready laughed, held out his hand towards Ignacio, and said to Irena, "There you go. See how much I like this woman?"

Irena smiled and rolled her eyes, then gave her husband a suspicious look. "What do *you* know about narcoleptic transvestites?"

"Nada," he responded with a laugh. "I just said it 'cause that shit sounds funny."

"Mommy!" yelled Aurora from the living room. "C'mere!"

Irena turned her head towards the living room. "What do you need, baby?"

"I spilt my drink!" she said.

"It wasn't my fault!" added Esperanza.

Irena laughed, and began to get up from the table.

Ignacio touched her hand and asked her, "You want me to handle it?"

"No, I'm already up," Irena said, "I'll get it." She walked over to a drawer, pulled out a hand-held wetvac, and walked into the living room.

Watching Irena exit the room, a look of fond affection appeared in McCready's eyes, and he commented, "You're one lucky man, my friend–'cause that is sure one special woman."

Ignacio knew McCready had something of a crush on Irena, but it had never really bothered him, since he knew the younger Freemon would never disrespect his familial boundaries. And in a way, the attention to his wife flattered Ignacio, and also served as a frequent reminder for him to appreciate what he already had. Ignacio nodded at McCready's comments, and replied, "Sí, I'm very lucky, patrón." Ignacio took another bite of his dinner, then looked back at the living room, made sure that Irena wasn't finished with the girls yet, and said to McCready in a hushed tone, "One thing I want to tell you about, Marc–but don't say anything about this to Irena."

McCready leaned forward and whispered, "Yeah, sure, man. What is it?"

"Earlier today," Ignacio said, "when I was at Deep Heat, I roughed up some blud named Tattoo–a middle-man amp dealer. Not a big-boy, but I know he's got *some* back. So if something happens to me in the next few days, I want to make sure you know who to look for. I doubt anything's gonna go down, but I'm letting you know about it just in case."

"Alright, yeah. I'm glad you told me." McCready paused, his face showing concern. "You don't think we should maybe just get him first?"

"No, no," Ignacio said. "I don't want to draw any extra attention to me being at the massage parlor. Everything should be chill, patrón, don't worry."

"Alright, Morris, if you say so... Though I-" McCready stopped his words, and casually leaned back in his chair.

"Those girls are a handful," Irena said with a laugh, as she entered into the kitchen. She set the wetvac atop the counter, and joined them again at the table. "But at least that's done with. Now we can relax and finish our dinner."

They all began to eat again, but were quickly interrupted when Esperanza asked, "Mamá? Can we have dessert now?"

Ignacio, Irena, and McCready all looked at each other for a moment. And then they laughed.

Together.

Δ

α

Chapter 8:
The Invisible Hand

*"The reality-masters did their very best to ensure that
enlightened individuals lost confidence in their own abilities.
Fear, terror, doubt, complacency, confusion...these were but a few of
the techniques exploited by them in order to destroy one's trust in
oneself. Diabolically, the masters took advantage of the fact that
without any confidence in self, the individual could achieve
nothing...and nothing could never be a threat to their control.
What could be a threat to them, and which they tried at all costs to
prevent others from truly knowing, was the fact that with full self-
confidence, the individual could achieve everything and anything,
for being in touch with oneself was akin to godhood.
And wasn't it God's hand which created the world?"*

Lifting the cup and saucer from the breakfast room table, Mason
asked, "And, gentlemen, what were the results of these findings?"

On the large uniview embedded into the wall before him,
were the images of Mr. Webber and Agent McCready, each occupying
one half of the currently split-screen. The Wednesday afternoon sun
was just beginning to burn through the gray, overcast sky, and through
the dining room's glass doors, a few, scattered patches of sunlight
could be seen dotting the lawns and gardens outside.

"Camera-records revealed Mrs. Huxton had no prolonged
exposure to a uniview screen," answered Mr. Webber, as the corner of
his implanted, metallic-red goggles glinted brightly from a nearby
light source. "Mall uniview-records showed no anomalous

transmissions during her visit." The rounded lenses of the gogs constricted momentarily, then dilated as the glint disappeared. "Eliminates possiblility of infection via uniview. Suspect usage of a time-delayed information release so as not to attract immediate attention. Passed through physical contact with your wife."

"I take it then, that you know who the attacker was?" Mason asked, bringing the small cup of espresso to his lips.

"Camera-records revealed six possible suspects," said Mr. Webber. "Narrowed to three after biochip search. Freemon can tell you more."

Mason looked at Agent McCready, and took a slow, careful sip of the hot mocha.

"Late last night," said the Freemon, who was currently seated on his living room couch, "I went down to HQ and looked into your wife's biochip data." Behind him, above the couch, hung a framed, Marilyn Monroe print by Andy Warhol. "From the camera-records that Webber sent to me, I was able to note the times in which your wife came into physical contact with someone, then match that up with her biochip's medical data." McCready's hand reached off-camera momentarily, then returned with a Folger's® instant latté. He opened up the can, took a drink, then continued, "At 3:36 on Monday afternoon, there was a sudden increase in your wife's cardiovascular and electrodermal readings. Also at this time, her freeread showed a lowering of amplitude and an increase in frequency. Since her bioreadings were normal and steady up to this point, we can safely say this was the time the information unloaded itself. But, as Webber said before, it was a time-delayed burst of information...a type of infobomb that's biologically untraceable up until the moment it actually attacks and releases itself–which means that the time she contracted the infobomb isn't the same time as when her bioreadings jumped."

Mason nodded. "And therefore you can't simply match the time of her abnormal readings with one of the incidents of contact."

"Right," McCready said. "In this case, infection and effect aren't simultaneous. So basically, your wife's bioreadings can't tell us *who* did the attack, but it can tell us who didn't." Taking another drink of his beverage, he said, "Since three of the people she came into contact with touched her *after* the abnormal bioreadings, we can eliminate them as possible suspects. That leaves us with three possibilties–a store employee who she'd come into contact with several times before, another who she'd never met, and one of her escorts."

"Mr. Webber," Mason said to his head of security, "which escort is he referring to?"

Adjusting the implanted, speaker-looking devices which served as his ears, Mr. Webber replied, "Benjamin, sir. Currently detained and being questioned. Interrogation to be conducted by myself at the conclusion of this conversation."

"Very good," Mason said. "Now, Agent McCready, these other two suspects–what information have you gathered on them?"

McCready picked up a remote, pressed a few buttons on it, and three faces–two males and one female–appeared in the lower corner of Mason's screen. "The person who she'd had previous contact with is Candace Wilson," the Freemon said, as the border around the attractive female's photo began to glow, "an employee at the cosmetics department at Nordstrom's®. Her files show no record of the type of memory augmentation that's required to hold an infobomb, and her only surgeries have been a tit, ass, and nose-job. I checked into the possibility of an illegal operation, but her biochip doesn't sense the presence of any non-documented implants or alterations." McCready set the canned latté down onto his coffeetable, and highlighted the photo of a clean-cut, Latino man. "The other suspect, Antonio Jiminez, works at Ben Bridge® jewelers, and he's had some brain modifications in the past–a few memory improvements, and an implant that regulates a tic he gets when he's nervous or anxious. I'd say him and your escort are the most likely suspects, since what's his name–Benjamin–used to to be a professional johnny-courier. Either of them could have had the infobomb download into their heads."

Mason placed one finger on his lip, thought for a moment, then said, "Agent McCready, when a courier transfers his data to another source, isn't there some indicator of this...informational release in his bioreadings?"

McCready lit up a cigarette and said, "Usually, yeah." He took a few puffs.

"Then can't you check the two suspects' bioreadings for that day, look for the indicator, and determine which one did it?"

"Nope," McCready said as he blew out some smoke. "Not with this kind of infobomb. As long as it's dormant, the biochip can't detect its presence. And unfortunately, when it's sitting inside the courier's head, it's dormant–same thing when it's transmitted. The biochip's basically useless until the information exposes itself."

"I see," Mason said, setting down his cup and saucer. "Then

what will be the next step?"

"Well," McCready answered, "next we'll do some data mining into the suspects' activities over the last few months–who they've come into contact with, where they've been, what they've bought, what they've watched, etcetera. That should give us some good leads. Webber's interrogation should give us some more information too."

"Most certainly it will," confirmed Mr. Webber. His mouth widened into a macabre smile which revealed the sharp, metallic teeth underneath. "Interrogation of the other two suspects surely would as well."

"Not just yet," Mason said. "Let's find out more about them first."

"Legal concerns?" asked Mr. Webber.

"No–future concerns." Mason reached forward, towards the large platter of fruits and pastries which sat on the table in front of him, and picked up a croissant. "Because it seems extremely improbable to me, Mr. Webber, that one individual planned this attack all by themselves. This entire situation *reeks* of conspiracy." He portioned off a tiny piece of croissant, placed it in his mouth, and began to carefully chew it. "And if there *is* a conspiracy afoot, then I want it–and every single one of its members–eliminated." He swallowed. "Completely."

Mr. Webber said, "Reasoning that one of the suspects might lead to a larger organization?"

"Precisely," Mason replied.

"That's not a bad idea," McCready said. "Obviously, the attacker doesn't suspect we know anything, or else they would have disappeared by now." He took another pull from his cigarette and said, "But if Benjamin turns out to be the attacker, then you're not gonna be able to do that–'cause now he knows you know. Why the different approaches?"

Setting the croissant aside and picking up a few champagne grapes, Mason answered, "Because I will not tolerate defection or betrayal within the upper-ranks of Ordosoft™, Agent McCready. Treachery is a weed that must be pulled immediately, lest it should spread and grow throughout one's entire garden." He delicately ate some of the miniature grapes, then said, "Besides, after spending a few hours with Mr. Webber, I am *quite* confident that Benjamin will be eager to tell us everything it is that he knows."

"Alright," McCready said. "So are you wanting me to carry

out the data mining on the other two suspects, or is Webber gonna do that?"

"Mr. Webber will conduct the rest of the investigation, then consult with you on his findings. I want *you* to be available to give full and complete attention to Ashley's safety–and conducting a thorough investigation would prevent you from doing that." Placing the remaining grapes back down onto the platter, Mason said, "Mr. Webber, I want you to assign two–and only two–other Ordocops™ to this case in order to assist you with the detective work. Do not tell them of the attack on my wife, merely inform them that we are conducting an investigation into the lives of these two individuals. Contact me should you find something of significance, otherwise...I'll be contacting you. That will be all for now, Mr. Webber."

Webber nodded his head, then his half of the screen quickly shrank in size until it disappeared completely. McCready's image immediately enlarged to fill up the rest of the screen.

"So tell me, Agent McCready," Mason said, making sure his vocal intonations sounded a bit less formal, "how are things going with Ashley?"

"You mean how is her safety," he asked as he leaned forward to tap off some ashes, "or how are we getting along?"

"The latter–I already know that she's safe."

"Well, I haven't pissed her off yet, she hasn't pissed me off yet...so I'd say things are goin' pretty damn good." McCready took a pull from his cigarette. "And actually, I'm even enjoying my time around her. Your daugher's a real sweetheart, Huxton."

"I'm pleased to hear you say that, Agent McCready. Though I knew you'd both be reluctant at first, I had a feeling that you two would enjoy each other's company once you got to know each other. You are, shall we say...of like minds."

McCready let out a small laugh. "That's one way to put it."

"Yes, and I believe that because of this, Ashley will come to respect you a great deal." Mason then said, in the same voice he used for sensitive business negotiations, "And that means that you could have a positive influence on her."

McCready smiled. "My influence has been called a lot of things, Huxton, but I think you're the first person to ever label it as 'positive.'"

Mason smiled back. "With Ashley, I believe it will be. You see, Agent McCready, despite my best efforts, my daughter has never been interested in becoming an integral part of Ordosoft™. She has an irrational...fear, so to speak–a trepidation of structure and order. You, on the other hand, obviously respect and appreciate these values, or else you wouldn't be in the line of work that you're in now."

"Not necessarily. Maybe I'm just too lazy to find another job," McCready said, leaning back on his couch and placing one arm up on top of its cushioned backrest.

"Perhaps..." Mason said. "...but I doubt it. I think you have more respect for order than you're willing to admit. Otherwise, the duties required of a Freemon would have pushed you away from the job a *long* time ago." He smiled. "Am I wrong?"

McCready took a few more draws from his cigarette, and didn't say anything in response.

"I would ask of you to please keep this in mind as you spend the next few days with Ashley, Agent McCready." Mason picked up a shiny, red apple, and began to polish its skin with a cloth napkin. "If you can influence her in any way towards seeing *our* point of view more clearly, it would be most appreciated. As a matter of fact, I would consider it a great favor." He took a bite from the apple, causing some of the juice to drip down onto his chin. Elegantly patting the liquid with his napkin, he said, "And fortune and prosperity always seem to follow those who do me favors." Mason smiled again, then replaced the barely-eaten apple onto the silver platter. "Please tell Ashley I said hello when you see her. I'll talk to you again shortly, Agent McCready. Good day." He severed the connection, and the image of the Freemon morphed into the Ordosoft™ logo.

"Marcel," Mason said to his butler, who was standing at the far end of the breakfast room, dusting a large bird-of-paradise plant. "I'm all finished with this," motioning his hand towards the replete platter of food. "You can dispose of it now."

"Right away, sir," Marcel responded, setting down his feather-duster and walking over to the table.

"Where is Dominique?" Mason asked.

Picking up the large, circular platter, Marcel said, "I believe that she's in the garden, sir."

Mason looked out through the glass doors, but didn't see any sign of his wife. "I don't see her, Marcel. Are you sure?"

"Excuse me, sir, I should have been more specific. She's in the *west* garden."

Turning his head from the doors, Mason asked, "And was she going out for a walk, or was she actually going out to garden?"

"Considering her attire, sir, I would say she was going out to do some gardening."

"Good," Mason said, nodding his head. "That's a very good sign, Marcel. Dominique always loved her gardening so."

"She did, sir." He coughed. "Or rather, she *does*."

"Indeed. I'll be in the west garden should you need me." Mason stood up from his breakfast room chair, proceeded through the kitchen and the adjacent, personal dining room, exited out of the house via the veranda, and began to amble around Xanadeux's expansive west garden. Within a few moments, he spotted Dominique, who was currently bent over on her knees, digging through a flower bed. His heart fluttered at the sight, as he recalled fond memories of his wife before her rebirth. He simply stood there for the next couple of minutes, watching her do that which she had always done. The familiarity was comforting, and it was showing itself at a most opportune time.

Since the infobombing—even before that, now that he thought about it—Mason had gradually been losing faith that the reborn Dominique could ever take the place of the original. Though he knew the rebirth wasn't always going to come along smoothly, he had expected that Dominique's innate characteristics would eventually begin to emerge and manifest themselves. However, as hard as it was for him to admit, the painful truth was that she was clearly turning out *not* to be the same person as before. I might as well be married to a complete stranger, he had caught himself thinking yesterday. But now, seeing this integral part of Dominique's personality appear, he was suddenly filled with a newfound hope; invigorated once again with the refreshing belief that, yes, things *could* be as they once were before. The joyful past could once again become the present. With a merry gait, he walked over to his wife and announced, "Good afternoon, dear." He bent down beside her, and affectionately placed his hand on her back. "Enjoying yourself?"

She let out a frustrated sigh, stuck her spade into the dirt, and released her grip on it.

"Dear?" he asked.

Dominique turned around, a defeated smile upon her face, and said, "I hate this."

"What...what do you mean?" he asked as he stood back up.

Dominique held up her soiled hands. "*This*," she answered. "I'm all dirty, I feel sweaty..." She wiped her forehead with her forearm. "And there's all these bugs that keep getting on me. I don't think I like gardening. Not at all."

FREQUENCIES

Mason said, "But gardening is something you love, Dominique. You always said that it helped you to relax and clear your mind."

"That's what Sophia said, also." She sat down on her rear and said, "So I decided I'd come out here and try it. I thought it might help me be who I'm supposed to be." Dominique shook her head, and scattered some dirt with the back of her hand. "But it's not working. I just don't like it, no matter how hard I try."

Mason's heart sank within his chest. All the newly-hatched hope that had been steadily growing and developing inside him, had rudely and abruptly been squashed back down, and now its crushed and mangled remains were writhing inside of him, metamorphosizing into an entirely different emotive creation—one born of anger and rage, of bitterness and resentment. The right-side of his nose began to twitch, he felt his blood-pressure rise, and his entire body began to violently shake. Mason breathed out heavily through his nostrils, and clenched both of his fists. He looked down at the pathetic, little creature seated before him at his feet, and it was all he could do not to strike his hand across that sickening, ungrateful face of hers. "You make me *sick*." he said disgustedly, spittle forcefully escaping from his mouth through the front of his teeth.

Her countenance immediately went from frustration to despondency, and she said, "Please don't say that, Mason. I'm trying to be who you want me to be." A whimper sounded from somewhere deep in her throat. "Really, I am. I'm trying."

Mason stared at her with wrathful eyes, and stated, "Then try *harder*." He turned away from her, and stormed off to the house. Upon entering into the personal dining room, he stopped, his mind awash in confusion, and tried to figure out what to do next. He was too angry to conduct any type of productive business affairs—and besides, he'd already delegated the day's duties in order that he could spend time with Dominique. But now the last thing he wanted to do was be around *that* pitiful creature. He needed to get away from here...from her...from it all. He needed to escape.

Mason reached down to his waist, unclipped his beeper, and brought it up in front of his face. Clicking a button on its side, he said, "Connect me to Burke."

A few seconds passed, then the tiny screen lit up with the image of his chauffeur. He was presently not in uniform, since Mason had told him earlier that he could take the day off. "Yes, sir?" he asked.

"Meet me at the front of the main house. Now."

FREQUENCIES

"I'll be right there, sir. Just give me a moment to get dressed."
Burke grabbed his coat and began to put it on. "Change of plans?"

"Yes," Mason said. "It appears that I *will* be needing to leave
Xanadeux today, after all."

"To Redmond?"

"No," he replied. "The Invisible Hand."

As Burke landed the limousine onto the roof of the monolithic
Seafirst® Columbia Tower, Mason tranquilly opened his eyes, and
slowly brought his head forward from the seat. The Diazecalm™
had now completely worked its way into his system, and he was
finding the drug's effects not at all unpleasant. The anger had been
quelled, and the desire to lash out quenched. He was once again able
to see things clearly and rationally, now that the previous, illogical
emotions had been chemically banished from his being. He still was
not satisfied with his wife, but he was no longer furious with her.
Blind fury would solve nothing. There were ways–orderly ways–to
remedy the situation. And after today, he vowed to explore
those possibilities.

"Open door," Mason announced. The limo immediately
responded. He stepped out of the Rolls®, into The Invisible Hand's
crowded parking lot, and walked up to the driver's window. As Burke
rolled down the tinted glass, Mason said to him, "I'll be in contact via
my beeper. You needn't wait for me up here, but make sure that you're
available to leave on my word."

"Will do, sir," Burke responded.

As the limo ascended into the air, Mason began to walk
through the rows of expensive vehicles, towards The Invisible
Hand's entrance located directly in the center of the roof. When he
had reached the gigantic, clear, plexiglass pyramid which served as
the exclusive establishment's entry point, he was greeted by two,
armed guards, both of whom he recognized.

"Good afternoon, Mr. Huxton," announced the human member
of the pair.

"Good day, Lex," Mason replied, reaching into his pocket
and pulling out the transparent ID card which only members of The
Invisible Hand Society™ were issued. "And a good day to you
too, Smith."

"Thank you, sir," replied the extremely human-like android,
as he held up his right hand with his palm facing out towards

148

Mason. "I'm pleased you could join us today." In the center of his palm, tattoodecalled onto his genetically-engineered skin, was the image of a pyramid with thirteen tiers. Levitating at the top of this pyramid, was a glowing, illuminated eye, framed in a triangular shape. Curving in a semi-circle around the lower part of the pyramid, was a rippled banner which contained the words: "Novus Ordo Seclorum." Smith said, "It'll be just a moment while I verify your card."

The ID was then magnetically sucked from Mason's hand, and it quickly flew over to Smith and affixed itself onto his tattoodecal. Both the android's hand and the transparent card's physical structure began to undulate upon contact. Their visibility became unsteady in synchronization with the wavelike motions, and then they completely faded from sight, and turned invisible. A holographic replica of the tattoodecal then shimmered into being, directly in between Mason and Smith. Simultaneously, a small bulge appeared underneath the android's skin, exactly in the center of his forehead, and began to grow larger. The skin on his forehead grew tauter and tighter until it finally split open–cleanly and with no blood–revealing the bulge underneath to be an oversized, human eyeball whose iris had an azure pigmentation. A bluish, white light emerged forth from the third eye's pupil, entered into the eye of the pyramid, and dispersed itself into a spectra of primary colors which bathed themselves over Mason's body.

A few seconds passed, the eyeball blinked (with the help of the forehead's seperated skin), the white light ceased emitting, and Smith said, "All finished now, Mr. Huxton." The skin grew itself back together over the eyeball, the bulge receded, the hologram disappeared, and the ID rematerialized. "Thanks for your patience."

"Of course, Smith," Mason replied, as the android handed him the see-through card. "I would expect nothing less. Security is of the utmost importance in a proper and civilized environment."

"Well put, sir," Smith said, as the triangular, double doors of the Plexiglas® pyramid swiveled opened behind him. "Please enjoy your visit."

"Thank you, my friend. I will." Mason entered through the opening and proceeded directly to the center of the impressive edifice, where a circular, glass elevator was located. He stepped into the elevator, and on to a GS platform which was very similar to the one at his Redmond office, only much larger in diameter. He looked up, through the clear roof of the elevator, through the transparent tip of the pyramid above it, and gazing at the now-blue sky overhead, he announced, "Down."

As the platform started its descent, his eyes remained fixed on the refracted heavens above, and he continued to watch until the overhead opening had fully closed itself. With the natural lighting now gone, the elevator's LEDs turned on, and the entire tube began to glow with a soft, blue hue. After passing through the stratum of shock-absorbent, reinforced concrete that served as a buffer zone between the roof and the establishment, the LEDs started to emit a reddish hue, and mere seconds later, he was inside The Invisible Hand.

The transparent elevator tube was centered directly in the middle of the enormous, circular area, so that one could take in a full, 360-degree view of the Hand's many levels as they descended into it. There were a total of thirteen levels, each one with a different theme, and all but one of them visible to the elevator's occupants. Barring the ground floor, the levels could not be reached by the entrance elevator, and each was located exactly thirty three and one-third feet away from the tube. This panoptic design ensured that one would not feel as if they were being watched as they entered into the Hand, but rather, allowed *them* to feel like the watcher.

Dropping down past the Las Vegas-like eleventh floor, Mason looked out at the members who had decided to spend their afternoon gambling, and considered that as one of the activities that he might like to engage in while he was there today. Past the ninth floor, which was almost completely comprised of private rooms, he could see numerous, alluring women and men walking along the outer hallway. Down further, he passed the seventh floor, and viewed members who were hooked up to various types of computer hardware and software, then the sixth floor, which was completely surrounded by a black wall, since every member had agreed that the fetish floor should be the one level that remained *completely* private from the elevator's view. After passing the second level, which served as the Hand's cigar bar and smoking area, and was enclosed by a clear, impenetrable plastic, the platform reached the bottom floor.

The elevator's doors opened quietly, and Mason stepped out into the noisy, bustling area which acted as The Invisible Hand's lobby, bar, and main social area. Fellow members of his social class, both male and female, mingled with each other at the numerous tables and counters which were spread about the capacious space. There were several bars to choose from, each one with its own particular theme and specialties. Mason had his own particular favorite, the one which specialized in vintage wines and ports, and he immediately made his way over to it. Sitting down on one of the plush, velvety, antique chairs that surrounded the bar, he was quickly attended to by an attractive waitress dressed in attire resembling that of a flapper from the 1920's.

"Hey, Mr. Huxton, how are ya?" she cheerfully asked in her high-pitched voice.

"Very well, Holly, thank you." And though he didn't really care, he asked, "And how are you today?"

Her face brightened up even more. "Better now–thanks for askin'! You're the first person who's asked me that all day." As Mason's eyes and mind wandered about the room, she said, "Sometimes it can feel like people don't even care about'cha at all. They treat ya like you were just an object–like you were workin' on the sixth floor, or somethin'!"

Trying to keep himself occupied while she delivered her terribly uninteresting soliloquy, he moved his eyes up to her breasts, and was able to mildly excite himself by focusing on her hardened nipples, which were barely showing their shape through the fabric of her top.

"It's so nice to see you're not like that, Mr. Huxton," she said.

He smiled, and dryly said, "Yes," though he was thinking, "Could you possibly be anymore uninteresting, you silly, little twit?"

"What can I getcha today?"

"Your finest tawny port, please," Mason responded, the Diazecalm™ greatly helping him to maintain his civility.

"Right away," Holly said, then mercifully took her annoyingly-happy presence away from him.

Mason looked around the vicinity of the bar briefly, then turned his gaze upwards. It was an impressive view, being able to look up thirteen stories above at the various levels of the Hand, and he often found himself taking it in while he was there. As he was staring up at someone leaning on the railing of the ninth level, he heard his name being called.

"Mason!" came the voice of Thomas Locke from behind him.

"Hello, Thomas," Mason replied, turning his head to face the large, corpulent man. "How are you today?"

"Quite well, thank you," Thomas said, as he pulled up a chair next to Mason. Barely managing to squeeze his obese rear-end into the chair, he asked, "And yourself?"

FREQUENCIES

"Well, also," Mason said. "Are you just getting here?"

"Yes, I arrived a few minutes before you did. Helped myself to a glass of Dom Perignon®," Thomas said, raising his champagne glass up as if he were giving a toast, "saw you over here, and decided to come and chat before I indulged myself into the Hand's *other* pleasures." He laughed, causing his double-chin to quiver in an odd sort of way, and took a hefty sip of the alcohol. "Aaaah, that hits the spot nicely."

Holly walked up to Mason, and handed him a full glass of port. "There ya are, Mr. Huxton."

"Thank you." Mason cupped his hand around the bottom of the port glass, its stem between his middle and fourth fingers, swirled it slightly, and brought it up to his nose for a careful sniff. Smiling, he said, "Put the charge on my account, please." He took a small sip, judged its flavor, then swallowed. "And give yourself a generous tip, my dear."

"Thanks, Mr. Huxton!" Holly said. "Let me know if ya need anything else!" She then turned, and walked back to the bar.

With hungry, predatory eyes, Thomas said, "Peppy little thing, isn't she?"

Mason nodded. "Quite."

"And she seems so innocent..." Thomas smiled diabolically. "So ready to be defiled." He licked his lips, then finished off his champagne with another large gulp. "What ungodly acts I could show her, Mason."

"I'm sure," Mason said with a smirk, knowing how much his contemporary enjoyed engaging in the iniquitous. After all, as president and CEO of Cytherea™, an extremely lucrative enterprise which specialized in pornographic products, it was Thomas' *job* to immerse himself into the world of sin. But for Thomas, it was much, *much* more than an occupation. From allowing himself to become grossly overweight (he believed it was a show of respect to some god of gluttony which he worshipped), to partaking in the most lewdest activities available at the Hand, it could veritably be said that it was a lifestyle.

Thomas laughed heartily at Mason's response, and asked, "Speaking of ungodly acts, which one brings you here today?"

"A rather tame and uninteresting one, I'm afraid." Mason took another small sip of the port. "Level seven."

"Ever the man of technology, eh, Mason?"

"Indeed."

FREQUENCIES

"Well, even on level seven, there's plenty of naughty things for you to do. In fact, we just supplied that level with a couple of new, *ultra*-intense sex sims about a week ago. One of them," Thomas said, excitedly leaning forward and lowering his voice, "can even make you have *multiple* orgasms."

Unimpressed, Mason said, "That's nothing new, Thomas. There's already ones up there that can do that."

"Yes, but how many of them can guarantee to make you orgasm at least *thirty* times per session, hmm?" Thomas leaned back with a smug look on his face.

Mason nodded, his eyebrows raised. "Yes, that certainly *is* something new, isn't it?" He let out a small laugh. "But, no offense to your impressive new device, I will be engaging in activites of a less...shall we say...arousing nature."

"To each their own, my friend. As for myself..." Thomas said, carefully squeezing himself out of the chair and standing up, "...temptation calls. Are you going up yet?"

"Yes, as a matter of fact." Mason stood from his seat, and sipped his port. "I'll join you on the elevator."

"Excellent," Thomas said.

As they walked through the crowd, over to the one of the elevators which granted access to the upper floors, Mason asked, though he already knew the answer, "Which level will you be going to today, Thomas?"

They stepped into the elevator, which no one but them currently occupied. He replied, "The sixth." Another diabolical smile as the doors shut behind them. "Of course."

"Of course," Mason repeated. He then announced, "Sixth and seventh levels, please," and the elevator began its ascent.

Thomas said, "Now, if memory serves, you've never been up to the sixth level, have you?"

"No, I haven't."

"Oh, you really should take advantage of this level some time, Mason." He rubbed his thin, trimmed mustache. "I guarantee that once you've tasted its impure nectar, you'll always come back for more." He smiled. "Your world will never be the same."

That's what I'm afraid of, Mason thought. "I'll consider it, Thomas," he lied.

The elevator came to a stop, and the doors parted open, revealing an extremely short hallway with a large, black door at its end. Thomas stepped out of the elevator, walked up to the door, and announced, "Open."

The black door raised up into the ceiling above it, and Mason caught a fleeting glimpse of a horrid, gengineered creation, the likes of which he had never seen before. It was essentially two men, grown together like Siamese-twins, dressed only in tight, black, metal-studded leather. One person stood upright, while the other was connected such that their shoulders were the other person's pelvis, and their body extended perpindicularly backwards, in a manner resembling a centaur. The lower person had no arms, and his head protruded out just above the other's privates. The upright one, who was wearing a studded, leather mask, was holding a whip in one hand, and with the other, was grasping the lower person by his hair, and forcing him to give themselves fellatio.

Thomas looked back at Mason, and asked, "Sure you don't want to join me, old boy?"

"Quite," Mason said.

The doors closed, and the elevator ascended to the next floor above. Reaching the seventh level, Mason left the elevator, and headed directly towards the area where the MUDs could be accessed. Walking past other members who were already hooked up to a sattelink, he looked for an empty booth, then entered into one when he had found it. He closed the soundproof door behind him, seated himself on one of the soft, comfortable couches, and set his drink down onto the small coffee table next to the couch. As he slipped out of his shoes, he picked up the headset which was resting on the table, and placed the lightweight, uncumbersome device atop his head.

His eyes were now covered by thin, wraparound gogs, his ears enclosed by surround speakers, and a small, miniature microphone wrapped itself from the left speaker around to the space just in front of his lips. He took a final sip of the port, then picked up the tipsets resting atop the coffee table. After placing each of the ten, thimble-like devices onto his fingertips, he laid back onto the couch, made himself comfortable, and said, "Voice-rec on."

The previously-transparent gog lenses filled themselves with light, and all he could now see before him were the images transmitted by the sattelink. At first, nothing but a blue void, giving him the sensation that he was floating around in a sea of nothingness. A combination ocean/static sound played through the speakers, adding to the vacuous effect. The Ordosoft™ logo then appeared from a vanishing point far in the distance, quickly shot forward, and began to head directly towards him. Just as it looked like the logo was going

154

to hit into him, it swiftly veered to the right, and zoomed past him with a whooshing sound. Behind him, he could hear it moving over to the left, and then it shot around past his ahead again, stopped a few feet in front of him, and morphed itself into The Invisible Hand's logo—a black outline of a hand facing towards the viewer, with the triangular, illuminated eye design set into the center of its transparent, invisible interior.

"Welcome to The Invisible Hand," announced a pleasant female voice (tinged with a slight British accent) which seemed to be emanating from everywhere around him. "Please select your destination." Various shapes, designs, and iconic graphics suddenly appeared—some slowly materializing into view, others popping up out of the void's thin air, a few growing larger from a small speck—then hovered there before him in the bluish vacuity.

Now that the Hand's computer had accessed his identity via the tipset's biochip reader, he was able to look down and see his arms, body, and legs, all virtually rendered to perfection. He closed his left hand into a fist, thumb resting on top of the index finger and pointing forward, and he began to move straight ahead through the void. The particular MUD icon that he wanted to reach was a bit to his right, so he rolled his wrist and thumb slightly in that direction, and his virtual body followed suit. Reaching the MUD icon—which depicted four circles in a square-like shape, each one linked to the other via six, solid, black lines—Mason released his fist, and his motion immediately stopped. He raised his right hand before the icon, pointed his index finger at it, and quickly tapped his digit forward two times.

"Thank you, Mr. Huxton," announced the omnipresent female voice. "Now accessing multi-user domain." The icon transformed into a black hole, which grew increasingly larger in size until it completely enveloped him. Mason found himself within a space-like dimension, filled with various types of stars, planets, and other celestial bodies. Floating directly in front him, were the six avatars which he most frequently used in this domain. "Please select an avatar for this session," the voice said.

Mason moved his index finger along the row of iconic identities, past the one that looked like himself, past one that resembled a figure from a Duchamp painting, past another which resembled King Arthur, then stopped when it was pointing at the one depicting a simply dressed, very ordinary, thirteen-year old boy. He double-tapped the icon, it rotated in place for a moment, and then it moved forward, morphed itself around him, and he became it.

"Where would you like to go today?" the voice asked, as different windows opened themselves up in the space surrounding him, each one a gateway to the virtual domain visualized within.

Mason moved his finger over the window showing a beautiful, ocean beach, and double-tapped. The next instant, the window increased in size, zoomed towards him, and he was immediately transported into the picturesque scene.

As he gently floated down from the overcast sky, he looked down at the peaceful domain below. On his right, a grayish-blue ocean, currently calm with waves no more than a couple feet high. A few sea stacks, ranging in height from approximately ten to thirty feet, jutted up through the water, their flora-covered tops providing a welcome refuge for the environment's avian occupants. To his left, was a large, ancient, evergreen forest, which grew all the way up to the fringes of the brown-sand beach. At some places, the change from forest to beach was gradual and level, while at others, it was quite abrubt and shear, with the trees and plants falling off into the ocean and creating sizable cliffs of soft earth. On the beach, which was directly underneath him, driftlogs and seaweed were randomly scattered about, as were the assorted tidepools which were just now beginning to reveal themselves. A menagerie of avatars currently occupied the ocean's sandy shores, some playing or talking together, others simply sitting alone and enjoying the view.

Once his virtual body had touched down onto the beach, Mason began to roam around the coast in search of familiar faces. Being that he was such a frequent visitor to this domain, it didn't take long for him to find some.

"Jeremiah!" shouted Anna, who was currently presenting as a scanned image of herself, dressed in worn, summer clothing. She smiled and gave him a friendly wave. "You made it!"

"Anna!" Mason said excitedly (his avatar voice sounding altogether different from his real one) as he waved back. He briskly made his way over to her and Demetrius.

"We didn't think you were going to make it today," she said.

"Neither did I," Mason said as he reached them. "I managed to get more work done today then I expected." He seated himself next to the two them. "And my supervisor is quite...chill about being telepresent. She doesn't care about set hours, provided that I get all of my work done."

"You're lucky, Jeremiah," said Demetrius, who was

presenting as his usual avatar–a large, bronze mask which was a caricature of the sun, set atop the scanned image of a statuesque body. "My bosses are *so* anal about set hours. We have to be telepresent even if we don't have anything to do. It's stupid." He shook his head, the dull sunlight glinting off his shiny, metal head. "It doesn't make any sense."

"That's because it's a *job*, Dee," Anna said with a laugh. "They're not supposed to make sense."

Demetrius laughed, his wavy, sunray designs around his head moving in unison with his voice.

Mason laughed also, though he didn't really agree with her statement. He could think of *plenty* of reasons why jobs made sense–but that was Mason, not Jeremiah. Jeremiah *would* understand what she was saying, because he was one of their kind, and he knew what they went through. So he continued to laugh, and as he did, he began to understand and agree with what she said. He became one of them.

He became Jeremiah.

And that was what he enjoyed about this place so much–he could *be* someone else, and escape from the stressful corporate life which he lived. Here, there were no business meetings, no agendas, no deals to be made, no ulterior motive behind every word spoken–here it was simple. Simple people discussing simple things in simple terms. Jeremiah loved it here. It was the world to him, literally all he lived for.

"It would be nice if they did, though," Demetrius added as he finished his laugh.

"It would be even nicer if there *were* no jobs," Jeremiah said with a smile.

Anna laughed. "You can say that again."

Jeremiah watched a wave crest...and crash down with a lovely splash. He said, "Then we could sit around and talk like this all the time." A seagull flew across the horizon, circled around one of the tall seastacks, and landed on top of it. "Without worrying about having to go back."

"Maybe it'll happen someday, Jeremiah," said Demetrius, as he drew some designs into the sand with a stick. "You never know."

For a few moments, nothing but the sound of the ocean, the birds, and distant voices of the other avatars visiting this realm. Then Jeremiah said, "I just realized...where's Noelani?"

"She should be back any time now," Demetrius replied. "I

IM'd her when you got here, and she said she'd be coming right up."

"But you know 'Lani," Anna said. "'Right up' could be a while."

"Oh," said Jeremiah, "she's in the ocean, is she?"

"You got it," Anna replied.

"And presenting as a mermaid?" Jeremiah asked.

Anna nodded.

Jeremiah smiled. "Then it certainly will be a while before she comes up." He ran his fingers through the sand, then said, "Maybe we should all join her. It certainly *is* beautiful down there. The reefs, the fish, the seals..."

"Sounds like fun," Anna agreed. "What do you think, Dee?"

"I'm game. That way, we-" Demetrius suddenly stopped mid-sentence, his sunny face showing a look of concern.

"What is it?" asked Jeremiah.

"Behind you," Demetrius said. "Look, Anna, that weird thing's back again."

Jeremiah looked back, and saw a thin, shadowy, human-like figure which was approaching them. It's entire structure was shaking and vibrating at an incredibly fast rate, as if a filmmaker was shooting a scene of someone having an intense epileptic seizure, but was making constant, jerky motions with the camera themselves. "That certainly is odd looking," he commented.

"And it's not just the way it looks," Anna said. "That thing gives off some really weird frees. It'll stare at you with these really disturbing faces..." she said as she watched it approach closer. "It should go to a different domain."

"Like one of the goth realms," Demetrius said.

"The goths aren't *that* scary," said Anna with a nervous laugh. "It would creep them out too. That thing belongs in a Lynchian domain."

"I guess we'll find out what it wants," Jeremiah said, "because it's most certainly coming our way." A few seconds later, the creature had reached them. Though it was still vibrating quickly, its proximity allowed him to see a better detail of its features.

An extremely-thin and elongated physique, with long fingers that ended in sharp points. Its entire body made purely of shadow, with no marks, designs, or clothing upon it. And then there was the head... A shadowy, featureless shape like its body (somehow managing to vibrate at an even faster rate), it would periodically flash with a disturbing image, but then the image would fade before the mind had a chance to completely understand what it was that it just saw.

The shadow creature stood there, looked over them, and didn't say a word. The silent image of a blood-spattered woman screaming in terror flashed across its face. The only sound emanating from it was the strange buzzing that accompanied its vibratory motions.

The three of them sat there, uncomfortable, unsure of what to do. Then Anna said to it, "Why don't you just go away? What do you want?"

The creature's head tilted slightly to one side at the question. A flash of a hanged-man's upper-body, his neck grotesquely twisted with his tougue sticking out. Its head then returned upright, and it began to slowly raise its hand forward. Its long, pointy index finger then uncurled itself towards Jeremiah. "Him," it said, in a barely comprehendible voice which was composed of the same vibratory sounds of his motion.

Shocked, Jeremiah asked, "Me?"

"Jeremiah?" asked Anna.

Buzzing laughter. "There is no such person here," it said. Mason's face flashed across the creature's head. "Jeremiah is the figment of an unhappy rich man's imagination."

Demetrius looked at Jeremiah with a confused look. "What's he talking about? Do you know him?"

"I've never met him before in my life," answered Jeremiah.

A flash of the Ordosoft™ logo, engulfed in flames, and the creature asked, "But you know what I'm talking about, don't you, Mason?"

Jeremiah/Mason wasn't sure how to respond. His world of escape was beginning to break apart and crumble, and he was afraid. He didn't want to lose it or his friends. Panicked, torn between two identites, he could only think to ask, "What is it that you want from me?"

Flash: a human skull, imploding. "Many things," it replied. "I want your friends to know the truth about you. About how you've lied to them all this time, and pretended to be someone else." Flash: Jesus on the cross, punctured and bloodied. "I want your inane fantasy to come to an end."

"Mason...?" Demetrius said in a perplexed tone, as he looked at Jeremiah. "Mason Huxton?"

With sadness and confusion in his eyes, Mason/Jeremiah

looked back at Demetrius, but said nothing.

"Yes," the creature said, "Mason Huxton." Flash: Mason's face again, with a crown of thorns atop his head. "One of the kings of the world, virtually slumming it with the commoners." It buzzingly laughed, feeling to Mason like a bumblebee forcefully entering into his ear canal. "Melodrama at its best."

"So what if he *is* Mason Huxton?" Anna asked with disgust. "Guess what, weirdo? I don't care! I'll accept him for who he is *here*, no matter *what* he is out there!" She picked up some sand, and threw it at the creature.

The sand harmlessly passed through its shadow-body. Across its face, a flash of a woman digging her eyes out with her fingernails.

Anna stood up angrily. "Go away! Nobody wants you here! Don't you understand?! You failed! You didn't accomplish anything!"

"Ah, but I did," it responded, with an image-flash of flesh being violently ripped from someone's face. "Whether or not you accept him is irrelevant. What matters is that he can never face *you* again." His head turned towards Mason, with a flash of the same face, flesh completely gone, muscualture now being torn apart. "The illusion is gone–it can never be the same for him." Flash: The final muscle torn, now just a skull. "Can it, Mason?" Flash: The skull, imploding.

Mason stood up, calmly dusted himself off, and stared at the creature fixedly. "I can assure *you* that it will never be the same." Outside of the beach-world, Mason said, "Command: Alert security to current domain."

Flash: Nazi stormtroopers, marching in perfect unison. "Trying to alert security?" the creature asked. "It's going to take them a while to get through my walls of fire and ice." A flash of a little girl burned with napalm, running from a village with tears in her eyes. He turned towards Demetrius and Anna. "Leave now, or I'll infect your brains with informational pus."

Anna and Demetrius looked at Mason, unsure of what to do.

"Do as he says," Mason told them. "I'll be fine."

Anna hesitated, but Demetrius grabbed her and said, "Let's go, Anna!" She looked at Mason's Jeremiah avatar for a long second, and then they both faded away.

The next instant, water from the ocean levitated over Mason and the creature, formed a dome, then solidified into ice. The inside layer of the dome then lit up with a fire that didn't melt the frozen saltwater. It was an impressive icewall/firewall combination, different than any Mason had seen before. Ouside of the domain, he said, "Command: Assume Arthur avatar," and inside the domain, he transformed into a likeness of King Arthur, complete with crown, armor, and sword.

"An old-fashioned duel," the creature said. A flash of two knights jousting, then one of them being impaled in the sternum by the other's lance. "Goody."

Mason raised Excalibur into the air, grasped its hilt with both hands, and stated, "Let's have at it then, creature." He swung the enchanted blade at the shadow, but its body unformed itself in the exact place that the sword was going to connect, then reformed the moment the weapon passed through the open space.

Flash: A surgeon's scalpel, opening up a pale, white man's chest. The creature lunged forward with its sharp fingers, and slashed Mason's chest, causing bright, blue sparks to fly off his armor.

Unphased by the attack, Mason swung his sword again, but the creature simply unformed and formed itself again.

They circled each other cautiously, both combatants trying to predict the best moment to strike. The creature acted first.

Another lunge, this time at Mason's face. A flash of the back of JFK's head being shot out. The claws hit an invisible barrier before they could touch him, and the creature immediately retracted its wounded hand.

Mason swung for its head, but the creature quickly ducked.

Still crouched down, it crawled back a few steps, and said, "Die." Its face flashed the bomb at Hiroshima, and a mushroom cloud exploded around Mason.

The cloud lifted, and Mason stood there, unscathed. "You forget I know Merlin," he said, then pointed the tip of his sword at the creature, and expelled out a shotgun-like spray of blue, photonic particles.

The shadow immediately fell down from the blast, its body becoming corrupted with the blue, Excalibur virus. Its vibration began to slow down and shift into focus. Its head however, remained the same. Flashing the image of American troops pulling out of Vietnam, it asked, "You think you've won, don't you?"

"Considering that you're lying there on the floor, incapacitated..." Mason stared at him coldly. "I'd say 'yes.'" He looked up above, at the barrier which was slowly dissipating. "And if I was considering the fact that security is already working its way through your walls, I'd respond with an *emphatic* 'yes.'"

FREQUENCIES

Flash: A whipped and bloodied slave, breaking his chains and escaping. "I'll already be gone by the time they get here."

"You think, do you?"

"I *know*." Across its face appeared images of the bombing at Pearl Harbor, then its head levitated from its corrupted body, and hovered there in the air. "You've heard the saying, 'lost the battle, but won the war?'" it asked. A flash of Adam's face.

Mason's expression grew dead serious, and butterflies of dread began to flutter within his stomach.

Flash: Adam's face, colored purplish-black, fat and bloated from the effects of decomposition. The beheaded creature said, in that horrible, buzzing voice, "You no longer have a son."

Then it vibrated even faster, dispersed itself into tiny fragments, and disappeared altogether.

$$\alpha$$

Ω

Chapter 9:
<u>Vicissitudes</u>

"To simply live one's life was an impossibility.
Life was not a simple thing.
Complex and convoluted, it was the universe in microcosm, rife with
infinite turns and twists, some expected, others not.

Twilight in the Emerald City.

    Across a sky stained with violent reds and redolent violets, the Polaris™ flew on automatic, due east to Issaquah. Its windows rolled down, A Tribe Called Quest's "Can I Kick It?" playing loudly on its stereo, it weaved its way around, over, and through the numerous holographic billboards which covered the city's skyscape, as the adsats overhead began to brightly display their graphics and slogans.

    McCready gazed up through the Chevy's® roof at the commercial constellations above, and asked, "N.J., am I still on hold, or did we get disconnected?"

    "You're still on hold, Marc," replied the cartoon Marilyn, currently attired in a black, see-through dress from *Some Like It Hot,* "though you have been waiting an unusually long amount of time. Would you like me to disconnect and call him back?"

    "Nah, doll, that's alright," he said, still staring up into space. "With the kind of day he's had, I'm sure that'd only piss him off more. I was just curious. Continue holding."

Twenty seconds passed, the volume of the song lowered, and he heard the voice of Mason Huxton ask, "Agent McCready?"

FREQUENCIES

Averting his eyes from a chip-shaped Doritos® adsat, McCready looked down at the console uniview, raised his seat forward from its reclined position, and responded, "Yeah, I'm still here. What's up? How is he?"

"Thankfully," Huxton said with a sigh, his voice showing signs of both weariness and relief, "much better than before. He's still groggy from the concussion and the pain relievers, but his memory appears to have fully returned."

"No permanent damage?"

"The doctors don't think so, no. The MRI's showed no bruising or tearing of the brain, and the other diagnostics yielded positive results as well. He'll be bedridden for a while, but they're expecting a full and complete recovery."

"That's good to hear. 'Cause I gotta admit, after I saw the video..." McCready's voice tailed off, as he recalled the streetcam images of the incident: Adam Huxton emerging from a limo, surrounded by two Ordocops™ and two Xandys. Taking a few steps from the car, he's suddenly grabbed and shielded by one of the Xandys, then pushed by the other, just as a full-size truck comes barreling into the entire entourage. Two Ordocops™ and one Xandy are brutally crushed underneath the speeding vehicle, as the android-shielded Adam goes flying up and over the grill, smashes into the windshield, and falls unconscious to the hard concrete. "...I was expecting worse news."

"Yes," Huxton said grimly, nodding his head in agreement, "so was I." He paused momentarily. "It's frightening to think what would have happened had Xanadeux not been there to take the brunt of the blow."

Your son would be roadkill right now, McCready thought to himself, feeling no fright whatsoever at the notion. "Well, at least it *was* there, so you won't even have to consider the alternative."

"True enough, Agent McCready." Huxton briefly looked back over his shoulder, and as he did, McCready was able to catch a glimpse of Adam lying in a hospital bed, his face badly bruised, his entire right arm housed within an exoskeleton. Looking back at the uniview, Huxton added, "Yet when one's child is involved, one can't help *but* think of the alternative."

"I guess I wouldn't know," McCready said, watching an ambulance fly quickly by, its annoyingly-loud sirens temporarily muting out all other ambient sounds. As the vehicular wailing faded away into the distance, he asked, "So did the OFT's end up matching with the biochip data?"

He nodded. "Only the owner had been in the truck recently."

McCready asked, "And you've already detained and questioned him?"

"Yes, but it was quickly apparent that he knew nothing about what had happened," Huxton said. "Moreover, his biochip showed that he was clear across town at the time of the attack, and there are numerous witnesses to corroborate the data."

"Hmm," McCready said, rubbing his thumb against the grain of his stubbly chin. "Definitely a remote-attack then. They must've jacked the truck's CPU and homed it in on Adam's biochip." He popped a few of his knuckles. "Which means there should still be some type of cyber-trail from the truck back to the location where the attack was programmed."

"There *should* be, yes," Huxton agreed. "But the unfortunate truth, Agent McCready, is that these terrorists appear quite adept at covering their tracks. So much so, that not even Xanadeux has been able to follow their trail."

Not even Xanadeux, McCready mockingly thought to himself. Huxton spoke about the androidal creation like it was a fucking god or something–like the AI was perfect, without any limitations or faults. But McCready had learned long ago that nothing was perfect. Not people, not places, not things. Not even God. He asked, "How long has he–or it–been looking into the case?"

"Ever since the attack occurred," Huxton said.

That would be about five hours now, McCready thought. Plenty of time for a good cracker to break some of the codes the terrorists were hiding behind. "And Xanadeux hasn't found out anything on *your* attack either?" he asked.

Huxton shook his head as he slowly blinked his eyes. "No."

"Have you considered the possibility that Xanadeux might be involved in the attacks?"

Mason scowled, and said, "I don't *consider* the impossible, Agent McCready. Xanadeux would never bring harm to myself or my family."

McCready couldn't help but let out a small laugh at Huxton's close-mindedness. Discussing Xanadeux with him was like trying to discuss the Bible with a Jesus freak–no matter what you said to them, no matter how logical, they'd always retreat back to some bullshit argument about how the Book is always right. Fuck the facts. "It's not impossible, Huxton," McCready said. "It's been known to happen in andys who've been programmed with emotions. They get jealous, angry, sad, depressed, etcetera. Just like anyone else."

"*Not* Xanadeux," Huxton said. "My father created it to be perfectly loyal." He solemnly looked at McCready. "And it is."

"Alright, if you say so," McCready conceded, not interested in wasting any more breath on Huxton's faith-clogged ears. "But let me make one suggestion."

"Certainly. Go ahead."

"Let someone else get a crack at finding their trail," he said. "A human."

"I take it you have someone in mind?"

"Yeah. Takura."

"Your fellow agent?"

"Right."

Huxton placed his finger on his lip, contemplated for a few seconds, then asked, "He's that good?"

Without hesitation, McCready retorted, "Are corporations greedy?"

Nothing but solemnity from Huxton. Then a subtle expression, something faintly resembling a smile, and he said, "I'll contact him immediately."

Now that Huxton, his son, and his wife had all been attacked, McCready knew that the head of Ordosoft™ wasn't going to be taking any chances with his daughter's safety. So when he reached Ashley's estate, and found an assortment of Ordocop™ vehicles and personnel–some ground-based, others airborne–stationed around its perimeter, he wasn't in any way surprised. Impressed maybe, by the sheer number of units armed and equipped to protect one, single woman–but not surprised. This was the daughter of one of the richest men in the world, for Christ's sake. Of course he'd use his corporate army to protect her. Especially, McCready decided, if his daughter happened to be Ashley. Funny thing was though, rather than having their hands full with terrorists, the Ordocops™ were instead having to deal with the flock of news crews that had vulturically descended down upon Ashley's Issaquah residence, eager to snatch up a fresh tidbit of morbid news.

Which didn't surprise him either–the buzz *always* grew quickly when a publicly-accessible streetcam caught something scandalous or disastrous happening to someone famous. By now, the grisly images of Adam's assault had been repeated, replayed, uploaded, downloaded–fuck, McCready thought, probably even masturbated to–thousands of times all over the uninet. And once word had gotten out that the security around Xanadeux and Ashley's had been significantly beefed up, not even Mason's influence could prevent the media from sighting their new target.

The story of the day had been found, and the news scavengers were hungry. There were the skyvans and Zoomcams™ of *Inside Edition, Eye Spye,* and the other tabloids, all carefully circling the area, making sure not to infringe upon the no-fly zone that existed above Ashley's estate. Local reporters, representing every station from KIRO to KOMO, were on the ground, incessantly picking at the Ordocops™ for more juicy information. Even CNN®, CNBC®, and the internationals were there, their sleek, self-contained RCC spheres whizzing to and from different people and spots around the area as needed. All of the commotion and chaos reminded him a little of the riot. Except in this case, people were being kept *out*, rather than *in*. And, McCready thought, when it's all said and done, the reporters get to go *home*.

After receiving clearance from the Ordocops™ to enter the estate, McCready had the Polaris™ do a quick fly-by of the arboreal area, just to make sure that nothing unusual was going on. Not that he could see much from above, since her residence was literally overgrowing with herbage and foliage–to the point that typical aerial reconnaissance was pretty much futile–but he made the token attempt anyways. Not surprisingly, the quickie inspection didn't reveal anything of a sinister or threatening nature. What it *did* reveal, he realized as he passed over her house that was composed entirely of pyramids, cylinders, and spheres, was that eccentricity must be a trait that W.A. Huxton had gengineered into all of his offspring. Either that, McCready laughed to himself, or they were all an example of what happens when you have too much money on your hands. You end up building weird shit like floating castles and homes with fucked-up geometrics.

Passing over the parking area, McCready said, "N.J., connect me with Ashley." He pulled out a Kamel® and placed it between his lips. "And go ahead and park over there by the green Lex."

Seconds passed.

The cartoon Marilyn tapped her fingernails onto an art deco table she was sitting at.

No answer.

FREQUENCIES

As the Polaris™ set itself down behind Ashley's Lexus®, it stated, "There's currently no response, Marc. Would you like to leave a message?"

"Try again," McCready replied, his tongue moving edgily back and forth along the butt of the cigarette. "And make sure she knows it's me."

More seconds passed.

Marilyn took a deep breath, then exhaled impatiently.

Still no answer.

McCready shifted in his seat, and uneasily grumbled, "Aw, fuck." Huxton had just spoken to Ashley about twenty minutes ago. Had she suddenly left? he wondered. Unlikely. She had promised him that she'd wait there until he arrived. Then why wasn't she answering? "N.J.," he asked, "is Ashley even in the house?"

Marilyn pulled a telescope out of thin air, looked through it, and replied, "Her biochip says she is, but she's still not answering."

The cigarette continued to waver between McCready's lips, its motion moving quicker with his thoughts. Had something happened since Huxton spoke with her? Could the terrorists have made their next move? When the next question, "Is she in danger?" passed through his mind, he was out of the car and quickly walking through the overgrown, garden pathway that led to the front of her house. With his palm touching the cold, steel handle of his holstered Colt® Python®, McCready emerged from the tall vegetation and trotted over to the front door. He immediately activated his emvest, causing a momentary ripple in the visual space around his upper body, removed the soggy, half-chewed Kamel® from his mouth, then touched his hand on the callscreen. "Ashley?" he asked, slipping the unlit Kamel® into one of his coat's front pockets. "You there?"

On the callscreen's oval monitor, nothing but an animated spiral, hypnotically swirling round and round to infinity.

Ten more anxious seconds passed.

"Ashley?!" McCready called out, his heartbeat quickening. He touched his wristcom, drew his .357 with his perspiring left hand, and said, "N.J., I need you to scan Ashley's biochip for location and vital signs. Now!" Pounding his fist on the wooden front door, he called out, "Ashley?! Are you in there?!"

"Marc?" queried the cartoon Marilyn.

Snapping a mini plasma torch from off of his belt, turning it on, and aiming it towards the door, he asked, "Yeah? What've you got?"

"Ashley is in the lower portion of the house," N.J. replied, just as McCready was about to press the "fire" button on the torch, "and her vital signs and frees are perfectly normal,"

He clicked the microtorch off. "So she's fine..."

"According to the biochip readings, that's correct."

"Well where the hell is she then?" he blurted out.

"She's currently moving through the house in a southerly direction, towards her callscreen," N.J. said. "In fact, she should be making contact with you right...about...now."

Within the monitor's oval frame, the swirling spiral morphed into a curious and slightly confused Ashley. "What's goin' on?" she asked. "Is everything okay?"

"That depends. Are *you* okay?" McCready asked, the tone of his voice falling somewhere between concern and irritation.

Ashley gave him a funny look. "Uh...yeah."

McCready snapped the microtorch back onto his belt and said, "Then why didn't you answer the UV?"

"I turned it off," she said. "I was meditating."

Meditating, he thought. Of course. With a smirk, McCready said, "I wish you would've told me you'd be doing that. You could've saved me some adrenalin." He replaced the Colt® into his shoulder holster, and adjusted his trenchcoat.

"Sorry about that," she said with a laugh. "I just figured you'd come up to the door without calling first." Reaching her hand towards the side of the callscreen, she said, "I'll be right there."

The screen morphed back into the psychedelic spiral. McCready placed his hands in his pockets, turned away from the door, and looked back at the giant evergreens which filled the southern part of the estate. As his eyes moved from the base of their fat, brown trunks, all the way up to their towering, needled tops, McCready was relieved to see that the compact forest had grown together thick enough so that its canopy almost completely covered the sky above–meaning that his "rescue" probably hadn't been caught on tape by one of the skyvans. That would have been all I needed, he thought. To spend my fifteen minutes of fame being known as the dumb fuck who made the world think another attack had happened. Hearing the turn of the deadbolt and the twist of the doorknob, he slowly turned back around, just as the oval door began to open.

"Hey there, Mr. Action Hero," Ashley said with a teasing smile. "Come on in."

"Action hero," McCready repeated with a droll laugh, as he

stepped through the doorway, and entered into the cylindrical entrance hall. Looking around at the curved, ivy-covered walls and ceiling, which appeared to be composed entirely of an electrochromic, plexiglass-like material, McCready commented, "Interesting place you got here."

"Like it?" she asked.

Be diplomatic, he had to remind himself. But not phony. "It's different," he said.

"Yeah," she agreed, closing the door and locking the deadbolt, "it is. That's what I love about it. Most Western architecture is so harsh and angular..." Drifting over to the wall, she softly ran her hand along its rounded surface. "I wanted something that was gonna be more curvy and smooth." Her fingers caressed the vines of ivy. "Something a little more natural, y'know?"

He acknowledged her statement with a few, small nods, as he continued to scan his eyes over the hall. "Who did the design?"

"My mom and I," she replied, cradling one of the green, spade-shaped leaves in the palm of her hand. She stared at it intently for a moment, her thumb circling gently round its soft edges, then smiled nostalgically. "We did it together."

"You an architect?"

"No, my mom is...was." Ashley laughed uncomfortably and shook her head. "Is." Moving past him, further down the long hallway and towards another oval door, she said, "I did a few rough drawings, told her what I wanted...but she was the one who designed the blueprints." Ashley took in a strong, bittersweet breath, and exhaled. "She was the one who made it real."

Sensing the hurt in her voice, McCready was tempted to say something comforting to her. He knew firsthand what it was like to lose a parent, and remembered how shitty it felt. But he wasn't very good with caring words, and he couldn't really think of the right thing to say. And he didn't want to think about his dad right now anyway–so he opted for small talk. "Must've been a lot of work."

"Yeah, it was," she said as she reached the northern door, this one less of a throwback than the other. "But she did it. She's amazing." Pressing her thumb onto a biochip scanner, she spoke the words, "Forty-two," and the oval door slid open with a hiss. "Oh yeah–there's one rule before you come in," Ashley stated.

Walking towards her, he asked, "What's that?"

Ashley pointed down to her bare feet. "You gotta take your shoes off."

"Nah," he said with disbelief, figuring she was kidding with him. He looked down at his Timberlands®, and saw a few pairs of her shoes lying on the floor. Looking back up at her, McCready asked, "Really?"

She laughed. "Yeah. Really."

"Alright," he said reluctantly, bending down to untie his boots, "just don't blame me if the CDC tries to place your hallway under quarantine."

Ashley rolled her eyes and smiled. "I'm sure your feet don't smell *that* bad, Agent McCready," she said, moving through the oval opening.

Slipping his feet out of his untied tims, McCready followed Ashley through the opened door, into another segment of the house—this one a huge, spherical room filled with more books than he'd ever seen, more plants than he'd ever want, and more art pieces than he could probably ever afford. "So how are you holding up through everything?" he inquired, as the door automatically hissed shut behind him.

"Okay, I guess," she replied, pushing aside a beanbag ottoman with her foot. "I mean, considering that my family's being terrorized and there's a media circus outside my house." She walked over to the east side of the sphere, where a spacious, cove-like kitchen area was located. "Do you want something to drink?"

"You got anything with caffeine?" he asked, examining a tall, spiral staircase which went up and through the domed ceiling, into another room above—more than likely the pyramid, if he was remembering the details of his flyby correctly.

"I'll check." Ashley touched a sensor on her cylindrical refrigerator, turning its opaque surface transparent. Peering into it, she said, "Looks like your only choices are between a green tea brew...and..." She laughed. "A green tea brew. That's it."

McCready moved over to the counter that separated the cove from the rest of the room, and seated himself on one of the cushiony stools connected to it. "If it's got caffeine," he said, as he doffed his Obsidians™ and placed them into his trench's inside pocket, "I'll take it."

Ashley touched another sensor, and the refrigerator doors slid open. She reached in, grabbed the brew, and set it down on the countertop in front of him. "There ya go. Caffeine."

"Thanks," McCready said, twisting the top off the bottle and taking a sip.

"You're welcome." Ashley closed the fridge, turned it back to its previous opaqueness, and served herself some water from the spigot of a green, ceramic cooler. "Y'know, Agent McCready,"she said, her face growing contemplative as she leaned against the counter next to the fridge, "right now...I think the reason I'm doing okay through all this...is because it kinda feels like I'm living in a dream. Or dreaming while awake...something of that nature." She sipped the water. "It's kinda like everything's real but at the same time it's unreal, y'know?"

McCready nodded, rubbing the bottle cap between his fingers. "I know the feeling. Like you're watching this incredibly fuckin' intense movie..." He raised the bottle to his lips. "Called your life." And took a swig.

Ashley smiled. "Exactly." She walked out from the kitchen area, rounded the counter, and seated herself onto the stool next to him. "These last few days..." she said, her legs brushing against his as she placed her feet onto the contoured, chrome footstool. "The last few months, really...so many major things have happened, it's like now I'm just *expecting* that the next day's gonna bring something deep with it. Almost like I'm not surprised anymore if my dad or my brother gets attacked...or if I'm suddenly told about all these things I never knew." She rotated her glass in place on the countertop. "But not in a numb way, y'know? It's more...it's more of an understanding that everything happens for a reason...and each person's placed here for a purpose."

"Destiny," McCready said.

"Yeah," she agreed, "destiny. And fate, synchronicity...all those things. The way everything just kinda falls into place the way it's supposed to, when it's supposed to." She took another sip from her glass, the simple act somehow appearing very elegant and attractive to him. "It's like how when you read something, it means you were always meant to be introduced to those ideas, or when you hear about something, it means that you were always meant to know about that information. Or when you meet someone..." Her eyes locking with his, him feeling a rush. "It means that you two were always meant to experience each other." She smiled warmly. "How could it be anything else? Things happen the way they're supposed to, and it's just a matter of us deciphering their meaning." Turning her eyes up towards the giant skylight which comprised half of the room's domed ceiling, she said, "And right now, with all these things that've happened lately...I think life's trying to tell me something,

Agent McCready. It's trying to bring something out of me. I'm not sure exactly what..." She looked back at him. "But it's something."

Before McCready had a chance to respond, he suddenly heard an odd noise. "What the hell was that?" he asked, perking his head up and instinctively reaching down towards his napper.

"What the hell was what?" she asked.

"That noise..." McCready stood up, set his drink down, and began to cautiously move towards the spiral staircase. "Coming from upstairs–sounds like a voice. And movement."

"Oh, *that*," Ashley said, exhaling with relief. "It's probably just Dawn waking up."

"Don?" McCready stopped his progress, turned around, and asked, "Who's that, your boyfriend?"

She laughed. "No, *Dawn*. D-a-w-n. Female."

"Your girlfriend?"

"My just-friend," Ashley said, still laughing, as she moved towards the base of the staircase. "You sure are curious."

Smiling, he said, "Have to be–it's part of the job description."

"Of course," she said, an incredulous grin crossing her face. Looking up the staircase, Ashley called out, "Dawn? You up?"

"Yes, no thanks to you," answered a feminine voice from upstairs. "I thought you said you were going to wake me up when you were done meditating."

"I was," Ashley said. "But I got kinda sidetracked."

A slender, curvy, strikingly-attractive redhead began to walk down the staircase. "You, the chaos queen? Sidetracked?" she asked, slipping a cellphone into her purse. "I don't believe it."

"Yeah, right," Ashley said playfully. "How was your catnap?"

"Divine," she replied. "Your bed is *so* absolutely amazing, sweetie. I want one of my own–kitties and all." Reaching the base of the stairs, Dawn gave Ashley a hug and a kiss on the cheek, and said, "Thanks for letting me sleep, Ash. I needed it."

"You're welcome," Ashley said. "Thanks for keeping me company."

"Isn't that what best friends are for?" Turning towards McCready, Dawn said, "Now, you must be the dashing secret agent I've been hearing about." Something vaguely familiar about her, but he couldn't quite place what it was. She daintily offered him her jewelled and manicured hand, and said, "I'm Amanda."

"McCready," he said, lightly grasping her soft, perfumed

fingers, his thumb touching a few of the small, implanted epigems. "Nice to meet you."

"The pleasure's mine," she replied.

He asked, "So should I be calling you Amanda or Dawn?"

"Amanda." She looked over at Ashley with mock irritation. "Only Ash still calls me Dawn."

Ashley laughed. "That's 'cause Ash still remembers when you wouldn't *let* anyone call you Amanda." To McCready, she said, "This would be *before* she went to Hollywood."

Familiar face, Amanda, Hollywood–now it clicked. "I thought I recognized you," McCready said. "Amanda Knight?"

"In the flesh," she replied. "You're familiar with my work?"

"I've seen a few of your films, yeah," he said. "Think I also did an interact that you starred in."

"And what'd you think?" she asked.

His hands in his coat pockets, McCready shrugged his shoulders. "Not bad."

Amanda raised her carefully-trimmed eyebrows. "Not good?"

"Not really," he said.

She burst out into laughter. "Ooh, I *like* it. A man who speaks his mind. Got any plans for tomorrow night?" she asked jestingly.

McCready and Ashley made eye contact, and he replied, "'Fraid so."

"Too bad," Amanda said, smiling sexily. "Maybe next time." She looked at Ashley. "Well, my dear, I should be heading home now. I want to make sure I have time to take a shower and freshen up a bit before the gathering."

"Mm-kay. Let me walk you out." Ashley picked up a light coat from the back of a futon, then to McCready she said, "I'll be right back, Agent McCready."

"Alright," he said, as Ashley and Amanda exited through the oval door. He walked back over to the counter, picked up his drink, and began to saunter around Ashley's pad.

Following the raised, outer rim of the sphere in a counter-clockwise direction, he browsed the various masks, artifacts, and plants that were hanging along the curved wall. Each item, including the living ones, seemed infused with an antiquity that made him feel a little bit like he was walking through a museum or gallery rather than a home. Passing by the mouth of another long, cylindrical hallway–this one leading to some sort of large, empty room with hardwood floors–then past more antediluvian wall decorations, he reached the entrance to a stairwell. McCready peeked his head into it, and looked up. There were tons of steps, spiraling all the way to the top of the tall, vertical shaft, and it was currently lit so that it gave the appearance that it ascended up into a black infinity. Recalling his flyby again, he figured this would have to be the tower that had the Kremlin-looking thing on the top of it, since that structure was the highest point on the estate. He pulled his head from out of the stairwell, took a sip of the brew, and continued walking in the same direction, towards a large, curved, sliding glass door which led out to the back part of the estate. As he neared it, McCready began to peer outside–and could have sworn he saw something flash by.

Something human-sized.

Moving swiftly to the door, McCready snapped a mini Maglite® off his belt, and shined it through the plexiglass, around the dimly-lit backyard area. Nothing but foliage, fountains, and the shining eyes of a few nocturnal animals. Wondering if it was just his imagination, he checked the label of the brew he was drinking, just to make sure it was only green tea, and not one of those mind-fucking Psilobrews™. Two yin-yang lizards, and the words, "Sobe®." Definitely only green tea. McCready took another look around the area, conceded that the flash was nothing but his eyes playing tricks on him, and replaced the light back onto his belt.

Turning from the sliding glass door, he stepped down from the outer rim, and into the sunken, center part of the sphere, which was filled with low-to-the-ground furniture such as futons, beanbags, and Gelaform™ loveseats, all looking like they'd been arranged by a tornado rather than a person–very chaotic, but just like Mother Nature, there was a certain, underlying pattern to the design. Scattered amongst the furniture, in an equally random way, were different types of artistic tools, including pencils, pens, sketchbooks, musical instruments, and laptops. He bent down by one of the wire-bound sketchbooks, and began to flip through its contents. Predictably, it contained a lot of abstract stuff, like spirals and wavy lines, and miscellaneous other trippy shapes and symbols. Unpredictably, it also contained a lot of carefully rendered, painstakingly detailed drawings of people, animals, and structures. Her artistic range was impressive, and when he had reached the end of the sketchbook, he found himself drawn to look at more. He picked up another spiral-bound book, this one smaller in size, and began to peruse its contents. Few pictures this time–it was filled with mostly writing. Not wanting to invade her privacy (somehow it seemed to him that words were more personal than pictures), McCready skipped further ahead to see if there were any other drawings.

No more drawings, but he did find a page of writing that he couldn't help but take notice of. On one of the book's creme-colored pages, in big, bright, red letters, it said: "WHERE IS ADRIAN WELLOR????"

His face grew gravely serious, and he looked up from the book. Adrian Wellor? Why the fuck was Ashley asking questions about *him*? And moreso, how did she even know about his existence at all? As far as McCready knew, all of Wellor's personal files, and any references made to him, had been edited out of the uninet's databases. The only place where information on him could be found, was within the private and secured databases of the upper-level government agencies, such as the Freemon or the NSA. And even then, the info was pretty scarce. All the files said about Wellor was that he was a scientist involved in the classified creation of the freereads, who then began to engage in terrorist activities. Soon thereafter, he completely and utterly disappeared, but since his body was never recovered, he was presumed to still be alive. Even to the present day, Wellor's capture–or the obtainment of any information that could lead to his capture–was considered a top priority. McCready looked back down at the enigmatic page. So what exactly did Ashley know? And what was he going to do about it?

Just then, out of the corner of his eye, he saw the flash of movement again. McCready immediately turned his head towards the door, and was startled by what he saw.

Standing there, staring at him through the glass with that horribly inhuman face, was one of the Xandys. Not motioning or moving–just staring.

And then he heard the oval door hissing open, and Ashley saying, "Sorry to keep you waiting, Agent McCready."

He swiftly shut the notebook closed, turned his head in her direction, and tried his very best to appear calm and composed.

Not paying much attention to what McCready was doing, Ashley took off her coat, and continued, "You get me an' Dawn together, and we can start talking for hours."

"Ah...right," McCready said, furtively dropping the notebook down onto a beanbag. "I know how that is." He looked back at the sliding glass door. Xanadeux was gone from sight. He asked her, "Did you know there's Xandys running around in your backyard right now?"

"Mm-hm," she replied, walking to the base of the bedroom's staircase. "My dad sent a few of them here for security. Did you just see one?"

"Yeah, one of 'em was just standing there outside your door, then split when you came in." McCready moved towards the staircase and said, "I hate those creepy little fuckers."

"I guess I'm kinda used to them," Ashley said, beginning to ascend the staircase. "But I could see how they'd be creepy."

"Where are you going?" McCready asked.

"To my bedroom," she said. "I'm gonna throw on something else before we go out."

He grasped his fingers around the staircase's polished, wood railing, looked up at her, and asked, "We're going *out*? You really think it's safe to be going out on the *same* day that your brother and father got attacked?"

Ashley stopped her motion, looked down at him through the open space between two of the steps, and replied, "Maybe, maybe not. But neither is here, *really*. If they wanna attack me, they're gonna find a way. And besides, I don't want to feel like I'm trapped in my own home. If this wasn't happening, then I'd be going out tonight."

"But this *is* happening," McCready reminded her.

Ashley laughed. "Oh well, then." She continued up the staircase. "I'm not gonna live my life in fear."

Brave words, he thought, walking over to the counter and setting down his empty bottle. Or maybe it was something else. Maybe she didn't *have* anything to fear, because she knew she wasn't going to be attacked. If she was asking questions about known terrorists, who was to say she wasn't somehow involved in the attacks on her family? She *did* seem to be handling it awfully well. Maybe Mason had been on to something, after all...

Though Ashley didn't know it, her father had hired McCready not only to protect her, but also to keep an eye on her activities. Mason knew how angry Ashley was about the situation with her mother, and reasoned that there was a remote possibility that Ashley had something to do with the attack on the clone. Unlikely, Huxton had said, but possible. McCready had doubted the scenario from the beginning–especially after getting a chance to spend some time with Ashley–but now he wasn't so sure. He certainly didn't *want* it to be true. Ashley was the most phenomenal woman he'd met in a long time. Maybe ever. And he was looking forward to getting to know her better. But now he had to seriously consider the notion that she was a terrorist herself, and that bothered him. Hella.

"Okay," Ashley said as she came down the stairs, wearing a different, slightly dressier outfit than before, "I'm all ready to go."

"I'm glad *someone* is," he muttered to himself, thinking about earlier, when Huxton had told him–in his polite, corporate, doublespeak way–that it would be McCready's ass if he let her go out tonight and something were to happen to her. As he and Ashley converged towards the oval door, McCready asked, "You realize what'll happen to me if something happens to you tonight?"

Opening the door, Ashley replied, "Do you realize what'll happen to *me* if something happens to me tonight?" She let out a short, exasperated sigh. "It's not like I have this burning desire to get attacked, or what." She exited the sphere, he followed, and they began to walk through the cylindrical hallway. "I'm just trying to retain *some* semblance of my normal life through all this craziness, okay?"

"Alright, alright," McCready conceded with a laugh. "No need to get your feathers ruffled." He pulled out his shades and placed them onto his face. "So where are you planning on taking us?"

Reaching the throwback door, she said, somewhat antagonistically, "I don't know. Maybe to get something to eat." She unlocked the deadbolt. "Then I might catch up with Dawn at the gathering. I'll just have to see how I feel." She turned the doorknob, opened the door, and said, "After you."

McCready smirked. "Thanks." He exited the house, and stepped out into the cool, night air. A breeze was blowing from the west, slightly moist, and altogether refreshing. And though there weren't any gray clouds yet, it felt like rain was on its way. "You got your emvest on?" he asked, as she closed and locked the door behind them.

"What do you think?" she replied, walking past him and towards the parking area.

"Honestly, sweetheart," he said, following her down the garden path, "I wouldn't be surprised either way."

Without stopping her motion, Ashley turned around towards him, opened the flaps of her chestnut-brown jacket, showed him the emvest underneath, and turned back around.

McCready smiled mischeviously. There was something about getting under people's skins that he enjoyed–particularly when he was attracted to them. "Anyone ever tell you how cute you are when you're angry?" he asked rhetorically, as they reached the Chevy®.

Walking around to the passenger's door, Ashley faced him, tilted her head forward and slightly to the side, looked at him with disbelief, and said, "You *didn't* just say that."

"I did," McCready said, as he opened up the car's doors.

She stared at him for a few more seconds, trying her best to keep a serious face. Then she reluctantly smiled, and began to laugh. "You're crazy, Agent McCready, you know that?"

"So I've been told, sweetheart...so I've been told." He seated himself inside of the car, and Ashley did the same.

Still smiling as the doors automatically closed shut behind them, she gave him a little nudge on his shoulder, and added, "But you're crazy in a good way."

A different, rarer kind of smile this time. McCready placed his thumb on the ignition pad, spoke his password, then suddenly realized that the last thing in the world that he would have wanted to say at that moment was something as impassive and indifferent as "whatever."

"Good evening, Agent McCready," the car announced.

"N.J.," he immediately said, "change password."

Marilyn snapped her fingers, and with a swirl of animated magic, her white dress transformed into the skimpy, coin-draped outfit of a Persian belly-dancer, while her 1950's backdrop was replaced with the desert cave from *Ali Baba and the Forty Thieves*. Clicking her finger-cymbals together, she told him, "Please state your new password now."

Not really sure exactly *what* he wanted to change his password to, McCready simply glanced over at the beautiful, entrancing woman seated next to him, took in the moment, and said the first thing that came to his mind.

"Fuckin'-A."

Now that was more like it.

$$\Omega$$

∞

Chapter 10:
<u>The Gathering</u>

And just as the universe itself, life's space was filled with millions of celestial bodies, each one wholly unique unto itself, a miraculous creation unlike any other.
Some were like planets, birthed in the same solar system. They orbited the same sun, shared similar traits, and produced corresponding frequencies which allowed them to resonate in harmony with one another. And while every planetary body had its own origins and evolutions, and each spun at their own, individual rotations, they were all drawn together by the same, guiding light.

Two hours later, having enjoyed a relaxing dinner at the most fabulous restaurant in the entire world, they sat together in satiated silence, as the Polaris™ smoothly carried them through the nighttime skies above downtown Seattle.

The moon nearly as full as her stomach, Ashley stared out at the silvery satellite, allowing her eyes to bask, unfocused, in its lovely luminescence. "Goddess," she said dreamily, both hands resting atop her tummy, "I love Ethiopian food."

McCready, who was lazily reclined back in his seat, his eyes closed, said nothing in response.

Music played softly through the car's speakers, something old and beautiful. A woman, her voice deep and rich and full of soul, backed only by the subtle strings of a piano and the occasional brush on a drum, singing about flying to the moon and playing amongst the stars.

FREQUENCIES

"That food *was* pretty damn good," McCready belatedly agreed, then slipped back into contented quietude.

For the next few minutes, neither of them said a word, and Ashley continued to space off into space, as she listened to the ethereal voice sing about her desire to sing. It was a peaceful moment, during which Ashley wasn't worrying or thinking about the fact that she could possibly be in mortal danger, or that she could be attacked at any moment. None of that mattered, because right then, she was warm and full and comfortable and everything felt okay.

"Who's singing this?" she asked, as a thin veil of cirrostratus clouds began to pass over the moon.

"Sarah Vaughn," he answered.

"Her voice...it's so pretty, isn't it?"

"Yup."

"It's like she's an angel..." Ashley said, watching a prismatic halo form around the moon.

"Amen," McCready replied, and they both lapsed into silence once again.

When the song came to an end, and another began to play (sounding like it was from the same era), McCready yawned, raised his seat forward, and said, "Well, if you're still planning on going to that gathering shindig, then I guess we might want to start heading over there."

"Yeah," Ashley said, somewhat disappointedly, as she stretched out her arms and legs, "I guess so." She looked at the uniview's clock. About half past ten...right about the time she'd told Dawn that she would meet up with her. Ashley was almost tempted not to go, but then she remembered that Dawn had mentioned to her that Seer would be there...and she definitely wanted the chance to talk to him about Wellor. Seer tended to know about all kinds of things–above *and* underground–and could probably shed some light on some of her questions.

"N.J.," McCready said, "disengage cruise mode."

On the uniview console, the old-fashioned low-rider that the Marilyn Monroe toon was driving around in bounced up and down on its raised shocks a few times, then lowered itself closer to its tires. "Where to next?" Marilyn asked, in that fabulous voice of hers.

"Over to-" McCready stopped, and looked at Ashley. "Where to again?"

"Third and Bell," she said. "The Tiger's Lair."

"The Tiger's Lair," he repeated to the car. "Third and Bell."

181

FREQUENCIES

At the same time the Polaris™ changed its course, the cartoon Marilyn raised her hand to her head, saluted them, turned off of the strip of road that she had been cruising back and forth on, and began to head in a new direction.

Ashley giggled and said, "I love your car's avatar, Agent McCready. She's so adorable."

He smiled. "Thanks. I dig her too."

"What site did you get her at?"

"None," he replied, pulling a small, cylindrical container out of his pocket. "A friend of mine at the bureau designed her for me." He twisted off its tiny, brass top, poured out a single, wooden toothpick, and twisted the top back on. "Same guy who's working on your family's case now."

Ashley looked up ahead, at the approaching Space Needle, and asked, "So what *is* my family's case right now, anyways?"

McCready placed the toothpick into his mouth, and put its shiny container back into his pocket. "What do you mean?"

"I mean, like, what do you guys think is going on? What's your theory behind the attacks?"

"Honestly, Ashley," McCready said, rolling the toothpick from one corner of his mouth to the other, "I think everyone's pretty much in the dark right now. Nobody's issued any demands, no one's claimed any responsibility, and last I heard, we didn't even have any solid leads. At this point, all we know is the obvious–someone has it in for your family. Beyond that?" He looked at her, the toothpick rolling back to the opposite corner. "We know jackshit."

As the Polaris™ flew past the Space Needle, Ashley asked, "Well what about these riots that are happening around Cascadia? Couldn't they have something to do with the attacks?"

"It's possible," he said. "But I doubt it."

Ashley stared at him for a second, expecting him to explain further. Realizing that he wasn't going to say any more without some prodding, she prodded, "And this is because...?"

"Because other than the fact that they both started happening at the same time, I'm just not seeing a logical connection between the two." The toothpick still in his mouth, McCready rolled it around in place a few times with his thumb and forefinger, and said, "It'd be one thing if the rioters were destroying some kind of commerce or infrastructure, or if they were trying to get behind the gates–*then* I could see there be some kind of connection. But all they're doing right now is fuckin' up their own neighborhoods and getting themselves arrested an' killed. That's not posing any kind of threat to the system–that's doing it a fuckin' favor." McCready shook his head, let out a frustrated laugh, and paused for a moment. "But those attacks on your family," he said, as the car began to descend down towards the street, "that's some shit that's gonna *freek* the establishment out. That's a real threat, right there–'cause if they can get to Mason Huxton, then that means they can get to *anyone*."

Stopping its motion, and hovering above a BMW® parked curbside in front of the Tiger's Lair, the car asked, "Marc, would you like me to find a parking space?"

"Nah, N.J.," he replied, "I don't want you parked while we're in there. You need to be ready to respond at a moment's notice."

"Where would you like me to let you out at?" Marilyn asked, blowing him an animated, goodbye kiss that fluttered through the air like a crimson butterfly.

"Drop us off at the corner up there," McCready said. The Polaris™ moved ahead over the row of parked cars, until it reached the tow-away zone at the end of the street. Then it lowered itself down a few inches from the asphalt, and came to a rest. "You ready?" he asked Ashley.

She smiled. "Ready as I'll ever be."

McCready touched his gun, patted a few different places on his belt, and said, "Alright. N.J.–open door, driver's side." He looked over at Ashley. "I'll come around to let you out." McCready exited the car and shut the door behind him.

From inside the car, Ashley watched him carefully scope out the area as he stepped out into the street. He rounded the front of the vehicle, and when he reached her side, McCready took one more cautious look around, and spoke into his wristcom.

The passenger door immediately opened up. McCready stood there, his hand extended towards her, and said, "Alright, let's go."

Ashley grabbed a hold of his gloved hand, and allowed him to help her out of the Polaris™. "Thanks," she said, stepping onto the sidewalk. "Everything seem okay?"

"Yeah," McCready said, watching a group of rowdy crossbreeds pass by them, the wolfen member of the party loudly howling up at the moonlit sky. "Relatively speaking." He touched his wristcom. "N.J., close door, and shadow us until we get into the club. Then circle the block until I tell you otherwise."

The Polaris™ shut its door, rose up about twenty feet, and as they started to walk down the sidewalk towards the Tiger's Lair, the car slowly followed overhead.

"See that Benzy over there?" McCready asked, supping his head towards a deep-green Mercedes® parked up the street.

Ashley nodded. "Mm-hm. It looks like an unmarked Ordocop™ car."

"It is. There's a few more of 'em parked back there," he said, raising his hand up, and pointing his thumb in the opposite direction. "They've been tailing us ever since we left your place."

She took a quick glance over her shoulder, saw a couple more Ordocops™, and said, "I guess just you isn't enough anymore, huh?"

"Nope," McCready said, taking the lead as they reached the entrance to the Tiger's Lair. "Not anymore."

"Sorry, guy," said one of the attractive, well-dressed bouncers, as she extended a baton in front of McCready's path. "You gotta be on the list."

"He's with me, Rachel," Ashley said, stepping out from behind McCready and into her line of sight.

"Ashley," the raven-haired woman said in a surprised tone. "I...I didn't think you'd be coming tonight. What with, you know-" She cleared her throat. "The stuff on the news."

Ashley nodded, and said, "Yeah, I didn't think I'd be coming either. But Amanda talked me into it."

"You're blowing this *way* out of proportion," said the other, orange-haired bouncer, who was currently talking down at a cellphone. "Oh, *please*. Like I'm suddenly gonna turn bi overnight?"

"Hey, Glyn," Ashley whipered to her, just loud enough so she could hear.

Glynda looked up from the screen, waved one hand, mouthed the words, "Hi, Ashley," then went back to her conversation. "What are you talking about, Sera?" she asked. "It was platonic. Pla-tonic. Does that word even *exist* in your vocabulary?"

"It's her girlfriend," explained Rachel. "She's a bit possessive."

"I guess so," said Ashley. "Oh yeah, Rache, by the way–this is McCready."

Shaking his hand, Rachel asked, "You the bodyguard?"

"You could say that," replied McCready.

"You look like it," Rachel said. "Nice to meet you."

McCready smiled, and said, "You too."

"Is Amanda already here?" Ashley asked.

Rachel shook her head. "Not yet."

FREQUENCIES

"Fashionably late, as usual," Ashley said, moving towards the revolving door that served as the entrance. "Well, tell her that I'm here, would you?"

"You got it," Rachel said. "Take care of yourself, Ashley."

"Thanks," she said, entering into one of the door's glass segments. "I will." As she followed the circular rotation of the door, she caught a brief reflection of herself in the glass, looked herself in the eye, then stepped out into the loud, smoky, Indian–motifed foyer of the Tiger's Lair, where she was immediately greeted by its doorman.

"Welcome, Ashley," said the tall, dark, and handsome man, extending both his hands towards her. "I'm glad you could make it. How are you?"

"I'm okay, Raj," she replied, grasping his hands with both of hers, thereby allowing his implanted sensors to read her biochip. "Thanks."

As McCready came through the revolving door, a few of the casually-attired members of security stepped forward to inspect him.

"Raj," said one of the burly guards, "he's projecting some kind of emfield that's disrupting the revolver's sensors. And she's got an emvest on." He looked at Ashley uncomfortably. "Hi, Ashley."

"Hey, Ally," she said.

Raj looked at McCready. "Well?" he asked, raising his eyebrows.

McCready pulled out his badge and handed it over to security. "Agent Marc McCready, Freemon. I've got clearance for everything. So does she."

Ally examined the badge and hologram with a hand-held scanner, then said, "He's legit, Raj." He handed the ID back to McCready.

"Good." Extending his hands to McCready, Raj said, "Welcome to tonight's gathering, Mr. McCready."

"Thanks," McCready said, shaking one of Raj's hands with his gloved one.

Raj eyed McCready curiously, and asked, "Why am I not sensing a biochip?"

McCready raised his left hand, and replied, "'Cause it's in this hand."

Grasping his ungloved hand, Raj smiled, and said, "Better." He released his grip, looked at Ashley and McCready, and motioned his hand towards the surroundings. "Please enjoy yourselves tonight."

FREQUENCIES

"Thanks, Raj," Ashley said. Her and McCready progressed into the spacious foyer, past tall, colorful statues of Vishnu, Brahma, and Shiva. "You wanna get a drink before we head in to the gathering place?" Ashley asked.

"Yeah, sounds good." As they walked towards the ornately decorated bar located at the establishment's east end, McCready said, "What setting is your emvest at?"

"Umm..." she said, grinning guiltily. "None."

"What?"

"I actually haven't turned it on yet."

McCready looked at her, dumbfounded. "Well turn it on already," he said, as they continued moving through the crowded place. "It's not gonna do you any good unless it's activated."

"I know, I know," Ashley said. She reached down, placed her fingers on the tiny knob, and hesitated. "You really don't think it's gonna disrupt me?"

McCready laughed. "Just do it, Ashley. C'mon, you'll be fine. I promise."

"Okay," she reluctantly agreed. Giving the knob a half-turn, she nearly lost her balance, as everything around her rippled and waved, the world suddenly turning into a giant, warped, fun-house mirror. "Whoa..." Ashley said, grabbing a hold of McCready. "I think...I think I just got disrupted."

"You're fine," he said reassuringly. "The effect's only temporary."

"Damn, dude," she heard a male passerby say, "that chick looks *curbed*."

"Okay..." Ashley said, letting go of her grip on McCready's trenchcoat. "The world is becoming solid again."

"Good," McCready said. As they approached two empty seats at the end of the bar, he shook his head, and began to laugh.

With a smile, she asked, "What are you laughing at?"

"The look on your face," he said, as they seated themselves onto the plush barstools. "That was fuckin' priceless. You really looked like you thought your molecules were about to scatter."

"You could of warned me that was gonna happen!" Ashley said with a laugh, pushing him just hard enough to move him backwards a bit. "Mr. 'don't worry, you'll be fine.'"

"Did I lie?" McCready asked, turning his palms up. "Are you alright?"

"I guess," Ashley said, picking up a thin, cardstock coaster.

"As long as my brain waves aren't all scrambled now."

Gazing directly at her, his face turned dead serious, and he said, "Actually, now that you mention it..."

"What?" she asked with curious concern, as he continued to stare at her.

"Your frees *do* look a bit odd right now."

"Really?"

"Nah." He smiled. "I'm just fuckin' with you."

With a relieved laugh, Ashley said, "You smartass." She tossed the coaster at him. "Now seriously, though–everything looks normal?"

"Yeah. Seriously, Ashley," McCready said, setting the coaster back down on the bar. "Your frees look perfectly normal. If some kind of scrambling effect had happened, I'd be able to tell." He placed his hand on her shoulder, lightly massaged it, and smiled. "So relax, alright? You're fine."

Though she wasn't entirely convinced–after all, no matter how advanced a technology was, it could never take *everything* into account–his touch at least comforted her. She smiled back, nodded her head, and replied, "Okay. But if the world starts to liquify again..." She pointed her finger at him. "You're in trouble."

As the bartender approached them, McCready pulled out a pack of Old Skools™, and said, "Fair enough."

"Good evening, Ashley," said the bartender, who was attired in an expensive, orange and black, silk outfit. "What can I get for you?"

"Hey, Rowan," she said. "Could I have a little glass of the anise liqueur, please?"

"Of course." To McCready, he asked, "And you?"

"Kahlua® and cream," McCready said, placing a cigarette into his mouth. "With a double shot of espresso."

Rowan nodded. "I'll be right back."

McCready lit up his cancer stick with an old-fashioned, flip-top lighter, and took in a slow, deep inhalation of the ignited tobacco. "This place seems cool," he said, exhaling the noxious fumes, and taking a look around. "Music's good."

"Mm-hm," she agreed, subtly moving her head and body to the Indian music's mystical rhythm.

"Mind you, I can't understand a fuckin' word of it," he said. "But it sounds cool."

Ashley smiled. "I can't understand the words either." She

picked up the coaster again. "But that's what makes music so powerful." Twirling the tiger-adorned coaster between her fingers, she said, "It transcends language barriers...and logic barriers, and all the other mazy bullshit that our minds get trapped in. It gets down to the core, y'know? The *real*, the feel, the primal..."

"The funk," McCready added, taking another draw.

Ashley laughed. "Yeah. The funk. I like that." Noticing that Rowan was bringing their drinks, Ashley put the coaster back on the counter.

"There you are," Rowan said, setting McCready's cloudy drink down onto the Tiger's Lair logo. Then, from a gorgeous, colored-crystal decanter, which reminded her of an Egyptian perfume bottle, he poured out a small amount of clear liquid into a port glass, and said, "And there you are."

"Thank you," Ashley said, making sure to make eye contact with him.

"Yeah, thanks, man," McCready chimed, as he snatched up his drink.

"Of course," Rowan said with a smile, then walked away.

Picking up both the small glass of liqueur and her train of thought, she said, "Yeah, music is *so* powerful." She sipped the sweet liquid. "If there ever *is* gonna be any kind of true revolution–or evolution, deevolution, whatever you want to call it–music's definitely gonna have to play a part in it."

Flicking his cigarette's ashes into a blown-glass ashtray, he asked, "In what way?"

"In a lot of ways," she replied.

"Like?"

"Well, for one, it's about the only thing that can still physically bring people together. Which is pretty amazing, when you consider how much of our lives are spent in isolation, immersed in the uniview or some other kind of convenience technology. I mean, yeah, we're always *tele*communicating with each other, and we're always *virtually* interacting with each other, but it's just not the same as being *physically* together. There's so much more energy created when five hundred people are in a club, than when five hundred people are in a MUD, y'know? It's a *completely* different phenomena. Like night and day." Ashley took another sip of her licoricey drink, and said, "So I just think there's an incredible amount of power in something that can still draw our physical energies together like that...which is what music does. Just look at here–it's a perfect example. Most of us are total strangers, yet we're *physically* gathering together, united through music. Same with any other club or concert."

"Alright, I can see what you're saying." McCready took a drink from his glass. "But I think you're overlooking something."

"What's that?"

"The fuck factor."

"The *what*?" Ashley asked quizzically.

"The fuck factor," he repeated. "Sex." He puffed some more tobacco. "I bet you half the people in here could give a clone whore's ass about the music, let alone a revolution. They're just comin' here to find someone to shag."

"Yeah, of course," she said. "I'm not overlooking that though–I think that's part of it. 'Cause right now, humanity is in *serious* danger of losing its physicality and its senses." Ashley laughed. "Losing its senses...that's fitting. Anyways, sexuality is one of the *major* advantages of physicality–and a *great* persuader for not relinquishing our physical existence to a virtual one."

McCready touched his glass to Ashley's. "Well, amen to that, sister."

Ashley smiled, and they both took a drink. Licking her lips, she said, "Yeah, at this point, I just see music and sensuality and anything that allows us to have fun and feel each other's vibrations as being part of the same cause. Anything that touches our souls, and taps into our collective unconscious, and lets us know we're *alive*." She took a deep breath. "'Cause in this cold, apathetic world, just feeling alive, and being happy, and knowing hope..." She paused for a moment, staring directly into the centers of McCready's sunglasses. "That's a revolution in itself, wouldn't you say?"

The end of McCready's cigarette flared up brightly. "I hadn't really thought of it that way." He took another swig of his Kahlua®. "Makes sense, though."

"I think so," Ashley said, noticing that a few of her friends across the room were waving to her. Waving back, she continued, "And I think that's why socialism, and communism, and so many of the other so-called revolutions failed in the past. They weren't really changing the vibe at all, y'know? They were too logical, and stiff, and serious...all stuck up in the same old, tired paradigms they were claiming to replace. I mean, c'mon, what's the point of a revolution if you're not having fun while you're doing it?" The glass stem between her fingers, she rotated the cup in her hand, counterclockwise, and said, "It's just time for something new–and I mean *completely* new. New signs, new symbols...new everything. Something that's beyond words...something *so* new and *so* different, that this restrictive English language can't even describe it." She raised the glass to her lips. *"That's* what I'm ready for."

As she took a tiny sip of the liqueur, McCready let out a puffy cloud of smoke, and coolly said, "Your thoughts are fuckin' beautiful."

She laughed, unsure of how to take that comment.

"No, I'm serious. They are. Literally." He took another pull from the cigarette. "When you were just talking there, the color patterns were shifting and swirling in this hella cool way," he said, his hand moving in smooth, wavy motions, the cigarette's embers making Mobius-strip tracers in the club's low-lighting. "It was fresh."

"Huh." Ashley took another sip. "That's interesting. I hadn't ever thought about the frees being aesthetically pleasing."

"Well, I don't think most Freemon think so, but at least for me it's been that way. It's always felt like I had this personal, sorta psychedelic light show happening right in front of my eyes." McCready inhaled some more tobacco. "And since everyone's thoughts are different," he said, blowing out a few perfectly-formed smoke rings, "and their thoughts are always changing," he continued, blowing a thin stream of smoke through the widening rings, "it never really gets boring to watch. It's like seeing each person paint their own frequential art piece." He drank from his glass, then pointed his two cigarette-holding fingers towards her, and said, "And you just painted a masterpiece."

"Thanks," she said. "So what'd it look like?"

"A lot of reds. Crimson and rose swirls. Splashes of deep-orange here and there. Very wavy, very soothing."

"And now?"

"Still wavy and smooth," McCready replied, drawing from the dwindling cigarette, while with the same hand, rubbing his thumb along the side of his stubbly chin. "But now you're using more yellows. And a few lush-greens. It's a nice composition."

"Wow..." Ashley softly said, marvelling at both the technology and the breadth of its user. "You must be so interesting. I mean," she quickly corrected herself, "that must be so interesting to see people's thoughts like that."

"Yeah," McCready said, "it is. But it all gets fucked up once I have to arrest someone based on their painting." He let out the same frustrated laugh as earlier in the car. "This world's fuckin' nuts,

Ashley," he said, shaking his head. He stood up, picked up his drink, and downed the rest of it. "Damn good drink," he said, forcefully setting his empty glass down onto the bar. He wiped his mouth with the back of his hand. "So we heading into this gathering place, or what?"

"I guess so," she said, standing up from her seat. "I wanted to wait for Dawn, but now I'm wondering now if she's even coming." Ashley looked around the foyer, saw no sign of her often-flaky best friend, and set her glass on top of the counter. "Okay, let's go." As they began to walk away from the bar, towards the hallway which led to the auditorium, Ashley asked, "You ever taken part in a gathering before?"

"Nah," McCready said. He snickered. "I've had to raid a few, though."

Ashley looked at him, slightly concerned. "You're not gonna pull any of that kinda shit tonight, are you?"

"Hell no, sweetheart," he said. "I'm off duty." He nodded at a dreadlocked white guy who walked by. "Right now, as long as it's not threatening you, I don't give a fuck *what* people want to think or do."

"Okay, good," she said, as they entered into the gorgeous, rounded hallway, which was completely covered with a painted montage of various scenes of India and Hinduism. Feeling the low, bass throb of the gathering's music beneath her feet, she noticed two people she recognized emerging from the auditorium's entrance. "Kaya, Gus," she said. "What's up?"

"Hey, Ash," Kaya said, giving Ashley a warm hug.

As they broke their embrace, Gus nodded at Ashley, his bearded face barely visible underneath his cloak's shadowy hood.

Ashley nodded back at him and smiled, then Kaya asked her, "You goin' in to watch Seer?"

"Is he already on?" Ashley asked.

"Yup," Kaya said. "We just got done doin' our thing with him. He's on his last few songs now. You better get in there if you wanna catch him."

"Yeah, I will," Ashley said, beginning to walk towards the auditorium again. "Thanks. I'll see you guys in a bit, okay?"

"Yeah, we'll be around," Kaya said, as her and Gus continued towards the foyer.

McCready asked, "The hooded guy always that talkative?"

"Usually," Ashley replied.

191

FREQUENCIES

When they reached the entrance to the auditorium, which was framed with an outline of the Taj Mahal, the painted door hissed open for them, immediately letting out the lively, infectious music coming from within.

"AaaAHHHH," the song's voices said, rising to a rousing crescendo. "Freek out!!"

As they entered into the pulsing, red strobe-lit auditorium, the song's voices echoed out, and a raw, thumping beat began to drop. "That's nasty," McCready commented.

"Yeah, it is," she agreed, her body already beginning to bob with the beat.

The place was packed. But not *so* crowded that there wasn't space to move around freely–which was how the gatherings were always organized, since the emphasis was as much on the crowd as on the performers. People were dancing in all kinds of different ways–a quick glance showed breakdancing, salsa, capoeira, jazz, triballet, and numerous freestyles–while others had formed drumming circles, or were just tapping out some drum rhythms by themselves. Then there were some who were just watching the performance, others who were talking, laughing, or smoking weed, and a few, stray souls who were simply walking around the place in a complete, drug-induced daze.

The gatherings were always something that fascinated Ashley, since they were essentially a refuge where the wealthy, well-off, under-40 crowd could come together, cut loose, and get freeky. It was an outlet for those who had clearance; an outlet for the minority of successful people–doctors, lawyers, actors, artists, professors, scientists, rich kids like herself, etcetera–who weren't quite satisfied with life behind the gates. Here, they could satisfy their rebellious urges in a legal, commercial way (membership in a gathering circle was *extremely* expensive), which wouldn't threaten the overlords of society. And usually the outlet worked. Everyone would get all riled up one night, half-heartedly talk about change and revolution, then go back to work the next day, not say a word about it to any of their coworkers, and forget the whole experience completely. Then they would come back next week, and repeat the same cycle all over again. Harmless fun for the well-to-do.

Occasionally though (in her opinion, not enough), they actually *were* a rebellious event, toeing the line between subversity and stability, and sometimes even crossing over it. Ashley had been to a few where she could sense a mass awakening happening; where a

192

new vibration was beginning to take hold–but unfortunately, those also tended to be the ones that got raided, since too many people started emitting similar, "dangerous" frees. These truly subversive gatherings were most likely to occur when the organizers brought in underground acts from outside the gates, rather than the safe, bubble gum fare they were supposed to bring in. When those acts came through, the vibe got *real* interesting.

And right now in the Tiger's Lair, the underground was representing in full.

Seer stood atop the jungle-motifed stage, energetically pacing back and forth from one side to the other, spitting rhymes into the wireless mic that he clutched in his hand. He currently looked like a young, six-foot African-American man with a skully, dressed in tiger-striped fatigues and black Karl Kani® boots–much different than the last time she had seen him, when he had appeared as an older, shorter Native-American, attired in a traditional Makah outfit, performing the ancient songs of that aboriginal tribe.

Ashley had no idea what Seer *actually* looked like, since he always wore an ever-changing hologram over himself. But his voice, which was very strong, resonant, and somehow able to be simlutaneously combative and peaceful, was something that she could always recognize. Walking closer to the stage, Ashley began to listen to his lyrics...

> *Just kickin' this verse*
> *thoughts disperse*
> *rhymes' gettin' freeky and they gonna get worse*
> *'cause I'm comin' to this spot, makin' it hot, as I inoc-*
> *ulate ya dome*
> *'gainst that wack propaganda that be flowin' through ya home*
> *on the unie, you need*
> *to check the time*
> *'cause there ain't no time to be walkin' 'round blind*
> *so*
> *now*
> *just*
> *take a look around*
> *what's goin' down?*
> *riots goin' on seem to me like a clown*
> *a dis*
> *and now*

FREQUENCIES

I-an'-I 'bout to get pissed
disturbed
a word
of advice to all'a y'all
wake ya ass up there's about to be a fall
'cause these devils be tryin'
these devils be lyin'
sayin' it's the people
when it's them who's connivin'

"This is trippy," McCready suddenly said in Ashley's ear.
"This guy's rappin' all this freeky shit, but his freeread is showing
something completely different."

Leaning towards McCready, Ashley asked, "So what's
that mean?"

"I'm not sure," he replied. "That's what's trippy. His
freeread must be malfunctioning or something."

"Maybe he just knows how to control his thoughts," she said.

"Yeah, right," McCready scoffed. "The day people figure out
how to mentally fool the freereads is the day *this* society comes
to an end."

Ashley simply smiled, said nothing in response, and began to
focus her attention on Seer again.

'Cause me na waan be on de uniview
steal ya soul like de devil go t'hell when it's tru
so me neva gon' be on de uniview
I say me neva gonna be on de uniview
me neva gon' be on de uniview
I-an'-I stay undaground whatcha gonna do?!

Finishing his verse, Seer immediately slammed his mic
down on the ground, and a raging fire began to burn around him. The
strobes started flashing faster, as the flames consumed his physical
form, reducing him to ashes in a manner of seconds. A fiery phoenix
then rose from the conflagration, up to the ceiling, and exploded into
a glorious blaze, leaving behind the words "SAY WHAT YOU SEE"
in its flaming wake. Then the lights abrubtly went out, leaving
everyone in complete darkness, save for the flickering letters
overhead.

When the lights came back on (no strobe this time, now a

steady, dim blue), Seer was nowhere to be seen.

As "The Freaks Come Out At Night" started to loudly play through the soundsystem, and holographic designs began to float in the air, McCready said, "That guy just completely disappeared."

"I know," Ashley said disappointedly, realizing she probably wasn't going to get a chance to talk to Seer tonight.

"That's fuckin' weird," McCready continued. "I had a bead on him, even while he was burning up...but then his freeread turned to static when the lights went out." He looked at Ashley. "And now he's completely gone. I don't get it."

"Yeah," Ashley said, scanning her eyes over the ends of the stage, hoping to find some sign of the musician, "Seer's a mysterious guy." She was about to give up, when she caught a glimpse of a familiar face–pony-tail, Chinese, handsome–one she'd seen Seer use before. To McCready, she said, "I'm gonna go say hi to someone real quick." She started to move away from him. "I'll be right back, okay?"

"Wait," he said, grabbing a painful hold of her wrist.

"Ow!" she shouted. "What the hell are you doing?!"

McCready immediately let go, and with a startled look said, "Sorry, I-" He raised his gloved hand and flexed it. "The bionics–they're imprecise. Sorry."

Ashley looked back, to make sure she could still see Seer. He was virtually in the same place, now talking to a few people. Turning back to McCready, she rubbed her sore wrist and said, "It's fine. What'd you need to tell me?"

He laughed uncomfortably. "Nothing, really. I...I was just gonna tell you to be careful. And watch out. That's it."

Sensing his sincerity, Ashley smiled, and said, "I will. Thanks." She then turned away from McCready, and briskly moved through the crowd, towards the far end of the auditorium where Seer was standing.

The moment she reached him, Seer immediately looked at her, and said, "Ní hao, Ashley."

"Ní hao," she replied. "Could I speak with you alone for a minute?" She smiled, somewhat apologetically, at the man and woman he was talking to.

"One moment," Seer said. To the two others, also Asian, he said something in Chinese that she couldn't understand.

The man and woman both nodded and smiled, then the woman said, "Wo dong le."

Seer smiled. "Xiexie. Hui jian." To Ashley, he said, "Let's move over here." He began to walk over to a less-populated section of the auditorium.

"I'm sorry to interrupt you," she said, following after him, "but I'm trying to make sense out of something that happened to me yesterday, and I really don't know who else to talk to."

"Apologies are unecessary," Seer said, reaching the area and stopping his motion. "We do what we must." He placed his hands in the front pouch of his robe-like outfit, and asked, "What is it that happened?"

"Okay," Ashley said, gathering her thoughts together, "yesterday...I met with a former professor of mine at the U-dub, and he told me about this man named Adrian Wellor."

Seer stared deeply into her eyes, as if to gauge her intentions, and asked, "The professor's name–what was it?"

"Brennan."

Seer cocked one of his eyebrows. "*Michael* Brennan?"

"Yeah," Ashley said, noticing that a few of the Ordocops™ were now discreetly patrolling the auditorium, maintaining their watchful vigil on her. "Do you know him?"

His eyes glancing to where Ashley's had been, he said, "I know that he speaks with a forked tongue."

"He seemed sincere."

"The devil usually does. What did he tell you?"

"He said that Wellor created the freeread technology, not him. And that Wellor never intended it to be used in *this* way," she said, touching her forehead.

Seer nodded a few times. "What else did he say?"

"Well, basically he said that he stole Wellor's idea, then warped it into what it is now by forming a commission..."

"The Brennan Commission," Ashley said, moving a few strands of her hair behind her ears. "I read about that in my research. That was where you formed the committee to study human FE's, right?"

"Correct," Brennan said. "After Wellor completed some of the initial prototypes, I suggested we form a commission to study the full implications of the technology, and its possible applications to society. The government eagerly agreed, authorized myself and others to begin the task, and allocated us the necessary funding to see it through." He turned his head away from the fountain, as a strong breeze blew some spray into his face. "As you can imagine, Wellor was quite thrilled when he heard the news. He thought his greatest dreams had been realized... I still vividly recall him coming up to me, hope and excitement gleaming in his eyes, thanking me for setting the wheels in motion." Brennan paused, wrinkles of guilt forming around the corners of his eyes. "But his excitement soon turned to horror, when he realized that the commission was only interested in mapping the *human* FE spectrum–and that we had no interest whatsoever in studying the interconnectedness or interdependence of all life. Which, as you know, was the entire motivating force behind his scientific endeavors."

"Goddess," Ashley said, "he must have been so angry. What did he do? Did he take his story to the media?"

"He couldn't."

"Why not?"

"That was the catch, you see," Breannan said. "When we formed the commission, we placed it under the protection of national security. Therefore, all of its members had to sign a contract of confidentiality in order to become part of the group–which meant that the unauthorized disclosure of *any* information pertaining to the commission's findings was considered to be an act of treason."

Surprised, Ashley asked, "And Wellor agreed to this?"

"Naturally," he replied. "If you had created a technology around which an entire commission was being built, wouldn't *you* want to be a part of it?"

"Yeah," she reluctantly agreed, feeling a hint of the frustration which Wellor must have felt. "I guess. I mean, I would have wanted to be a part of it, but still... I don't think I would have signed the contract. It would have seemed suspicious to me."

"I don't doubt that it would have," he said. "But Adrian did not share your distrust of the government, Ashley. He believed in America and its institutions, and he believed in academia. And more than anything else...he believed in me. He trusted me with all his heart." Brennan paused, his teeth grinding together uneasily. "And why shouldn't he have? I was his mentor, for God's sake. I was supposed to be the one person he could trust above all."

"So why did you betray him then?"

"I was cold...power-hungry...weak..." Brennan said. "And the temptation was too strong for me to resist. I saw an opportunity to impact the world, and to cement my place in history...so I took advantage of it, and devised ways in which I could legally take hold of Wellor's creation."

"Like the contract."

"Yes, that was one of the final steps, but there were many others leading up to it. And because I was his mentor, they weren't very hard to put in motion. He greatly respected my opinion, and therefore it was a rather simple task to influence his choices in one direction or another. All I had to do was lie to him."

"Wow," Ashley said flatly. "You sold your soul, Professor Brennan."

"If only you knew," he said under his breath, turning his eyes towards the ground. "If only you knew."

There was silence between them.

Brennan dejectedly stared down at the concrete.

Ashley stared at him, amazed at the evil this seemingly-gentle man had once committed. Granted, everyone had their dark side, but raping someone's idea and then knowingly turning it into a device which raped people's thoughts...that wasn't a dark side, that was a *demon* side.

Breaking the silence, Ashley asked, "So what happened to Wellor?"

"I have no idea," he said, still gazing down at the ground.

"You must have *some* idea."

"I wish I did." Brennan looked up at her. "But the truth is, I don't. The last time I even saw him was at the turn of the century, shortly before the committee's end. By that time, he realized that his ideas had absoutely no hope of ever being implemented. So one day, he politely threatened to expose us all, and quietly excused himself from the meeting. We immediately sent FBI agents out to his residence to detain him–but he never showed up." He twisted his cane around in place. "And we've never heard from him since."

"Nothing?"

"Nothing substanstial," he said. "Since this was before the Frequency Emissions Act, he was never biochipped, so we were never able to track his movements. We assume that he's dead, but his body has never been recovered to confirm it. It's an enigmatic situation, to say the least."

Ashley thought about his response, then commented, "You said nothing *substantial*. What did you mean by that?"

Brennan smiled, letting out a small laugh through his nostrils. "I did say that, didn't I?" he asked. "Well, since his disappearance, various rumors have surfaced from time to time concerning his existence and whereabouts. I've heard some colleagues say he simply assumed another identity and lived out a normal life, and I've had others tell me that he comitted suicide in a remote part of the world. Yet others have said that he went underground, and is still currently plotting his revenge against us. But none of these rumors have ever been substantiated. The truth of the matter is, even to this day, the question of what happened to Adrian Wellor remains a complete and utter mystery to us."

"And that's essentially what he had to say," Ashley said. "Though I'm not exactly sure what to make of it."

His arms folded, his chin resting on his right hand, Seer thought for a moment. "This is odd," he said.

"Tell me about it," she agreed.

"He told you the truth..." Seer said, his facial expression showing that he was still cycling through various thoughts. "Which I find much more suspicious than if he had told you a lie. What were his reasons for revealing this information to you?"

"He said that it was his way of making amends. He hoped that by telling me, Wellor's dream wouldn't die with him."

Seer smiled, placed his hands back in his pouch-like pocket, and said, "He needn't worry."

"Why not?"

"Wellor's dream is in no danger of dying."

"Meaning that Wellor's still alive?" she asked.

"Meaning that-" Seer paused, his eyes darting quickly towards the auditorium's entrance and back. "I can tell you this much, Ashley," he said, as the "The Freaks Come Out At Night" seamlessly blended into a song much darker in tone. "What was once a dream, shall soon become reality."

A cryptic response, but it conveyed the message...and further confirmed what she'd already been feeling. Change was on its way. "That's what I wanted to hear," she said.

"For now though," Seer said, "you should be most concerned with the Presence."

"The Presence?"

"The entity that's attacking your family." Seer looked towards the entrance again, this time his gaze remaining fixed. "It's a powerful ally, but its methods are crude and reckless. You're likely to get caught in its path, simply because of your heritage."

FREQUENCIES

Ashley looked in the direction he was. Six people, whom she'd never seen at any gathering before, were standing together, looking in their direction. Two women, two men, and two crossbreeds, all very starchy and rigid–obviously not here to enjoy the vibe. Watching them, she asked, "So what should I do?"

"Stay alert," he responded, as the six individuals began to walk towards them, the tall, dark, and beautiful member of the sextet taking the lead.

Ashley's heart began to race. She looked for McCready or the Ordocops™, but then the lights abruptly dimmed down to a deep-puple, and she could no longer make out any faces in the crowd.

"Be prepared." Seer's image started to flicker and blink, like a uniview rapidly changing channels.

The attractive female, who was clad in glossy-black, skin-tight plastic, continued to move forward, and was now outstretching her arm towards them.

Ashley breathed in deeply through her nose, reached her left hand over to her right, placed her fingers around the twisty-fit, and rotated it–twice–then turned her emvest up to full power.

"And expect the unexpected." Seer flickered, flashed, and blinked out of existence. "I'll find you," his invisible voice said, then she felt a rush of air as he left her presence.

One of the crossbreeds suddenly turned into a blur, and moved in the direction that she had felt Seer move in. A split-second later, the mustached, Latino member of the group did the same.

"Stay where you are!" the woman commanded Ashley, her ghostly, white eyes as harsh and severe as the tone of her voice.

"Freeze!" yelled an Ordocop™, as he and the other two undercovers drew their laser pistols on the quartet. "Don't move!"

"This is governmental jurisdiction!" shouted the older, salt-and-pepper-haired member of the quartet, as he and the Asian woman pulled out their pistols, and faced the Ordocops™. "Lower your weapons and back off!"

The crowd began to notice, and was quickly becoming alarmed. The ominous music felt like it was getting louder.

Ashely instinctively started to retreat, walking backwards while still facing the threatening woman.

"You think I'm playin', girl?!" A pulse of clear energy suddenly shot from the woman's hand, directly at Ashley's head, and burst into a spectrum of color just a few inches from her face.

Ashley raised her hands up as the colors dissipated, and the fun-house mirror effect began to happen again.

Lasers began to fly, as the government agents and the Ordocops™ began shooting at each other indiscriminately.

The crowd panicked, and people went running everywhere.

"Her emvest's too strong!" the pupil-less woman shouted above the cacophony, as the ripple effect ceased, and Ashley's vision returned to normal. "Time to get physical! Rex!" She looked over at the short, man-creature who was crouched next to her in a feral manner, and as her emvest blocked some type of rear EM attack, she pointed at Ashley, and screamed, "Sick her!"

Rex immediately bounded towards her in an ape-like fashion, as the woman turned towards the Ordocops™ and began to exchange fire.

"Oh, shit," Ashley said to herself. Raising her fist at the incoming crossbreed, she fired the laser on her ring, but it harmlessly reflected off his chest in a similar display of colors. Just as Rex was about to reach her, she remembered that emvests protected only the head and trunk, and aimed towards his legs.

The same flash of colors at his knees, and Rex had grabbed a tight hold of both of her hands, while his simian feet grabbed a hold of her ankles. "Nice try, lady," he gutturally said, his wet snout glistening with his mouth's movements, "but my entire *body* is an emvest. And now that I'm inside *your* emfield," he whispered loudly as his eyes began to glow, "say goodnight."

A thunderous gunshot suddenly rang out, and the flesh on Rex's arm ruptured violently, spraying a mist of blood into the air, and revealing beneath it a silvery alloy. He didn't scream or release his grip on her, but merely looked in the direction of the gunshot.

Ashley did the same.

McCready calmly walked towards them, his smoking revolver aimed at the simian man, and said, "Let her go now, you fuckin' Cro-Magnon–or I'm puttin' the next one in your fuckin' head!"

Ashley struggled, but she couldn't break free of the crossbreed's powerful grip.

"I call your bluff, McCready!" Rex said, as his eyes began to glow again. "You're out of your jurisdiction!"

"Last chance, fucker," McCready said, keeping his aim and closing his ground.

Rex's orbs grew brighter, and twin lasers shot from his eyes at McCready's gun. A prism of emfield colors appeared around the antique weapon. "What?" Rex asked confusedly, then a bullet split open the flesh on his forehead, sending streams of blood down into his glowing eyes.

Ashley backed her head away from the gore, and dry-heaved a few times.

"There's an emfield in the handle, dumbfuck," McCready said, firing another shot into Rex's face, this one lodging itself into one of his eye sockets, reducing the eyeball inside to a whitish goo.

Rex let go of Ashley, and rushed at McCready with a furious, primal scream, its long, hairy arms flailing wildly about.

Unruffled by the showy display, McCready shot off two rounds into Rex's chest, temporarily slowing the creature's progress. As Rex began to move forward again, McCready swiftly reached down to his belt, grabbed a hold of something small, and threw it towards Rex as if he was tossing a mini Frisbee®.

Rex immediately lifted up and off of the ground, his body becoming weightless, but his motion continuing towards McCready.

As Rex struggled to remove whatever it was that had been attached to him, McCready rushed forward, cocked his bionic hand way back, and delivered a crushing blow to the creature's bloodied face, instantly sending it backwards through the air at an unreally fast speed–and its motion didn't cease until it had slammed into the auditorium's wall, located about twenty feet away from McCready's fist.

"That's not gonna stop him for long," McCready said to Ashley, motioning for her to follow him. "Let's get out of here."

"What the hell's going on?!" she asked, moving towards McCready, as she looked back at the Ordocop's™ battle with the government agents–a conflict which the corpos were obviously losing.

"I don't know," McCready said, as they started to run up the stairs which led to the jungly stage, "but now's not the time to find out!" Weaving their way through the Indian foliage, they rapidly proceeded backstage in search of an escape route. "There's gotta be an exit here somewhere!" he shouted, as they hopped around and over the various musical equipment that was scattered about the backstage. To his wristcom, he said, "N.J., show me a blueprint of this place with my position, and lock on to me!"

Quickly realizing that there wasn't any back exit, Ashley said, "Shit! This is a dead end!" She looked back, just to make sure the ape-creature hadn't already caught up with them. Not yet, but she knew it was on its way. Looking at McCready, who was still staring down at his wristcom, she said, "There's no exit back here, McCready!"

"Then we'll have to make one!" he responded as he looked up from the tiny screen, and faced one of the walls. Pulling a device from his belt, and aiming it towards the wall, he said, "Cover your eyes!"

Ashley shielded her hand over her eyes and looked down towards the ground. An extremely bright light began to fill the darkened area, flashing and pulsing in various degrees of intensity, causing her to squint tightly. Hearing a searing, crackling sound, she asked, "What is that?"

"Plasma-torch," he said. "I'm cutting us an exit. And I'm just...about...finished. Alright," he said to her, as the burning sound ceased, "you can look up now." McCready walked up to the molten-lined, makeshit exit, forcefully kicked it out, then reached for another device, and cooled the top of the opening in order to prevent any magma from dripping down. "C'mon, let's go," he said, allowing Ashley to exit first. "Just watch the sides–they're hot."

Ashley carefully stepped through the hole, out into the wide alley located behind the club. The rain was falling down from the sky as a fine mist, and there were a few, cigarette-smoking onlookers nearby, their mouths agape with surprise.

McCready threw down a pellet that exploded into a thick cloud of smoke, and joined her outside, just as the Polaris™ began to descend from the skies. "Open doors," he said to the wristcom.

The Chevy® landed perfectly in front of them, its doors opened, passenger-side facing Ashley. She hopped into the car, and N.J. immediately closed the door behind her.

McCready quickly slid across the hood, landed on his feet, and joined her inside the vehicle. He exhaled a sigh of relief as his door shut closed, and said, "That was close."

Then Rex suddenly slammed into Ashley's window like a rabid dog, his bullet-torn face leaving a reddish smear across the transparent plexiglass.

Ashley let out a startled scream, as Rex's fists began to slam into the window, causing the plastic to fissure and crack.

"Lift off, N.J.!" McCready said.

The car instantly ascended into the air, and rose up high above the alleyway–with Rex on its hood.

The simian creature stared in through the windshield with one eye, futilely shouting something at them while gripping his long arms around the vehicle's sides.

"Seatbelts," McCready said, and the car automatically

strapped both of them in with its belt and shoulder harnesses.

Rex's lone eye glowed red, then he creepily looked at Ashley–the ripped flesh hanging from his forehead, his eye socket still bleeding pale biomatter–and fired a laser directly at her.

"Oh my goddess!" she said, trying to lean her head and body away from his line of fire, as the window slowly began to melt.

"Hold on to your stomach," McCready said to her, then shouted, "N.J.–roll!"

The car rolled over in place, and they were now looking at the world upside down, held in place by the secure seatbelts.

Unfortunately, Rex was still on the car, his fingers and toes sticking to the hood as if he was Spider-Man®, his single laser still burning its way through the windshield.

"No way," Ashley said with disbelief, just as Rex reached his hand through the hot plastic and into the car's interior.

"Jesus fuckin' Christ!" McCready said. "Pulse him, N.J.!"

As Rex's seared hand was about to grab Ashley, there was a sudden look of surprise on his bloodied face, as an electromagnetic pulse coursed outwards from the car. Rex instantly lost his magnetic grip, and began to rapidly plummet to the alleyway below.

Ashley tilted her head upwards–or downwards, in this case–and through the Polaris'™ clear roof, she watched Rex brutally smash down onto the unyielding concrete. "I think you just killed him," she said, feeling more than slightly sick to her stomach, as McCready rolled the car back into its normal position.

"Nope," he said, pointing his finger to the lower-right quadrant of the rear-view screen, which currently showed Rex standing up in a staggery manner.

"What *is* that thing?" Ashley asked, glancing her eyes from the screen, to the windshield, to the blood-smeared window.

"A Rex," McCready replied, manually flying the car away from the Tiger's Lair at a moderate speed. "Reconnaissance Escort–Xi series. Tough little fuckers."

"Shyeah," she agreed, touching her fingers around the windshield's melted hole, which had been sufficiently cooled by the rain that was now coming down in much thicker droplets. "I'll say."

"Watch your fingers," McCready said. He waited for her to pull her hand back, then pressed a button on the dash, causing the damaged windshield to drop down into the hood.

Watching a new, undamaged windshield emerge from the hood to fill the empty space, Ashley said, "So what the hell is going on, McCready? Was that really the government, or was that the Presence posing as the government?"

"The Presence?" he asked confusedly. "What are you talking about? God?"

"No," she said, realizing that McCready had no clue about the Presence's existence. "I'm talking about the thing that's attacking my family. Was that just part of its plan or was that really the government?"

"I don't know," McCready said. "But I'm gonna find out. N.J., connect me to-"

"Marc," the cartoon Marilyn interrupted, as she held up a bright, yellow caution sign. "I detect a rapidly approaching vehicle from behind. Would you-"

"Fuck," he said, immediately stepping on the accelerator, and jumping the vehicle's speed to well over eighty miles per hour. "Here we go again. How about some theme music, N.J.?"

"Any requests?" the car asked.

"Rock 'n' roll, baby," he replied.

"737 comin' outta the sky!" growled the singer's gravelly voice through the car's speakers, as McCready quickly dropped the vehicle's altitude, and narrowly flew between two buildings.

Ashley looked back to catch a glimpse of the pursuing vehicle, but all she could see were its two HID lamps, blindingly shining themselves at the Chevy®–that is, until the red and blue sirens began to flash atop its hood. "It's the government again," she said over the loud music.

"Or the terrorists," he countered, deftly maneuvering the Polaris™ through the airborne traffic. "We still don't know which."

"So how are we gonna find out?"

Dropping down into a tunnel meant only for gravity-bound vehicles, he said, "I'm still workin' on that one."

The governmental vehicle–which she could now see was some type of Ford®–followed them into the tunnel, and both cars began to narrowly pass over the traffic below.

"Marc," Marilyn said, pulling out and pushing in some cables from an old-fashioned switchboard. "The driver of the vehicle is attempting to open a line of communication. Should I answer?"

"No," McCready said, increasing his speed further and causing an annoyingly-big knot to form in Ashley's stomach. "It's too risky–that might be their way of infecting our systems. I'm just gonna have to ditch 'em for now."

"McCready..." Ashley said uneasily, bracing herself against the back of the seat with the vehicle's increasing speed.

"N.J.," he said, as they neared the end of the tunnel, "prepare the afterburners for firing."

"Afterburners?" she quietly said to herself. "...shit."

As they reached the end of the tunnel, and entered into an open-spaced area which separating them from the next tunnel, McCready said, "Hold on." He then released his foot from the accelerator, pulled back hard on his gravity-lever, quickly spun the car around 180 degrees, and shouted, "Fire, N.J.!"

Just as their backwards momentum was about to send them careening into the gigantic, glass sculpture which sat atop the next tunnel, the rear jets kicked in, and immediately propelled them up and into the opposite direction, straight towards a glimmering skyscraper.

"Kill the jets!" he shouted, spinning the wheel all the way to his left, and somehow managing to barely miss the wide structure.

Emerging from the side of the building unscathed, they suddenly found themselves in the middle of oncoming airborne traffic. "Oh, Goddess," Ashley said, closing her eyes as a GS Winnebago® headed directly towards them. Feeling no impact, she reopened her eyes, but was not all relieved to see more vehicles coming at them.

Darting in and out, above and below, McCready finally maneuvered the swiftly decelerating Polaris™ to a safe, cruising level. "Motherfucker," he said, touching the car's tires down onto the road with a loud screech, and switching it to its gravity-bound propulsion system. He wiped his brow with his sleeve. "I need to think for a minute... N.J., activate cloaking field."

The cartoon Marilyn clicked open a Star Trek® communicator, and transported herself into the cockpit of a spaceship. "Cloaking field activated," she confirmed, as the spacecraft turned invisible.

Running her fingers through the top of her hair, Ashley said, "I think you just melted the world's largest Chihuly sculpture."

"That's not what I fuckin' need to hear right now," McCready said in an agitated tone. Shaking his head, he added, "Man, those better have been terrorists, or I am in *deep* shit."

As McCready pulled into a near-empty parking lot on the outskirts of downtown, the falling rain became a downpour, and Ashley said, "Don't worry, McCready. If you get in any kind of trouble, my dad'll find a way to get you out of it. Believe me–I know from experience."

"Yeah, we'll see," he said, as the car came to a rest. "N.J.,
kill the music please."

Marilyn, now playing lead guitar at a crowded concert, raised
her instrument over her head, and smashed it down onto the stage.
"Music deactived," she said, as the rock-and-roll ceased.

McCready gave Ashley a look of concern, and said, "Release
seatbelts."

"Seatbelts released," the car confirmed, retracting its straps.

"Oh, no," McCready said, quickly reaching over to Ashley's
side of the car and manually opening her door. "Get out!"

"What?" she asked.

"Now!!" he said, pushing her out onto the wet concrete, and
immediately scrambling out the same door after her.

As they stood to their feet in the pouring rain, Ashley
brushed herself off and asked, "What did you do that for?"

"Her system's been corrupted" McCready said, taking a
careful hold of Ashley's hand and backing away from the car. "I
turned off the vocal confirmation yester-" He stopped mid-sentence,
as the car began to quickly rise up into the air. Contnuing to move
away from the spot N.J. was parked at, he said, "I think the
terrorists just made their next move."

Through the heavy rain, she watched the Polaris™ rise
higher and higher into the air, and said, "Wow, I don't think
it's gonna stop. It looks like–oh, wait–I think it's coming back
down. Fast." Her and McCready turned, began to run, and didn't stop
until they heard the deafening impact of the Chevy® crashing into
the ground and exploding behind them.

Turning to face the flaming wreckage, a look of gloom came
across McCready's rainsoaked face, and he dejectedly said, "N.J...."
He touched his wristcom, and asked, "N.J.?"

But there was no answer on the other line.

McCready said nothing further, and simply stared ahead,
the bright, orange flames flickering across the wet, black lenses of his
Obsidians™.

Seconds later, the Ford® came speeding into the parking lot,
accompanied by another Polaris™ and four SPD squad cars. The
vehicles surrounded them in a circle, landed, and then their occupants
all swiftly emptied out, their weapons drawn and pointed towards
Ashley and McCready.

"Stay where you are, Agent McCready," said the driver of
the Ford®–the same, older man who had been leading the sextet

inside the club. "You too, Ms. Huxton."

The Asian woman, who Ashley also recognized from the club, said, "McCready, I hope you have a good explanation for all this."

McCready let out a deadened laugh, and under his breath he said, "Yeah, Jung. Me too."

Approaching them, the older man, whose hair was graying at the temples, clicked open a one-handed umbrella, pulled out his badge and said, "I'm Agent Carter Stone of the DCC–I'm gonna need you both to come down to the station with us."

Her entire body soaking wet, Ashley wrapped her arms around herself, and looked at McCready. Shivering slightly from the cold, she offered an unsure smile, and said, "I think it's safe to say these aren't the terrorists."

$$\infty$$

Δ

Chapter 11:
Anamnesis

Others were like black holes, allowing no light to escape
their pull, and choosing to forever exist in a perpetual, vacuous
void of darkness.
Or did they?
When encountering a black hole, one could not say for sure, for one
knew not the mysteries contained within them.

The six of them entered into the loud, hologram-filled auditorium of
the Tiger's Lair, which was packed nearly as tight as Essence in her
body suit. Ignacio looked down at his wristcom, and said, "Ey, I'm not
seein' a Ray Davis on this anymore. You sure he's still in here?"

The older REX glanced back at Ignacio, and in a voice that
could only be produced with inhuman vocal chords, he replied, "He's
not. Ray Davis is gone." Returning his gaze forward, he added, "But
the man we seek is still here."

"Come again?" Essence asked.

"He's changed identities," said Carter Stone, his eyes
surveying the area like a famished hawk. "It's still the same perp,
but he's fooling the biochip system."

"If he's able to do that, it's no wonder you've had so much
trouble catching up with him," Jung commented. "He might as well
be invisible."

"Invisible or not," said the younger, fiercer-looking REX,
forcefully exhaling a spray of moisture from his nostrils, "he still
has a scent."

FREQUENCIES

Pointing his wet snout up towards the ceiling, the older REX swayed his head back and forth, sniffed the air a few times, and said, "I think I have something, Agent Stone."

"Yes?" eagerly asked the DCC agent.

"I detect a smell that matches the olfactory information you downloaded into me," said the REX. "It must be him."

A smile appeared across Carter's clean-shaven face. "Good."

"I smell him too," said the younger REX, his nostrils flaring in timed pulses. Taking the lead, he said, "This way."

As they followed the REX to the left-hand side of the crowded auditorium, Ignacio was approached by a couple of twentysomething frat boys, their eyes watery and bloodshot, their bodies rapidly shaking, both obviously as amped as a transistor.

"Hey, man," one of them said, tugging on the sleeve of Ignacio's leather jacket. "Are you a freeker? Hunh?" He laughed maniacally, his frees sporadically spiking back and forth from gamma to alpha. "You freekin' too?"

Ignacio glanced down at the spot on his sleeve where the man had touched it, saw an oily, viscous residue that had been left behind, and angrily looked up at the wannabe freeker. The next instant, quicker than than the eye could see, Ignacio backhanded the rich punk with a closed fist, then slammed the same hand into the other side of his drugged-out head.

A stunned look of incomprehensibility passed across the frat boy's face. His knees buckled, and he began to stagger around like a crippled drunk, the amp being the only thing keeping him up on his feet.

Wiping his sleeve onto his pants, Ignacio rejoined the others. "Wildlife troubles?" Jung asked.

Ignacio rubbed his knuckles. "Not anymore."

"I've found him," announced the lead REX, as they reached a less-crowded area of the club, located near its northern wall. "There. Cheng-tao Bankei," he said, pointing ahead to an Asian man garbed in a simple robe, who was currently speaking with an attractive white girl, "is Ray Davis."

"Wasn't Ray supposed to be black?" Essence asked.

"Ray is," Carter said, "but Cheng isn't. His appearance changes with his identity."

Essence stared at Bankei. "Holograms? Then why aren't I sensing any?"

"Because that's the level of technology we're dealing with,"

210

Carter said. Still looking ahead, he began moving forward, and said, "Damn. He just noticed us. Freemon Ignacio, T-REX–you two are the quickest–cover Bankei when he tries to make his break."

"I'll make sure he doesn't get far," said the younger REX.

"Freemon Sommers," Carter continued, as they all began to walk forward. "Take the lead–attack on my cue."

Essence moved to the front of the group.

"D-REX–you're on the woman he's talking to–make sure she doesn't escape. We need to find out if she's really Ashley Huxton."

As Bankei's image started to flicker, Essence raised her hand, and Carter said, "Freemon Kwong, stay with me. We're probably going to have to deal with the Ordocops™ to our right–they've already noticed us and they're moving in." He reached towards his belt, and said, "Sommers, get read–"

Before Carter could give the word, Bankei suddenly bent the light around himself and turned invisible.

"Follow me!" T-REX shouted, taking off in a flash of hyperspeed, heading in a southeasterly direction.

Ignacio immediately followed,
the
world
slowed
down,
and as he started to snake his way through the mannequin-like crowd, he said into his wristcom, "Activate aural IR." Without disrupting his normal vision, a colorful aura appeared around every person or object which transmitted infrared radiation. He could now see Bankei as an animated, reddish-orange, humanoid outline, which was just shooting through one of the auditorium's emergency exits.

T-REX jammed through the opened door after the invisible quarry, and Ignacio did the same. They spilled out into a wide alleyway, rapidly ran its length, and then the three of them started to zip their way through the busy city streets.

The cars, while moving noticeably faster than the people, were still fairly slow in comparison to their hyperspeed, and it didn't take much effort to avoid contact with them–just a whole helluva lot of concentration. Because all it took was one slip-up, one lapse out of hyperspeed, and the world would instantly be returned to normal. And Ignacio would instantly be turned to roadkill.

Erratically dodging back and forth between same-way and oncoming traffic, Bankei was making the chase as tough as possible.

FREQUENCIES

Whenever it seemed like Ignacio or T-REX were about to catch him, Bankei would throw some wild juke worthy of an ESPN® highlight, and quickly regain his lead. But, as they turned on to the freeway-like Madison Avenue, Bankei started to run out of gas–which was a godsend for Ignacio, since he was already running on empty himself.

The REX on the other hand, showed no signs of hydrocarbon shortage, and was swiftly gaining on the see-through silhouette.

Bankei overtook a monstrous semi, made a sharp turn in front of it, and T-REX followed.

Pushing himself to his limit, Ignacio also rounded the semi, and as he did, he was surprised to see the REX being crushed underneath the truck's massive frame–evidently the victim of some type of speed-slowing attack.

Moving off the busy thoroughfare and onto a sidestreet, Bankei reached his limit, and slowed down to a near-normal speed.

Ignacio felt like he was about to hyperventilate, and desperately wanted to slow up also. But he realized if he did that, he'd lose Bankei for good–so he kept his concentration as focused as a laser's beam, and zeroed in on his target like a living smart bomb.

The next instant, he exploded into Bankei, sending them both crashing down to the sidewalk, where they tumbled along its unyielding surface until they reached the entrance to an alley, and slammed into the side of a building with a painful thud. Luckily for Ignacio, Bankei took the brunt of the structure's impact.

Gasping for air as a misty rain began to fall, Ignacio rolled over on top of the transparent outline that was Bankei, pinned him down by his throat, and began to reach for his disruptor.

As he was detaching the device from his belt, the red-orange aura suddenly filled in again. But it wasn't Bankei this time, it was Ignacio himself–albeit about twenty years younger with a holographic symbol painted in bright-red onto his forehead.

$$\delta$$

"Lo siento," his younger self said, his eyes full of sadness.

A feeling of déja vu passed over Ignacio, and he found himself releasing his grip on his likeness, unable to look away from the symbol.

FREQUENCIES

δ

"If you're hearing me right now," his younger self continued in Spanish, "then it means you're about to capture one of us, and we've been left no other choice but to awaken you."

"No..." Ignacio whispered, his mind trying its best to avoid the veracity of his own words. "No."

"Please try to relax," he soothingly said to himself, gentle waves of energy emitting forth from the symbol, "and take a deep breath. You're about to learn the truth."

His self uttered the wordsounds,

The symbol became brighter; losing its color, becoming all colors.

Then a flash of white light, and

there was con

fu

FREQUENCIES

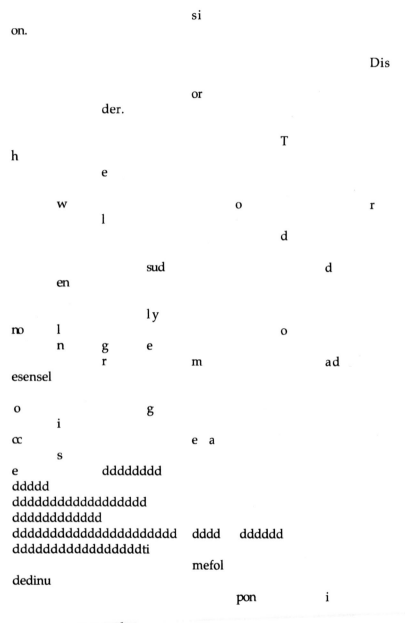

si

on.

Dis

or

der.

T

h

e

w   o   r

l

d

sud   d

en

ly

no   l   o

n   g   e

r   m   ad

esensel

o   g

i

oc   e   a

s

e   dddddddd
ddddd
dddddddddddddddddddd
ddddddddddddd
ddddddddddddddddddddddd   dddd   dddddd
dddddddddddddddddddti

mefol

dedinu

pon   i

tsel

FREQUENCIES

fandmemoryslowlyreturned,

andtheloss
of forgetfullness
commenced.

And Ignacio began to remember...

In a darkened room–a basement, maybe–with rubble, dust, and
cobwebs all about–somewhere in Seattle.

Too large for a basement, actually.

In a darkened room–crushed brick and mortar strewn about, an
antiquated smell of mustiness and dust in the air, archaic spiderwebs
and aged patches of moss hanging from every corner and
crevice–somewhere underneath downtown Seattle.

The old underground, amongst the earthquaked ruins.

A chiselled, fortysomething, African-American man sits
across from him at a dilapidated, wooden table. The man's face,
while handsome, reveals much wear and tear.

Wellor.

Adrion Wellor is his name. He asks a twenty-two year old
Ignacio, "You do realize what you'll be sacrificing by doing this,
don't you?"

"Sí," Ignacio replies with a nod. "Myself."

"Yourself," Wellor says. "Yes." Elbows resting on the dusty
table, he leans forward and says, "You will *completely* lose the
essence of who you are now. The person inside you who wants to see
change, who wants to see revolution–will be gone forever. And he will
be replaced by a man who wants nothing more than to uphold the
system and maintain the status quo." Wellor wets his lips, and
continues, "You will become someone you despise. Someone you loathe.
Possibly even hate–because you will take advantage of the weak and
you will protect the strong. Laws will mean more to you than morals.
Order will be more important than freedom. You will arrest people
because of their thoughts. You will be violent. And most
assuredly–you will be responsible for the deaths of innocents."

Wellor looks deeply into Ignacio's eyes, and states, "You will
become the gestapo." His jaws clench, his nostrils flare, and he
breathes in. "Now, Morris Ignacio, I ask you again–is this what you
want? Is this movement so important to you that you would sacrifice
your own self?"

FREQUENCIES

Ignacio's stomach feels queasy. Nervous. Uneasy. Then he thinks of his cousin, Ernesto, and his friend, Andre. In workcamps for their thoughts. It shouldn't be like this, he knows. But it will take great sacrifices to change it.

"Well?" Wellor asks.

Becoming the beast to fight the beast. Nobility through ignobility. The one sacrificing for the many.

"Does it mean that much to you?"

Self-sacrifice. He thinks of Jesus on the cross. The rest of his life, for a better, more just future. He sees children laughing. People living free. The light of God shining down on all. The fear and loathing pass through him, hope and strength enter in. His stomach settles, he nods his head, and answers, "It does."

God's light shines down upon him.

A flash of white light again.

Ignacio found himself on his hands and knees in an alleyway, staring down at his partial reflection in a small pool of water created by the falling rain. Why was he here? Why did he look so old? Was that rain running down his face? Or tears?

Water everywhere. And white light.

A walkway on the water, cedar chips underfoot. Leaning against a wooden railing, trees behind him, Lake Washington in front. The University of Washington. The arboretum's waterfront trail. Dawn.

Someone standing next to him. A fellow U-dub student. The one who introduced him to Wellor. He's talking to Ignacio right now.

"Un momentito, Griffin," Ignacio interrupts, as he watches a few kayakers in the distance. "Hold up. If I'm never gonna be in contact with any of you *ever* again..." He looks at Griffin. "Then how am I supposed to get you the surveillance information you need? What good is a sleeper if he doesn't report back?"

Griffin smiles. "That's what's so fucking brilliant about this, Ignacio," he says in his native English accent. "You don't have to." He waits for a jogger to pass, double-checks his white-noise generator, and says, "We'll be able to remote-view the information via your signature pattern, while you're sleeping. Without you ever knowing that we're doing it."

Ignacio gives him a look of disbelief. "You're sayin' that

you're gonna be inside my head?"

"Yes. But only while you're dreaming."

"Why not when I'm awake?"

"Because your frequential state of consciousness is too jumbled then," Griffin says. "There's too much interference–too much stimuli. The signature pattern becomes nearly impossible to lock onto, let alone decipher." The floating walkway gently bobs up and down a few times, as a large boat passes by. "We have to wait until you've achieved dreamstate," he continues, "when your frequencies become relaxed and focused, and your SP emerges clearly. Then we can lock on to the pattern, enter your consciousness, and obtain the data from that day."

Ignacio laughs. "Privacy isn't one of the pluses of this assignment, ey?"

"Unfortunately, no," Griffin says. "Each time that we tap into your SP, we'll see what you saw, feel what you felt, and think what you thought. Your life will become like an open book."

There is nothing but the sounds of lapping waves, distant boats, and waterfowl. The word sacrifice won't leave Ignacio's mind. The sun beginning to glow brighter, he asks, "So when does all this begin?"

"As soon as we finish the frequential testing."

"How long's that gonna be, Griffin?" Ignacio says. "It feels like this is takin' forever."

"I'm sure it must, Ignacio, and I apologize. But it'll take a few more weeks of testing in order to precisely get your signature pattern down. It's a lengthy and complicated process."

"I know it is," Ignacio says, "but...when you make a decision like this, you just want it to begin. You don't want to have to keep thinkin' about it. You'll start second guessing yourself, and I don't want to do that. I want to be sure of this." He stares off into the morning sky and exhales a deep breath. Shaking his head, he says, "This better not be for nothing, Griffin. That's all I'm saying."

"It won't be, my friend," Griffin says, placing his hand on Ignacio's shoulder. "You have my word."

Ignacio briefly looks into the bright, rising sun and squints his eyes.

White light.

A car drove by. It was raining. Ignacio was in an alley,

FREQUENCIES

huddled near a dumpster, violently vomiting onto the wet pavement. The alley seemed familiar, as if he'd been there before in a dream.

A flash of lightning.

A flash of white light.

In the basement again. The city's basement, weeks later. He and Wellor are not alone this time. Other people–fellow revolutionaries–are in the room also. A few are focusing their attention on him, most are engaged in other activities.

As Wellor removes an electrode-laden device from off of his head, Ignacio blinks his eyes hard, sits up in the recliner, and asks, "Is that it? I didn't feel anything."

Wellor smiles, places the device onto a monitor, and says, "Good." The monitor's screen is filled with colorful, frequential animation–pulses, waves, spikes, vibrations, oscillations. "You're not supposed to."

"I-" Ignacio looks around. Different faces than when he was placed under hypnosis. Jesse still there, but not Griffin. Or Jason. "How long have I been out?"

Jesse runs a scanner over him, glances at its display, and replies, "About twenty hours."

"Say what?" Ignacio asks.

She sets down the scanner. "Twenty hours," she repeats, walking over to him and touching his cool forehead with her warm hand.

"But I don't feel like any time passed," he says, as she places her fingers on the underside of his wrist, closes her eyes, and gently applies some pressure. "I remember closing my eyes, you saying some things...and that's it. I don't remember anything else. No dreams, no images, no waking... Nada."

Her eyes still closed, her fingers moving back and forth along various pressure points on his head and forearm, Jesse nods, and says, "That's normal for this kind of frequential hypnotism. It acts like a spiritual anesthetic."

"Your true essence was temporarily submerged," Wellor says, "so that the new essence could enter in to you. Thus, you–the *true* you, the one I'm speaking to now–has no memory whatsoever of the consciousness transfer. You could say that you were away while it happened..." He rubs his finger along a purplish energy pulse upon the monitor's screen. "Deep within the realm of your subconscious."

FREQUENCIES

Jesse continues to rub his pressure points. Ignacio feels waves of energy rush over him. "Que bueno," he whispers, closing his eyes. "So where is the new me?"

"It has retreated to your subconscious, just as your true self has emerged forth," Wellor says. "And there it will stay, until next you sleep."

"Then?" Ignacio asks, seeing bluish-purple colors in his mind's eye, harmoniously corresponding with Jesse's fingertips.

"Tomorrow you will wake," Wellor says, "and you will be a new man. You will have absolutely no interest in subversive activities, and you will find yourself with an undeniable calling to pursue a career with the FBI. You will have no recollection of ever encountering any of us, and this chapter of your life shall fade from your mind completely." He paused. "Like a dream that never existed."

A flash of white light.

A flash of lightning.

Leaning against a wall, Ignacio slid himself up to his feet. There was soggy vomit near his shoes, and his stomach muscles were sore. His throat burned, and his mouth felt acidic.

He was crying, it was raining, and he wanted to go home. But he couldn't remember where home was, and there was this overwhelmingly bright light suddenly emanating from within his mind.

The basement. Hours later.

Jesse stands in front of him, a thin paintbrush in her hand. "Almost done," she says, then leans forward, her sandy-blonde tresses swaying softly with her motion, and adds a few, final strokes onto his forehead. The holographic paint feels cool. Soothing.

"There," she says, removing the brush from his forehead. She stares at him. Her eyes squint. "Perfect." She sets down the brush and hands him a mirror. "Have a look."

Ignacio looks into the mirror. A bright, red, 3-D symbol painted on to his forehead.

δ

FREQUENCIES

"Arabic?" he asks, shifting in his chair.

"No," she answers. "Greek. It's a delta."

He smiles. "Delta. Sleeper. I get it." Still examining the symbol in the mirror, he says, "Isn't this supposed to be shaped like a triangle?"

"Only if it were an upper-case delta," she says, setting up some kind of camera-like device in front of him. "That's lower-case."

"Why not the triangle?"

"It's too linear and shallow. The dimensions aren't right." She adjusts a knob around the camera's lens. "Memetic triggers work best when they're housed within curves and circles," she says, peering into a viewer. "Which is exactly what the lower-case design provides."

Ignacio watches her tinker some more with the camera-device, then says, "So, Jesse–if we end up needing to use this..." He looks at himself and the symbol in the mirror again.

$$\delta$$

"What's gonna happen to me?"

Jesse stares at him for a second, saying nothing. Then she says, "First of all, Morris, the possibility that you'll actually capture another one of our agents is-"

"Jesse," he interrupts, setting the mirror down. "Just tell me."

Her bottom lip wraps around her lower teeth, she bites down lightly, and nods her head. "Okay." She walks over, kneels down beside him, warmly places her hand on his, and says, "If awakened, your true essence is going to emerge forth from within your subconscious, and then it's going to begin to merge together with the implanted essence. They'll continue to combine until both essences' memories are fully integrated, then..." She pauses. "Then the old essence reasserts itself. You'll once again remember the entirety of your life, know all of your implanted essence's memories–but now you'll feel like your true self again. You'll be who you are now–with additional memories."

Ignacio thumbs his mustache, and says, "Then I won't be who I am now. Memories make you who you are. I'm gonna be different."

"Well, yes," Jesse says, "of course. But your essence will be the same as it is now."

He looks away from her, and uneasily says to himself, "It's

220

gonna be a miracle if I manage to stay sane through all this."

She rubs the top of his hand with her thumb. "You will, Morris. You'll make it through. I promise." She grasps his hand firmly and hugs him. "Trust me. You will." She slowly releases her embrace, then walks back to the camera. "Don't forget–in all likelihood, this is never going to happen. This is just a precaution. The whole point of our sleeper system is to allow you to experience a normal life. And needless to say..." She smiles compassionately. "Awakening you would really mess that up."

Ignacio smiles, as he looks at the sincerity in his compatriot's face, and says, "I'm gonna miss you, Jess." He looks over various parts of the gigantic room, at all of the others, realizing that these are some of his last moments being around them. "I'm gonna miss all of you."

Jesse laughs uncomfortably. "C'mon, Morris," she says, her voice slightly strained, "I'm trying to get through this without crying."

He laughs, touching the corner of his eye. "Yo se. Pero...I just wanted to let you know."

She swallows hard. "I'm going to miss you too, Morris. We all are." Clearing her throat, she says, "Alright. Now...look at the lens, and imagine you've come face to face with your awakened self. You're confused, disoriented, and you're looking for answers." Jesse looks into the viewer. "What do you tell yourself?"

Ignacio stares into the lens, and imagines the situation. "Lo siento," he says, tears still present in his eyes. "If you're hearing me right now..."

A flash of white lightning.

White light. Still there. Not flashing, but a subtle ebb and flow of informational luminescence.

Back in the ((chase.bankei)) alley. Back? Was he here ((yes)) before?

Head up at the ((wednesday.night)) night sky, droplets of rain ((seeing himself.delta.remembering)) splashing off his face. Slapping at his face. Someone slapping at his face.

"Mo!" she shouted, one ((morris)) of her hands holding him up by the collar, the other ((FBI)) grasping his face at the cheekbones. Shaking him, she made ((freereads)) eye contact and asked, "What the hell's wrong with you?"

FREQUENCIES

It looked like the woman ((she.didn't)) had no pupils. He focused his eyes. He knew ((freemon)) her. From where?

"Ignacio!" she shouted ((essence)) louder, shaking him ((morris.ignacio)) harder. "What happened?"

Too much information, his brain awash in a sea of frequential data.

"What happened?" he repeated after her. Home. He knew he had ((irena.children)) to get home.

Information overload.

"Carter," she says into ((dcc.terrorists)) a wristcom. "Ignacio's alive but incoherent. His frees look ((wellor.training)) funny and his eyes are starting to roll up into his..."

Systems crash.

Fade to black.

<<irena.children>>
        <start.>
<<irena.children>>
        <received.>
<<irena.children>>
        <today.>
        <breakfast.
        carter stone?irena asks.is he new?

        no,ignacio says,placing some beans, chorizo, and eggs into a warm tortilla.he's one of the dcc guys i was telling you about yesterday.one of the bureau's big boys.he sprinkles some fresh cilantro onto the burrito filling.he'll be heading the riot investigation.

        so they're sure it's terrorism?irena asks.

        looks that way,ignacio says,wrapping the tortilla into a burrito.

        terrorism,irena says.she takes a bite of hash browns.i hope it's not that.my mother told me some horrific stories about the terror years.

        he dabs some hot sauce onto the top of the burrito.it's never gonna get that bad again,irena.we've got too much control now,he says.we can nip any insurrection while it's still a bud.he bites into the burrito.all this'll blow over before you know it.

        irena picks at her food.she asks,when was the last time the bureau sent a dcc agent to work with you?

FREQUENCIES
he thinks for a moment.never,he replies.>

"Never," he said ((ignacio)) groggily.

"Ignacio?" she ((essence)) asked. "You up now?"

It took a considerable amount of effort for him to open his eyes. He was in the backseat ((freemon.polaris)) of a car. She was looking ((beautiful)) back at him from ((beautiful?)) the driver's seat.

"We're heading back to HQ to meet ((beacon.hill)) up with Carter and((dcc.terrorists)) Kwong," she said. "We're gonna ((jung-ran)) run some tests on you to see ((frequential)) what happened. Are you getting this?"

The sea of information, rolling over him.

"Sea," he ((memory.integration)) muttered.

"Good," she said. "'Cause they also nabbed your boy McCready while ((marc.trustworthy.friend)) they were chas-" She stopped.

Drowning in information.

"Aw, shit, Mo," she said. "C'mon!"

Submerged. Sinking.

Dark.

<<dcc.terrorists>>
       <start.>
<<dcc.terrorists>>
       <received.>
<<dcc.terrorists>>
       <today.>
       <headquarters.

how reliable is this informant?ignacio asks the female dcc agent.

very,janet vegas responds.if he says davis is going to be at the tiger's lair tonight,then that's where he's going to be.

and you really think wellor is behind all this?ignacio asks, taking a sip of coffee from his black mug.after all these years?

carter solemnly looks at ignacio,and says,we don't think he's behind it,freemon ignacio.we know.

ignacio moves over to the room's window, and gazes at the busy city outside.i still think we're jumping to conclusions here, carter,

FREQUENCIES

he says.even with all the evidence you say you have.

neither of the dcc agents say a word.

watching the vehicular traffic fly by,ignacio says,we're ignoring possibilities.how are we supposed to even fully understand this case if we're not looking into all the possibilities?he turns from the window,and faces them.

vegas asks,you're still bothered by the policemen issue?

of course,ignacio replies.don't you find it strange that your superiors have extradited all three of them back to dc?and denied us access to their frequential records?he laughs.c'mon, these are the cops who set the riots off in the first place–they're the first ones we should be talking to.

ignacio,carter says, cutting the air with his hand.relax.we've got everything under control.>

His arm ((ignacio)) was placed around her ((essence)) shoulder, and he was being dragged through ((freemon.hq)) a well-lit hallway.

"We're almost there," she said ((frequential.testing)) to him.

"Terrorism," he ((dcc.riots.propaganda)) mumbled. "Control."

"What?" Continuing to ((dcc.lies)) move him forward, she said, "Damn, Mo, they fucked ((himself.underground)) you up good."

His head dropped ((wellor.training)) forward and down.

Consciousness retreated.

<<wellor.training>>
      <start.>
<<wellor.training>>
      <received.>
      <an image in his mind's eye.
      a bright,green electromagnetic pulse.
      pulsing.soothing.speaking.
      wellor's voice.
      think before you speak,it says(wordswithinwordscompresseddata).be calm.control your frequencies.allow memories to integrate.will help asap.sleep.make peace with old life.prepare for new.remove biochip/freeread.find safe haven.wait for contact.>

FREQUENCIES

Ignacio realized that his eyes were open. They felt dry. He felt tired. He ((memory.integration)) blinked. Slowly.

Very slowly. He was lying on his ((hq.medical.ward)) back, and there were others in the room with him.

"Everything seems normal," the man in ((freemon.doctor)) the white coat said, lowering a scanner. "I think he's okay now."

"So what happened to him?" she ((essence)) asked.

"My ((richardson)) guess is that he got hit with some kind of synaptic disruptor. One that ((memetic.trigger)) wasn't very powerful either, because his frees have already attained normality."

"You don't think it might have been something worse?" Essence asked. "Like ((compressed.information)) an infobomb? His frees were buggin' ((delta)) about twenty minutes ago."

Richardson looked at a large ((frequential.images)) monitor, and said, "I noticed that, but..." He continued to stare at it. "It's just not the right pattern ((rapid.oscillations)) for an infobomb. And I'm not seeing any residual traces. I think that was just his mind's response to being ((true.self.emergence)) synaptically disrupted."

"He must'a been having some fucked-up dreams then."

Richardson laughs. "Probably." Turning his gaze to Ignacio, he asks, "Were you?"

Ignacio said ((yes)) nothing, but smiled slightly.

Essence looked at Ignacio. "Is he up?"

"He can hear us now," Wilson said. "But he's going to need a lot more sleep before he's fully ((almost.integrated)) cognizant."

"How long's this gonna keep him out of action?"

"At least until ((next.awakening)) the end of the week. We'll have someone notify his wife that ((irena)) we'll be keeping him here overnight. That way, we can run some more tests ((frequential)) on him in the morning, after he's had some rest." Richardson moved across the room towards Ignacio, a small, metallic device in ((sleepscan)) his hand. "For now though," he said, setting the device onto Ignacio's forehead, "he needs ((final.integration)) to sleep."

Ignacio felt it stick to his ((magnetic adhesion)) forehead. It began to emit soothing ((frequential.sleep.induction)) undulations of ((electromagnetic)) energy.

His eyes started to feel heavy. He closed them. Slowly. Ignacio fell asleep.

<<final.integration>>

225

FREQUENCIES

<start.>
<<final.integration>>
<received.>
<<final.integration>>
<in.progress.>

$$\Delta / \delta$$

α

Chapter 12:
<u>Checkmate</u>

Other celestial bodies, however, were less of an enigma. Like stars or suns, they shined for all to see, their intentions as clear as day. They announced their presence to the world unabashedly, and showed all who gazed upon them their power and glory. These radiant displays allowed them extraordinary pull, and other masses gravitated towards them in great numbers.
And while this sometimes had the effect of drawing unwanted objects and bodies into their orbit, it rarely, if ever, posed a threat to their existence. For, the starlights were a force to be reckoned with, and only a select, few, cosmic entities could challenge their strength."

Inside Xanadeux's subterranean nerve center, Mason sat comfortably in the contoured chair, looking up at the gargantuan uniview screen that stood before him.

On the screen was a beautiful Tibetan woman, dressed in a long, thin, orange cloth which had been carefully and delicately wrapped around her body. She was sitting in a lush, tropical garden, filled with flora and fauna from around the world. Visible in the distance behind her, were the jagged, snow-capped peaks of the southern Himilayas. Stroking an ocelot which was lying next to her, she asked, "Are you sure you don't want to leave a message for him?"

"Yes, Lhasa," he said. "I'm just checking–*again*–to make sure he hasn't been attacked."

She smiled and said, "No attacks, Mason. Gonpo is just busy. But he'll appreciate the concern."

"I doubt it," Mason said.

"You know how your father gets when a project comes to fruition," Lhasa said, as a toucan flew onto the branch of an African mahogany tree behind her. "He can't think of anything else."

"Yes, but it would be rather nice–not to mention courteous–if he at least took the time to check in with his family when they're experiencing a crisis."

"He thinks you can handle it on your own, or else he-"

"Yes, yes," Mason interrupted. "I saw the message. But a call? A simple call? Is that too much to ask?"

Lhasa smiled. "Well..."

Mason shook his head. "I know. Don't answer. I'll see you Friday, Lhasa."

"Friday," she said. "Take care." The screen transformed into the Ordosoft™ logo.

Mason swivelled in his chair to face Xanadeux, who was standing right behind him. "That man absolutely confounds me sometimes, Xanadeux," he said.

"Your father *is* a difficult man to get a hold of, sir," the android agreed. "But judging from the message, this project's results will be well worth the lack of correspondence."

"Yes, but one would think..." Mason began. "Bah. What one would think rarely applies to my father."

"Rarely," said Xanadeux.

"Well," he said, swivelling back around in his chair to face the giant screen, "enough time on that matter. There's work to be done. Xanadeux, please connect me with Mr. Webber."

"Certainly," said the AI.

The Ordosoft™ logo morphed into the face of Mr. Webber, who was standing in a brightly-lit laboratory. A few doctors and scientists were in the room with him. All were dressed in black. "Good evening, sir," he said, smiling his ferocious smile. "Good news."

"You've made a breakthrough?" Mason asked.

"More," Webber said. "Nature of attack has been determined." Behind him, a bruised, male body was lying on an operating table. The body was completely nude, save for a thin, black veil which covered its face. "Carrier identified."

Mason leaned forward. "I'm impressed, Mr. Webber. Please continue."

Mr. Webber nodded, and began to walk towards the body, whose head was being attended to by two of the masked scientists.

FREQUENCIES

The camera's POV then switched perspectives. Rather than seeing from behind Webber, Mason was now seeing directly through the head of security's cybernetic eyes. "Extensive interrogation revealed Benjamin knew nothing," Webber said, looking over the entire length of the badly mutilated body. Missing toes, contused skin, numerous bite marks, damaged genitalia, broken fingers–it was a horrible sight.

Mason cringed in his chair.

Webber's gaze passed over the body's veiled face, and stopped at the top of its head. The body's brain was exposed, and was brightly glistening under the lab's abundant lighting. Scores of extremely thin, fiber optic tubes had been inserted into it. "Technocyte deployment and subsequent brain examination revealed him to be the carrier," Webber said.

"Then he...he didn't know he had been infected?"

"Correct," Webber said, as one of the scientists pulled one of the long tubes from out of the wet organ. "Infobomb uploaded itself without subject's knowledge."

"I see," Mason said, momentarily turning his eyes away from the screen. "Were you able to gather any evidence from his augmentations?"

"Negative," he replied. "Infobomb wasn't carried within subject's augmentations."

A look of puzzlement crossed Mason's face. "Pardon?"

"Infobomb was housed within subject's brain cells."

"What?" Mason asked.

"Interesting," Xanadeux commented.

The body's head twitched slightly, as another tube was pulled from out of its brain. Webber's gaze averted from the brain, and he began to walk away from the body, towards another scientist who was inserting one of the tubes into a tall, wide, cylindrical device. "Report for Mr. Huxton," stated Webber.

The goggled, masked scientist nodded his head towards Webber, and said, "Hello, Mr. Huxton. At this point, we've determined that the informational infection found within the subject's brain is one of a previously unknown nature–a biological infobomb that requires no implants or memory augmentation in order to carry it." He turned to a monitor near the device which housed the tubes, and touched his gloved finger upon the image of a magnified, cellular object. The cell image grew larger in size, past its membrane, past its cytoplasm, until it reached the nuclei. Pointing to one of the bluish growths attached to the cell's nucleotides, he said, "This is it."

"A virus?" asked Mason, whose voice was projecting through a microspeaker attached to Webber's lapel.

"Yes," the scientist replied, looking directly at Webber. "A genetically-specific, viral infection which somehow allows an informational attack to be stored within the host's RNA. We've found traces of the virus in the subject's brain cells, spinal fluid, blood, lungs... It's penetrated his entire body."

"Odd," Mason said, rubbing his chin. "Is it transmitted like an ordinary virus?"

"That's very probable, sir, though at this point, we're not quite sure. We're going to need some more time before we can give you a definite answer."

Mason nodded. "I understand. Thank you for the report."

"You're welcome, sir," the scientist replied, and turned back towards the monitor.

The camera switched perspectives. Mason was now looking at Mr. Webber again.

"Would like to make a suggestion, sir," Webber said.

"Certainly, Mr. Webber. Proceed."

"Since infobomb is a biological virus," he said, "recommend quarantining Mrs. Huxton until tests can be done on her. Possibility that she may have contracted virus, and that virus may be programmed to attack you also."

Mason said, "Isn't it a bit late for that? I've already come into contact with her numerous times."

"Nature of virus is still unknown. Possible that it requires lengthy gestation period in host before it can attack. Recommend that you remain in nerve center until Mrs. Huxton is isolated and Xanadeux can check for virus' presence within your home."

Mason turned to Xanadeux. "What do you think?"

"Mr. Webber has a good point," Xanadeux said. "It's better to be safe than sorry."

"Very well," Mason said, facing the screen once again. "Thank you for the suggestion, Mr. Webber. Keep me updated on any new developments."

"Of course, sir," he replied, and transformed into the logo.

"This doesn't make any sense, Xanadeux," Mason said. "If these terrorists are wielding weapons such as these, then why haven't they simply tried to kill me?"

FREQUENCIES

"It would seem that they're playing a game of cat and mouse, sir," Xanadeux said.

"But why? For what end?"

"Why does one climb a mountain?"

"Hm," Mason said. "Just to do it. That's a possibility...but I'm sure it's something more. It has to be something more." He swivelled to face the screen. "Where is Dominique, Xanadeux?"

"In her studio, sir," the android said, as the image of Dominique appeared upon the screen. Her back was facing the camera, and she was painting thick, harsh strokes onto a large canvas. "I'm currently on my way there."

Mason nodded, as he watched his surrogate wife continue to paint her bleak picture. It was all blacks and blues, randomly scattered across the painting's fabric. Nothing like the bright, effervescent work which Dominique *used* to produce. "You poor creature," he said to himself.

Two Xanadeux androids entered into the room. "Mrs. Huxton?" one of them asked.

Startled, she turned and said, "Yes?"

"I apologize for the inconvenience, but I need you to come with me right now."

She set her paintbrush down. "What-what for?"

"There's some tests that need to be done."

"Now?" she asked. She looked at a nearby clock. "Can't they wait until the morning?"

"Unfortunately, no," it replied, taking a few, methodical steps towards her.

She stood up, and took a few, panicky steps away from it. "Where's Mason?"

"Patch my voice through," Mason said to Xanadeux.

"Go ahead," the android's voice said from behind him.

"Dominique?" asked Mason's voice through Xanadeux's vocal speaker.

"Mason?" she asked.

"Yes, it's me, dear. I'm busy in the nerve center right now, or else I'd come up personally."

"What's going on?" she asked, her face full of fright.

"We just need to run some tests, Dom," he said. "That's all. Please go with Xanadeux. I'll join up with you shortly."

She began to cry, as she dispiritedly walked towards the androids. "What's going on?" she whispered through her

231

tears. "Nothing makes sense."

"Don't worry, dear," Mason said. "Everything will be fine."

She said nothing, and exited the room with the two androids, leaving the dreary painting the centerpiece of the camera's cold gaze.

"This has all gone so wrong, Xanadeux," Mason said. He wiped his face with both hands. "All I wanted was to be with my wife again..."

Xanadeux comfortingly placed its hand on Mason's shoulder.

"...but this has all gone so horribly wrong..." he said, his palms rubbing his eyes.

"Sir?" Xanadeux asked.

Mason sighed. "Yes?"

"I realize that the timing of this is unfortunate...but there's something you should see." Upon the screen appeared an image of a darkened, crowded nightclub. Obnoxiously loud music started to blast through the nerve center's speakers. Two Ordocops™ were in front of the camera's view, their weapons drawn and aimed towards a motley group of four individuals.

"Freeze!" shouted one of the Ordocops™.

"What is this?" Mason asked.

"The club where Ashley is at," Xanadeux replied.

Mason felt his heart sink. "Oh, no."

The next instant, lasers began to fly through the air, the shouting increased, and chaos descended down upon the club.

Mason shot up from his seat. "No!" he shouted. As it became increasingly harder to see what was happening, he turned back to Xanadeux, and asked, "What's going on?"

"Apparently our security forces have been forced to fire upon a group of government agents."

"What?" He looked back at the screen, but all he could see were people running every which way. Sounds of panic joined the blaring music. "But why?"

"Apparently they were threatening Ashley's welfare. She was talk-" Xanadeux suddenly stopped.

Mason's face drooped. "What now?"

"I've just been contacted by something calling itself the 'Presence.' It claims responsibility for the attacks, and would like to speak with you."

"That bastard," Mason said. "This is all his fault."

On the screen, the battle continued. An Asian woman pulled out a nunchaku-like device, whose chain greatly extended when she flung it forward, so that one of its ends wrapped around the legs of one of the Ordocops™. She then pulled back on it, and swept the Ordocop™ clean off of his feet.

"Can you put him through without compromising your security?" Mason asked.

"Yes," Xanadeux said.

"Then do it–but disable the outgoing cameras."

The shivering, black creature from the MUD appeared onscreen. "Hello, Mason," it said in its buzzing voice, its face showing the streetcam image of Adam being hit by the truck. "Remember me?"

Mason clenched his fists together. "I'm going to kill you, you bastard," he said to it.

"Oh, you would love that, wouldn't you?" it asked. A flash of Mason as Arthur swiping his sword at the creature. "But I'm not so easy to kill, am I?" Flash: the creature's head rising up from its corrupted body, then disappearing.

"Everything in time," Mason said. "You obviously want something. What is it?"

Flash: the Ordosoft™ logo in flames, the American flag in flames, the United Nations' flag in flames. "Isn't it obvious? I want to play a game."

Mason turned to Xanadeux and mouthed, "Is Ashley alright?" Xanadeux nodded.

"What kind of a game?" Mason asked loudly.

"A game of chance," it said, as a DISORDER pulse of ENTROPY words shot across its ANARCHY face at a DESTRUCTION subliminal pace.

Mason couldn't catch the rest. He asked, "The stakes?"

"You know," the creature replied, half of its face a living, human fetus, the other half a close-up of an abortion in progress.

"I want specifics," Mason said, placing his hands behind his back.

Flash: A SWAT team, kicking in someone's back door. "Stalling?" it asked.

"Hardly. I simply want to know what I have to gain."

"What you're trying won't work," it said, accompanied by the images of a man graphically stabbing another man in his spine.

"The odds, beast. What are they?"

Its face showed a satellite, a wristcom, a shackle, then a police car. "You can't trace my physical location."

"I'm waiting," Mason said impatiently.

It laughed, a swarm of insects in a psychotic frenzy. "Your

attempts to distract me are amusing, Mason." A flash of a woman laughing, then suddenly coughing up blood and choking. "But much like your attempts to find me, they're futile."

"We'll see about that."

"Don't believe me?" Flash: A priest, slipping his head into a noose. "Just ask your android slave."

Mason looked back at Xanadeux.

"Go ahead," the creature said.

"Well?" Mason asked the AI.

Xanadeux shook his head. "I'm sorry, sir. I can't seem to pinpoint where it's transmitting from."

"Damn," Mason said gloomily.

The creature laughed again.

Turning to the screen, Mason shouted, "Just tell me the stakes, damn it!"

"Alright, old man," it said, showing an image of a gray-haired man, sprawled on a tile floor, clutching his chest in pain. "Don't have a heart attack. Here's the odds: You win, and I leave your family alone." Flash: A photograph of Mason's family, posed for a publicity shot. "You lose..." The same photo, but now they were all desiccated corpses, still posing for the camera.

"And the game?" Mason asked.

"Since you're so fond of medievalism," it said, showing an image of a man being stretched upon the rack, his skin just beginning to split and tear. "I propose a quest. An immersible, cyberquest for the king." Flash: Hundreds of lesioned bodies, all infected with some type of plague. "You *do* have an immersible, don't you?"

"Of course," Mason replied, looking over at the giant, fluid-filled sphere which occupied the eastern section of the nerve center.

Flash: A man submerged in an immersible, the intelligent fluid around him solidifying into a blade and slicing open his gut. "And it's capable of inflicting realtime damage?"

"It is," Mason said.

The image of a woman being burned at the stake. "Good," it said. "Then you accept my challenge?"

"No details?"

"Details come when you get to the domain." An image of a man being guillotined. "Take the offer..." The man's severed head, rolling away from its body. "Or leave it."

"Very well," Mason said. "I accept."

"Of course you do," it said. "I'll send the domain's location to your slave." Flash: A handcuffed man being raped with a soiled plunger. "See you there." The creature's vibrating body scattered into thousands of tiny, black particles, which filled the entire screen until it was completely dark.

"It's gone," Xanadeux said, turning the uniview off.

Mason stood from his seat, still fixedly staring at the blank screen, the game's monumental stakes weighing heavily upon his mind. Were he to sustain enough damage while inside of the domain, it could mean permanent–or worse–mortal injury. Were he to fail, it could mean the death of his family. But were he to succeed...

Mason started to undo his tie.

"Would you like me to prepare the immersible?"

"Yes, Xanadeux," Mason said, slipping off his tie as he began to walk towards the large sphere. "Let's put an end to this madness."

The lights at the bottom of the sphere turned on, causing the clear, intelligent fluid inside it to glow with a greenish hue. It then did a few, multi-directional rotations upon its magnetic axes, and came to a rest with its entrance facing the ground.

As Mason reached the immersible, another android emerged from behind it, and said, "All systems are go, sir,"

"Good." Mason tossed his jacket aside. "We can't afford any mistakes." He removed the rest of his clothes, save for his briefs.

The android extended its upturned palm towards Mason. A small, rounded, black disc rested atop it.

Mason picked up the disc with his thumb and forefinger, pressed in and held the two, tiny buttons on its sides, and placed it on top of his chest. He released his fingers, and the disc magnetically adhered to his skin.

"Shall I activate the suit?" Xanadeux asked.

Mason nodded. "Go ahead."

The android placed its index finger in the center of the disc. The device glowed for a brief moment, then hundreds of extremely-thin, black tendrils began to sprout out from it in every direction. They quickly grew themselves along Mason's trunk, arms, legs, and head, forming a complex, interconnected web of neurological stimulators and receptors. Within a manner of seconds, his entire body was covered with a technorganic neural net. The tendrils ceased their growth, and Xanadeux asked, "Does everything feel alright, sir?"

Mason flexed his electrode-covered fists, wiggled his neural-netted toes, tilted his wired head from side to side, and replied, "Superb."

FREQUENCIES

"Excellent," Xanadeux said. It handed him the immersible suit's headpiece. "Here you are."

Grasping the black, plastic/magnetite mask with his right hand, Mason held it up before his face. His eyes passed over the large, obsidian lenses, whose sideways-teardrop shape caused them to resemble the eyes of a graylien; the silvery, metal material that covered the mouth and nose, shaped like an oval and looking like it was comprised of near-microscopic links of chain mail; the speaker components on each side, which had been custom-molded to precisely fit the shape of his ears. "'Twas armor he donned..." Mason said, bringing the mask to his face, "...a king or a pawn?" After it had magnetically adhered itself in place, he asked, "Can you hear me?"

"Perfectly, sir," answered Xanadeux through the headpiece's speakers.

"Then I'm ready to be immersed," Mason said. He walked under the sphere–which was raised about eight feet from off of the ground–and placed himself directly beneath its entrance. The transparent opening slid open, and the intelligent fluid inside began to gently ooze out and around him. As it seeped over his head and shoulders, down past his hips, he could feel it smoothly, logically molding itself around him. When he was completely engulfed by the viscous liquid, he said to himself, "Here we go..." It then sucked itself back into the sphere, with him now inside it. The entrance closed below, and it brought him to the center of the immersible. "Activate all systems," he stated. The mask immediately started to pull the air from the fluid that surrounded him, while the visor lit up, and began to project images directly onto Mason's retinas, so that his entire field of vision was now taking place within cyberspace.

He saw before him the east garden of Xanadeux. Tulips, roses, carnations, and a plethora of other flowers encircled him. The sounds of wind, birds, and insects came through the mask's speakers, sweet, familar smells emitted themselves via the olfactory processors, while a soft breeze blew lightly at his face, courtesy of the IS's neural net. Mason bent down, picked a single, yellow buttercup, and as he did, he could feel the stimulators within the suit and the surrounding liquid perfectly mimic the sensation of grasping and plucking the flower's stem. And as he moved in cyberspace, so did he move in realtime, suspended by the intelligent fluid such that he could maneuver any which way he wanted, but always remain centered in the middle of the sphere. Mason stood up, the transmutable fluid solid beneath his feet, and brought the flower to his nose, the fluid around his arms as light as air.

From behind him, he heard Xanadeux's voice ask, "Stopping to smell the roses, sir?"

Mason turned to face the android, the retinal projectors scrolling along with his motions perfectly, and cracked a miniscule smile. "Actually, the buttercups. You've already received the domain location?"

"Yes, along with the Presence's instructions."

"Which are?"

"That you may enter into the domain as the avatar of your choice, but you may not change once there, nor access anything from the outside." Xanadeux held out its palm, and various avatars that Mason had used in the past started to holographically rotate over its opened hand. "And, you must remain within the domain until the challenge's end. Otherwise, the deal is off."

"That's it?"

"That's all."

"Hmm," Mason said, examining the avatars. "Walking blindly into battle..." He raised a single finger above the choices. "Arthur would be best prepared." He touched the miniature figure, and was instantly transformed into the Arthur avatar.

"A good choice," Xanadeux said. "Especially considering the Excalibur program's previous performance against the Presence."

"Yes," he agreed, touching the hilt of the regal sword which rested at his hip. "Not to mention its new additions." Placing the single buttercup into a leather pouch attached to his belt, Mason said, "Shall we begin?"

"At once." Xanadeux waved its hand, and a prismatic, swirling portal opened up in the fabric of virtual reality before them. The android motioned its hand towards the opening, and said, "After you, sir."

Mason nodded, and stepped into the portal.

Xanadeux followed after him, and together they began their journey towards the Presence's realm.

It was an odd sensation, traversing the virtual tunnel, much like walking through thick, soft, ankle-deep mud...but with the hallucinogenic addition of bright, kinetic colors all around, and a foundation that simply would *not* stop moving. Mason imagined the experience to be what LSD or psilocybin would feel like, but had no idea if this was the case, since he had never chosen to dabble in the province of illegal narcotics. Nearly tripping on the spinning floor, he commented, "Of course it couldn't be a *simple* portal."

"Of course," Xanadeux agreed, its arms resting comfortably at its sides, as it easily floated its way across the tunnel's shifting surface. "The Presence seems to enjoy making things as complicated as-" The android paused, as a large shape suddenly began to morph up from the ground below. "-possible," it finished.

Mason immediately drew Excalibur, and readied himself for battle with the unknown entity.

The multicolored, liquidous shape quickly congealed into a gigantic, human head...one which he recognized...as the head of...

"George Washington?" Mason asked out loud.

"You're free, Mason," boomed the voice of the president, as the portal abruptly stopped swirling around them.

"What?" Mason said, doing his best to maintain his balance on the now-stable ground.

"Free, Mason," the head repeated, its voice slowed down to the point that its words became incredibly distorted. "Free to leave now." It smiled, its mouth full of rotten, wooden teeth. "Leave now, and I'll even spare one of your children–your choice which."

"Are you reneging on your challenge?"

"No." Within its pupils, Mason could see the image of a young George Washington, chopping down a cherry tree with a large axe. "I *never* go back on my word." It blinked, and now its eyes showed an older George Washington, ruthlessly chopping into a Native-American woman and her baby. "I'm merely offering you a deal."

"To hell with your deal!" Mason said, and sliced his sword through the presidential mockery.

Its pupils showed the image of Mason's blade splitting George Washington's skull into a bloody mess. "Your choice..." it said, then liquified back into the colorful ground.

The tunnel began to swirl once again.

"Madness, Xanadeux," Mason said, putting Excalibur away, and continuing to trudge towards the portal's exit. "Sheer madness."

"Indubitably, sir," the android replied.

They soon reached the end of the phantasmic passage, and emerged forth from it onto a grassy hilltop which overlooked a vast forest. "Here we are," Xanadeux said, as the tunnel closed behind them.

"But where is here?" Mason asked, his breaths exiting into the cold air like fog as he scanned his eyes around the area.

"Good question."

An ominous, three-pronged castle rose up directly before them, beyond the forest's clearing. Its architecture was strange, very gothic and mysterious, with elements of both the medieval and the modern. A small, dirt path led down the hill towards it. Behind them was more forest, but much denser, and an aquamarine ocean could be seen far, far in the distance beyond it. Another dirt path led down the hill to their right, into a thinner strip of the all-surrounding forest, and continued out of it towards an impressive mountain range, in which Mason could see several, gigantic caves. To their left, were dark, gray clouds, and monstrous patches of fog. From this direction, it was possible to see a small portion of the forest, and not much else.

Turning to Xanadeux, Mason asked, "The creature's allowing you to stay?"

"It hasn't informed me otherwise," it replied.

"Good," he said, watching an unusually large bird fly through the skies overhead. "Now, the question remains, what is our challenge?"

The galloping of hooves could suddenly be heard in the distance. Two horses–one white, one black–appeared upon the hill's horizon, from the direction of the fog. An armored man was riding upon the black one, holding a tether which was connected to the other horse's muzzle. "Arthur!" he wearily shouted, barely able to remain seated upon his ebony steed. His armor was badly damaged, his face bruised and battered, and his entire body splattered with blood. "Arthur!" he yelled again.

With a bewildered look, Mason glanced over at Xanadeux, and was even more surprised to see that the android now appeared as a gallant, black-haired knight, dressed in splendid, white armor, with a long, shining sword at his side.

"I'm not sure what the challenge *is*, sir," Xanadeux said, curiously looking over its appearance, "but I believe it *has* begun."

"Indeed," Mason said. He reached down to draw Excalibur, but found in its place an ordinary sword. "What?" he asked.

"What is it?" Xanadeux said.

"Excalibur..." Mason checked the other side of his belt, but found only the leather pouch, the flower still safely tucked inside. "It's...it's gone."

Realizing that they could not retrieve the Excalibur file without breaking the rules of the game, Xanadeux said, in a low, hushed tone, "Oh, dear."

"Arthur," the knight said as he neared them, blood and

saliva trickling from his mouth. Mason could now see that the knight's damaged armor had been ripped and torn, as if by the claws of some great beast. Reaching them, the knight slumped off of his horse, and hit the ground with a loud clang, still clutching within his hand a weathered scroll.

Moving over to the fallen knight, Mason drew his sword, and asked, "What's happened?"

"Perceval and I," he stammered. "We-we were ambushed by hellhounds in the Forest of Fog. I managed to escape, but he-" He pounded his armored fist onto the frozen ground. "I'm sorry, my liege, I tried but I..." He looked at Xanadeux, and said, "I failed, father. Our mission succeeded...yet I failed to save Perceval."

"Father?" Xanadeux asked.

Mason turned to Xanadeux, eyed his white armor, and said, "You're Lancelot."

"Of course," Xanadeux said. "Arthurian legend."

To the knight, Mason said, "Galahad?"

He grimaced with pain. "Sire?"

Mason planted the sword of his blade into the ground, kneeled beside the wounded knight, and said, "The mission–you've found the Holy Grail?"

Galahad laughed. "The Grail?" He laughed harder, and began coughing up blood. A few, crimson droplets splashed off of the frosted ground, and onto Mason's boots. "Surely you jest, sire."

"Why would I?" Mason asked.

"Because-" His face grew deathly serious. "Because you removed the Siege Perilous..." He hacked up more blood. "...and abandoned the quest for the Grail."

"That doesn't make any sense," Mason said. "Why would I do such a thing?"

Galahad wiped his mouth, and replied, "You said that God no longer exists."

Mason looked at Xanadeux curiously.

Xanadeux said, "It appears the legend has been twisted."

"To put it mildly," Mason said. "Sir Galahad, what of this mission?"

"The mission," he repeated, extending the scroll towards Mason with an unsteady hand. "We were told by the witch, Kundrie, that upon this parchment..." He started to cough again, spraying red mist everywhere.

Mason took the scroll, and stepped back from Galahad.

240

"...is written the answer..." More coughing from the knight, yielding more blood. "...to where Excalibur is." He rolled over on his back, and his head dropped down onto the cold, hardened ground.

"Galahad?" Mason asked, peering over him.

His eyelids barely open, Galahad stared into the sky above. "The Grail..." he whispered. "Do you see it?"

Mason looked up at the sky. "I see nothing."

Galahad continued to stare at his vision. "Then I pray for you, my liege." He then closed his eyes, placed his hands together, and said, "I'm ready." The youthful knight's body went limp, and he discontinued breathing.

Xanadeux asked, "Is he...?"

Mason nudged him with his bloodstained boot, but Galahad didn't respond. He nodded, and said, "He's gone."

Xanadeux walked over to the body to examine it for itself. "What does the scroll say?"

"We'll see." One of its spools in each hand, Mason unrolled the scroll, briefly inspected it, and said, "Hmm. The message reads:

> Though a king of rhime and reason
> shall know the nature of what is betwixt
> Exceptional swords of the finest calibre
> lie within the stronghold of the demon son
> A king must know his given name
> should he wish to receive the lady's gift

"Demon son..." Mason said, looking up from the scroll at Xanadeux. "Merlin."

"And that would have to be his stronghold," Xanadeux said, pointing his sword towards the techno-medieval structure.

Mason nodded. "Where we can find 'exceptional swords of the finest caliber.'"

"Excalibur."

"Yes," Mason said. He stared at the castle, then looked down at the scroll again. "But that's far too simple. And there's still the other verses." He read over the lines once more. "'A king of rhime and reason...shall know the nature of what is betwixt.' The nature of what is between..."

Xanadeux moved over to Mason, quickly glanced at the scroll, placed a finger onto the middle two lines of verse, and said, "Looking at the number of syllables per line as a numerical code, these don't belong here. It reads: 8, 10, 12, 11, 8, 10." It lifted its finger off of the parchment. "The 12 and 11 are out place."

"Meaning there's no rhyme to them," Mason said.

"Or reason," it added.

"Therefore, the nature of the 'betwixt' verses is illogical. False. Look," he said, pointing to the fourth line, "the word 'lie' is even embedded within this verse. Thus, if we eliminate the nonsensical lines, the stanzas now rhyme:

> 𝕿hough a king of rhime and reason
> shall know the nature of what is betwixt
> A king must know his given name
> should he wish to receive the lady's gift

"And we have a poem which makes sense," Mason said, utterly immersed within the riddle. "Now, the giv-"

"Sir?" Xanadeux said.

He looked up from the scroll. "Yes?"

Xanadeux pointed down at Sir Galahad, whose body was shaking in jerky, spastic motions, and whose flesh had turned gruesomely pallid and purpled.

Mason asked, "He's alive?"

Galahad's movements became more spasmodic, and thick, mucosal blood began to flow profusely from his nostrils and out of his mouth, spilling down his face and neck as a river of gore.

Xanadeux raised his sword. "Not exactly."

Mason pulled his sword from the ground, the opened scroll still hanging in his other hand, and prepared himself for battle.

A low, infernal rumbling started to sound from somewhere within Galahad's throat, and his body suddenly shot up into the air, and began to hover about two meters off of the ground, a weightless, reanimated corpse. "The kingdom is dead!" he shouted in a demonic voice, vomiting up something which could only be a portion of his viscera. "Your world is dead and you don't even know it!"

Mason clenched his jaw, and tightened his grip on his sword.

Galahad's digestive juices began to eat their way through his stomach, dumping food and bile all over himself and the ground. "You're all walking dead men, dressed in shrouds of lies!" he hellishly moaned. "Infecting everything you touch with your lifeless ways, your need to conquer, your need to capitalize, your nee-"

Mason's blade cut a clean swath through the possessed

242

knight's neck, sending Galahad's severed head rolling along the grassy knoll. The headless body immediately dropped to the ground, splashing malodorous fluid in all directions.

After shielding himself from the miasmic spray, Mason surveyed the scene. The body was no longer animated, and the head was sitting a few feet away, its blank, expressionless features facing towards them. "Well," he said to Xanadeux, "that's that."

"Dead!" shouted the head. "Dead!"

The decapitated body suddenly grabbed a hold of Mason's leg with its left hand, as its right hand grasped the bottom spool of the opened scroll, and tore off the majority of the parchment.

Mason let out a startled yell, swung his sword, and chopped into the arm gripping his leg, leaving only a severed forearm behind.

A forearm that wasn't releasing its grip.

The head screamed, "Your world is dead!" as its body stuffed the ripped scroll into its opened stomach. It moved to its knees and attempted to stand, but Xanadeux swiftly sliced through one of its knees, sending it back down to the frozen turf.

The forearm tightened its grasp on Mason's leg, and began to crush his enchanted armor.

Outside the domain, the liquid turned solid as steel, and tightly squeezed itself around Mason's shin. Before it could break his bones, he let fly a few, well-aimed swings, and the body's forearm was soon reduced to nothing more than segments of twitching fingers and flesh, which Mason then proceeded to ferociously trounce upon with his armored boots.

"You've killed everything!" continued the head.

The body, with only one good arm and one whole leg, attempted to upright itself, but Xanadeux once again slashed it to the ground, this time dismembering it at the thigh.

Mason severed its other arm, chopped it into smaller pieces, then he and Xanadeux started to work away at the torso.

"Genocide!" shouted the head. "Genocide! You always have to resort to genocide to achieve your goals!" It laughed maniacally.

Mason angrily looked over at the head, and began to walk towards it, his sword and armor splattered with blood.

"You were given Eden!" it screamed.

Passing one of the horses, Mason pulled a flanged, silver mace from its saddle, and tossed his sanguine sword aside.

"And you turned it in to Hell!"

Mason stood before the shouting head, grasped the mace's

shaft with both hands, and calmly settled himself into his customary golfing stance.

"You butchered every living thing you could!"

He sized up the shot, swung the mace back...

"Raped and pillaged and violated and desecrated–"

And teed off. The smashed head went flying into the distance, down the hill, and towards Merlin's castle. Mason held his follow-through for a moment, then flipped the mace onto his shoulder like a club, a satisfied expression upon his face, and walked back towards Xanadeux.

There were now quivering pieces of Galahad scattered everywhere, and the scroll was lying in a heap of coagulated blood and spilled bile. "I take it you have the verses memorized?" Mason asked, eyeing the revolting substance.

His white armor now not so splendid, Xanadeux replied, "I do. 'A king must know his given name.'"

"Pendragon," Mason said. "Arthur Pendragon."

"'Should he wish to receive the lady's gift.'"

"The Lady of the Lake gave Excalibur to Arthur..." Mason looked around the vicinity. "I see no lakes though, only ocean." His gaze stopped at the giant caves. One of the large, winged creatures he had seen earlier was circling the area around the caverns. "Pendragon... Dragons live in caves." He placed the mace back into the saddle holster, mounted the black horse, pulled its reins towards the caves, and said, "That's where we'll find Excalibur. Let's go."

Xanadeux climbed onto the white steed, and they started down the hill's path, into the forest, spurring the horses to move as fast they possibly could.

Mason and Xanadeux exited the forest, and entered into a rocky terrain that was covered with shrubs, brush, and a few, small trees. The caves rose up from the earth a few hundred yards in front of them, dark and foreboding. There were three, gigantic caverns, plus countless others that were much smaller in size. The dirt path led directly into the largest cave, which was located in the direct center of the mountain range.

Nearing the central cave's entrance, they came upon a shallow pond which had been created by a previous day's rainfall. The horses stopped at the pond, and began to drink. "I suppose we'll leave the horses here," Mason said, dismounting his steed, "and continue into the cave on foot."

Xanadeux hopped off its horse. "You're sure this is the dragon's cave?"

Mason knelt down, and picked up one of the large, plate-like scales that were scattered about the vicinity. Showing the shedded piece of reptillian skin to the android, he said, "Positive." He tossed the scale aside, and drew the mace from the horse's saddle. "Do we have any torches?"

Xanadeux searched its horse's saddlebag , pulled out two sticks of resinous wood, and said, "We do." It grabbed a handful of small rocks from the same pouch. "And also some flints."

"Good," he said, eyeing a glistening pool of water which had formed in a hollowed tree stump. As Xanadeux began to strike the flints against the hilt of its sword, Mason walked to the nearby water source. Peering into it, he saw a perfectly still, crystal clear surface, which reflected his kingly image like an aqueous mirror. The water then started to ripple, his reflection shimmered, and the image of Ashley dashing into a car appeared. "Xanadeux, come here!" Mason shouted.

Xanadeux ran over to him, two lit torches in its hands. "What is it?"

"This pool..." Mason said, as he watched some type of simian crossbreed jump onto the hood of the car, which he now recognized to be McCready's Polaris®. "Ashley's still in danger...the creature's breaking the deal."

"Actually, sir, it's not," Xanadeux said. "The Presence only said it would leave your family alone *if* you won the challenge." The image of McCready's car, falling to the ground below and exploding. "And we've yet to do that."

"True," he said, relieved to see Ashley and McCready running away from the car's flaming wreckage. Looking up from the realtime window, he said, "Let's get to it then."

Xanadeux handed him a torch, and the two of them marched into the daunting, darkened cave. It was damp and musty, and the earth was soft and muddy beneath their feet. The temperature was cool and chilly, though an occasional, warm, sulfuric breeze blew from somewhere up ahead. The rustling of bats, rats, and other cave-dwelling creatures could be heard all about, as well as other, unidentifiable noises. The torches provided enough light for them to see the path ahead, a bit of their periphery, but none of the roof above. How high the cavern rose, they could only imagine.

FREQUENCIES

Deeper and deeper they moved into the cave, passing skeletons, ragged remains of clothing and armor, and the occasional piece of treasure. They often saw smaller, divergent paths, but since none of them were really "dragon-sized," they chose to remain upon the larger, main path. As the cave grew warmer, and the sulfur smell became stronger, Xanadeux stopped its motion, and said, "Do you hear that noise?"

Mason stopped and listened. "Yes," he said. "It sounds like...like smacking."

Moving in the direction of the wet, noisy sounds, the light from their torches revealed a thin, greenish, wart-covered creature who was dining on the fresh remains of a human being, its long tongue repeatedly dipping into the person's cracked skull.

"A troll," Mason said, keeping his distance.

Lifting its mouth from the body's brain, the troll looked up at them with its beady, black eyes. "Them pyre...never diet," it growled, sputtering saliva-drenched gray matter down its pointy chin. "Roam and...I wander...fit dice..." It pointed a long, bony finger at Mason. "Wilt chew?" It licked the specks of tissue from its jaw.

"Let's leave it to its meal," Mason said, seeing that the deranged creature was speaking nothing but nonsense.

"Let's," Xanadeux agreed.

The two continued on their way, and soon reached a slope that ascended to an area which glowed with a gorgeous, golden light. Climbing the rocky incline, they came to a humongous, treasure-filled lair which reeked of sulfur, and was somehow, magically generating its own luminosity. The sweltering heat, which also had no visible source, caused the jewels, coins, weapons, and other valuables to appear like a mirage. Mason stepped in, coins clinking underfoot, and said, "I believe we've found the dragon's lair." At the far end of the den, embedded halfway into a large stone that rested atop the treasure pile, was Excalibur. "And our prize."

"And the dragon," Xanadeux added, pointing up to a gigantic, red dragon that was perched on a ledge above.

"Congratulations," it said in a thunderous voice. "You've found the sword." It spread its leathery wings, swooped down on top of the treasure, and blocked the way to Excalibur. Blowing smoke through its nostrils, it added, "Now all you have to do is get it."

Mason cast aside his torch and quickly picked up a nearby shield, just as the dragon released a torrent of fire from its mouth. He ducked behind the large, triangular shield, but could still feel the blistering, burning heat building up all around him. In realtime, the immersible increased its temperature to a near scalding level, and had it not been for the enchanted armor he was virtually wearing within the domain, the heat would have kept increasing, and Mason would have been boiled to death right then and there.

When the dragon had ceased its fiery attack, Mason peered his head around the partially-melted shield, and saw that Xanadeux was already off and running towards the sword. "Dragon!" he shouted, hoping to draw its attention away from the android. He discarded the useless shield, and again yelled, "Dragon!"

The dragon paid him no mind, its eyes fixed upon Xanadeux.

Mason hurled his mace at the reptilian creature, but the weapon harmlessly bounced off of its thick, scaly hide.

"Yes?" the dragon asked, calmly watching Xanadeux reach the sword. "Something on your mind?"

Xanadeux grasped Excalibur's handle, pulled it with all of its might...but the sword would not budge.

"Only Arthur can draw the sword, Lancelot," the dragon said. It whipped its muscular tail into Xanadeux, and the android went rocketing clear across the room. "Or hadn't you heard?"

"Damn," Mason said, picking up a long, sharp spear as he watched Xanadeux crash headfirst into the treasure pile.

The dragon turned towards Mason. Nostrils flaring, it bared its ferocious teeth, and said, "Your turn." It then rushed forward, its gargantuan claws digging into the golden ground, its huge wings flapping in the hot, humid air, and roared with prehistoric fury.

Mason's eyes widened, and his heart began to race. He quickly started to backpedal towards the cave's entrance, hoping to lure the dragon outside of its lair. But when he turned to face the opening, he found that there was now a colossal pile of boulders blocking the way. "Uh, oh," Mason said, looking back to see the wide-open jaws of the dragon coming right at him. Realizing that he had nowhere to run, Mason jumped straight into the creature's mouth, just as its sword-like teeth snapped down on the space where he had previously been standing. As everything went dark around him, he landed on top of a slick, wet surface, nearly slipped, but stabbed his spear into the soft, fleshy floor in time to regain his balance.

A combustive, booming sound started to reverberate from somewhere behind him, the smell of sulfur became extremely pungent, and it suddenly felt like he was standing inside of a broiling oven. Bright, yellowish-orange light started to illuminate from the back of the dragon's throat, and the next instant, an enormous fireball exploded forth from its gullet. As the dragon's jaws began to open once again, Mason firmly gripped the spear with both hands, planted it deeper into the living floor, pole-vaulted himself high into the air, and rode the explosive wave of fire out of the creature's mouth.

Landing without injury onto a cushioning mound of gold pieces, Mason swiftly scrambled towards a battle axe located a few feet away from him. He grabbed a hold of it, stood to his feet, turned around to face the dragon, and was rudely slammed to the ground by one of the creature's gigantic feet.

His head barely sticking out from the webbing between two of its toes, the dragon lowered its head towards him, dripped some blood from its maw, and said, "That hurt." It increased its pressure upon him, and began to squeeze its scaly toes around his neck.

Mason felt the immersible's fluid strangling him, as his armor crushed beneath the monster's weight. He started to feel dizzy, and was about to lose consciousness, when Xanadeux suddenly rushed forward, and drove a long lance deep into the dragon's ear canal.

The beast screamed in agony, and began to wildly flap its head and wings in an attempt to dislodge the implanted weapon.

The dragon's frantic motions caused it to raise off of the ground a few inches–just enough for Mason to roll out from beneath its crushing grip. Dazed, he looked up and saw that Xanadeux was still hanging on to the lance, even though the dragon was thrashing its head about in a frenzy. As the blood started pumping back into his brain, Mason took a deep breath, sprang to his feet, clenched his battle axe, and began to dash as fast as he possibly could towards Excalibur. He was within twenty feet of the sword in the stone, when suddenly the treasure before him magically rose up, and transformed into four, armed soldiers. Gold pieces as their flesh, jewels and gems for their eyes and mouth, equipped with armor, shields, and weapons, they began to charge forth at Mason.

The lead soldier, armed with a cutlass and buckler, was quite sloppy, and Mason was easily able to slice his large axe through its ruby eyes, and revert the animated creature back into treasure. The next one, wielding a thin rapier, wasn't much better, and he disposed of it just as quickly. The other two, unfortunately for Mason, were *much* more skilled in battle.

The soldier dressed in plate mail, wielding a morning star and shield, smashed its heavy, spiked weapon at Mason's chest, rending open his already-damaged armor. As Mason reeled back from the blow, the other treasure-soldier fired a quarrel from its crossbow directly at his exposed chest, and hit him in the shoulder, just below his collarbone.

The bolt's impact knocked Mason off of his feet, and he crashed hard into a sizable treasure box behind him, sending splinters of aged wood flying in every direction. In realtime, the fluid had brutally forced itself though his flesh and remained there, exactly like the arrow in the domain. Mason gritted his teeth from the pain, and swiftly hurled his axe at the soldier with the crossbow, just as it began to take aim once again. End over end, the battle axe raced through the air, and hit the soldier dead between its sapphire eyes, before it had a chance to fire another shot. It instantly fell apart, its bodily coins jangling to the ground like a slot machine's jackpot.

The final soldier ran forward, raising its enormous, spiked mace high above its head.

Wounded and weaponless, Mason had no other choice but to run. Grimacing with pain, he attempted to head in the direction of Excalibur, but before he could fully get on his feet, the armored soldier smashed its morning star into him once again. Mason tumbled back down into the treasure, his ribs cracked and bruised. He scanned around for a weapon, but saw only gold pieces and jewelry. He looked back at the soldier.

The armored creature stood directly over him, its morning star aimed at his head.

Mason raised his forearms in front of his face.

It began to swing the weapon forward.

And then an unconscious Xanadeux came flying into the soldier, and shattered it into a thousand gold pieces. The spiked mace immediately fell from its grip, and landed roughly one inch from Mason's head.

As armor and gold rained down all around him, Mason immediately, painfully clambered towards Excalibur. Within seconds, he had reached the stone, but when he reached his hand for the sword, he was slammed clear across the lair by one of the dragon's immense wings. He rapidly arced up through the air, and smacked into the pile of boulders with a dull thud. Barely conscious, Mason rolled down the rocky incline, and slumped to the treasured ground, his face falling straight into a pile of of smooth, cut diamonds.

He heard the dragon approach him, and could feel its hot, sulfuric breath, as it said, "We've reached the end of the game, Arthur. Any last words?"

"Y-yes..." Mason said, his face contorting with pain as he pushed himself up with his good arm. "I..." He shakily knelt down on one knee, reached into his leather pouch, and pulled out the single buttercup. "...I humbly ask for your mercy." He gently set the flower down onto the heap of treasure in front of him.

"A flower?" the dragon asked. It laughed, like rolling thunder, as wisps of smoke puffed out its mouth and nose. "All this treasure, and you expect to bribe me with a *flower*?"

"It's...it's a buttercup," Mason said, grasping his bleeding shoulder. "A...a special kind...inspired by Alice in Wonderland."

Unimpressed, the dragon growled, "And...?"

"And, well..." he said, as the pink flower began to sparkle, "...it's special."

A cheshire grin appeared in the air above the flower. "How are you getting along, dear dragon?" it asked, as Mason crawled behind one of the large boulders.

"Trickery!" shouted the dragon, exhaling a gust of flames towards the grin and Mason.

The heat passed deathly close to him, and reduced the protective boulder to mere ashes.

"Are you blind?" asked the grin, which was now to the dragon's left. "I'm over here!"

The dragon whipped its head in that direction, blowing fire as it did.

"No," it said, as another grin appeared to the dragon's right. "Over here."

"I'm over here, silly!" said the one directly in front of the dragon's face.

The dragon angrily snapped its mighty jaws at the grin.

"Over here!" another said from behind it.

As multiple grins popped up everywhere, all of them taunting and teasing, the full, black-and-white, cheshire cat began to form in front of Mason. "Grab a hold of my tail," it said, its pencil-drawn lines starkly contrasting with the vivid, colorful detail of the Presence's domain.

The dragon took notice of the cat.

Mason grasped its soft, furry tail.

The red beast drew in a titanic breath.

The cheshire cat and Mason turned incorporeal, just as the dragon exhaled a mountainous gust of fire. The blaze harmlessly passed through their fading forms, but utterly destroyed everything

250

else around them, turning treasure into slag and boulders to dust.
The next instant, Mason and the cat reformed–right beside Excalibur.

Realizing they had teleported to the stone, the dragon quickly turned around, but it was already too late.

Mason had drawn the sword.

"No!" shouted the dragon, retreating a few steps backwards.

"Yes," the cheshire cat said with its enormous grin.

Mason pointed Excalibur directly at the dragon. "You lose."
Bright, blue energy burst forth from the enchanted blade like lightning, and immediately spread itself all over the dragon's frame.

The creature screamed, thunder and lightning everywhere, as its entire body became corrupted by the Excalibur virus. It started to transform into pure, blue energy, and tried in vain to flap its wings and fly away. It grew brighter and brighter...brighter still...and then it let out a final, earth-shaking scream.

And its light died out completely.

Mason dropped to his knees, still clutching Excalibur.

"We did it," said the cat.

"We...we did," Mason said, letting out an exhausted sigh.

"And if Xanadeux and I updated the virus properly," the cat said, slinking its tail back and forth, "the Presence...well, to put it nicely..." It smiled at Mason. "Should no longer exist."

Mason slowly nodded, and looked over to where Xanadeux had landed earlier.

The android was shaking its head, and lifting itself up from the treasure.

"Are you alright, Xanadeux?" Mason asked, clutching at his wounded shoulder.

"Fine, sir," it said, brushing off its damaged armor as it walked towards them. "Just a tad shaken."

"But not too stirred, I see," added the cat. To Mason, it said, "Mr. Huxton, I do believe we can call it a day."

"Indeed, Agent Takura," Mason replied, wincing as he stood to his feet. "Indeed."

When Xanadeux had reached them, the cat sat on its hind legs, extended a fore paw to each of them, and said, "Take a paw. But watch the claws–they're sharp."

Mason and Xanadeux each grasped a paw.

"And away we go," the cat said.

The three of them started to fade from the domain, their legs first, then their bodies, then their heads, until all that remained were their mouths.

"I thought we were going," Mason said.

"We are," the cheshire grin replied. "I just like the effect."

The mouths then rippled, vanished entirely, and they triumphantly exited the arena.

Game over.

α

Ω

Chapter 13:
<u>Everything Changes</u>

"It is said that the only constant in life is change.
I understand this now, better than I ever have before."

"Ms. Huxton, Agent McCready," Carter Stone said, seated across from them at the black table, an opened laptop sitting in front of him. "Please keep in mind as you answer our questions that you *are* being frequentially monitored, and we *will* be able to tell if you're lying to us."

An extremely annoyed look upon his face, McCready stared straight at the DCC agent, unblinking. Like I didn't already know that, you fuckin' cretin. Get on with it already.

"And needless to say," Stone said anyway, "lying will only make things worse."

McCready and Ashley were being detained inside one of the claustrophobic interrogation rooms located within Freemon headquarters, sitting in rigid, metal chairs which were already making his ass sore and his patience thinner. Behind them, was a large uniview screen which projected their frees so the interrogaters could see a more detailed image of their thoughts.

"We just want the truth," added Janet Vegas, the butch DCC agent who was leaning against the corner of the table, next to Stone. "That's all."

"Alright, already," McCready said with an irritated laugh. "Get on with the fuckin' show, or the truth's gonna get hella bored and leave."

Ashley laughed.

Vegas sucked her teeth at McCready.

McCready smiled.

Stone tried to throw a hard stare at him. "Okay, Agent McCready," he said, slowly nodding his head, "let's begin then." Stone looked at his laptop. "Are you aware that you attacked and damaged a federal agent tonight?"

"Tonight?" McCready asked. He checked his wristcom. "It's past midnight. Don't you mean last night?"

"Fine, McCready," Stone said. "*Last* night, were you aware that you attacked a federal agent?"

"Yup."

"And are you aware that's a punishable offense?"

McCready stared up at the white ceiling. "Yup."

"Then why did you do it?"

"Why the fuck do you think I did it?" McCready asked, pulling a toothpick from his trenchcoat's pocket.

"That's what I'm asking *you*, smartass," Stone said. "Answer the question."

"Because I was hired to protect Ms. Huxton," McCready said, placing the toothpick between his lips, "and your little ape-boy attacked her. That's why."

Vegas said, "But if you knew it was a federal agent who was attempting to detain her, then you also must have known that Ms. Huxton was in no real danger."

"Bzzt," McCready said. "Wrong answer, lady." He leaned back in his chair. "First off, since I *am* a federal agent, I know that Ms. Huxton *was* in danger at that moment. Maybe you hadn't noticed, or maybe you don't want to notice, but we 'accidentally' fuck people up all the time when we're 'detaining' them."

Both of the DCC agents had shocked and surprised looks upon their faces.

"Secondly," McCready continued, his tone doused with acid, "the terrorists that have been attacking Ms. Huxton's family have already proven that they can do so from a remote location. So it didn't seem that far-fetched to me that they may have overtaken the REX's OS and used it to attack Ms. Huxton."

"Okay," Stone said. "At least that makes some sense."

"Um," Ashley said, lifting her hand, "I'm wondering...can we just call me Ashley? I know you want to be formal an' all, but this Ms. Huxton thing...it feels like you're talking about someone else."

"The interrogation records will list you as Ms. Huxton," Vegas said, "so that's what we're going to call you."

"Okay," Ashley said. "Just thought I'd check."

McCready said, "I'll call you Ashley."

She smiled. "Thank you."

"Now, Agent McCready," Stone said, "once you had escaped from the REX, why did you ignore my attempts to contact you, and why–why–did you pull that stupid, reckless car-chase stunt?"

"Same reasons," McCready said. "I wasn't sure if fielding your call would infect my car's systems, and I wasn't even sure if your car was really being controlled by you. I was just trying to get Ashley to safety so I could figure out what the fuck was going on. But you fuckers never gave me the chance. And besides, why the fuck were you chasing me?"

"We knew your car had cloaking capabilities," Stone said. "We didn't want to lose you."

McCready chuckled. "It's not like you couldn't have asked me later. You know where I live."

Stone said, "But we had no way of knowing whether or not you two were planning on disappearing."

"Disappearing?" McCready asked, rubbing his eyes. "What the fuck would we do that for?"

Vegas stood up, her arms crossed. "Maybe Ms. Huxton could better answer that question, Agent McCready."

"Me?" Ashley asked. "Why me?"

"Let us ask the questions, Ms. Huxton," Vegas said.

Ashley laughed. "Okay. Go ahead."

"Prior to all hell breaking loose," Stone said, "who was the man you were talking to inside the Tiger's Lair?"

"The Asian guy?"

"Yes."

"I don't know his name," she said. "He's just a guy who I've seen around at different gatherings."

McCready wanted to turn around and see her frees for himself, but since that could have made her–or himself–look suspicious, he resisted the urge.

"You have no idea who he is?" Carter asked.

"Not really," she said.

Stone studied the screen in front of him, then said, "What were you talking to him about?"

"Um, let's see..." she said, her eyebrows raising slightly.

"Life, death, love, frequencies...the past, the future...Zen, the present..." She smiled. "Y'know...the usual."

"You're saying you *always* have conversations like this with people you barely know?" he asked.

"Umm..." She thought for a moment, looking out of the upper-corners of her eyes. "Yeah. Pretty much. Yeah."

"Interesting," Stone said, tapping out a few notes onto his laptop's keyboard. "Now, you say you were talking about frequencies and the past. Could you be more specific?"

"Like...?"

"Did you talk about any particular events or people...mention any names–that sort of thing?"

"Let me think." Ashley closed her eyes, and breathed in slowly through her nose. Opening her eyes, she shook her head, and said, "Hm-mm. We didn't get into any specifics. It was more of a general kind of conversation...real holistic, y'know? It was neat."

Stone stared past her at the large screen, carefully scrutinizing the detailed images of her frequencies, then looked at Vegas, and raised his eyebrows in a questioning manner.

Vegas nodded, and continued looking at the large screen, lightly tapping her finger against her chin.

Ashley circled her index finger round and round on the table, gazing directly at both DCC agents with a look that McCready could only describe as defiant.

Stone exhaled loudly, obviously frustrated. "Okay, Ms. Huxton. Let's get straight to the point."

"Sure," Ashley said. "Which point?"

"I think you know," Stone said, watching the wall's screen. She smiled. "You think?"

Stone squinted his eyes, and said, "During the course of the quote 'holistic' conversation you had tonight–" He paused. "Did the name 'Adrian Wellor' ever come up?"

McCready looked at Ashley.

"No," she assuredly responded.

Vegas asked, "Have you ever *heard* of the name 'Adrian Wellor'?"

"Hm-mm," she said, shaking her head. "Should I have?"

McCready turned his eyes from Ashley, his mind trying to figure out what the hell was going on. Why wasn't she telling the truth? What did she have to hide? He looked at Stone and Vegas, who were carefully studying her frees on the screens. And what were they going to do, now that they knew she was lying?

Stone closed the laptop. "Well, Ms. Huxton," he said, "it appears you're telling us the truth. I apologize for the inconvenience. You're free to go."

McCready stared at Carter, an obviously confused look upon his face. Ashley knew about Wellor–so why weren't they busting her on her lie?

"Thanks," Ashley said, standing up from her chair and stretching her lower back. To McCready, she asked, "You coming?"

"Actually," Stone said, "we'd like a few words alone with Agent McCready."

"Oh," Ashley said. "Okay." She looked back at McCready. "I'll wait for you outside?"

"Nah, it's fine," McCready said, still puzzled as a jigsaw. "Xanadeux's already here...it's already hella late. You should get home and get some sleep."

"I'm a night owl, Agent McCready. I won't be asleep for a while. And besides, you're gonna need a ride," she said, painfully reminding him of N.J. "I'll be outside, 'kay?" She smiled warmly.

"Alright," he said, his mind wondering, who the hell are you? as Ashley walked past him, lightly brushing her hand along his shoulder.

Vegas opened the door, and Ashley exited the room. "You two have a little thing going, don't you?" Vegas asked as she closed the door.

McCready set his toothpick on the table, and said, "Whatever, chick. Just get to the point, alright? I'm fuckin' tired."

Vegas smiled and shook her head. "You must be a bitter man, Agent McCready."

"Yup. So fuck off."

"Enough of this childish bullshit," Stone said, standing up from his seat. He placed his palms on the table, stared at McCready, slowly leaned forward, and asked, "Agent McCready, are you working for Adrian Wellor?"

"No," McCready said indignantly. "What kind of a fuckin' question is that?"

"A logical one," answered Stone, quickly glancing up at the screen. "Now let me ask you something else. How long have you known Ms. Huxton?"

"Not very. Maybe forty...forty-eight hours."

"And has she done anything suspicious while you've been

with her?"

"No, not really," McCready said. "I mean, the girl's a trip, for sure. She's definitely a freeker, but...whatever, right? She's got money, she's got clearance...she's free to do that."

"Is she lying to us?" Stone asked.

McCready stood up and stretched his arms. "I don't know, man. You got the fuckin' freereads right now, what are you asking me for?"

"You're avoiding the question, Agent McCready," Vegas said.

"Does she know about Adrian Wellor?" Stone asked.

"I-" McCready laughed. "I have no fuckin' idea, alright?"

They both stared at the screen behind him.

McCready turned around and looked at the screen. Yellow with patches of bright orange, erratic pattern changes, and some occasional, tiny spiking–it was frequentially obvious he was lying.

"That's what I thought," Stone said. "You're in deep shit, Agent McCready."

He turned from the screen. "Yeah, well, I guess that makes two of us, hunh? 'Cause *your* ass is on the line, too," he said, pointing his finger at Stone. "You attacked Mason Huxton's *daughter*, genius. In the midst of a family crisis, no less. And then, you had the fuckin' audacity to bring her down here, badger her...and now what the fuck do you got? Jackshit, Stone. Jack. Shit." McCready snickered. "You fucked up, man, and now all you got to look forward to is a big, fat-ass, Ordosoft™-sized lawsuit."

Stone stared at him, unphased by the verbal barrage. "We'll see about that, Agent McCready," he said. "You're forgetting this is a matter of national security. Different rules apply."

"I guess we'll see, won't we?" McCready put on his shades. "So, are you two wanting to sit around here and shoot the shit all night? Or can I go now?"

"You can go," Stone said. "For now."

"Alright then," McCready said, adjusting the collar of his trench, and walking towards the door.

Stone placed his arm in front of him. "But let me remind you of something, Agent McCready."

"What's that?"

"The *only* reason you're not sitting in a cell right now," Stone said, "is because you pulled this stunt while you were under the employ of Ordosoft™. But that doesn't mean you're getting off scot-free. We're going to press civil charges against you for the damage you caused to federal and city property." He moved his arm out of the way. "And pending further investigation, you're being placed on suspension."

McCready moved to the door. "Whatever, man. I'm already on leave."

"Not anymore," Vegas said. "Now it's going on record as a suspension." She smiled. "Meaning your income has come to a stop."

Opening the door, McCready said, "Well, guess what?" He pulled out his badge, and dropped it on the floor. It opened on impact, his picture facing up. "I quit."

"You can't just quit the Freemon like it's an ordinary job, Agent McCready," Stone said, raising his voice as McCready left the room. "There's procedure to be followed!"

"Fuck your procedure," McCready said, walking down the hallway to where Essence and Jung were standing.

The door shut loudly behind him.

"Looks like that went well," said Jung.

"Peachy," said McCready. "How's Ignacio doing?"

"He's alright," Essence replied. "They're gonna keep him here overnight, then run some tests on him in the morning."

"Did anyone call Irena yet?"

"Richardson did," Essence said. "After he diagnosed him."

"Alright, good," McCready said. "So what did the doc say happened to him?"

"He thinks he got hit with some type of disruptor," Essence said. "A mild one."

"What'd the contact records show?"

"Nothin' but static once Mo caught up to the attacker. No audio, no video–nothin'."

"Fuck," McCready said. "Well do you at least know who attacked him?"

"In a way," Jung said. "We know it's the guy who the rich girl was talking to."

"Great," McCready said, wondering how this day could possibly get any worse.

"But we don't know *who* he is," Jung added.

"What, he had some kind of biochip scrambler?"

"If only," Jung said. "This guy can change identities, McCready. Instantly. Holographically *and* on his biochip. He's good."

What have you gotten yourself into, Ashley? he asked

himself. Hell, what have *you* gotten yourself into, Marc? "Alright,"
McCready said, beginning to move, "I'm outta here. I gotta go fuckin'
sleep. Tell Ignacio I'll call him tomorrow, alright?"

"Sure," Jung said. "Take care of yourself, McCready."

"I'll try," he said, walking off in a pissed-off hurry. Choosing
the quickest route out of the building, he reached the exit, pressed his
thumb onto the scanner, and entered into the parking lot, where a
long, white, stretch limo was waiting for him. Xanadeux stood
outside of it. "This is fuckin' surreal," he muttered, as he approached
the Rolls®.

"Good evening, Agent McCready," Xanadeux said, opening
the rear doors without touching them.

"Yeah, right," he said with a laugh, reaching the vehicle.

Ashley was seated inside of the opulent and spacious interior,
a bottled water in her hand. "Hey," she said. "Everything go okay?"

"Are you serious?" he asked, slumping into the cushy seats
across from Ashley.

Xanadeux shut the door behind him.

She took a sip of the Evian®. "That bad, huh?"

"Worse." Between them was a small table, which contained
below it a small liquor cabinet. McCready opened it up, and began to
rummage through it.

The car moved slightly, as Xanadeux seated itself in the
driver's seat and shut the front door.

McCready looked behind him. There were three Xandys in
the front seat, all staring directly ahead. The tinted partition began
to raise. "Take me home, Jeeves," he said, just before it closed.

Ashley asked, "Wanna talk about it?"

Going back to the rummaging, McCready pulled out a mini
bottle of Jack Daniels®, and said, "Nope." He opened the bottle
and took a sip.

As the limo's engines started up, Ashley asked, "You sure?"

"Yup." He downed the rest of the bottle, set it on the seat, and
reached for another.

The Rolls® lifted into the air.

Twisting open a bottle of Bacardi®, McCready looked out the
window, and watched the Beacon Hill headquarters become smaller
as they ascended. He toasted the bottle towards the window, touched
it against the glass, and downed all of the rum in a single swig.

"My dad said the attacks are over," she said.

He placed the empty bottle next to the other, and reached for a regular-sized bottle of wine. "They caught the terrorists?"

"Apparently so."

Digging at the bottle's foil wrap, he asked, "How?"

Ashley sipped her water. "I'm not sure," she said. "He didn't go into details."

McCready tossed aside the shredded foil. "At least that's one less thing to worry about. You got a corkscrew?"

"You don't need one," she said.

He looked down at the bottle's top, and saw that it was a pull cork. He popped it off, and examined the front of the bottle. "Port?" he asked. "This shit any good?"

"Not to me, but I don't really like alcohol."

McCready took a sip. "It's alright." Then another. "It's hella sweet, though."

"It's a dessert wine," Ashley said. "You really don't want to talk?"

McCready leaned back in his seat, and kicked his boots up on the table. "I really, really don't want to talk," he said, resting the bottle on his stomach while holding it with both hands.

"Okay," Ashley said, also leaning back. She looked at him for a few moments, just to make sure he wasn't going to talk.

He wasn't.

She turned on some soft music, and closed her eyes.

McCready looked out the window at the bright city lights below, and took a long, slow sip of the port.

When the car had settled onto the ground, McCready sat forward, and said, "Well, I guess this is it."

Ashley sat up. "I guess so, huh?"

The doors opened up.

"It's been fun," he said, scooting towards the exit. "I think I can honestly say..." He laughed. "I'll never be forgetting these last two days." He laughed harder as he stumbled out of the limo.

She moved to the doors, and said, "Agent McCready?"

"Agent who?" he asked, turning around. He took another drink. "I'm just Marc now. Call me Marc."

"Okay. Marc..." she said, taking a way-too caring hold of his hand and smiling that fuckin' gorgeous, pure smile. "Thank you."

Her touch felt amazing. And comforting. So he pulled his hand away from her. "Don't mention it," he said. He started to turn away, then turned back towards her.

Ashley's eyebrows lifted.

He was tempted to spill his guts. Open up to her, he thought. Let her in. "Ah..."

"Yeah?"

Then he remembered what happened the last time he decided to do that. Fuckin' bitch ripped his heart out. Holding up the bottle, McCready said, "Care if I take ol' porto with me?"

She laughed. "What do you think?"

Shrugging his shoulders, he replied, "Fuck if I know." He began to stagger backwards towards his house, bottle in hand.

"Are you sure you're gonna be okay?" she asked.

"Ask me tomorrow," McCready said. He turned from her, and continued towards the house. Taking a few, unsteady steps along the path, he heard the door shut behind him, and the limo begin to take off. As the car flew by overhead, rising up and over his house, McCready placed his fingers onto his lips, blew a kiss towards the vanishing taillights, and watched his best chance at happiness fly away into the night.

Then he went inside, got as shitty drunk as he possibly could, and passed out on his living room couch.

McCready awoke to the sound of ringing.

"Wha..." he muttered, struggling to open his eyes. His head was throbbing.

Ringing.

He dizzily looked around the area.

It was the fucking uniview.

"Fuckin' shit."

It was early morning, he was on the couch, he had a massive fucking hangover, and there was an incoming call on the uniview. Turn the motherfucking ringer off when poisoning self with alcohol, he reminded himself as he grasped the remote control. Putting the display right in front of his blurry eyes, he touched a button.

The ringer turned off.

He put the remote down.

He went back to sleep.

McCready didn't wake up again until late afternoon, this time of his own volition. He was still groggy, but at least the throbbing in his brain wasn't so severe. And he wasn't covered in puke. That was good.

He sat up slowly, thumb and middle finger rubbing his temples, and grumbled something incomprehensible. Resting his head against the couch's cushioned back, he sat there for a few mintues, simply staring at the walls of his living room in an attempt to get a hold of his bearings.

The black-and-white, framed glossies of James Dean, Audrey Hepburn, Clint Eastwood, Brigitte Bardot, Marlon Brando–and Marilyn. Norma Jean. Fuck. He loved that car.

A Dali print of melting clocks. Time out of joint. Him out of job.

A poster of the album cover to Earth Wind and Fire's <u>That's the Way of the World</u>. Ain't that the truth? McCready thought, standing up from the couch. He walked to the bathroom, and took a much-needed piss. It was relieving, but his head still hurt. He zipped up, and opened the cabinet above the sink without looking in the mirror. He grabbed a bottle of Tylenol®. Extra Strength. He popped a few in his mouth, drank from the sink's faucet, walked back out to the living room, and plopped onto the couch. "Voice-rec on," he said.

The thin wallscreen immediately lit up. A message in its upper-corner noted that the ringer was off.

"Ringer on," he said. "Who called today?"

The screen listed seven calls. Five messages. Two of them he erased without viewing–the one from a telemarketer, and the one from an ex-girlfriend. The ones from Harold Moore he put on save. When he reached the one from Mason Huxton, he said, "View message."

The head of Ordosoft™ appeared on the screen, attired in a velvety robe, sitting in his breakfast nook. His face looked like it had been scratched or something. "Hello, Agent McCready," he said, pouring himself some orange juice. "I hope your morning is going well."

McCready let out a short, audible, "Ha."

Huxton continued, "As I'm sure you've already heard from Ashley, the terrorist attacks against my family have been remedied, and life has begun to return to normal." He took a sip of orange juice. "This was due in large part to the efforts of Agent Takura, and I wanted to personally thank you for the recommendation." He set down the juice, and carefully picked up a scone. "I also wanted to thank you–sincerely thank you–for protecting my daughter during this whole, wretched affair. You went above and beyond the call of duty, and I mean to compensate you accordingly for these sacrifices."

McCready sat up a bit.

Huxton crumbled off some of the scone and primly put it into his mouth. "Your director has informed me that you've been placed on suspension, and that there are some lawsuits which are going to be brought against you." He smiled. "You needn't worry, Agent McCready. You will have the full and complete backing of Ordosoft™, its lawyers, and most importantly, its finances–meaning that everything will be settled out of court in a quick and timely manner...without *anything* going on your records."

"Alright," McCready said out loud, "I like the sound of this. Keep going."

"Mind you, this is simply restitution, Agent McCready–not rewards. *Those* are something that I would like to discuss with you in person." Huxton set down the scone, and gently brushed his hands together. "Therefore, I am offering you an invitation to spend the weekend with Ashley and I in Tibet."

McCready's brow scrunched up. "What?"

"There, we can go over some of these things in detail, and you can have the opportunity to learn a bit more about Ordosoft™. It should be a...rewarding experience. For both of us." Huxton picked up a white, cloth napkin, and dabbed it at the corners of his mouth. "I will be preparing for the trip most of today, but you can reach me at any time with your decision." He set the napkin onto his lap. "I look forward to hearing back from you, Agent McCready. Good day."

Huxton morphed into the message display.

Somewhat stunned, McCready walked over to the fridge, pulled out a canned latté, and popped it open. He felt like his headache was receding, but maybe it was just that all these thoughts were suddenly displacing it. Rewards. Tibet. Ashley. Tibet? Unreal. Was he still going to quit the Freemon? Fuckin' DCC bastards. Is she really involved with Wellor? Have to call Ignacio. Wonder how Irena's doing? But Tibet? *Tibet?*

McCready walked back into the living room and sat on the couch. "Call Ignacio," he announced. He took a sip of the coffee while he waited.

Seconds later, Irena answered, looking naturally beautiful as usual. "Marc?" she asked. Her face appeared concerned. "You okay?"

"Yeah," he said, a bit surprised by the question. "Why?"

"You don't look so good."

"Oh, right," he said, realizing that he must look like shit.

FREQUENCIES

"Long night. How are you doing?"

"Better, now that Morris is back," she said. Aurora and Esperanza ran by behind her, chasing each other. "But I'm a still a little worried about him. He came home about an hour ago, and he just..." She paused. "He just didn't seem himself."

"What do you mean?"

"I-I can't really explain it, Marc. He just felt distant."

"I'm sure it's only the aftereffects of the disruptor, Irena. It takes a couple of days to get over 'em. I'm sure he'll be fine."

"Yeah," she said unsuredly. "You're probably right. He'll probably feel a lot better once he's done resting."

"He will, sweetheart," McCready said. "I promise. But just remember it takes a while."

Irena nodded, her expression revealing that she was obviously more troubled than she was saying.

"You gonna be okay, Irena?" he asked. "You need me to come over or anything?"

She smiled. "No, it's alright, Marc. I'll be fine. My sister's gonna come by in a little, so I'll have some company. I'll be fine. But thanks."

"Alright then," he said, not entirely convinced. "But you call me if you need anything, okay?"

"I will, Marc. Thank you."

"You're welcome, Irena. And tell Ignacio to call me when he wakes up, alright?"

"Sure."

" I'll talk to you later, then. Bye-bye."

Irena disconnected, and the message screen appeared again.

McCready sipped the latté, then looked to his right, through one of his living room windows. The sky was a light, gray color. Overcast, but not overbearing. A contemplative cloud cover, full of possiblities.

And of course, decisions.

He looked back at the screen, at the saved messages from Director Moore. He knew he couldn't go back to the Freemon. Regardless of whether or not Huxton could fix everything. Not after her. Not after Ashley. She'd shown him things. Things new, and things he once knew, but had let himself forget. And now he felt different. About everything. He felt...felt...he *felt*. That was it all boiled down to–feeling. Whether she had blessed him or cursed him, he still hadn't decided, but she'd changed him. That much was undeniable. She was the catalyst, she-

The uniview started to ring.

She...

The words "Ashley Huxton" appeared, blinking, upon the screen.

She was calling.

McCready rubbed his fingers through his tangled hair. Was he ready to talk to her yet?

The uniview continued to ring.

Maybe he should wait and call her back–after he'd had a shower and some time to think.

Her name continued to blink.

That way he could figure out what the hell it was that he wanted to say to her. Give him a chance to put things in perspective.

Still ringing.

Let alone the chance not to look hungover. Plus, he could...

Still blinking.

He could watch the taillights fly away again. "Aw, fuck it," he said, setting down the latté. "Answer call."

The ringing stopped.

Ashley morphed into view, her hands on her hips, wearing a sports bra and a pine-green leotard. "You're there," she said. "I was just about to hang up."

"Yeah, I was just, ah," he said, smoothing out his hair, "doing some–sorting some things out. Basically." He covered his mouth with his fist and cleared his throat. "How are you?"

"I'm good," she said, placing her palms together as if she was praying, and stretching her wrists. "You?"

He grabbed a lighter and the pack of Kamels® on the coffee table in front of him, and said, "Not bad."

"Long night, huh?"

McCready smirked, as he lit up a cigarette.

Ashley smiled, relaxed her arms to her sides, and said, "Me too." She looked down briefly, placed her hands behind her back, and said, "I think we should talk, McCready."

He blew out some smoke while nodding his head. "Yeah. Probably should." He inhaled. "Where were you thinking?"

"Here, I guess," Ashley said. "Unless you wanted to go somewhere else."

"Nah," he said, tapping off some ashes, "your place is cool. What time?"

FREQUENCIES

"Whenever. I'm just gonna be here dancing, so...whatever's good for you."

"Alright. Let me take care of a few things here–shower up, get something to eat–then I'll head over."

"You don't need a ride?"

He laughed, then drew in some clobacco. "Actually, yeah."

"Mm-kay," she said. "I'll send my car over now. That way you can come whenever you want."

"Cool. You want me to call first?"

"Hm-mm. Just come on over."

"Alright then. I'll see you in a bit."

Walking towards the screen, Ashley smiled, and said, "You will. Peace."

The message screen appeared, and he said, "Uniview off."

The screen went black.

With a relaxed expression upon his face, McCready turned from the uniview, gazed out at the overcast skies, and enjoyed the rest of his smoke.

Light, gray puffs, full of possibility.

McCready stood at the front door of Ashley's house, staring at the swirling spiral.

The intercom turned on, but the whorl remained.

"McCready?" she asked, the sound of water all around her.

"Yeah," he said. "It's me."

"I just got in the the shower," she said. "Come on in." The doorknob turned, the deadbolt unlocked, and the oval door opened. "I'll be out in a few minutes."

"Alright," he said, stepping into the ivy-covered hallway.

"Just make yourself at home," he heard her say, as the door shut behind him.

When he reached the row of shoes sitting next to the cylindrical wall, the second door hissed open. He took his boots off, placed them neatly beside her footwear, and entered her place, his least-raggedy pair of socks adorning his feet. The lighting inside the sphere was subtle and soft–candles, the overcast sky, and a few, dimmed, full-spectrum lamps. There was background music playing, not very loud, but very present, since the music was coming from numerous microspeakers located around the sphere. The sounds of light drumming, with a cello and a sax. From a nearby room, he could

267

hear the flowing water from Ashley's shower.

McCready stopped at the bedroom staircase, and slowly looked around the room, deciding how he was going to make himself at home. When his eyes reached the tall bookcase, he had his answer. He walked over to the curved, wooden shelves,and started to browse some of the library's titles. He ran his finger along the spines of a row of books, past one titled <u>Valis</u>, another called <u>The Man in the High Castle</u>, and pulled out a tattered, hardcover volume whose spine read: <u>Pools–Collected Reflections</u>. He opened its yellowed pages, and scanned over its table of contents.

"Still Waters." Page 5. "Nothing Can't Happen." Page 41. "Silent Majority." Page 88. "Behind the Sphere." Page 113. "Reality, Inc." Page 139.

McCready turned to page 88, and began to read the first page of the story.

An unshaven, but neatly dressed man is pacing around a room. His face shows signs of distress and conflict, his movements emulating these same conditions, fists clenching and unclenching repeatedly. The room also mirrors his state, books and clothes strewn about chaotically. He looks at the desk sitting in the far corner of the room. A wire-bound journal sits upon it, open and ready to be filled with the thoughts from his mind. He walks over to the desk and seats himself at the chair in front of it. He picks up a pencil and begins to write...

My name is Phil Martin. I'm a writer. I'm thirty two years old, single, and living in Atlanta, Georgia.

And oh yeah, I'm in deep shit.

Like deep enough to suffocate me.

I write science fiction. Alternate realities, possible futures, that kind of thing. Visions of what may come or what might never be.

McCready turned the page, and skipped ahead.

268

FREQUENCIES

After two years of writing, I finished it, and many rejection letters later, the novel was picked up and eventually published. It didn't do as well as I had hoped, but some people did pick it up.

The wrong people.

Now I'm forced to make a huge decision, one that will affect my life forever. But I'm getting ahead of myself here. Let me tell you about how it all began, or rather, me being a writer, why don't I tell you a story about how it all began? It's the story of this writer, Marty Phillips we'll call him, who sets out to write a novel to open people's minds...

Feeling the dryness in his throat, Marty Phillips reached into his backpack and pulled out his water bottle. He drank for a few seconds, wiped his mouth, then returned the bottle to the backpack. It was Tuesday and business was fairly slow at Disc Haven.

Sensing a long intro, McCready jumped ahead a few more pages.

The ride went by quickly. Marty was removed from the car and taken up what felt like a neverending flight of stairs.

When the stairs finally did finish, they came to a door. One of the men opened it. They entered.

An old, gruff voice stated, "I hope your trip was as pleasant as possible. Please have a seat, Mr. Phillips and we will begin."

They sat Marty down, then removed his blindfold.

Seated directly in front of him at a table was an older man. Slightly fat and slightly balding. He wore a black and white suit like the other men, but his was of a different style. The blonde man was standing behind Marty, and the mustached man was standing to his right. He looked around the room. It appeared he was in a hotel suite. All the windows were shut, but judging from the stairs, Marty knew they were fairly high up.

The old man's left hand was moving back and forth across a hardcover book, caressing it's cover. With his right hand, the old man picked up a glass filled with an amber colored liquid, most likely alcohol, and took a sip. He then said to Marty, "Mr. Phillips, I'm sure you're wondering why you are here."

Marty nodded, "To say the least."

"Yes." The old man tapped the book. "Your book. We found it very interesting. You have some very innovative ideas in it."

Marty said nothing.

"We especially enjoyed the chapter in which the 'villanous' government creates that new form of population control...what was it that you called it?"

Marty rubbed his eyes. "Silent Majority."

"Yes, 'Silent Majority.' That was an enlightening concept."

McCready turned the page, and skimmed to its bottom half.

"But that's the whole reason I wrote the novel," Marty said. "To get people prepared in case you tried to do something like that. Don't you remember in the last chapter, when the protagonist explains to his friend how to defeat the strategy?"

"Yes, I remember," he said. "But there are two things you didn't take into account, Mr. Phillips. Number one, most people don't read fiction to understand their society and reality. They read fiction to escape from their reality." He sipped his drink. "Number two, as I said before, we are modifying the ideas to suit our purposes. When we finally implement your 'silent majority,' you may not even know that we are doing it. We will have

270

modified it that much."

McCready heard the sound of water being turned off. He skipped to the last two pages of the story, and continued reading.

"There is no such thing as a sure thing, Mr. Phillips," he said. "Only a fool believes that." He leafed through the pages of the book. "We always have a need for people like you."

"But if my intention was to help people, why would I start writing propaganda for you? Why would I do that?"

The old man took another sip. "You know the answer. Because of Karen. Because of your mother and father. Because you don't want anything to happen to them. You wrote about that in the first chapter."

Marty put his face in his hands, and sighed a breath of frustration.

"You don't really have a choice, Mr. Phillips. But we'll let you sleep on it tonight. Give us a call in the morning and let us know your answer. I'm sure you'll make the right decision." He looked at the other two men. "Gentlemen, please escort Mr. Phillips back to his house and give him the phone number which he can reach us." He looked back at Marty. "I needn't remind you to stay silent, Mr. Phillips. Good day."

That was last night. End of story.

Now what do I do? The only definite thing is that my life as it was before is now over. Even if their job allowed me to keep the same relationships, I'm still going to have to lie to everyone around me. My whole life will be a lie. I'd probably end up killing myself, I'd be so ashamed. I can't believe this has happened. I mean, I can, since this is the stuff I write about, but at the same time it's unbelievable. By setting out to reveal oppression and control, I inadvertently created it. And now they want me to do it intentionally.

But maybe I can salvage something out of this. Maybe I can give them ideas that I know will ultimately fail. Craft the ideas in a way to make them seem like they would work. Conceptual trojan horses.

Yeah, right. They'd probably catch anything like that *long* before they'd ever implement it. I'm sure of that. But... What was it that the old man said again? That's right. "There's no such thing as a sure thing."

The man puts down the pencil and closes the journal. He walks over to the nightstand next to his bed. He opens the drawer, and pulls out a lighter.

Walking towards the phone, he picks up the journal. He puts it and the lighter in one hand, and with the other picks up the telephone receiver. He lets it rest between his ear and shoulder, then grasps the lighter. He flicks it on. The dial tone hums. He raises the flame to the journal's pages.

They begin to burn. He puts the lighter on the desk, right next to the number given to him by the two men in black. As he dials the number, he throws the ignited journal into the metal wastebasket, watching the ideas within it burn away.

THE END

McCready stared at the empty space at the bottom of the page. That's it? Not much resolution. And the prose wasn't anything to rave about, that's for sure. He closed the book shut.

As he was returning it to its place on the shelf, Ashley emerged from the bathroom, dressed in nothing but a brown bathrobe, and said, "What'cha readin'?"

"Short story collection from some 20th century hack," he said, wedging the book back into place. "Never heard of him."

"Pools?" Ashley asked, walking directly to the bedroom staircase.

"Yeah," McCready said, as he watched her wind her way up the spiral. "How'd you know?"

"It's the only short story collection in that section." Nearing the top of the stairs, she said, "I'll be right down, 'kay?"

"Yeah, sure." McCready walked over to the sunken center of the domed room, to one of the large bean bag chairs, and seated himself into it. He looked up at the half-dome skyview above, and saw that the clouds had turned a darker shade of gray. The color of rain. He molded himself into the chair, relaxed his eyes on the cloud gestalt, and waited for Ashley.

When he heard her coming down the stairs, he said, without moving from his seat to face her, "This chair's bomb."

"You look comfortable," she said.

"I am," he said. "I don't want to get up."

"Then don't," Ashley said. She moved around in front of him, and seated herself on a nearby futon. She was now dressed in light, baggy sweatpants and an oversized T-shirt, both a similar shade of dark-green. "It's good to relax." Ashley set down a wooden cigar box on the cushion next to her, stretched out her arms, and said, "I know I'm ready to."

"Yeah," he said, sitting up slightly in the chair. "'Bout to fall asleep though, if I relax any more."

She smiled, placed the box onto her lap, opened it, and placed her fingers inside of it. "How much did you drink last night?"

McCready laughed. "No comment."

She looked up from the box. "Did you get sick?"

"Nah," he said, catching a whiff of the box's herbal contents. "But I still got a fuckin' headache."

Ashley pulled out a hemp Zig-Zag®, and began to crumble some weed onto the paper. "You're welcome to have some herb with me," she said. "It's good for hangovers."

"Cool," he said. "Thanks."

As she rolled her joint, she said, "So... Did you talk to my dad today?"

"About Tibet?"

"Mm-hm."

"I got his message, but I haven't called him back yet. I'm still deciding."

She acknowledged his words with a nod, smoothly rolled up the joint, and delicately licked the paper. Putting on the final twist, she said, "You have any plans for the weekend?"

"Nothin' special," he said.

Ashley rolled the joint between her fingertips, while lightly blowing on it. "You should come then."

McCready scratched his chin. "Yeah, maybe." He glanced up at the skyview. Tiny sprinkles of rain, pitter-pattering against its surface.

"Decisions..." she said, pulling a flameless lighter from the box. "Always decisions." She closed her eyes, took in a deep breath, released it, then placed the joint between her lips. When she opened her eyes, Ashley ignited the tip, and flared the embers up in slow, sensuous pulls.

McCready watched the wisps of white smoke dance and whirl as they released from the burning end, rising into the air until they were freed of their form.

Exhaling the minty vapors like she was blowing a gentle kiss, she passed the joint to McCready.

Cigarette-sized, the smoke felt natural between his fingers. He watched it burn for a moment, then placed the moist end on his lips. And breathed it in.

Ten seconds later, the boundaries at the edge of his mind began to ebb. And flow. The flow of the music more evident now, the flow of his heartbeat too. Sensorium expanding. Senses extra marked. Sensorium, he wondered, is that a word? Fuck it. He took another pull, smoky herbal air passing over his tongue, down his throat, and into his lungs. He extended the joint towards Ashley. "Thanks," he said, their fingertips pressing together as the joint changed hands.

She smiled. "You're welcome." She drew in a small puff, and asked, "You want anymore?"

"Nah," he said, watching the smoke curve and flow around her lips. "I'm good."

"Me too," she said, reaching underneath the futon's edge, and pulling out a round, ceramic ashtray. She placed the joint's cindery end into the center of the ashtray, then gradually put it out by tracing a spiral outwards to the ceramic's edge.

As she set the ashtray back under the futon, he asked, "What is it with you and spirals?"

"Me and spirals?" she asked with a laugh. "What is it with you and Marilyn?"

"Nah, c'mon," he said, smiling, "I asked you first. They're everywhere. What's the deal?"

"Well, let's see..." Ashley said. "To put that into words..." She licked her lips, and said, "The spiral, to me, is like...the best visual representation...of whatever infinity, life...Goddess and

forever is, y'know?" She concentrated, her eyes squinting slightly.
"Like a two or three-dimensional representation of everything."
Ashley touched one of her silvery earrings, two spirals shaped into
an "s," glanced at him with a smile, and said, "That's about as good
as I can do with words."

Tripping off her response, he said, "Good enough. Shit."

"So what about you?"

"What about what?"

"Marilyn," she reminded him.

"Oh, right," McCready remembered. He tried to concentrate,
but his thoughts were becoming more tangential. "I'm not sure,
really..." He latched onto the closest tangent, and said, "She *looks*
cool. That's one thing I can definitely say. She's visually
appealing..." Suspending from the first tangent, he reached up for
another. "But, ah, beyond that...I don't know. It's just that whole era
or something...it's like beautiful and tragic at the same time. And I
guess she represents that." He shrugged his shoulders, and laughed.
"Whatever that means."

Ashley said, "It means what it means, y'know? It is
what it is."

McCready nodded and smiled, no verbal reply necessary.

The raindrops' sound as poetry.

Horns and strings conversing.

Stories written upon each other's faces. No words needing to
be said, and yet...

"Damn," McCready said, leaning forward, forearms resting on
his knees, and staring down at the patterns of movement shaded into
the thick carpeting. "I wish there wasn't so much shit going on right
now. I want to be able to relax and just kick back, but I got all these
fuckin' questions runnin' around my head...about the attacks, last
night at the club..."

"Me?" she intuitively asked.

"Yeah," he said. "And about you."

"I understand," she said. "I'd be curious too."

McCready nodded. "So where do we begin?"

"I don't know...just ask the first question that comes to mind."

"Alright," he said. Different things he wanted to know, but
out came the initial doubt, "Did you have anything to do with the
attacks on your family?"

Emphatically, she answered, "No," her face revealing
her repulsion towards the notion. "Have you *really* been worried

about that?"

"Not really. But the thought had crossed my mind," he said, neglecting to mention Mason's influence on the query.

"Wow," she said with a small laugh. "Attacking my own family...that would be pretty crazy." She looked at him curiously. "I'm almost afraid to ask, McCready, but... What else have you been wondering about me?"

He thought for a moment, then said, "Last night, with the DCC, why di-"

"Okay," Ashley interrupted. "Hold up. Before we talk about last night..." She paused. "I need to know if I can trust you, McCready." She stared him straight in his eyes, and said, "Straight up–tell me now, and look at me when you do. Can I honestly, *truly* trust you?"

Without wavering, McCready met her gaze, and replied, "Yeah. You can trust me."

Ashley continued staring into him, then nodded her head. "Okay then," she said, her eyes no longer checking his. "Ask away."

McCready gathered his thoughts, and asked, "Last night, why did you lie about Adrian Wellor?"

"What makes you think I lied?"

"You said you'd never heard of him, but I saw his name in that sketchbook over there," McCready said, pointing to the same one he'd looked through yesterday. "So that means either you've never seen the pages inside that book...or you're lying. Why?"

"Why?" Ashley repeated. "Maybe because I think my thoughts should be my own...because I think the 'authorities' don't need to know *everything*." She paused. "Because *I'm* still trying to figure out what's happening right now..."

"Alright," he said. "Fair enough. But can you at least try to give me *some* sense of what's goin' on with you? 'Cause this shit is confusing the hell out of me, Ashley. I mean, you're talking to people who the DCC is after–the *same* ones who happened to have attacked my best friend–you obviously know something about Wellor, you're fooling the fuckin' freereads..." A short laugh, and he said, "What's the deal, sweetheart? What are you involved in?"

"I don't know," she said. "It's like I'm telling you...I'm still not sure." Ashley stood up, ran both of her hands through her long, brown hair, and rested her hands on the back of her neck. Gazing down at the floor, she said, "It's...it's like I've always been on the fringes of this...this *something*. This feeling, this movement. It's like an undercurrent of change that I've always sensed...but I've only been getting my feet wet in it, y'know? I've only been playing around its edge." She paused. "But now the current's rising, McCready..." She released her hands and looked at him. "And I think I just started swimming in it."

"Swimming?" he asked. "Or are you getting swept away?"

"No," she said. "I'm swimming. There's no doubt about that." Sitting down on the futon, she smiled, and said, "I'm just not sure where the current leads."

Precipitation falling harder now, rivulets of rain running along the skyview above them.

"Alright, so let me try to get this straight." He paused, the webbing of his left hand on his brow, attempting to piece the puzzle Ashley together. Fragments of evidence, waiting to be joined...

The sketchbook. "Something has made you want to look into Adrian Wellor," he said, "or else you wouldn't have been asking yourself where he is. The fact that you *don't* know where he is, means that you aren't that involved with anything he's doing." He looked at her. "Am I close?"

"Yeah," she said.

"Good."

Two more fragments, the rapper and Jung's update about the identity changer. He said, "So you go to the Tiger's Lair, looking for information. You talk to the guy in the robe, because you know he has some connection to Wellor."

"Actually, I didn't know for sure," she said. "I just knew he was someone who knows things."

"That's pretty lucky," he said, somewhat skeptical.

"Yeah, I know. But that's been the theme of my week, McCready. Synchronicity after synchronicity...things just keep on falling into place. It's bizarre."

"I guess so." His tongue moved around his cottony mouth. "You care if I get some water?"

Standing up, she said, "I'll get it. I need some too."

As she moved over to the kitchen cove, he asked her, "So now, the rapper...he's the same person as the guy in the robe, right?"

"Right," she said, opening the fridge and pulling out a pitcher of water. "And you think he attacked your friend."

"That's what the evidence says."

Pouring two glasses full of water, she said, "I don't think he did it, McCready. It's not his way." Glasses in hand, she walked back over. "Seer's not a violent person."

"Anybody can get violent when they're cornered."

"Maybe." She handed him a glass. "But I doubt it."

McCready took a big sip of the cold water. "Oh, man, that's good." He took another drink, swished it around his mouth, and swallowed. "I had some serious fuckin' cottonmouth. Thanks."

"Mm-hm," Ashley said, taking a drink. "So is your friend gonna be okay?"

"Looks like it, yeah. Fortunately." He drank more fluid. "He's just gonna need some rest."

"That's good, at least." She paused momentarily, then said, "McCready...do you know why they want Wellor so bad?"

He shrugged his shoulders. "They probably think he has something to do with the riots. That's what they were flying in from D.C. to investigate."

"Hmm." She took a sip of water. "So what are you guys taught about Wellor, anyway? What do the Freemon records say?"

"Not a whole helluva lot," he said. "Just that he was one of the scientists involved in the creation of the freereads...and that at some point, he turned seditious and went underground."

"That's all they say?"

"Basically. I mean, they also talk about how they pulled his files from the public database and what not, but that's just general stuff. That applies to anyone who's been labelled an enemy of the state."

Ashley shook her head. "Wow..." she said. "So you guys don't even know."

"Know what?" he asked. "What are you talking about?"

"A conspiracy, McCready." She laughed. "A really, big, huge, fucking conspiracy."

"Which is...?"

"Wellor wasn't just involved with the the frequency emission technology...he created it."

"History says it was Michael Brennan," McCready said.

"Yeah," she said. "But history's bunk."

"Well, yeah, I'm not gonna argue with you on that one," he said. "But, ah, in Brennan's case...that's sort of like saying Einstein didn't come up with the theory of relativity."

"Maybe he didn't," she said.

McCready laughed, finished off his water with one large gulp, and said, "So where did you hear about this conspiracy?"

Completely serious, she said, "From Michael Brennan."

His brow wrinkled. "*What*?"

"Yeah," she said. "I met with him the day before yesterday, and he..." Her voice tailed off, her body language revealing that she was still trying to comphrehend the situation. "He spilled it all to me."

"Are you sure it was actually him?"

"What do you mean?"

"It could have been one of Wellor's group in holographic disguise."

Ashley put her finger on her lip, much like her father would, and ruminated on the possiblity. "I guess anything's possible, but...it had to have been Brennan. I'm positive. It was him."

"And you think he was telling you the truth?"

"Yeah," she said. "I don't see any reason why he'd lie to me. There'd be nothing for him to gain." She drank the rest of her water. "Not to mention the fact he's been a friend of the family for as long as I can remember...it just wouldn't make any sense for him to lie."

"Trippy," McCready said, the implications of her words mingling with the herb to make him feel extra budded. "But why did he decide leak the truth *now*? After all these years?"

"I think it was just time. He's getting old, and I think he's scared of dying with all that guilt. Telling me was like...a way to purge himself, I guess."

"That is fuckin' trippy." He rubbed his eyes and laughed. "This world is *so* fuckin' nuts, Ashley. It never fuckin' stops."

"I feel you," she said, picking up the lighter and the joint. "Fully."

"Oh well," he surrendered, as she relit the ashy end. "Whatever. Fuck all the nonsense and all the bullshit. Fuck jobs, fuck terrorists, fuck the DCC–you're here, I'm here, the vibe is cool..."

Ashley handed him the joint, holding in the smoke with a smile on her face.

"So let's just have a good fuckin' night," he said, then took a strong fuckin' hit. Holding it in, he smiled, and added, "Alright?"

Ashley laughed as she exhaled her smoke. "Alright."

Minutes flowed into hours, moments into montage...

"What if," Ashley said, breathing out the joint's final hit. "Do you ask yourself 'what if' questions a lot?"

"Like 'what if your life is just a dream' kind of shit?" he said.

"Mm-hm."

"Oh yeah," McCready said. "For sure. You too?"

Ashley laughed. "Constantly."

"Were you just thinking of one?"

Nodding, she said, "A second ago, when I was talking to you, I started thinking, 'what if I'm saying something *completely* different than what I *think* I'm saying? What if the words coming out of my mouth aren't the same ones I'm hearing in my head?"

McCready laughed. "I know what you're saying. I've tripped on that before." He paused, then laughed again. "I remember one time, when I was about...fourteen, I think...no, fifteen–it was fifteen. Anyway, I had this one 'what if' that just kept trippin' me out for *days*."

"What was it?"

"Well, it was while we were learning about the electromagnetic spectrum and gravity shielding, and...I started trippin' on 'what if somebody built this big, fuckin' GS device around the Earth?' One that totally shielded the planet from gravity's effects. Like utterly and completely shielded it."

"Sounds like you were a little freeker," she said.

He smirked. "Yeah, so like for days, I had these nightmares about people and animals, and oceans and cars, and just fuckin' *everything* floating up into the sky, and then into space, and..." He laughed. "Now it's just fuckin' funny to me, but ah, back then...man, that shit freeked me out."

"Yeah, I hate 'em too," McCready said, as they strolled through the forested backyard of Ashley's estate. "They're fucked up. I had to use one a few years back with this one girl I was dating, 'cause she was so paranoid about germs. Every single time we had sex, I had to put one on. It was fuckin' brutal."

Ashley said, "I take it you two didn't last long?"

"Nah, not at all," he said. "It ruined the whole experience." He chuckled. "This one guy I knew, when I was on the force, he had the absolute best fuckin' line I have ever heard about condoms. He said that wearing a condom is like eating your favorite food with a balloon on your tongue."

She laughed. "That's good."

"Yup, that pretty much sums it up." He looked up at the

darkening sky. "I can't even imagine what sex was like before the AIDS vaccine."

"AIDS," she said, shaking her head. "Don't even get me *started* on that one."

"Why not?" he asked.

"It just pisses me off, that's all," she said. "It was such an obvious example of genocide, and no one even talks about it. They always try to pretend like it was Mother Nature's way of controlling the population. Bullshit, y'know? If nature wanted to halt human growth, she would have started AIDS in Europe or America, *not* Africa. And she would have started it in the cities, not the forests."

"So you think it was gengineered?"

"Oh, no doubt," she said. "I mean, doesn't it seem a little shady to you the way the vaccination didn't appear until *after* the AIDS virus had decimated the African population?"

Placing a cigarette in his mouth, he replied, "Shady as venetian blinds."

Popping the orange slice into his mouth, McCready sat on one of the barstools, and said, "Way I see it, society's just one, big, fuckin' con. 'Cause there's two things that they sell us on, and both of 'em are a scam." He held up one finger. "Security." He put up a second finger. "And convenience."

"The dreaded 'C' word," she said, biting into a kiwi. "Quite possibly the most dangerous word in the entire English language."

"Well, there's gotta be an 'S' word too then, sweetheart, 'cause security's just as dangerous a' notion."

Ashley smiled. "I can accept that."

McCready smiled back. "So the world controllers, they're the con artists, right? 'Cause these fuckers know that there's *no* such thing as security and convenience, but they sell it to us anyway. They know that no matter how many gates they put up, and how many laws they pass, we're still not gonna be any more secure, 'cause *they're* the ones who are making the poverty and creating the fuckin' crimes in the first place."

"True," she said.

"And convenience, shit–how the fuck is it more convenient to always have an electronic leash with you at all times? How is it more convenient to be reached on your wristcom or cellphone twenty-four hours a day? Shit, convenience is just another word for slavery." He popped another piece of fruit into his mouth. "I'm tellin' you,

Ashley, without those two scams, society as we know it..." He peeled off another orange segment. "Falls apart."

"I don't mind," Ashley said. "Ask away."

He looked at her curiously. "How'd you fool the freereads?"

With a smile, she said, "You won't believe me."

"Try me," McCready said.

"Okay," she said. "It's a technique someone taught me."

He gave her a funny look. "Seriously?"

"Yeah. It's kinda like meditating."

"Well," he said with a laugh, "you were right–I don't believe you."

She shrugged her shoulders. "Told ya."

"She told him," Ashley said, as she rolled the joint in the palm of her hand. "She gave him fair warning....but he didn't listen." She smiled, shaking her head. "And so the second he reached his hand around her thigh and touched that sensor she installed...the alarm went off." Ashley laughed. "*Really* loud. It was hilarious."

"I bet," McCready said, laughing. "Right in the middle of the fuckin' movie. Damn, he must've felt stupid."

"Yeah, he did. He just sat there for a minute, not sure what to do..." Ashley blew on the joint. "And then he got up and left."

"I'm taking it their relationship didn't last long?"

She smiled. "Not at all. They broke up that night." She took a sip of water. "Which was just fine with Dawn. 'Cause even then–even at fifteen–she *demanded* respect. And she was always smart enough and strong enough to know how to get it. Which is probably why she's been so successful in Hollywood." Ashley paused, then said, "Hey–I just thought of a good 'what if.'"

"Yeah?"

"Mm-hm."

"Alright then. Let's hear it."

"What if..." she said, looking him in the eyes with a playful grin, "...we were just characters in a movie? Or a book?"

"Well," McCready said, "then whoever wrote my life story had a lotta angst, or something."

Ashley laughed. "Okay, so..." she continued, still smiling at his comment, "...if we were just characters in a movie...then that would mean an audience was watching us *right* now, talking about them and how they're watching *us* talking about them." She put the joint in her mouth. "It'd be a weird infinity effect, wouldn't it?"

"Now watch this," Ashley said, passing him the joint as the lights dimmed down. She touched a few more buttons on the holographic remote, and the skyview above started to glow with thousands of psychedelic hues. The pouring rain reacted with the colors, forming infinite droplet patterns across the sensitive surface, as the sound of every single raindrop was transmitted through the room's speakers.

"Whoa," he said, easing back into the beanbag and taking a toke. "That's fuckin' sweet."

Ashley laid back on the beanbag next to him, their shoulders touching together, and said, "Yeah. Chaos is beautiful, isn't it?"

"It is," he replied, the misty rain sprinkling lightly upon his face. They stood on the balcony of her Kremlin-like tower, staring out into the night sky, at the city lights, the adsats, and the air traffic laid out before them.

"Even though it's all crazy," McCready said, "there's still something beautiful about it. There's no denying that." His eyes passed over the full moon, which currently had the red, Coca-Cola® wave projected across its surface, the slogan "Always Coca-Cola®" written around its lower rim, then he looked over at Ashley, and said, "I'm having a good time tonight."

She smiled, and moved in closer to him. Leaning her head against his shoulder, she said, "Me too."

He placed his arm around her, and the two continued to watch the night unfold.

Unfolding the blanket that sat underneath her pillows, Ashley shifted, causing the water beneath McCready to roll from one end of the bed to the other, gently rocking him back and forth. As she wrapped the crocheted blanket around herself, she looked down and said, "I still miss her so much."

"Yeah," he said, petting one of the two cats that was sharing the spacious waterbed with them, "it's hard to lose a parent." He thought about being nine years old. "Real hard."

She studied his face for a moment, and said, "You sound like you're speaking from experience."

He nodded slowly, surprised he was doing so.

"Recently?" she asked.

"Nah," he said, rubbing the edges of his sleeve. "It happened when I was nine."

"Your mom or your dad?"

" My dad, he, ah...he..." His lip quivered slightly. "He got taken away. Right in front of me an' my mom. They fuckin' smashed the door in..." He cleared his throat. "And they fuckin' took him."

"Oh my Goddess," she said, covering her mouth with one hand, holding his hand with the other.

"They killed him, Ashley. Those fuckers killed him."

She placed her other hand on top of his, and said nothing.

"And you know what's so fuckin' sick about it all?" he asked. "What makes me so fuckin' sick I just wanna die sometimes? I..." McCready struggled to let out the words. "...I fuckin' became one of 'em, Ashley. I became the thing I hated most." He breathed out hard through his nostrils. "I became a Freemon."

She gently placed her hand under his chin, and said, "But then you quit, McCready. You changed. You're *not* that anymore."

McCready looked away from her, shook his head, and stared at the pyramidical walls through bleary, tired eyes.

"You took the first step," she said. "And now all you need to do is forgive yourself...and accept. Life doesn't always make sense...believe me, I know..." Her voice cracked a little. "'Cause I'm still trying to understand why my mom was taken away... But life happens the way it does for a reason. It really, truly does." She grasped his hand. Comfortingly.

He looked back at her.

Bittersweetly, she smiled, saying, "And when someone dies...it just means it was time for their energy to change form...and time for their life vibrations to change their frequency." She closed her eyes, and breathed in deeply. "But they're still part of the life spectrum, y'know? Forever." Her eyes opened, sparkling, shining with life. "That's what's so beautiful." A tear trickled down her face, around the corner of her smile, and she said, "Nothing ever really dies...it just changes."

And much to his amazement, McCready started to cry. The most genuine, heartfelt cry to come out of him in a long while. Years of cynicism and apathy melting away in the hopeful glow of her eyes. A timeworn veneer of indifference dissolved by inspiration.

He felt exhilarated. But also exposed.

Unmasked.

Bared.

And she could tell. So she smiled back reassuringly.

FREQUENCIES

Soothingly.

Lovingly.

Instinctively, driven by the desire to comfort her, as much as the want to be comforted himself, he slowly leaned forward, closed his tearing eyes, and they kissed each other. Passionately.

Both looked into each other's eyes for the briefest of moments, and then like polar opposites coming together, they embraced each other tightly, for what felt like a magnetic eternity. Human electricity combining. Positive and negative currents intermingling. Polarity reversing within him.

Nothing dying.

Everything changing.

An eternity later, they lay next to each other, a light, silk sheet draped over their naked bodies.

Her inner thigh resting comfortingly on top of him, Ashley kissed him lightly on the cheek, and said, "So...are you gonna be okay?"

"What?" he asked.

"I asked you that last night, and you told me to ask you tomorrow." She smiled. "Tomorrow's here. Are you gonna be okay?"

McCready smiled, laughed a little, and nestled the back of his head into the soft, down pillow. "Yeah," he replied. "I'm gonna be fine."

Ω

∞

Chapter 14:
The Wizard of Is

"It is time.
I must go away, far away, on a journey which shall lead me to my
salvation.

The front door slid open, revealing a nicely decorated, though not too tidy, living room. Rumpled blankets strewn across the black, leather couch, beer and latté cans on the glass coffee table, and a gorgeous, hardwood floor in need of a good vacuum.

McCready looked at Ashley, scratched the back of his neck, and said, "Excuse the mess. I, ah..." He laughed as he walked into the house. "Wasn't really expecting to have company."

It was Friday morning, and the sun was shining.

"Don't worry about it," she said, following him inside. "I wasn't expecting you to expect me."

"Yeah, even so, it's still a little embarrassing." He moved over to the coffee table, and scooped up the empty cans with both hands. "Place looks like a fuckin' pig sty."

"C'mon," she said, nudging him as he walked towards the kitchen. "It's not *that* bad."

Arms full, he reached the recycler, dropped the cans in, and gave her a halfcocked smile. "It is. But thanks for trying." Rounding up some stray dishes, he asked, "You want anything to drink?"

She shook her head, as her eyes passed over the room's twentieth-century-themed decorations. "Hm-mm. I'm fine."

He opened the dishwasher, and placed the dishes inside.

"Alright then," he said, moving back into the living room. "I'll just go ahead and throw my shit together real quick, and we can bounce out of here." He passed by her, and began to walk down the hallway ahead. Stopping suddenly, he turned around, and said, "I still can't believe I'm going to fuckin' Tibet."

"Yeah," she said, smiling. "You're going to fuckin' Tibet."

McCready shook his head and laughed. "Crazy." Turning back around, he continued down the hallway, still laughing.

The SST's door slid open, just as they reached the top of the stairs leading up to it.

"Good morning," Xanadeux said. "Welcome aboard."

"Thanks," Ashley said, stepping into the plane's ample interior.

"Yeah, thanks," McCready said, following her in.

"My pleasure," the Xandy replied. To Ashley, it said, "Your father is in the rear of the aircraft."

"As usual," she said, moving into the lobby, which was beautifully decorated with rugs, couches, chairs, paintings, chandeliers, and more, all specially designed for air travel.

Xanadeux said, "He'd like you to join him before takeoff."

"Okay," Ashley said.

"This is a fuckin' baaadass plane," McCready said, touching the soft material on one of the couches. "You guys fly in style, I gotta say that."

Walking to the bar, Ashley said, "Yeah, it definitely beats coach."

The Xandy at the bar asked, "What would you like to drink?"

"Just cranberry juice," she said. "On ice."

It turned to McCready. "And you?"

"How about..." He looked around at his surroundings. "How about a martini?"

"This early?" Ashley asked.

McCready smiled. "Seems fitting."

As the Xandy at the bar prepared the drinks, the one who greeted them motioned towards a set table, and said, "Breakfast will be served at the dining table once we've reached our cruising altitude, and we should arrive in Tibet shortly thereafter. In the meantime..." It bowed its head towards them.

"Enjoy," said the Xandy at the bar, as it set the drinks down onto the counter.

"I plan on it," McCready said as he picked up his martini.

Picking up her glass, Ashley moved past a spiral staircase, and towards the door at the far end of the room.

"What's up there?" he asked.

"Stargazer lounge," she said, approaching the door. "We'll go up there after we say hi to my dad."

"Sounds good to me."

The door slid open as they approached, and they stepped into the conference room, which had a very businesslike atmosphere to it. Sparsely decorated, it contained numerous wallscreens, a round meeting table in its center (the Ordosoft™ logo prominently displayed upon it), with twelve chairs surrounding it. Passing through without stopping, they reached the tail of the aircraft, which was just as palatially decorated as the lobby. The only significant difference in design being a giant, transparent window which formed the entire back end of the tail, so that a perfect view of the surrounding airstrip could be seen in front of them.

Her father sat in a large, Ordosoft™-green armchair, his back turned towards them, facing the view. "You're here," he said, the seat immediately beginning to rotate around towards them. When it faced them, the chair's motion stopped, and he stood up from the chair with a pleased expression upon his face. "It's good to see you both." Walking towards her with a slight limp, he said, "Ashley." He placed his cheek next to hers, and kissed towards her, his lips not touching her skin. "It's so good to see you safe."

"You too," she said. "How are you feeling today?"

"Much better," he said. "Thanks to the nanotech therapy, I'm nearly one hundred percent." He looked at her for a moment and smiled. "Thank you for asking." He then extended his hand towards McCready, and said, "And Agent–rather, I should say, *Mr.* McCready..." They shook hands. "I'm pleased you could make it. You're in for a quite a treat this weekend."

"I'm lookin' forward to it," he said, sipping his martini.

"Splendid." Her father looked at them both. "Will you be joining me back here for takeoff?"

"Actually, I'm gonna show him the stargazer," Ashley said.

"Very well," he said. "Then I'll see you both at breakfast."

"You will." To McCready, she said, "C'mon. Let's go upstairs."

288

FREQUENCIES

"Alrighty," he said, munching on the martini's olive. "Lead the way."

As the SST's engines began to hum louder, they exited the tail, walked through the conference room, and climbed the stairs leading to the top floor. "Here we are," she said upon entering the stargazer lounge, which contained, among other things, recliners and chairs that allowed its occupants to stare up at its transparent ceiling. "Where do you wanna sit?"

"The middle," he replied, walking to the center of the lounge.

Ashley sat down in one of the comfy chairs, set her drink down in the armrest's cupholder, and said, "Good choice."

McCready finished off the remains of his drink, and sat down next to her. "Do these recline all the way?"

Leaning back all the way in the chair, she said, "Of course."

"Bomb," he said, joining her in her reclined position, as the aircraft began to move.

The sky above was blue, with lots of fluffy, white clouds scattered about. "I love this kind of sky for takeoff," she said, watching the cumulus shapes pass by.

"I can see why."

"Please prepare for takeoff," Xanadeux announced over the loudspeaker.

"You gonna wear your seatbelt?" McCready asked.

"No," she said. "You?"

"Nope."

The plane began to move faster, as did the clouds above. "Here we go," she said.

"Alright," McCready said, as the SST rose up from the ground, and her stomach dropped slightly. "We're off to see the wizard."

The aircraft dropped its altitude and speed as they reached the Himilayas of southeast Tibet, and began to skim over the snowy, jagged peaks which topped the spectacular mountain range. Standing in the lobby before one of the large, lookout windows, Ashley, McCready, and her father gazed out at the breathtaking view below.

"Goddess," Ashley said, watching a herd of yaks move across the wintry landscape. "Nature is amazing."

"Indeed," her father said.

McCready was simply speechless.

FREQUENCIES

They passed over summits and lowlands, villages and towns, bridges and monasterries, surveying the sacred land from their heavenly viewpoint. When they reached the valley where her grandfather's retreat was located, Ashley pointed down to it, and said to McCready, "There it is."

A small, gleaming city, nestled into the snowy terrain, encapsulated within a gigantic, iridescent dome. Completely protected from the harsh elements, it contained within its barriers small jungles, forests, and deserts, all aesthetically interwoven into the fabric of the city, all sustained by the magical technology wielded by her grandfather.

"Spectacular, isn't it?" Mason asked.

McCready nodded. "Fuck yeah, it is."

As they neared the winter wonderland, the plane reduced its speed even more, and Ashley said, "It always reminds me of one of those little Christmas-scene bubble-toys you get when you're a kid...the ones that you shake up and watch the snow fall." She smiled. "Except all the snow is on the *outside* of this one."

A portal in the dome swirled open, allowing entry.

"And you can go inside it," McCready added, as they entered into the city's airspace.

Joined by two security-escort vehicles, the SST switched to its GS mode, circled around the area, and utilizing its VTOL capabilities, descended down onto a wide landing pad located on the outskirts of the desert domain.When the aircraft came to a complete rest, her father let go of the gold, overhead handrail, and said, "Here we are."

Outside the SST, the desert air was warm and dry, and the artificial sun was shining brightly. They were greeted by four, crossbred security guards, each attired in their own, distinctive uniform, which was reflective of the region from whence their animal traits came.

"Tashidelek," the humanoid cobra said, slithering to the fore, his skin-hood flaring out as he did. Bowing his head towards them, he placed one arm across his underbelly, the other behind his back, and added, "Tibet welcome to."

"Thank you, Dorje," her father said, as the Xandys began to load their luggage onto the open-aired SEVs. "It's good to be here."

To Ashley, Dorje smiled, and said, "Long time has it been."

"Two years," she said.

"Time flies how," he said. "Welcome back."

She smiled. "Thanks."

Turning his reptilian eyes to McCready, he said, "I've before met you not. I Dorje am."

"McCready," he said with a sup. "Good to meet you."

Dorje nodded. "You well as." Motioning back to the other guards, he said, "Allow me my guard to introduce." His scaly hand pointing towards the antelope-like crossbreed, he said, "Kudu."

"Greetings." Kudu reverently bowed his head, his corkscrewed horns dipping down as he did. "And salutations."

Dorje pointed to the next guard, and said, "Gila."

The black and orange-skinned, lizard-like woman, flicked her tongue, and said, "Pleasure to meet you."

"And Canis."

The jackal, clothed in regal Egyptian dress which made him look like a living hieroglyphic, merely nodded, and uttered no words.

Dorje said, "We will to the palace your escort be." He looked over at the two SEVs, which were now loaded with their luggage, then at her father. "We shall go?"

"Let's," he replied, and they all began to walk towards the circular vehicles.

"We will four to a ship ride," Dorje said. "Two Canis and I with, two other Gila and Kudu with. Preferences any?"

"Why don't you take Ashley and Mr. McCready," her father said. "Xanadeux and I will ride with the others."

Reaching the vehicles, Dorje said, "It so be," and the two groups branched off.

Canis walked up the vehicle's ramp, onto its flat, circular platform, and moved directly to its center.

Dorje followed right after. He slid up the vehicle's ramp, turned back towards Ashley, extended his arm, and said, "Aboard welcome"

"Thanks," Ashley said. She grasped his smooth, scaly hand. Always an interesting sensation...cool, reptile skin with human bones beneath it.

As he walked up the ramp after Ashley, McCready held up a pack of Kamels®, and asked, "Can you smoke here?"

"You can," Dorje replied with a charming smile.

"Alright," McCready said, tapping out a cigarette with satisfaction. "This place just keeps getting better and better." He walked over to the four-foot railing that surrounded the circular vehicle, and leaned his butt against it. Lighting up the cigarette, he looked around at the SEV's dimensions, and said to Ashley, "You feel like you're on a giant coaster?"

Ashley laughed, as her father's SEV began to lift off of the desert sand. "It does kinda look like that," she said.

Canis then gestured his hands in a sorcerous manner, causing a plant-like stalk to grow up from the SEV's center, straight out of the metal floor. It stopped growing when it reached the height of Canis' chest, and its top formed into a gelatinous, emerald-colored substance the shape of a sphere.

"What?" McCready asked.

Canis placed both of his fur-covered hands atop the sphere. It morphed around his hands, then quickly reformed itself.

Dorje turned to McCready, and said, "Interface organic."

Moving his fingers around the inside of the soft sphere, Canis lifted the ship off of the ground.

Though the platform barely lurched as it rose into the sky, Ashley still leaned back a little past its railing, just to test the invisible barrier that she knew surrounded the vehicle. It was soft, like a cushioning, rather than a wall, and gently prevented her from going too far, while keeping the wind off of her face.

Noticing the effect, McCready pushed his back against it, and said, "Cool."

As they cruised over the golden sand, Ashley could see all kinds of desert plants and animals below them. The range of species was so diverse, she imagined that a sample from every major desert of the world must have been represented there. Far off in the distance to her right, where desert became jungle, she could just barely make out rainclouds. To McCready, she said, "It's raining in the tropics right now." She pointed in the gray clouds' direction.

He took a puff from his Kamel® and moved forward. "So over there, there's all these jungle animals and plants?"

"Mm-hm," she said.

"Underneath the same dome..." He blew out some smoke, the lack of air resistance causing the wisps to drift in front of him as if they were in an enclosed room. "That's fuckin' incredible." Noticing the way the smoke cleared—not a smooth dissipation, but more of an abrupt disappearance—he looked at Ashley, and asked, "You're seeing that too, right?"

She smiled. "Oh yeah. Get used to it. There's always more to come."

They could now see the palace up ahead, its domed architecture curving along the horizon. "Kinda looks like the Taj Mahal," McCready said.

"Yes," said Dorje. "Lama by that influenced was."

"Lama?" McCready asked.

"My grandfather," Ashley said.

"Your grandfather's a *camel*?"

Laughing, she said, "Buddhist."

"Oh, right," McCready said. He laughed, then looked at the two crossbreeds. "It wouldn't have surprised me."

"Me neither," Ashley said, watching a coyote chase after a jackrabbit.

"So, Dorje," McCready said, walking towards him. "Is it just you guys out here, patrolling this whole place?" He scanned the horizon. "Where are the other security ships?"

Canis looked at Dorje, and they both gave each other a knowing smile.

"Everywhere security is," Dorje said. "Rest assured."

When they reached the palace, the SEV's hovered a few feet above the ground, and extended their ramps.

Ashley waited for the others to disembark, then she walked down the SEV's ramp, and onto the palace's marbled steps. "Thanks for the lift," she said to Dorje and Canis, who remained behind on the platform.

"Our pleasure," Dorje said, as the two SEV's began to ascend. "Your stay enjoy."

After Ashley joined the rest of the group—consisting of her father, Xanadeux, McCready, and Kudu—a beautiful Tibetan woman, adorned in the ochre oufit of a Buddhist lama, emerged from the palace's entrance. In one of her hands, she was balancing a wide silver tray. Six, long, white scarves were draped across it. "Nga-to delek," she said as she reached them. Removing her hand from underneath the tray (which continued to hover in the air without her support), she picked up one of the scarves, draped it across both of her hands, and walked over to Mason. She smiled, and placed the fabric around his neck.

"Thank you, Lhasa," he said.

"You're welcome." Lhasa proceeded to perform the same welcoming ritual to each of the Seattle group, and when she reached

Ashley, she said, "It's so good to finally meet you."

"Thanks." Ashley bowed her head slightly to allow the kata to be placed around her neck. "It's nice to meet you too."

Lhasa nodded, and said, "I've heard a lot about you."

"Really," Ashley said, wondering to herself exactly who this woman was, since she had never seen her before on any previous visit.

Lhasa smiled. "Yes." She walked over to the silver tray, and brushed her hand along its underside, causing its molecules to dissipate into the air. Then to everyone, she said, "Please follow me. Gonpo is being inside."

As the group began to follow, McCready drifted back to the rear with Ashley, and asked, "Gonpo is your grandfather?"

"Mm-hm," she said. "It's his honorific name."

"What's it mean?" he asked, slowing down to examine a marbled pillar which had leaves and branches growing out of it.

"Sorcerer," she said. "Or protector. He likes both translations."

Touching the palace's floral growth, McCready said, "This building...it's growing things." He looked at her. "It's alive."

"Yep," she said, beginning to move. "It has roots too."

"Unreal," he said with disbelief, as the two of them caught up with the others.

Inside the palace's courtyard, which contained streams, waterfalls, fountains, and other types of flowing decor, plus an interesting menagerie of small, uncaged animals, Lhasa led them over to a large pond that was filled with orange and white carp.

Across the pond, Ashley's grandfather was kneeling at the water's edge, clothed in a robe which synthesized the designs of those worn by Buddhist and Christian monks. His eyes were closed, and his hands were folded together before him. He looked younger than the last time she had seen him.

"Gonpo," Lhasa said respectfully.

Ashley's grandfather nodded his head, his eyes still shut, then cupped his hands, reached into the water, and washed his face. Standing upright, he motioned his hands in a manner similar to Canis, opened his eyes, smiled, then stepped out onto the water's surface, and began to walk across it towards them.

"Jesus," McCready said, startled by the display.

The water rippling slightly with each step he took, her grandfather said, "I'm so pleased you all could make it." As he neared the water's edge, he allowed a sparrow to land in the palm of

294

his hand, and said, "Welcome."

"Hello, father," Mason said, moving towards him.

Gonpo handed the sparrow to Lhasa. "Hello, my son," he said, grasping both of his hands with Mason's. "How are you?"

Touching his forehead to his father's, Mason replied, "Good. Thank you."

"Excellent," Gonpo said, as they released their embrace. He looked at Xanadeux, bowed his head, did the same with Kudu, and moved over to Ashley. She held out her hands for him, as he said, "Granddaughter."

He grasped her hands, they touched foreheads, and she said, "Gonpo."

He asked, "How are you?"

She said, "I am."

Gonpo smiled as he pulled his forehead from hers, nodded, and said, "Yes, you are."

"You look younger," she said, their hands releasing.

"Do I?" he asked rhetorically. Turning to McCready, he bowed his head, and said, "Welcome back for the first time."

"Thanks," McCready said, a slightly confused look upon his face as he bowed his head. "It's quite a place you have here."

"It is what it is," Gonpo said. He then walked to Lhasa, turned around, and said to them all, "Let us show you the rest of the phodâng. Then we will have some cha. Come."

Gonpo began to walk. All began to follow.

After the grand tour of the palace, and after the tea and lunch in the garden, Ashley was inside of her room, unpacking her suitcase's contents into the curvy, wooden dresser that sat near the open window. A warm, nighttime breeze blew through it, very calm and relaxing, a perfect blend of temperature and humidity. Placing the last item of clothing into the top drawer, she closed it, walked over to her canopied bed, sat down, and looked around the room.

The accommodations were exactly what she wanted. Simple yet elegant, it was candlelit, with a minimum of objects–just a bed, a dresser, a wicker chair, a Persian rug, a jade, spiral sculpture, and a colorful oil painting of a Lorenz attractor. No clocks, no univiews, no cellphones, no nonsense...perfect. A true vacation from Metropolis.

She laid back on the soft bed, stretched her arms and legs to their fullest, then relaxed and closed her eyes. Just about to fall asleep, she heard a knock outside her doorway.

"Ashley?" McCready asked.

"Yeah?" she said, sitting up and yawning.

"Is it cool if I come in?"

"Yeah. Go ahead."

McCready stepped through the rows of green, hanging beads that served as her door, and Ashley's eyebrows raised. He was dressed in a hunter-green, silk, dress shirt, khaki slacks, and his usual pair of tims. His wet, black hair was combed back, and for the first time since she'd known him, his face was clean-shaven.

Scooting to the end of the bed, Ashley smiled, and said, "Look at you."

He laughed, picked up the wicker chair, and brought it next to the bed. "Figured I'd dress nice for dinner."

"You look great," she said, as he seated himself in the chair.

"Thanks," he said, pulling out a pack of Old Skools™ and a lighter from his shirt's front pocket. "So do you."

Ashley looked down at her casual, summer dress, and said, "I'm not even dressed up yet."

"Yeah," he said, placing a cigarette between his lips, "but you still look beautiful." He flicked his silver lighter open.

She smiled as he lit the cigarette. "Thanks."

"It's the truth." He looked around the place as he inhaled the tobacco. "Your room's a lot different than mine."

"I'm sure it is," she said. "What's yours like?"

McCready smiled. "It's fuckin' bad-ass, Ashley. I got a Wurlizter® in there, Marilyn photos, neons, an old TV that plays old movies–it's fuckin' incredible." He took a puff. "Is your granddad an antique collector or something?"

"Not really."

"What's up with my room then? It's so perfect."

"Yeah," she said, lighlty rocking back and forth, her legs hanging over the edge of the bed. "they usually are. He creates the rooms specifically for each person."

"But how?" McCready asked. "I didn't even decide I was coming until this morning. He couldn't have had time to fly all those antiques into here."

"He didn't," Ashley said. "He created it all today."

He gave her a funny look. "What do you mean 'create?'"

"Just that. Create."

Watching the smoke at the end of his cigarette magically

disappear, he asked, with a deadpan delivery, "What is this place, Ashley?"

"That's hard to say..."

"Well, what's the first word that comes to your mind?"

She thought for a brief second, then answered, "Alive?"

He leaned back in the chair, and breathed the tobacco in deeply. "Alright." He blew it out. "Please explain more."

"Okay." Ashley tried to figure out the proper words, and when she did, she said, "This entire place, is...it's kinda like the ultimate, nanotech heaven. Everything's alive and interconnected, and Gonpo can shape and mold it in any way he wants to. He's like God here." She laughed. "Or Satan, depending on your perspective."

"Holy shit," McCready said. "That's nuts. Seriously?"

She smiled. "Yep."

"Holy shit," he said, looking away from her momentarily. "So that's why my cigarette is burning like this? The air *knows* to turn the smoke into more air?"

Ashley nodded.

"Jesus," he said, taking another puff. "And that's why the security seems so lax–it really *is* everywhere. They weren't joking."

"Huh-unh," she said. "The moment you enter into here, it enters into you. You become a part of it."

"Meaning that Gumpa can play God with your fuckin' molecules."

"Basically," she said. "And it's 'Gonpo.'"

"Gonpo," he quickly corrected himself. "Right." McCready sat forward, and cautiously looked around the room. "He couldn't hear that, could he?"

She laughed. "Don't worry, McCready. Gonpo's not petty."

"You sure?"

"Yeah."

"Alright." He leaned back, and took another comfort puff. "I think it's gonna take me a sec to get used to this."

"Well, you've got plenty of time before dinner. So relax, McCready..." she said, rubbing her toes along the inside of his thigh. "You're on vacation, after all."

He smiled, nonchalantly flicked his cigarette aside, and gently placed his hand around her calf. "Thanks for the reminder," he said, softly running his hand along her taut muscle.

Watching the cigarette fade from existence before it reached the ground, Ashley said, "You learn fast."

McCready moved his mouth to her bare leg, and replied, "I've got a good teacher."

McCready plunged his fork into the pork chop, cut it with his serrated knife, and took a large bite of the juicy, white meat.

"How is it?" Ashley asked, bringing a small, steamed carrot to her lips and blowing on it.

Still chewing, McCready said, "Luscious."

Dinner had just been served in the palace's regal dining room. Ashley, her father, McCready, Gonpo, Lhasa, and Xanadeux were sitting around a circular table which had been beautifully crafted into a yin-yang symbol. Each of them had their particular dinner in front of them, while the table was filled with all kinds of fruit and appetizers for them to share. Above them, dozens of GS chandeliers hung magically in the air, each one comprised of a different kind of precious gem. Around them, streams flowed, plants were, and birds sang, as Kudu played the flute, lying in a lace hammock that was attached to nothing but air.

McCready swallowed, and said, "Man, this is the best fuc-" He cleared his throat. "This is the best pork chop I've ever had. No lie." Beginning to cut off another piece, he looked at her grandfather, and said, "This meal is beyond words, Mr. Huxton."

Gonpo smiled, as he scooped up some baba ghannouj with a piece of pita bread. "There could be no better compliment." He bowed his head. "Tujay-chay."

"Everything *is* fabulous, father," Mason said, cutting into his bloody-rare filet mignon.

"I'm pleased to hear that." Gonpo took a small bite of his food, and said, "Now, back to what we were discussing before we were served..."

"Okay," Ashley said with a smile. "I'm into that." She crunched down on a broccoli crown.

Digging his fork into his baked potato, her father said, "Two sides of the same coin, you two." He laughed. "You both could debate up until your final breath, I swear."

"But not you?" Lhasa asked, sipping some juice.

"I don't enjoy debate," Mason said.

"He doesn't like people to question him," Ashley added.

"This is true," Mason said.

Lhasa laughed. "I see."

"So where were we?" Ashley asked.

Gonpo said, "You had just said that you didn't see the point of immortality since there was no such thing as time."

"No," Ashley said, "we were past that."

"Autoevolution and transhumanism," Xanadeux said.

"That's right," Ashley said, the train of her previous thought returning. "Thanks, Xanadeux."

"My pleasure," it said.

"Okay," Ashley began, "so you were essentially saying that humans have to evolve out their bodies, right?"

"I said that intelligent life should not be *limited* to human form," Gonpo replied. "That doesn't mean we *have* to evolve out of our current form, it just means that we should not be limited by it. We should be willing to explore the possiblities that technology presents to us."

"Like uploading our consciousness into a CPU?" Ashley asked.

"Among other things," he said. "Yes."

"Aren't you worried that something's gonna get lost in the translation?" she asked.

"Not if we're using the proper technology," Gonpo said. "Everything is pure information–including ourselves–and it's simply a matter of deciphering that data and transferring it to a new host."

"That's not a simple matter," Ashley said.

"Simpler than you would think," he said, taking a sip of tea.

"Alright, I got a question," McCready said to Gonpo. "Say you transfer our consciousness into a computer... What then? Would we just live inside the uniview forever, or would we live in cybernetic bodies? What would we do?"

"Anything we wanted," Gonpo said. "When immortality becomes possible, then the possibilities become endless. We'll be limited only by our imagination. We could do any of the things that you mentioned, we could transfer our intelligence into a completely new, gengineered lifeform... Anything."

"And what would you do with the technology, father?" Mason asked, cutting off a thin slice of his red meat. "What would be your personal choice?"

Gonpo took a sip of tea, then answered, "I would upload our intelligence into von Neumann probes."

"A noble endeavor," Mason said. "Not the first thing *I* would choose, but noble nonetheless."

"Von Neumann probes?" McCready asked. "What are those?"

FREQUENCIES

"A way to spread our infection into space," Ashley said.

"Or a way to spread intelligence throughout the universe," Gonpo countered.

McCready said, "So what do they do?"

"They build intelligent life wherever they land," Gonpo said, filling his teacup with a wave of his hand.

"That's putting it euphemistically." Ashley looked at McCready, and said, "They're galaxy colonizers."

McCready dabbed some Tabasco® onto his fried catfish. "Interesting. So how do they work?"

"I'll show you," Gonpo said. He motioned his hands, and a hologram of the Earth and its solar system appeared over the dinner table. "The idea is that these probes will be able to travel to other solar systems and land on a planet or a moon." The hologram showed multiple probes being ejected from Earth in all directions. It then began to follow a single probe, as it hurtled its way through space. When the probe reached another solar system and landed onto a green planet, Gonpo said, "Each probe would contain within it the most advanced molecular assemblers available, and its stored records would contain consciousness uploads from a comprehensive sample of Earthlings and their technology." The probe opened itself up, released a few clouds of foglets, and began to create a biosphere which resembled her grandfather's. "Utilizing the planet's indigenous materials," he continued, "the assemblers would create an environment hospitible to human life..." The foglets started to create a multi-racial mix of cybernetic humans. "And then they would actually begin to *build* human life. After this bio/technosphere is completed, and intelligent life is established, the foglets would then build replicas of the original probe, and launch those off into the next solar system, where they proceed to do the exact same thing."

The POV pulled way back, showing the probes spreading, virus-like, throughout the cosmos. "And since the probes will be programmed with a metahuman level of AI, they will constantly evolve and update themselves and their creations as they travel further and further across the universe." As the hologram continued to mirror his words, Gonpo said, "Life will evolve into posthuman forms which we can barely fathom with our current level of intelligence. Plasmodial humanoids, intelligent stars, suns, and planets, cognizant wavelengths, sentient cosmic rays..."

"So you wanna become the universe," McCready said.

"I want the universe to become intelligent," Gonpo said, as

the POV pulled back again.

"It already is," Ashley said. "You just don't recognize it."

"I do, granddaughter," Gonpo said. "But I want to *increase* its intelligence." The massive stars within the holographic universe began to burn out, transforming themselves into black holes and neutron stars, as its overall shape began to shrink. "Because currently, at some point in time, the universe *will* collapse and be destroyed."

"And you think an 'intelligent' universe will decide not to collapse upon itself?" Ashley asked.

"Yes. Intelligent life preserves itself."

"That's a good point," Mason said.

"But what if the intelligent universe comes to *accept* the cycle of birth and death?" she asked. "What if it understands that everything exists always? Once was, will be...you taught me that, Gonpo."

"And it *will* understand that, Ashley," he said, as the cosmos continued to shrink. "But it won't have to accept it. It can choose to break out of that cyclical loop of forgetfullness, and remember everything." The hologram became smaller and smaller. "This is a crucial step in evolution, because every time a universe reaches its omega point, it loses all of the information that was previously contained within it." The hologram turned into a single, small point, then disappeared. "All of its data is completely obliterated, and intelligent life can only *hope* that it will be recreated after the next alpha point." The universe appeared again, as it was before the stars started to burn out. "But, if we avert this collapse," Gonpo continued, "all of that infinite data is preserved. Intelligent life can evolve forever, learn forever, and the universe can become omnisicient. Omnipotent. Life can become immortal within itself, and the ultimate aims of both science and religion are achieved." Gonpo waved the hologram away. "We truly become one with the universe."

"Sounds like we become God," McCready said.

Gonpo smiled. "Call it what you will." He scooped up some more of his roasted eggplant, took a bite, and said, "Mmm..." He slowly chewed, and swallowed. "Food is wonderful, isn't it?"

Her father picked up a slice of fresh sourdough bread, and said, "Indeed."

"Better enjoy it while you can, daddy," Ashley said with a mischievious smile, as she moved some peas around on her plate. "'Cause God don't eat dinner."

FREQUENCIES

The next morning, Ashley awoke to the sounds of birds singing.

She rubbed the sleep from her eyes, yawned, and stretched her arms into the air. Pushing the light, silky sheets from off of her, she crawled to the edge of the king-sized bed, opened the canopy, and looked towards the opened window. Three little birds were perched upon the sill, paying no attention at all to her movement. As they continued to sing their pure, cheerful melody, Ashley got off the bed, walked to the dresser, and was surprised to find that there was a book sitting atop it. She stared at it for a moment, wondering how it got into her room. Silly question at Gonpo's, she realized. Things just happen. She picked it up.

It was an old, blue book with a black tape binding, much like the ones people used to use in lab classes. There was no writing on its stained, weathered cover. She flipped it over. Nothing on the back, either. Ashley skimmed through the lined pages within. The words were handwritten in various colors of ink, sometimes cursive, other times printed. It was a journal of some sort. She turned to the first page, and looked at the inside of the front cover. In the lower, right-hand corner, was scrawled the initials: "A.W."

She began to read the first page.

Life is never quite what it seems, is it?

One thinks they know everything, and in the blink of an eye, the turn of a phrase...they realize they knew nothing. Their paradigms are shifted in ways which they never would have imagined, even in their wildest dreams...

Or their most terrible nightmares.

Unfortunately, circumstances surrounding the Brennan Commission have caused in this life just that—a paradigm shift of nightmarish proportions.

Those who claimed to be mentors revealed themselves to be Judases. Academic institutions which purported to exist for the good of humankind, showed themselves to be tools of the devil. A government claiming to pursue life, liberty, and happiness, in truth only seeks death, oppression, and misery.

Ashley looked back at the initials.
"A.W."

Her eyes widened.

It was the journal of Adrian Wellor.

The book still in her hand, Ashley rushed through the hanging beads, and out of her room.

And crashed right into Lhasa, spilling the silver breakfast tray she was carrying, and its contents, all over the floor.

"Oh my Goddess!" Ashley said, bending down and attempting to pick up some of the mess. "Lhasa, I'm so sorry!"

"Don't worry," she said reassuringly. "It's nothing."

Ashley continued to pick up the spill. "Yeah, but-"

Lhasa touched Ashley's arm. "Really." The spilled food began to disappear. "It's nothing."

Ashley looked up at her. "I guess not, huh?"

She smiled. "Are you alright?"

"Yeah," she said, standing up. "I'm fine. Do you know where Gonpo is?"

"He's in the courtyard, meditating."

"Is it okay if I go talk to him?"

"Of course," Lhasa said. "He's expecting you."

"Of course," Ashley said. "Thanks." She turned from Lhasa, and began to jog through the winding hallways until she reached the palace's courtyard. Finding her grandfather at the pond's edge, meditating in the lotus position with his eyes closed, she said, "Gonpo?"

"Ashley," he said without opening his eyes. "You found the gift."

"Is this for real?" she asked, tapping on the journal. "Or is this just one of your creations?"

"It's as real as you or I."

Ashley stared at him for a moment, then asked, "How did you get this?"

Not moving from his meditative state, Gonpo replied, "How I obtained it is unimportant. What *is* important, is that you now have it."

"Okay..." she said. "Why?"

"Why what?"

"Why are giving this to me?"

"So that you may do with it what you will."

"I don't get it," she said.

"You do," he replied, only his lips moving. "You just haven't realized it yet."

303

"Wanna give me a clue then?"

Gonpo smiled. "No."

Ashley laughed, slightly frustrated. "Why not?"

"Because."

"Because why?"

He let a few, long seconds draw out, then said, "Because you have those rare and special qualities, Ashley."

A rush passed through her body.

Her mind flashed back to her meeting with Brennan.

"Ashley," Brennan said, as he stood up from the bench and straightened out his coat, "you have those rare and special qualities that are required to make a positive difference in this world, and I encourage you wholeheartedly to do just that–make your presence felt and let your voice be heard." He picked up his cane. "Your privilege and status, combined with your intelligence and intuitiveness, allows you a very unique position within this society, and I hope that you do fully and truly realize that..." He paused, looking into her eyes. "And then act upon that realization when it's time."

Ashley stared at him, unsure of what to say. Why was he telling her all this? For what purprose? Curiouser and curiouser... Brennan looked at his watch. "I must be going now, my dear. I have a conference to attend in Los Angeles, and my flight leaves in a few hours." He patted her gently on the shoulder, and said, "Take care of yourself. We'll speak again soon." Then he walked away from her without saying another word.

She watched him climb the steps leading towards Red Square, and... Did he just flicker?

"It was you..." she said. "But how? He...you touched me."

"Hard-light hologram," Gonpo said.

Ashley was silent then, trying to take everything in. She heard a fish break the surface of the water, and asked, "So was any of it the truth?"

"All of it," he replied, his eyes still closed. "Minus the part about the wife and the regret. Brennan regrets nothing. And he's still married."

She laughed, shaking her head. "What...?"

"His motivations for telling you wouldn't have been

believable without a logical catharsis. Divorce seemed sufficient."

"That's crazy," she said. "Why didn't you just tell me yourself?"

"I enjoy games," he said. "Don't you?"

"Uh...yeah, but I kinda like to know when I'm playing one."

"You've known."

"No, I haven't."

"Yes, you have."

"*No*," she repeated, "I haven't."

He smiled. "You have."

Ashley didn't bother to respond again, realizing that Gonpo wasn't just talking about the Brennan situation.

He let a few seconds pass, and said, "You've known the game since an early age, granddaughter. It's a very, very old game, and it's been played many, many times throughout history." He paused. "And now you must decide what part you're going to play in it."

"And you're showing me what that part is," she said.

"Maybe," Gonpo replied. "Or maybe I'm leading you astray. Time will tell." He smiled. "If you can tell time. Now go. I must meditate. And so must you."

Ashley didn't move. She just stood there, her mind contemplating, her eyes moving back and forth from the book to him to her surroundings.

"Yes?" he asked.

"You know," she replied.

Gonpo nodded once. "Yes."

Ashley left his presence, and in the distance behind her, she could faintly hear him saying, "You're welcome."

∞

δ
Chapter 15:
Mo Better Blues

I will leave everything behind, and undertake this odyssey with myself as my only companion. Alone, I will walk away from yesterday's failures and yesterday's regrets, strengthened by the knowledge that I have learned the lessons that my past was meant to teach me.

I will not make the same mistakes again.
I will not be blind or ignorant to what is happening around me.
I will not place my trust in those who are not worthy.
I will not forsake my dreams.
I will die without regret.
The eternal present now awaits me.

At 2:17 a.m., on Saturday morning, Ignacio finally awoke.

Not just a partial awakening, like the ones he'd been doing for the past few days, stirring just enough to sip some fluids or go to the bathroom–but a full and complete cognizance of where and who he was.

And what he needed to do.

He looked over at the woman lying next to him in bed. Irena Alma Ignacio was her name, and she had been his wife for eleven years. Yet despite all that time, he didn't really know who she was. He'd only had the opportunity to experience her through someone else's eyes. Though memory resonances from his previous self allowed him to know the particulars of their life together, he currently had no feelings with which to associate those memories. It was like trying to hear laughter with no ears, or trying to love with no heart. The consciousness mergence had left him with no emotions from his previous life, just hollow and empty reminders of what was, and what could now never be.

Only the facts remained. Cold, raw data, callously bequeathed to him by himself.

As he laid there, watching Irena sleep, he was filled with a profound sense of sorrow. These were the last moments that he would be spending with her, and he couldn't help but feel mournful, even for a life he hadn't ever really known. Endings were never easy, and the fact that this one had no real beginning didn't make it any easier. In many ways, it only made it worse. But the worst part of it all, by far, was the guilt. He was about to violate her and her family. Take from them a husband, a lover, a father, and a friend. *His* family, he reminded himself, as hard as it was to do. It was still his family. Her...and the children. God, the children. He knew their names, ages, what they looked like...but he didn't know *them*. Their essences. His body had experienced time with them, but *he* hadn't. Yet somehow, he had, because he saw their beautiful, little faces in his mind. *His* girls.

Ignacio felt queasy. He had to leave. Now. Before they woke. "Esposa," he whispered to Irena, softly removing her arm from off of his chest. "Lo siento."

She smiled dreamily, letting out a small, nonverbal sound as he carefully sat up, and got out of bed.

Dressed only in his boxers, he crept in the darkness over to his dresser, and quietly pulled out a change of clothes. He then moved to his closet, and grabbed a large backpack. Without looking at her again, he left the bedroom, walked straight past his daughters' room, and went down the stairs. He entered into the bathroom, and dressed himself. He opened the medicine cabinet, reached for a pack of razor blades and a bottle of rubbing alcohol, placed them into his backpack, and walked into the kitchen. Ignacio opened the fridge, and pulled out some cold leftovers. Without heating them up, he ate as much as he possibly could, as fast as he possibly could. He put the nearly-empty container of rice and beans back into the refrigerator, then walked to the cupboard, and filled his bag with two cases of Power Bars®.

Food necessities taken care of, he exited through one of the kitchen's two doors, and entered into the adjoining garage, where his Harley® was parked. He opened the hoverbike's right-hand, side compartment, removed the spare, Freemon utility belt he kept stored there, and put it around his waist. Ignacio was about to place the pack onto his back and leave...but he couldn't bring himself to do it. Not without seeing his little girls with his own eyes.

He set the pack onto the Harley's® seat, and entered back into the house. He walked to the stairs, and climbed them slowly, his palms sweaty with trepidation. As he approached their door, he felt a shortness of breath. He paused outside of it, swallowed hard, and entered.

There they were, sleeping in their beds. Two, beautiful, little souls which his body had brought into this world. Which *he* had brought into this world. Him.

Ignacio approached them. Standing right in between both of their beds, he watched them sleep. So peaceful, the expressions on their faces...but so different it was going to be once they found out their father was missing. This was all so fucked up and crazy. It should never have happened. He cursed himself for ever becoming a sleeper. Now he would never rest easy again.

And neither would his loved ones.

"Aurora," he woefully said, dropping to his knees. "Esperanza..." He placed a hand on each of their shoulders, bowed his head, and began to weep. "Please forgive me for what I've done... Te quiero mucho. Siempre." His sobbing increased, and he could say no more words.

Nor could he stay any longer.

Ignacio stood up, took one, long, last look at his babies, and just as he was about to leave, Irena entered the room.

"Morris?" she asked with concern. "What's going on? Why are you dressed?"

Unable to hold back his tears, he said, "I'm sorry, Irena. I'm so sorry."

Confused, she asked, "What? What's wrong? I don't understand."

He walked to her, and embraced her tightly.

"Tell me what's going on, Morris," she said, rubbing the back of his neck with her soft hand. "Let me know."

He wanted to. But he couldn't. It would only make things worse than they already were. Still holding her with one arm, Ignacio reached down to his belt with the other, and snapped off a sleepshot. He pressed his face against hers, placed the hypospray against her neck, and fired it. Irena instantly fell asleep in his arms.

He picked her up, carried her to the room, and placed her back into the bed. He kissed her on her forehead, tucked her underneath the covers, and said, "Cuídate, Irena." He turned off the alarm that was on the nightstand, so that only the girls or herself could wake her up mañana. She deserved a final night of restful sleep. God, she deserved a lot more than that, but he couldn't give it to her. Pulling his hand away from the alarm, he noticed the framed, 3X5 portrait of his family that sat atop the same nightstand. He picked the photo up, stared at it momentarily, then placed it in his leather jacket's pocket, and walked back down to the garage. He strapped his backpack on, mounted the Skyhog™, and activated its computer.

"Voice-rec on," Ignacio said. "Open garage."

The large doors parted, unveiling the open road before him.

Placing his thumb on the scanner, he fired up the Harely's® engine, and looked around his garage, fully aware that this was the last time that he would be seeing it. He then revved the throttle a few times, cruised out of the garage, and left his home for good.

At 3:09 a.m., Igancio set his Skyhog™ down in a Denny's® parking lot near Capitol Hill. He removed everything of value from its compartments, placed them into his backpack, and walked into the 24-hour restaurant. He sat down at a booth, ordered a black coffee, and paid for it right away. He drank it quickly, and kept to himself. There was nothing he had to say to anyone. Nothing to say, only things to do.

When he finished the hot drink, he picked up his backpack, and went to the bathroom. He went into a stall, and locked the door behind him. He placed the backpack onto a hook, reached into it, and pulled out a razor blade, a Band-Aid®, and a bottle of rubbing alcohol. He put the razor blade and bandage into his pocket. Kicking the toilet lid down, he opened the alcohol bottle, and poured it over his right thumb. The liquid trickled off his digit and splashed down onto the bathroom's sticky floor. He set the bottle on top of the toilet lid and pulled out the razor blade. With the other hand, he pulled off his microtorch, and sanitized the razor's steel. As he clicked the torch back onto his belt, he heard someone enter into the bathroom. He looked through the stall's thin slit.

An employee walked to one of the urinal's and took a piss. Ignacio waited until the man had washed his hands and left the bathroom, then he turned his thumb towards himself, and readied the blade between his thumb and forefinger. He examined his fingerprint, followed the epidermal spiral to its very center, and placed the razor's egde upon it. He pressed it into his flesh. A rush of pain and adrenaline shot through him, as he began to carefully dig the blade around inside his thumb. He clenched his teeth and growled. Blood dripped off of his palm, joining the spilled urine and alcohol on the tiled floor. When the razor touched the tiny, embedded microchip, he cut a circle around around it, then scooped it and the surrounding flesh from out of his thumb. He picked up the alcohol bottle, kicked opened the toilet's lid, and dropped the blade, biochip, and excess tissue into the bowl. He poured the alcohol over his bloodied, gored thumb, and grimaced as the liquid fire started to burn intensely.

Tossing the bottle aside, Ignacio reached into his pocket, and pulled out the Band-Aid®. Ignacio wiped the back of his thumb against his backpack, and placed the bandage around the wound. He then reached into the pack, and pulled out a headfield. He placed the device–which resembled a banded necklace with a small, dialed pendant–around his neck and activated it. His head was now protected with an emfield, and most importantly, his freeread's capabilities had now been disrutped. He put his backpack on, flushed the toilet with his foot, and left the bathroom.

Entering back into the dining area, his stomach dropped, as he saw two police officers talking to his waitress. The biochip must have already notified them of its removal, and since Ignacio was databased as a Freemon, they were probably here to make sure that nothing had happened to him. But they might as well have been there to capture him. Once Freemon HQ was contacted, either motive would lead to the same result.

The cops were holding a hand-held uniview, and showing her a picture of something, more than likely a photo of him. She looked down at it, nodded, then pointed her finger towards the bathroom. At him.

The officers looked towards Ignacio, and before they even had a chance to figure out what was going on, he had rushed up to them, and rendered them both unconscious with a sleepshot.

Without slowing his hyperspeed, he ran through the exit door, and distanced himself from the establishment. He now had a few minutes to get to where he was going, before more cops were called, and before they started sweeping the streets for him. He alternated back and forth between hyper and normal speed, and reached his Central District destination in less than two minutes. It was an old, two story house which had been recently renovated and refurbished. Its windows were tinted, and surveillance cameras were located at various positions around its lawn. A black gate fenced in the property from the sidewalk, and there was a sign posted on it that warned: "Trespassers will be obliterated."

Ignacio walked up to the gate. He paused to catch his breath, then pressed the intercom button, and said, "Jack. It's Ignacio."

A few moments passed. A groggy voice said, "Ignacio. It's three in the morning, man."

"I know," Ignacio said, cautiously looking around his surroundings for any rollers. "I need that favor, Jack."

"*Now?*"

"Now."

"Can't this w-"

"No," he interrupted. "It can't."

Ignacio could hear a man's voice in the background, and Jack whispering something back to him.

"Tell him to fuck off," he heard the whiny voice say.

"Jack," Ignacio said firmly.

The whispering more intense now, Jack telling his boyfriend to be quiet.

"You owe me," Ignacio said. "Remember?"

Silence at the other end of the line, as Jack was undoubedtly remembering the time Ignacio had saved his ass from going to prison.

The locks on the gate clicked.

"I remember," Jack said.

The gate swung open.

"I'll meet you at the door."

"Bueno," Ignacio said, walking through the gate, and up the short, concrete path that led to the front porch. He waited at the front door, his fidgeting causing the wooden floorboards to creak underfoot. Police sirens wailed away in the distance. A cold wind kicked up, swaying the porch bench so that its chains grated noisily. He walked over to it, and stopped its motion.

The front door opened.

"Ignacio?" Jack asked. He stretched his violet-haired self around the corner. "There you are." He motioned with his head. "Come on."

Ignacio entered the house.

Jack closed the door behind him. He touched Ignacio's

backpack and said, "What's with this? Your old lady kick you out?"

"I wish," he replied, moving to his left, and walking into Jack's comfortable living room. He set his pack down, and seated himself in the middle of a large, neon-blue couch.

"Have a seat," Jack sarcastically said, sitting down across from him in a matching loveseat.

Ignacio reached into his backpack and pulled out a couple Power Bars®. "Thanks," he replied in the same tone as Jack, tearing open the wrapper on the guava-flavored one and biting into it.

Jack adjusted the sash on his silk robe, and asked, "You know I'm not in the business anymore, don't you?"

"That's what I've heard," he said. "But I know you still got connections." He voraciously devoured the rest of the energy bar. "Jack Jax *always* has connections–whether he's still a fence or not."

Scratching the violet hairs on his forearm, Jack looked down pensively. "What is it you need?"

Ignacio unwrapped another Power Bar®. "I need to get rid of my freeread." He bit into the concentrated food. "Immediately."

With a bewildered look, Jack asked, "What the fuck did you do, man?"

"It's a long story, Jack. And I don't have time to go into it. I need it out. Now."

"So you're a fugitive right now?" His lip curled up. "Motherfucker! You're gonna bring the heat to my house!"

"Jack–calm down. They can't trace me." Ignacio raised his right hand and showed him his bloodied Band-Aid®. "My biochip's already gone..." He lifted the necklace. "And this is a Freemon-issue headfield. You're safe. Everything's chill. ¿Comprende?"

Calming down a little, he said, "Yeah. Okay. But you're still putting me at risk here, man. Aiding and abetting a felon's no small offense."

"I know. And I wouldn't be doing this if I didn't have to. But I do." Ignacio leaned forward. "Now–can you help me?"

"I don't know, man. Freereads take time," Jack said, one leg anxiously bobbing up and down. "Not a lotta people have an extractor, and even if they do they usually re-"

"Can you?" Ignacio said impatiently. "Or can't you?"

Jack stared at him, his leg stopped bobbing, and he said, "This is it, man. If I do this for you, I don't owe you shit anymore. Is that straight?"

Ignacio nodded. "Sí."

"Okay then." Jack stood up, walked over to a coffee table, and picked up a remote. He sat back down and clicked it on. A holographic, 2-D uniview screen projected into the air between them, both of its sides showing the exact same image. He widened the screen's size to about forty inches, and said, "Call Otto." Jack looked around the screen, and said to Ignacio, "If anyone can do it at this hour...it's Otto."

When Jack moved back behind the screen, the image of a man in a black fedora appeared upon it. His face was very pasty and angular, and his cheekbones prominet. A pair of thin, round, wire-rimmed glasses rested at the edge of his nose. The lenses were tinted a dull gray. "Jack," he said without emotion. "Since when did you become a vampire?"

"Since never," Jack replied, almost defensively. "That's your bag, Otto. I'm just not sleeping well tonight."

"Surely," Otto said, scratching the corner of his mouth with his pinky finger's long, black-painted nail. "What's the problem?"

"I've got a headache," Jack said. "A bad one."

"And you want me to come over and kiss it." Otto lowered his gaze. "And make it all better."

"Yeah."

"You naughty boy, you," Otto said. "I'll be there within the hour. Be still."

His face disappeared from the screen, and Jack clicked the hologram off.

"Strange character," Ignacio said.

"That's an understatement," Jack said. "But he gets the job done." He stood up. "I'm gonna go back upstairs, man. My boyfriend's waiting for me. I'll listen out for the door, and we'll deal with Otto then. Meantime..." He tossed Ignacio the remote. "Mi casa es su casa."

"Thanks," Ignacio said, as Jack walked out of the room, and back upstairs. He waited a moment, then clicked the screen back on. "Directory assitance," he said, setting the remote aside.

The screen displayed the US West® logo, and asked, "For what city?"

Reaching into the front of his pack, and pulling out a silver pen, he said, "Seattle."

"For what listing?"

"Rosario. Raquel Rosario."

"Thank you," the feminine voice said, displaying Raquel's address and phone number in bold, black letters. "Would you like to download this information for later use?"

"No," he replied. "Leave onscreen. Voice-rec off." He touched the 'record' button on the pen, and began to speak Raquel's address and phone number into its microphone. When he finished, he pressed the button again, and replaced the pen into his backpack. He picked up the remote, slouched down into the loveseat, and started to flip through the thousands of channels as he waited for Otto's arrival.

At 4:31 a.m., Otto showed up.

Dressed in all black. Black, tweed coat. Black slacks. Black Doc Martens®. Black everything. Expect for his pallid skin, which practically glowed in contrast to the darkness of his attire. As he walked into the living room, he removed his fedora, placed it under his arm, and said, "Good night. You must be my client."

Ignacio turned off the uniview. "Sí."

Jack said, "Ignacio, this is Otto. Otto, Ignacio."

Ignacio started to stand up, but Otto said, "No need to get up." He extended his hand towards him, his long, painted fingernails pointing towards him like little, black daggers. "I prefer my clients to be seated."

"Fine with me," Ignacio said as he shook the pale man's hand, which was much warmer than he had expected. Almost hot. Nothing like the icy, corpse-like hand he thought he'd be grabbing. "I just want it out."

"Surely," Otto said, releasing his strong grip. "Now, the details..." He clicked his fingernails together. "What do you have to offer in collateral for my services?"

Ignacio handed him his utility belt.

Otto held the belt by one end, and looked over its devices. "This is not police issue."

"Freemon," Ignacio said. "Everything's there but the laser."

"No matter," he said, running a finger along the napper. "Lasers are easy to come by." He draped the belt over the same arm that was holding his hat. "What else?"

"This." Ignacio touched his necklace. "It's a headfield."

Otto crouched over, and brought his face right up to the apparatus. "*Very* intriguing..." He pulled back slightly, and moved his hands in the space around Ignacio's head. "Yes, very nice..." he whispered, his breath smelling like a combination of dust and ginseng. He stood back up, and said, "You have a deal."

"Bueno."

Otto set down the belt and his hat next to Ignacio, and asked, "Are you ready to begin?"

Ignacio checked him up and down with a curious look. "Where's your extractor?" he asked.

Otto smiled. He parted his light-pink lips, and slowly let out his long, grayish tongue. It undulated like a centipede, then its tip unfurled, revealing within it something that resembled the mouth of a leech.

Disgusted, Ignacio said, "What the fuck?" He scowled at Jack. "What kind of maricón fag shit is this, Jack? Hunh? What the fuck?"

Jack replied, "It's what'll get that fuckin' freeread out of your head, man, that's what."

Ignacio pointed his finger at him, and stared him down. "If this is some kind of bullshit, Jack, I'm gonna fuck you up. You hear me?"

"Yeah, man," Jack said. "I hear you. It's not. He's legit, okay? Fuck."

Ignacio looked back at Otto, whose tongue-thing had retreated.

"Well?" Otto asked. "Do we still have a deal?"

Ignacio shook his head, and reluctantly said, "Sí. Let's just get this shit over with."

Otto walked behind him, and said, "Please lean your head back."

Beginning to rest his head, Ignacio asked, "This shit's not gonna turn you on, is it?"

"Truthfully?" Otto asked, as his hot hands touched Ignacio's temples.

"Forget it," Ignacio said. "Just get it out."

"Surely," he said, lowering his lips towards Ignacio's head. "Now just relax...this won't hurt a bit." Otto's open mouth pressed against his skin, and he softly began to suck, spreading his warm saliva all around Ignacio's forehead.

As calm as he possibly could, Ignacio asked, "What the hell are you doing?"

"Sterilizing the area," he said between kisses. "My saliva's a disinfectant...and an anaesthetic. Now...don't move."

Ignacio felt Otto's opened mouth press down firmly. The tongue-thing started to ripple around on top of the enclosed area, and when it reached the exact center, it too pressed itself down. He felt the tip open up, and then there was a slight, tingling sensation. Otto quietly moaned, as his hands continued to massage Ignacio's temples.

Ignacio had the urge to pull away, not because it hurt, but because he was actually finding the experience tolerable. He wanted to hate it, but he couldn't. The reality was, Otto was somehow making him feel comfortable. It didn't make sense. But that was seeming to be the theme of his life.

There was a subtle pull on his forehead, and then the tip of Otto's tongue began to move back and forth rapidly. This continued for about fifteen seconds, and then Otto retracted his tongue, sucked up the excess saliva, and released his hands from Ignacio's head.

"It's gone," Otto said as he stood upright.

Somewhat in a daze, Ignacio leaned his head forward to its normal position. He touched his forehead. There was no mark whatsoever. He checked his fingers. No blood either.

Circling around in front of him, Otto said, "A mechanical extractor would have left a scar." He picked up his hat and the utility belt from off of the loveseat. "I don't." He placed the hat on top of his head. "The rest of my fee, please."

"Right." Ignacio touched the headfield's dial, deactivated it, and removed it. Handing it to Otto, he said, "Here."

"Thank you," he said, placing it inside his coat's inner pocket. "It was a pleasure doing business with you." He smiled fiendishly. "I'm sure we'll talk again."

"I doubt it," Ignacio said, rubbing his numbed forehead.

"You never know," Otto replied. "Stranger things have happened." He turned to Jack, and said, "Good night, Jack. I'll let myself out."

"Go ahead," Jack said.

Otto exited the living room, and then the house.

As the door shut closed, Ignacio said, "You should've warned me it was gonna be like that, Jack. That shit was fuckin' extraño."
"Hey," he said. "Beggars can't be choosers, man. I got you what you needed, didn't I?"

"Yeah, you did," Ignacio said. "I'll give you that."

"And maybe a 'thanks?'"

"Sí. Gracias, amigo."

"You're welcome, man," Jack said, rubbing one of his violet eyebrows. "I owed it to you. Are we even now?"

"Almost."

Jack frowned. "What do you mean, 'almost?'"

Ignacio stood up and said, "Let me use your shower first. I got another man's spit all over my head."

"That's it?" Jack let out a relieved laugh. "That's easy. C'mon." He started to walk out of the living room. "You had me worried there for a minute, man. I thought you were going to go back on our deal."

Ignacio picked up his backpack. "That's not mi estilo, Jack. I follow through." He trailed after him. "Believe me, boy–I follow through."

At 5:49 a.m., Ignacio was standing in the shadows, across the street from the brownstone building that matched Raquel's listed address.

The journey there had been somewhat precarious, since he had to duck every single birdie and roller that he saw. And there was a lot of them. His previous self had never realized how many cops there were everywhere. Ignacio looked up in the sky to the east, and saw a birdie shining its redeye on the streets below, searching for any signs of biochipless citizens. It was the eighth one he'd seen on his journey to her Georgetown residence–way more than the routine. They were obviously looking for someone in particular, more than likely him.

Ignacio checked for any signs of cars, then zipped across the street at hyperspeed. He stood before the complex's callscreen, and rubbed the top of his now-bald head. The air felt cool against his newly exposed scalp. Same with his upper-lip. Remembering the information from his recorder pen, he touched the part of the screen that would ring #11. He waited, but there was no answer. He pressed it again. And waited. And pressed again.

"Go away," Raquel's voice suddenly said through the speaker.

"Raquel," he said. "It's me." He looked into the camera's eye. There was a long pause. "Iggy?" she asked.

"Sí. I need to talk to you."

"I can't believe you're actually here," she said.

"Me neither," he said. "Can I come up?"

"Yeah," she said. "Of course. I'm on the third floor."

The glass entry door buzzed open. Ignacio walked into the rundown lobby, headed straight for the stairwell, and climbed to the third level. When he reached her apartment, the door immediately opened.

"Iggy," she said, giving him a strong hug. "You came."

He hugged her back. "I did."

"You're cold," she said. "Come inside, sweetie. You need to get warm."

He entered into Raquel's well-heated apartment. It was a small place, with not a lot of amenities, but it was clean and well-kept. There was a living room with a kitchen built in to it, a bathroom, and it looked like there were two bedrooms. "You live with someone?" he asked.

"Pam," she said, as they walked over to an old, reddish couch. "My roommate. But she's down in Tacoma for the weekend." She sat down, and patted the seat next to her.

Ignacio set his pack aside and seated himself.

She rubbed her sleepy eyes, and tried to smooth out her hair. "Sorry if I look crappy right now."

"You look fine. Don't apologize."

Raquel smiled. "Thanks." She crossed her legs, and asked, "So what made you decide to come and see me?"

Ignacio thought about various things he could say. Stories that would make things easier. But the last twenty-two years of his life had been a lie, and he was *more* than sick of them. "I'm in trouble, Raquel," he said. "I need a place to stay for a day or two."

"You can stay here as long as you need, Iggy," she said, taking his cold fingers into her tiny hands, and warming them up. "What happened?"

"It's a long story," he said. "But what it all amounts to, is that I know too much."

She blew her warm breath onto his hands, and asked, "But how? You're a Freemon."

"Not anymore."

Her eyes widened. "*Really?*"

"Sí."

"Jeez, Iggy," she said. "I can't believe it. So you're trouble with the *law?*"

Ignacio nodded slowly.

"Jeez," Raquel said. "I can't believe this..." She touched his upper lip. "That's why you have the new look, huh?"

He nodded again.

She let out a small laugh.

"What?" he asked.

"It's funny..."

"What is?"

"I was always thinking you were gonna come and rescue *me*." She smiled. "And now here I am..." She embraced him lovingly. "Rescuing you. Funny, huh?"

Allowing his exhausted self to fully collapse into her arms, Ignacio said, "Hilarious."

They laid back on the couch together, and Raquel began to rub the back of his neck. "It's nice to have you here, Iggy," she said.

"It's nice to be here," he replied, and fell asleep shortly thereafter.

δ

α
Chapter 16:
Futurosity

I eagerly embrace today, with a careful, hopeful eye on the future. Everything will be as it should."

As McCready joined Mason and Dorje aboard the SEV, he asked, "Where's Ashley?"

"She's still inside the palace," Mason replied, shining a golden delicious with the bottom of his tan, lightweight safari-shirt.

"She didn't want to go?" McCready asked, as Dorje formed the organic steering column.

"She said she had to catch up on some reading." He bit into the apple. "She'll join us for dinner when we return."

"Alright," McCready said, walking to the area of the SEV where Mason was standing. "Just the guys, hunh?"

"So it seems." Mason motioned his hands towards the abundant fruit basket that hovered in the air next to him. "Fruit?"

"Nah," he said, leaning back against the vehicle's railing, "I'm good. But thanks."

Mason savored another bite of the scrumptious apple. "Suit yourself." Still chewing, he looked at Dorje, and said, "We're ready to go now, Dorje."

The humanoid cobra nodded. "It so be." The SEV smoothly lifted off, and began to cruise forth in an easterly direction, hovering about twenty feet above the ground as they headed into the savannah. Their destination, the tropical rainforest, was visible far ahead. There were light rainclouds hovering over some portions of the jungle environment, but for the most part, the weather in that area of the dome looked perfect for a Saturday afternoon safari.

"So what do you think of the duds?" McCready asked, tugging on his beige, nylon jacket. "Lhasa whipped 'em up for me this morning."

Mason nodded approvingly, as he looked over McCready's nanotech wardrobe. It consisted of a white tanktop beneath the jacket, multi-pocketed cargo-shorts, thin, wool socks, and a pair of Timberlands®. "Very nice," he said. "You look well prepared for a jungle excursion."

"Yeah, seems like it." McCready reached into one of the shorts' compartments, pulled out a Swiss Army® device, and said, "There's even a bunch of gadgets in the pockets."

He smiled as he took one more bite of the apple. "What will they think of next?" He tossed the half-eaten piece of fruit aside, allowing the ambient intelligence to disassemble its molecular structure.

McCready smirked as he watched the apple disappear. "I'm not sure I wanna know." Averting his gaze to the forested horizon, he asked, "So there really are tigers and pumas out there?"

"And jaguars," Mason said, adjusting his thin Seattle Sombrero™. "And leopards and boars... monkeys and macaws..."

"Boas," added Dorje. "Anaconda, python..." He smiled, his fangs showing slightly.

"All types of jungle creatures," Mason said. "It's miraculous."

"Hunh," McCready said, still staring out at the rainforest, as they passed a herd of elephants. "This is gonna be a trip."

"Indeed," Mason said.

They continued towards their destination at a relaxed pace, exchanging few words between them, both men content with the language of the scenery. It said so much more than mere words. The totality of his father's domed creation could not be faithfully described–only beheld. It was truly a miraculous gift to the world. A wonder that could rival even the pyramids of Giza...and it was his father who had created it.

When they reached the halfway point of their journey, McCready asked, "What are those?"

"What?" Mason asked, turning and walking in McCready's direction.

"Those," he replied, pointing his hand holding his cigarette towards an outcropping of white, geodesic domes that could barely be glimpsed upon the southern horizon. "The Disney World® things."

"The geodesic domes, you mean?" Mason said.

"Right," he said. "What are they for?"

"Laboratories," Mason replied.

McCready took a draw from his cigarette. "Gonpo's?"

"Yes. Though visiting scientists often work there as well."

"Hm," McCready said, scratching his temple. "They don't fit with the rest of the place."

"That's the idea," Mason said. "They're the only part of this place that's not affected by my father's thoughts."

"Why's that?"

Mason said, "It would alter the results of the experiments performed there."

"Interesting." He blew out some smoke.

"Isn't it all?" Mason asked, watching zebra and impala bound across the grasslands.

McCready nodded, and said, "No doubt."

As they passed a pride of lions on the prowl, Mason said, "I suppose, Mr. McCready, this is as good a time as any for us to discuss your compensation."

"Uh...yeah," he said, taken a bit surprised by the suggestion. "Sure. Sounds good."

Mason rested his hand atop the railing's edge, and said, "I have two offers to make you. The first is a short term one, which consists of a single, lump sum payment of seven hundred and fifty thousand DC's, credited to the account of your choice."

"Seriously?" McCready asked, his cigarette dangling from the edge of his lip.

Mason looked at him. "What do you think?"

"Whoa..." McCready removed the cigarette from his mouth. "Thanks, Huxton, I ah..." He laughed. "Thanks."

Mason nodded. "The second option is a long term offer...one which I will straighforwardly tell you I prefer. You see, Mr. McCready, you've proven yourself–on many levels–to be quite a...valuable asset, shall we say. So much so, that I would be very, *very* interested in retaining your services."

McCready rubbed his chin. "What did you have in mind?"

"A job offer," he said. "I'd like you to work for Ordosoft™."

Raising the cigarette back to his lips, McCready asked, "Doing what?"

"Various security-related duties, depending on the needs of

the company and myself."

"What, like an Ordocop™?"

"No, not at all," Mason said. "The job would be much more prestigious than that, and you would yield *far* more power than they do...and much more freedom. You would be my...utility man, so to speak, doing various jobs as the need arises. And barring any emergency situations, you would be able to set your own schedule as you wish."

"Alright," he said, flicking his cigarette aside. "I'm listening. What's it pay?"

"Annually..." Mason said. "Two million."

McCready's eyebrows raised. "Two million DC's? A *year*?"

"Yes."

"Holy shit."

"Indeed," Mason said. "And in addition to the salary, all living and food expenses will be covered, and a vehicle will be provided for you." He paused, a confident look upon his face. "When I told you I was prepared to reward you generously for services rendered..." He smiled. "I wasn't joking."

McCready laughed a little, and said, "I guess not."

As they reached the outskirts of the jungle, and the air became more hot and humid, Mason said, "Well, Mr. McCready...which would you prefer? Option one? Or option two?"

McCready thought for a moment, nodded to himself, then answered, "Two. Definitely two."

The SEV started to descend.

"I'm pleased to hear that." Mason extended his hand to McCready.

He firmly grasped his hand. They shook on the deal.

Mason smiled. "Welcome to the company, Mr. McCready."

"Thanks," he said.

The vehicle hovered over a small clearing in the thick canopy, descended into its forested shroud, and stopped its motion about five feet above the ground.

Mason said, "We'll iron out the details back in Seattle. But for now..." He motioned his hand towards the surrounding jungle. The wails of howler monkeys could be heard in the distance, as well as countless other birds and insects. Rainforest smells wafted through the humid air, and Mason breathed them in. "We have better things to do." He looked back at McCready. "Wouldn't you agree?"

FREQUENCIES

McCready, whose wide-eyed gaze was fixed upon the tropical paradise in amazement, simply replied, "Word."

Mason and McCready returned from their day trip about six hours later, arriving just in time to shower up before supper.

As expected, the results from the jungle trek were very positive. Both he and McCready had thoroughly enjoyed themselves, shared many miles and stories with one another, and for the first time since he'd hired him, Mason could honestly say that they both had developed a full level of mutual respect for one another. It wasn't strictly business anymore, but an actual friendship.

Which was just fine with Mason. After all, not only was McCready trustworthy, brave, and very good at what he did, but his influence on Ashley had already been considerably noticeable, and Mason expected that, in time, it would only increase. As would his influence over McCready...and thus, ultimately, Ashley.

Despite the week's chaos, the future was falling into place nicely. Structures were reasserting, and matrices were reappearing. Mason was seeing, quite clearly, the ways in which he could better organize his family and his corporation. He felt inspired, invigorated, and ready to take on the future.

Order had returned.

After they had showered and dressed, Mason and McCready met up with Ashley and the others for dinner. And as was fitting for their final night there, the dining experience was spectacular. They ate a royal feast outside the palace, and were joined by all of the dome's humanoid residents. It was an open-aired celebration, filled with things and events which would best be described as magical. Luminescent faeries dancing in the night sky, avian crossbreeds singing songs older than humankind, photonic guitars playing alongside cowhide drums, holographic tone poems materializing and dematerializing in the air around them... It was a magnificent display of innovation and control; a celebratory exhibit of informational dominance, the likes of which only his father could have dreamed up and actualized.

Many hours later, when the bonfires ceased burning and the music stopped playing, after the indigenous creatures went home and the four moons hung high overhead; after McCready and Ashley had left for their midnight stroll, and Xanadeux and Lhasa had returned to their rooms, Mason was descending the onyx stairs leading down to the palace's basement. A goblet of ruby port in his hand, humming a cheery tune he knew not the name of, he soon reached the end of the stairs, and entered into the treasure room-like substructure. He began to walk amongst the eclectic collection of objects, some of which were ancient, others which were novel, and a few which were impossible to tell. He stopped occasionally to examine a particular item or thing, but never stayed so long as to delay his meeting with his father.

He was much too excited to linger.

"We will speak tonight of the events of the past week, my son," his father had told him earlier at dinner. "What has happened and what it means. And we will also speak of the future...of what is to come."

Reaching the far end of the basement, he approached a wide, ten-foot high, brass mirror that was leaning against the black, chalcedony wall. He looked at his reflection, placed his knuckles against the glass, and knocked a particular pattern of sounds onto it. He waited a few seconds, then stepped into the mirrored surface, causing it to ripple and wave.

Through the looking glass, he emerged into his father's study, which was a room that wasn't a room. A polychromatic space which seemingly had no beginning or end; an everchanging, colorful dimension which made Mason feel as if he was in the heart of another galaxy, with different natural laws than those of his own. There were no visible floors or walls, yet he could feel the ground beneath his shoes, and see the various objects suspended upon its nonexistent walls. He could look down, underneath where he was standing, see forever into infinity, and do the same when he looked above and side to side.

Endless, varicolored space, all around.

And though he was used to these types of sensations in virtual space, it was an entirely different experience when it happened in realtime, and it always took Mason a few moments to fully adjust.

"Watch your step," his father said, seated low to the ground in front of a short table which was completely transparent, save for its thin, glowing, red outline. The items on top if it appeared to be hovering in the air, perfectly still.

"Believe me," Mason said, carefully maneuvering around the furniture which, like the table, were also only outlines, "I am."

"So you are," he agreed, as Mason reached the chair in front of the table without any major trouble.

Taking a sip of his port, Mason sat down in the luxuriously

soft chair, and kicked his feet up onto its ottoman. "Made it," he said.

His father smiled. "You did." An iridescent meteor shower occurred in the distance behind him. "And now we can begin." He took a sip from a teacup, and said, "Ask me whatever you would like to know, and I will try my best to answer."

Mason placed his finger on his lip, tapped it a few times, and asked, "Why didn't you answer my calls this week?"

"I thought it best not to."

"Why not? I could have used your advice on how to handle the terrorist situation."

"It was better for you to handle it alone."

"But I've always consulted with you on major issues that affected the family or company. Why, when something was affecting them both so severely, would you decide to change that?"

"It was time," he said, cupping his hands around his ceramic teacup. "Did you not handle the situation by yourself?"

"Yes, I did, but-"

"No buts then," he interrupted. "If you did, you did, and if you did, then you didn't need. Correct?"

"I suppose," Mason reluctantly said. "Though I would have at least liked to have spoken with you about it in *some* manner, even if it wasn't in regards to how to deal with it."

"You can do that now," he said. "The opportunity hasn't passed."

"Yes, but people sometimes like to speak to loved ones *while* the crisis is occuring, father. Comfort, support...those kinds of things are nice sometimes, you know."

He smiled. "Yes. But so is change."

"It *can* be..." Mason drank from his silver goblet, while staring off into the mesmerizing colors. "Depending on the situation." He wiped his lips, and said, "On to the next...I take it Xanadeux has informed you of the details surrounding the attacks?"

He nodded.

"What do you make of it?"

"Which aspect?"

"All of it," Mason replied.

"It is what it is," his father said.

He gave him a semi-mock look of annoyance. "Could you be a *bit* more specific, father?"

"Yes, if your questions were a bit more specific."

Mason sighed. "Very well," he said. "What do you think it

was that attacked the family?"

"Tell me your theories first, and then I will tell you mine."

"You're impossible, you know that?"

"So I hear." He picked up a kettle from the table and poured himself some more tea. "Well?" he asked. "No theories?"

Mason chuckled. "You know, father, sometimes I think its amazing that I turned out as well as I did, considering that I've had to deal with..." He playfully stammered, as he motioned to their otherwordly surroundings. "...with *this* all my life."

"Miraculous, I'd say," his father replied. "Theories, please?"

"All right," he sportively said. "I'll indulge you." He drank from his cup, and said, "When the attacks first occurred, I thought that they were being committed by a group of crackers...possibly underground, possibly hired by a rival corporation...possibly former temps or other disgruntled employees..." His words tailed off as a particularly bright color pattern caught his attention. "Whatever the case," he continued, "I assumed it was something of a conspiratorial nature, conceived and carried out by a group of people in order to strike out against Ordosoft™." He took another sip of the sweet liquid, and said, "But as this 'Presence' further revealed itself to me, it felt less and less like it was a group creation, and more and more like it was just one, single person...or thing."

His father waited for him to continue.

"You see," Mason said, "neither Agent Takura, nor Xanadeux, could find a single, realtime port that the Presence might have used, nor could they find even the faintest trace of a connection to the real world. All of the attacks had been carried out from *within* the uninet–not from without...meaning that no human was giving the orders." He finished his port, and set his cup onto the table. "The three of us then came to the conclusion that whatever the origins of this Presence may have been, by the time it attacked me, it only existed within cyberspace. It was a creation which had no corporeal, realtime form... A true ghost within the machine."

His father nodded a few times, and said, "I agree with your theory."

"You do?"

"Completely."

"Well," Mason said, surprised his father didn't have his *own* spin on things. "I'm pleased to hear that. My question for you then wou-" He stopped mid-sentence, noticing for the first time a small, clear square which sat atop the table. Inside of it, was a swirling collection of energy, resembling the shape of a black hole, but with much more color. He reached forward, touched the top of it, and asked, "What is this?"

"A wormhole," his father replied.

Mason picked it up, and stared into the kinetic whorl. "Fascinating."

"That one leads to some sort of microscopic, pocket universe," he said. "I only recently sent a probe into it, so I haven't fully had a chance to understand what's on the other side."

He looked up from the square at his father. "You mean you have others?"

"Yes," he said. "But they're much larger than that. Now, back to what you were saying..."

"Of course," Mason said, still staring at the miniature wormhole as he set it down on the tabletop. "The Presence..." He collected his thoughts, and said, "The thing about it that was terribly confusing, and which none of us can quite figure out–and I'm hoping you can–is why this ghost chose to haunt *our* family in particular. And why it did so in the way that it did. It had numerous opportunities to kill us, yet it only sought to terrorize, and...the only word to describe it is 'play.' It was as if this creature was playing a game with us the whole time...not really interested in destroying us, but in...I don't know. I can't fathom its reasoning, father. There's no logic to it."

His father nodded. "Maybe that's the answer."

"That it's illogical?"

"Yes."

"If it is, then that's a very unsatisfying answer," Mason said. "It doesn't explain anything."

"But it does," he replied. "Who or whatever created this entity, whether they realized it or not, brought into this plane a living chaos equation. An extremely powerful entity whose sole purpose appears to be the disruption of order." He sipped his tea, and asked, "And what represents order more in this world than the corporation?"

Mason thought for a moment, nodded, and said, "That *would* explain why it chose Ordosoft™. After all, we've been as instrumental as any force in achieving world order...and I suppose even our name would tempt it, not to mention the control we have in our market. But still..." He paused. "That doesn't quite explain its behavior. It wasn't chaotic *enough*. The Presence was too calculated, its actions too deliberate for it to have been a being of pure chaos."

"Is there not order within chaos?"

"There is," Mason agreed.

"And were a being to act *only* in random and haphazard ways, wouldn't it then be somewhat predictable? If it never calculated or planned, could it still be called a creature of chaos? Or would its adherence to randomness now make it predictable and ordered?"

"I see your point," he said. "Considering the infinite targets available to it, were it only to attack at random, it would achieve nothing."

"Precisely. Some order is needed to disrupt order."

Mason mulled over the possibilites. "Say that Xanadeux and Takura's attack didn't really destroy the Presence...and it's still alive, somewhere in the net... Am I to believe that it will keep its word about not attacking our family?"

"Maybe," he said. "Maybe not. That's chaos."

"That's unnerving, is what it is," Mason said. "How can I deal with something that doesn't make any sense?"

"You just do."

"That sense of unknowing doesn't bother you?"

"No. I accept it as a part of life."

"Then you're not at *all* worried that this creature might come for you as well?"

"I consider the possibility," he said. "And then I let it go. It weighs naught upon my mind. Whatever will be, will be, and the future...will unfold as it will."

"The future..." Mason said. "You mentioned that earlier at dinner. You said we'd be speaking about...how did you put it... 'What is to come.'"

"Yes," he said. "And now we've reached that time." He set his teacup down, and when he did, the room immediately transformed into its actual state. Mason could now see the walls, the ground, the furniture, other doors...everything as it truly was.

A sense of reality returned to the moment.

His father said, "I have two things with which to discuss with you, my son. One is a forewarning, the other, a gift. Which would you like first?"

His eyes still adjusting to the candlelit lighting, Mason said, "Work before play. The warning first."

"Certainly." He paused momentarily, then said, "I believe

the appearance of the Presence was a sign...an omen of things to come. Order has ruled supreme for nearly this entire century–for the last *few* centuries, even–and I believe it is now come time for its rule to be challenged. In the coming months, you must prepare yourself for events which will shake the very foundations of your world."

"I've already had that happen," Mason said, thinking of Dominique in particular.

"I'm not referring to your personal world," he said. "These events will affect the entire Earth."

Mason looked at his father intently, studying his face for any sign of humor. There was none. "How do you mean?" he asked.

"Let me explain," he said. "When chaos fully descends upon this plane, innovation and confrontation will increase exponentially, leading to a period in humankind's history which will be as volatile and unstable as any that has been experienced before. I would dare say it may even be *the* most volatile period in human history, especially when taking into account the realities of a global government. On one side," he said, extending his hand out like checking for raindrops, "we have the power of worldwide security and scientific cooperation." He raised his other hand, palm also facing upwards. "On the other, we have an interconnected system of nations that is vulnerable to attack from any place on Earth. And if one should fall...will the others follow?" He moved them up and down, as if he was balancing the air. "We shall see."

Resting his hands upon his lap, he continued, "As an agent of order, your role will become more important than ever. You must be as a rock in a storm, steadfast and unyielding, for others will look to you for guidance. You must become stronger than ever, my son, and learn not to be reliant upon anyone else but yourself. Ultimately, no man, woman, or construct can help you through this coming time. Only *you* can help yourself. While certain individuals may aid you at certain times, it is essential that you remember where the true power lies... Within you. Always." He stared directly at Mason without saying a word, and asked, "Do you understand what it is that I'm telling you?"

Still grappling with the weight of his father's words, he said, "I...I believe so, father. It seems...so unreal to think of this scenario, but...but I understand what you're saying...about my role." As the thoughts sunk in, his voice became more confident. "And I'll fulfill that duty if it comes time. I'll be ready for the future."

He nodded encouragingly. "Then that is all I have to say on

the subject," he said. "At least for the time being. And now, the gift."
He stood up, and walked around the table to Mason. "A project that I
have been cultivating for a *very* long time has finally bore its fruit,
my son." He set his hand on Mason's shoulder and smiled. "Prepare to
be astonished." His father snapped his fingers, and one of the room's
doors began to slowly open.

Mason stood up from his chair, his head tilted to one side in
attempt to sneak a peek. "What is it?" he eagerly asked.

"My son..." his father said.

A familiar figure emerged from behind the door.
"Consciousness uploading has been achieved," his father's other body
said, as the door closed behind him.

"What?" Mason asked, taken aback by both the sight of two
fathers and the words they were speaking.

"He is me," the emerging father said, as he seated himself
where the original father had been.

"And I am him," said the father standing next to him. "Our
consciousness is one and the same."

"I don't believe it," Mason said with awe.

"Believe it," they both said.

He looked back and forth between the two of them. "You're
exactly the same?"

"Identical," the father next to him said.

Mason felt rush of adrenalin pass through him, as he thought
of its applications to Dominique. "You're *completely* sure, father?
Without a doubt?"

"Yes," the seated father said. "Otherwise..." He pulled out a
small device, and aimed it at the other father. "Would I let myself
do this?" The next instant, he fired a laser beam at the original
father, instantly splitting him in half from head to toe.

Horrified, Mason stepped back.

The original father's bodily halves fell to the ground, jerked
a few times, and ceased their motion.

"I'm still me," the seated father said. "Don't worry."

Mason looked at his father, adrenalin borne of excitement *and*
fear now passing through his being.

"I apologize for the grotesque theatrics, but it seemed the
simplest way to convince you." He peered over the table at his other
body. "May I clean up the mess now?"

Without looking at the body again, a nauseous Mason replied,
"Please do."

His father motioned his hands, and the ambient nanotech cleaned up his remains. "There," he said. "Much better."

Mason stood there, motionless, attempting to quell his sickness.

"Son?"

He looked at his father. "I feel sick."

"No..." his father said with a subtle laugh, drawing out the word as if Mason was a boy again. "There's no reason to."

"No reason?" Mason asked. "Father, I just watched you *die*."

He laughed. "No, you didn't," he said, still speaking to him like a child. "You saw one of my bodies die." He poured himself some tea. "There's a world of difference between the two. You must stop thinking of this breakthrough in yesterday's terms. It won't do you any good. This is the future, son." He raised the tea to his lips. "Get used to it."

Mason seated himself back in the chair. "All right," he said, "just give me a moment." He picked up his goblet to take a sip, but quickly remembered there was nothing left in it. "Damn," he muttered.

"Allow me," his father said, motioning his hands.

Mason's cup filled up with fresh port. He took a sip, then asked, "Could I have something a bit stronger?"

"Of course." He twinkled his fingers.

The ruby liquid turned amber. Mason drank a large gulp. "Much better," he said, the old fashioned's aftertaste soothingly lingering in his mouth.

"I took the liberty to mix in a little Diazecalm™, too," his father said.

Feeling its calming effects already, Mason replied, "Many thanks."

His father nodded with a smile.

When Mason's mind was completely settled, he once again thought of the implications of his father's technology, and why it was such a gift. "This is really happening, father?" he asked. "This isn't a hologram or a test of some sort?"

"Not at all," he replied. "This is my gift to you."

"Then..." Mason's heart filled with excitement. "Then that means you can bring back Dominique."

"I can."

"Thank you, father," he said, bowing his head and closing his eyes. "Thank you." He breathed in, then looked back up at the miracle-maker seated in front of him. "You don't know what this means to me."

"I do," he said.

Mason smiled. "Yes. You do, don't you?" He shook his head with disbelief, and said, "Dominique..." His mind was whirling with images of his beloved wife, their time spent together, the times to come...

And that was when reality rudely reasserted itself. "Dominique..." Mason repeated, this time more gravely, as he thought of his reborn wife back in Seattle.

"You're thinking of the clone." his father said.

"Yes. The..." He couldn't believe he was saying it. "...the clone. That *is* all she is, isn't it?" Mason asked unsuredly. "All she ever was?"

"And nothing more," he said. "But now you can have the real thing."

He somberly stared at his father, and said, "You realize what this means, don't you?"

His father nodded slowly. "I do."

Mason sighed heavily. "God forgive me."

α

α
Chapter 17:
<u>Brief Lives</u>

"There could be no other way than this one.
Old things must pass, in order that the new may come forth.

They arrived back in Seattle on a cold, wet, and thoroughly miserable Monday morning.

After they had said their goodbyes at the airstrip, and parted their separate ways, Mason immediately attended to his dreadful duties. There was no time to waste.

The future was now.

As he entered into the quarantine area, Dominique's clone smiled at him from behind the thick, plate glass, walked towards the barrier, and enthusiastically said, "Mason."

"Hello," he replied, as coldy as possible.

She was in a medium-sized room, furnished with a few possessions from their house, but not nearly enough to make it feel homey. The walls were stark white, and combined with the harsh fluorescents to make everything–including her–unrealistically bright. "I'm so glad to see you," she said, pressing her palms up against the glass. "It's been so lonely in here."

"Yes," he said.

Noticing his distance, her face frowned, and she asked, "What's wrong?"

"Nothing," he said, unconvincingly.

"Did they find something bad, Mason?" she asked. "Did they?"

He was unable to reply, as he was too caught up in his own internal conflict, tempted to try to save her somehow, but knowing that simply was *not* a realistic option.

"Please tell me what they're saying about me," she said worriedly. "All they tell me is that they need to run more tests, but I know they have to know something by now. Tell me, Mason, please...what's happening? When can I go home? I don't want to be here anymore..." She rested her forehead against the glass and began to cry.

Mason timidly reached his hand towards the clear barrier, and placed it next to her face. His hand was shaking, as he told her, "You won't be here much longer, Dominique."

She looked up at him, a small trace of hope in her eyes. "Really?"

"Yes," he said truthfully.

"Then I can go home soon?"

He nodded, a low murmur building in his throat. "Yes," he managed to say. "You'll be...going home..." He traced his finger along the glass outline of her smiling face. "Soon. I promise."

She closed her eyes as if he was actually touching her, a look of peace upon her face.

"I have to go now," Mason said, stepping back from the barrier.

She nodded, and wiped her eyes. "I understand."

Mason stared at her for a moment, then said, "I'll see you soon, Dominique." He swallowed hard. "And I promise everything will be better."

"I believe you." Both palms still pressed against the glass, she said, "I love you, Mason Huxton."

"I..." He whimpered painfully. "I...I'm sorry, Dominique," he said, and without uttering another sound, he left the room.

Xanadeux was waiting outside. "Sir?" it asked.

"Don't speak to me," he said, covering his eyes. "Just walk."

They moved quickly through the quarantine wing, out of the hospital, and to the limo parked out front.

The rain was still falling.

"Sit in the front," Mason said to Xanadeux, as the back door opened for him. "I need to be alone."

"Of course," the android said.

Mason climbed into the backseat, and the door shut softly behind him. He leaned forward, reached his hands up to the top of his head, and tightly grasped at his hair.

"Where to, sir?" Burke asked.

"Just drive," Mason cried.

The car lifted off the ground.

Mason rocked himself back and forth at the edge of his seat, as the warm rain continued to run down his face.

Webber had assured him it would be painless, he rationalized. An injection in the day, that wouldn't act until the night. She would pass quietly in her sleep, and feel nothing. "Cause of death," his head of security had told him. "Aftereffects of the informational infection."

A flawless story. No one would dispute it.

But Mason would always know the truth.

He released his hands from his head, and reached towards the mahogany cabinet situated in the center of the backseat. He opened it up, and pulled out the alpha-covered, green cube and its accompanying headpiece. He placed the neural net onto his head, and twisted the cube at its fissure. The headpiece magnetized to his skin, and the technorganic tendrils grew out of it, quickly forming their intricate network over his scalp.

Mason leaned back in the soft, cushioned seat, closed his eyes, and twisted the cube again.

Virtuality blossomed before him.

The day could not have been more perfect.

$$\alpha$$

δ

Chapter 18:
Life After Death

A seed must shed its shell so that it may grow once again.
I am but a seed.
Growing."

Morris Ignacio was dead.

At least as far as he was concerned, that identity had been laid to rest. Put into the ground and covered with dirt.

"I've seen your face on some of the public unies, Iggy," Raquel said, as she set a bag of groceries onto her countertop.

Unfortunately, the law was already attempting to dig it up.

"They're really lookin' for you."

"I know," Ignacio said, turning off her uniview with the remote. "I'm all over the local news." He stood up from the couch, and walked towards her. "There's already been a few national mentions, too. I guess it's the first time in a while that a Freemon's defected."

She smiled as she unpacked the groceries. "Didn't you always want to be famous?"

"Famous, maybe," he said. "Infamous, never." He kissed her on the cheek. "Thanks for shopping, Raq."

"Te nada," she said, as he picked up a blue banana and unpeeled it. "It's actually kinda nice to be shopping for someone else. Me an' Pam always get our own stuff."

Biting the azure fruit, he asked, "She's supposed to come back today, ey?"

"That was the *original* plan, yeah." Raquel placed some food items into her small refrigerator. "But she called me on my cell while I was shopping and said she wouldn't be coming back 'til Wednesday." She looked over her shoulder at him. "So you're clear to stay here for a few more days."

"Bueno." He walked behind her, placed his hand on her back, and said, "Let me get this, Raquel. You've done enough already."

She laughed, as she continued to pack the fridge. "All I've done is gone shopping, Iggy."

"You've done more than that," he said. "You saved my ass." He gently took an Odwalla® from her hand, set it onto the refrigerator's top shelf, then placed his hand under her chin.

She looked up at him with her beautiful, brown eyes.

"Thank you, Raquel," he said. "From the bottom of my heart. Gracias."

"Thanks," she said, almost sounding surprised. "It's um...I'm not really used to people telling me things like that." She stared at him for a moment, then hugged him tightly. "I love you, Iggy," she said.

Ignacio held her in his arms, and pressed his lips against the top of her head. "I love you too, Raquel," he said.

And that was from the heart.

The previous memories he had of her were all positive ones, and now that his true self had gotten a chance to know her, and had the chance to experience her compassion personally, the memories synergized with the feelings to make a complete whole. It was like knowing a lover for a long time then suddenly being able to experience their freshness and newness all over again.

"I really do," he said, softly releasing his embrace. "Let me put these away, okay?"

Raquel smiled. "Okay." She walked over to her couch, and plopped down on top of it. As Ignacio started to put away the remaining groceries, she asked, "You know how you were telling me last night about this group you were a part of? The ones that sent you undercover?"

"Sí."

"Are you supposed to join up with them again?"

"That's the idea," he said, putting a box of Frosted Flakes® into the cupboard.

"But if you don't have any chips, then how are they going to find you?"

"Through my thoughts," he said. "They can pinpoint

338

individual frees like they were GPS transmitters."

Raquel adjusted a big pillow behind her head, and said, "How do they do *that*?"

"I have no idea," Ignacio said, placing the final item away. "But they can." He walked over to the couch, sat down next to her, and put her feet on of top his lap.

"So why haven't they contacted you then?"

"My frees are still stabilizing right now from the awakening," he said, massaging her tiny foot with one of his hands. "It's like there's still a lot of static in my head. Once the static's gone, and my frees stabilize, then they'll be able to tune in and find me."

"And then what?" she asked.

"I don't know," Ignacio said. "I'll cross that bridge when I get there."

Raquel placed her hand on top of his. "I hope we'll still be able to see each other."

"Me too, Raquel," he said, staring down at their interconnected hands. "Me too." He looked over at her and smiled. "You're a beautiful soul, you know that?"

"No." She smiled. "But I'm learning."

"Bueno," he said, laying down, and cuddling up next to her. "Por que eres."

Her smile widened, as his arm wrapped around her waist. They began to kiss.

And despite the numerous issues his awakened mind still had to deal with, Ignacio felt content with the present. The future may have been uncertain, but one thing in this new life was for sure–he would know love.

And that was enough for now.

δ

∞

Chapter 19:
<u>Overstandings</u>

"When the tale has been told, and the lines have been drawn, what then remains? When all is said and done, and the facts and the truths and the lies and the dreams have been presented before us, what are we left with?

We are left, as always, with but one, single, thing.

In the end, it all boils down to choice.

We choose how to interpret the tale, and how the tale will affect us. We choose how to perceive the lines, and what they will mean to our being. We choose for ourselves what will be fact, and what will be fiction; what will be lie, and what will be truth; what will be reality, and what will be dream.

We choose with whom we will trust.

We choose with whom we will love.

We choose with whom we will do battle.

We choose with whom we will build.

We choose how to live our lives. Fate only acts after a choice has been made. Destiny is written by our own hands.

We create our world.

And though other forces, whether they be individuals or institutions, will try to persuade or dissuade us in the decisions we make along our life's journey, in truth, that is all they can ever really do: try.

Only we can do.

So do.

Do what must be done, and do it without fear. Do what you know is right, and do it without hesitation. Do what you must, and you shall set yourself free.

True freedom lies within you.

FREQUENCIES

Awaken it.

Now.

For tomorrow may never come, and time waits for no one. Act before it is too late, while understanding the paradox that it is never too late to act. While there is still breath, there is still hope.

I know this for a fact. All seemed hopeless around me, my dreams turned to dust. Yet I still drew breaths, and I dreamt new dreams.

And I have seen that dreams become reality for those who are willing to believe in them.

Do you believe in dreams?

I do.

And so should you, because in your hands you're holding one. Feel its weight? Feel its substance?

The dream is real.

The choice is yours.

Choose wisely.

—Adrian Malcolm Wellor

Ashley stared at the journal's final entry.

"Choose wisely," she said to herself. She closed the book, and looked up at the lush, green, Tiger Mountain scenery surrounding her. Ferns and spruce...moss and lichen...birds, streams, rocks, and earth...

Gaia in her full splendor.

After the week's events, the forest was the perfect place for Ashley to come and think...and relax...and decompress. So much had happened in so little time. So many confirmations. So many revelations.

So many choices...

She looked down at the stream beside her, into the fresh, mountain water. Everything was so clear. She could see things coming to the surface. Other things moving on. Others approaching nearer.

The current of change.

Ashley placed the journal into her backpack and cinched the top closed. She dipped her fingers into the cold water and swirled them around in it. Then she took off her hiking boots, her wool socks, and pulled her Nanopôr™ stretch pants up to her knees. She slowly lowered her bare feet into the stream...

It was chilly, but refreshing. She wiggled her toes around, allowing the undercurrent to pass between them. It felt good getting her feet wet, and she enjoyed the sensation. It was a way for her to feel alive. And free.

But somehow, it wasn't quite enough. Not anymore.

Ashley took off her polar fleece sweater, set it on top of her pack, and placed her hands underneath the water's surface. She leaned forward, cupped her hands, and brought the cool water to her face...

Wonderful.

She did this a few more times, then pulled her feet from the water. She put her knees beneath her, and placed her hands at the stream's edge. Ashley closed her eyes, and gave thanks to life.

For everything.

She slowly took in a breath, then immersed her head into the gentle current. The amplified sounds rushed around her. Beautiful, flowing, chaotic music. She delicately swayed her head to the melody, and danced until she was out of breath.

She emerged from the water, and breathed in again. She smiled. She opened her eyes.

A thrush was singing from a cedar's branch. A squirrel scampered into a blackberry bush. Life was all around.

A black and red butterfly flittered by, dream-like.

But was it her dream? Or the butterfly's?

Ashley laughed.

It didn't matter. Either way, the dream was real.

That was what mattered.

She wrung the excess water from her long hair, and put her polar fleece back on. Then the socks, and then the shoes. She tied the laces, picked up her backpack, and stood to her feet. She faced the trail leading back down the mountain, and walked towards it.

There was work to be done.

People to network with. Things to be changed.

Old structures to bring down, and new ones to build.

Ashley stepped onto the path without hesitation.

The choice was hers.

∞

Ω
Chapter 20:
<u>Ad Infinitum</u>

"No way," McCready said, as he eagerly stepped out of the limousine. "No fucking way."

In his driveway, was parked a gorgeous, cherry-red, '57 Chevy®. Mint-condition. Freshly waxed. In *his* driveway.

He quickly walked up to it, and stood there before the machine in amazement.

Xanadeux followed behind him. "Mr. Huxton wanted you to have a surprise bonus, Mr. McCready," it said. "I hope that you approve of my suggestion."

He looked back at the android. "*You* suggested this?"

"Yes."

McCready laughed, and said, "Xanny, if I did hugs, I'd hug you right now." He turned back around to the car, and lightly rapped his knuckles against its sides. "Steel. This is so fuckin' bomb."

"I'm pleased to see I made the right choice," it said.

"Me too," he replied, running his fingers along one of the fins. "So does she actually run on gas?"'

"She does. And her tank is currently full." McCready heard a jingling noise, as Xanadeux said, "Here are your keys."

"Keys," he said, as he grasped the Chevrolet®-logo keyring. "Sweet." He closed his hand around them, and said, "Alright, I gotta know–is this baby actually mine, or am I just borrowing her?"

"She's yours, Mr. McCready."

"Fuckin'-A," he said, walking over to the front door and opening it. He touched the red, vinyl interior. "I am in the *sweetest* dream right now." He clicked on the antique radio's knob, and dialed it up and down the different stations. "Does this only pick up FM/AM?"

"Yes," the android said. "But we could have it modified if you would like."

"No way," McCready said, as he clicked off the tunes. "An old radio fits her just perfect."

"Good," it said.

McCready climbed into the front seat, and shut the door behind him. He put the key into the ignition and turned it forward. The engine roared to life. He pushed his feet on the gas pedal, and revved it a little.

The sensation was awesome.

Xanadeux tapped on the window.

McCready rolled it down. "Yeah?"

It reached its hand towards him, palm facing upwards. "You'll need the proper permit to drive a leaded, gasoline-burning vehicle."

"Oh yeah, right," he said, placing his thumb on top of the small scanner located in the center of the android's palm. "I got it?"

It nodded. "You now have it."

"Great." He pressed his foot on the brake, and shifted the car into reverse.

"Mr. McCready," Xanadeux said.

He held his foot on the brake. "Yeah?"

"A few more things before you go."

"Sure. Go ahead."

"Your company car will be delivered shortly, after we make some final modifications on it."

"Alright," he said.

"And Mr. Huxton has requested for you to meet with him tomorrow morning to discuss the details of your employment."

"But I'm free today, right?" McCready asked.

"Correct," Xanadeux said. "Also, with your permission, I can load your bags into your house."

"Fine with me. Is that it then?"

"That's all for now," it said.

"Then I'm gonna go cruisin', Xanny," he said, releasing his foot from the brake.

"Enjoy yourself," Xanadeux said.

"I will," McCready said, as he backed out of the driveway and into the street. "Believe that."

FREQUENCIES

For the next four hours, McCready cruised around various parts of the Eastside and Westside, listening to an oldies station that he found on AM. He would have stayed out cruising all day, but he only had so much gas, and he didn't want to ask Xanadeux for a refill already.

He'd wait until tomorow. That'd be enough time.

Entering into his apartment, McCready still had a child-like grin stretched across his face. He couldn't help it. It was like he'd found a little piece of heaven on Earth.

He set his keys onto his counter, went to the bathroom, then walked over to his uniview. Time to tell Ignacio the good news.

"Voice-rec on," he said. "Call Ignacio."

He waited for about fifteen seconds, but there was no answer.

"Would you like to leave a message?" the unie asked.

Before he could answer, his doorbell sounded.

He said to the screen, "Yeah, leave message. Ignacio, this is McCready. I got some good news, amigo. Call me when you get this. Late." He touched the screen and disconnected the call. "Show door camera," he said.

Ashley appeared upon the screen.

McCready smiled. "Open door," he said, and walked around the corner to greet her.

"Hey," she said with a bright smile, as she entered his place. "How are you?"

"Awesome," he said, as they hugged each other. "How 'bout you?"

"Same." She kissed him on the lips, and walked into his living room. "Today's been incredible."

"Yeah, it has." McCready sat down on the couch. "Did you see the car?"

Ashley sat down next to him, and placed the book she was holding on her lap. "Mm-hm. I like it."

"Did you know they were gonna give that to me?"

She shook her head. "No...but it doesn't surprise me."

"Surprised the hell outta me," he said. "I was like a kid on Christmas, Ashley. You would've cracked up. I hopped right in that baby, and just..." He flattened his palm, moved his hand forward like a plane, and made a whistling noise. "*Cruised*. It was bomb. It was like I was in a movie, or something."

"That's neat," Ashley said.

"Yeah, it was. So what did you do after the airport?"

"I went over to Tiger Mountain, and hiked for a few hours...

345

Relaxed, thought about things..." She held up the book. "Went over this a little more."

"The journal?"

"Mm-hm," she said, opening it up and thumbing through its pages. "There's really some amazing stuff in here."

"I bet," McCready said. "You'll have to show me some of it."

"Definitely," she said, continuing to look through the journal. "There's actually this one part in here I wanted to read you... It really sums up a lot of what I feel right now. And the way he put it was just really perfect."

"Cool. I'd love to hear it."

"Okay," she said, "let me find it."

As Ashley searched through the journal, McCready leaned against the side of his couch, and peeked out the window. The rain had completely stopped, and the sun looked like it was about to come out.

"Here it is," she said, leaning her head back onto his lap and kicking her feet up and over the opposite end of the couch. She looked up at him and smiled. "You ready?"

He lightly touched her damp hair, and smiled back. "Shoot."

"Okay." She propped the book in front her of face. "So he was talking about the way that our lives go through cycles, and the way that one thing always leads to the next. Like how one door will close and then another door will suddenly open."

McCready said, "Like how you'll quit a job and then all of a sudden get offered one that's even better?" He laughed. "Like that?"

"Exactly," Ashley said. "So that's basically what the theme of this entry was. But what I liked about it so much, was the *way* he said it. So here it goes, his words now: 'We each write our own individual stories as we move through the years of our lives, filling them with events both good and bad, things both right and wrong, and people both loved and loathed. But unlike fiction, our tales have no simple resolution. Though chapters of our life may have their particular conclusions, the overall story keeps on going, ad infinitum. For, even when we reach our last heartbeat–even then–does the tale really end? Do our frequencies truly stop vibrating? Or does our energy simply change form, and loop back into the life spectrum, where it can commence its story all over again? Who is to say? Ultimately, we can only answer these questions for ourselves.'" She paused for a moment, noticing the room growing brighter.

McCready glanced out at the sky.

346

FREQUENCIES

The sun had pierced the clouds, and its energy was now shining through the window and onto them. The warmth felt good.

They both smiled, and she continued, "'This then, is what *I* have come to know: There are no such things as endings. Only infinite beginnings.'"

Ashley closed the book.

Ω

OMEGAPPENDIX

TABLE OF CONTENTS

ΩΩΩΩΩΩΩΩΩΩΩΩΩΩΩΩΩΩΩΩΩΩΩΩΩΩΩΩΩΩΩΩΩΩΩΩΩΩΩΩΩΩ

Freekspeek:
A glossary of frequential terms
ΩΩΩΩΩΩΩΩΩΩΩΩΩΩΩΩΩΩΩΩΩΩΩΩΩΩΩΩΩΩΩΩΩΩΩΩΩΩΩΩΩΩ

AAS: See **Automatic Anti-collision Systems**.

ADD: See **Attention-Deficit Disorder**.

Adsat: *n.* An orbiting or **geostationary** sattelite which is used to display slogans and/or advertisements that can be viewed by the naked eye from the surface of the Earth.

Aeonomics: *n.* The study of how economics will be affected by a world populated with immortals.

AI: *n.* Artificial Intelligence.

Alpha-beta: *n.* **Freemon** term for someone who thinks within the acceptable range of **FE**'s for normal citizens.

Alpha point: *n.* The beginning of the universe; the **big bang**.

Alpha wave: *n.* A frequency transmitted by a source (a **uniview**, a radio tower, etc.) which induces a feeling of calm and complacency. Also, the **frees** emanated by someone when they are calm or "normal."

American Empire: **Headquartered** in the United States, this empire directly or indirectly controls the Earth's entire Western Hemisphere and also has influence or dominion over much of the Eastern Hemisphere. Has been compared by many to the **Roman Empire**.

American Revolution: Also known as the **Revolutionary War**, this conflict led to the creation of the **American Empire**, which was officially founded in 1776, and is still active to the present.

Amp: *n.* A powerful, illegal stimulant which is a synthesis of epinephrine, ephedra, cocaine, and concentrated caffeine. –*v.* To be on amp or to act in a hyperactive manner.

Anamnesis: *n.* Latin term meaning "the loss of forgetfulness."

Anasazi: *n.* A term used for the Native American culture that once inhabited Colorado, Arizona, Utah, and New Mexico. Descendants of the Pueblo, the Anasazi are often associated with basket-making, cliff dwellings, and petroglyphs.

Androidal: *adj.* Of, or relating to an android.

Armas: *n.* Spanish for "weapon" or "arm."

Arthurian: *adj.* Of, or relating to King Arthur.

ASAP: As soon as possible.

Astral travel: *v.* To leave the body and travel over physical or mystical distances in spirit form.

Attention-Deficit Disorder: *n.* The label branded upon children who exhibit signs of hyperactivity or restlessnes, especially when in a scholastic setting. Treatment for the "disorder" usually involves a form of **neurochemical** therapy.

Aural IR: *n.* A device which displays infrared radiation as an outline surrounding the object being examined.

Auto: *adj.* Automatic.

Autobus: *n.* Public transportation buses which are programmed along specific routes and contain no human driver.

Autoevolution: *n.* Evolution controlled by intelligent **lifeforms** rather than **natural selection**.

Automatic Anti-collision Systems: *n.* An intelligent technology that prevents **GS** vehicles from coming too close to one another during their operation. Required by law and standard-equipped in all **GS** vehicles and crafts.

Avatar: *n.* The icon which someone uses to represent themselves in a virtual domain or setting.

Baba Ghannooj: *n.* A Middle-Eastern dish consisting of roasted eggplant, tahini, garlic, lemon juice, and spices.

Babylon: *n.* A place containing an abundance of luxury and conveniences which have been gained through the exploitation and oppression of human and animal beings. –**Babylonian:** *adj.* Utilizing the methods of, or having the traits associated with a Babylon.

Back: *n.* Back-up; reinforcements.

Banistered: *adj.* Containing a banister.

Barre: *n.* A rounded bar, usually wooden, used in ballet for stretching exercises.

B-chip: See **biochip**.

Benzy: *n.* A Mercedes-Benz®.

B/free scanner: *n.* A device which can simultaneously sense both **biochip** and FE information. The **Freemon** are equipped with **B/free scanners** (usually housed within contacts or implants) so that they can directly gauge a suspect's **frees** without having to rely on the **freeread**'s data. Since a **freeread** senses its owner's **frees** and then transmits the information via **sattelink**, there is much more room for error with it than with a B/free scanner.

Bi: *adj.* Bisexual.

Big bang: See **big bang theory**.

Big bang theory: The theory that the entire universe originated from a singular, infinitely-dense state of being.

Biochip: *n.* A tiny microchip (less than half the size of a grain of rice) which is encased inside of a **biocompatible** material and painlessly injected under the skin at birth. Once inside the body, it becomes surrounded by a thin sheath of protein which securely holds it in place for the duration of its owner's life. Usually located on either thumb, the **biochip** contains all of its owner's personal, financial, and medical records, their bank accounts, credit cards, and **digital cash**, their electronic keys and passwords, **live-feed** biological information, a **GPS** transmitter, and a **sattelink** hookup which allows them to perform countless other functions and duties via the **uninet**. Also commonly referred to as a **B-chip**. Less commonly referred to as the **Mark of the Beast** (see **freeread**). –*v.* To inject, or to be injected with a biochip.

Biocompatible: *adj.* Having little or no adverse effects upon a biological organism. Usually used in reference to vertebrates.

Bioinformatics: *n.* The study of how **information theory** and technologies are applied to the fields of **biotechnology** and genetic analysis research.

Biological fundamentalism: The belief that death is a natural, essential part of the life equation which should not be removed. –*n.* Biological fundamentalist: One who adheres to the principles of biological fundamentalism.

Biomatter: *n.* Biological material.

Bioreadings: *n.* The data provided by a device or apparatus during or after the examination of a biological organism.

Biostasis: *n.* The complete suspension of an organism's biological functions and activity in order to perfectly preserve it until a later date. Also called **suspended animation**.

Biotech: See **biotechnology**.

Biotechnology: *n.* The synthesis of biology, medicine, engineering, and technology and its applications (see **gengineer**). **Biotech** is the most profitable industry of the 21st century.

Birdie: *n.* A police or law enforcement helicopter.

Black Panther Party: An organization founded in 1966 by Huey Newton and Bobby Seale in the hopes of bettering the welfare of their community (i.e., free breakfast programs, protection against police brutality, etc.). One of the favorite targets of the **FBI's COINTELPROs.**

Blud: *n.* Man or fellow; dude.

Blunt: *n.* A hollowed-out cigar which has been filled with marijuana. Also, a large **joint** which has been rolled up in a tobacco leaf.

Borg: See **cyborg.**

Bounce: *v.* To leave or go somewhere.

Brennan Commission: A think-tank formed in 1999 by **Michael Brennan** to explore the implications, possibilites, and applications of the **FE** technology. The commission was comprised of **Brennan, Dr. Adrian Wellor, W.A. Huxton,** members of the **FBI, NSA,** and **CIA,** and certain, carefully selected biologists, physicists, sociologists, psychologists, anthropologists, political scientists, and **futurists.**

Brennan, Michael Jude: Born 1943. Founder of the **Brennan Commission,** and the official creator of the **FE** technology. One of the most respected men in all of science, Brennan still conducts reasearch and occasionally teaches upper-division courses at the **UW.**

Bubble gum: *adj.* Having no substance or depth; sugarcoated.

Budded: *adj.* Under the influence of marijuana. –*n.* Budder: one who partakes in the consumption of marijuana.

Bugged: *adj.* Strange, odd, or unusual; **trippy.**

Bumbaklaat: *n.* Jamaican slang which roughly translates to "bullshit." Also is used as a verb or an interjection.

Bueno: *adj.* Spanish for "good." –*interj.* "All right," or "okay."

Bureau, the: The **Federal Bureau of Investigation** (see **FBI**).

Butch: *adj.* Being a, or having the characteristics of a masculine lesbian.

Bzzt: *interj.* Used to voice disapproval with someone's statement, opinion, or response.

Cabróna: *n.* Spanish for "bitch."

Callscreen: *n.* A closed-circuit **uniview** which is located at the entrance of a residence and is used primarily to screen visitors.

Cancer stick: *n.* A carcinogenic cigarette.

Canny: *n.* Cannabis; marijuana.

Capoeira: *n.* A Brazilian martial arts/dance with heavy African influences. Pronounced "Ka-pway-da."

Casa: *n.* Spanish for "house."

Cascadia: The region consisting of Southern British Columbia, Washington, Oregon, and Northern California.

Cauterizer: *n.* A device that uses a combination of laser light and protein solder to weld a wound shut.

CDC: See **Centers for Disease Control.**

Centers for Disease Control: Founded in 1946 and based in Atlanta, Georgia, the **CDC** is a major division of the United States Public Health Service, and is responsible for many programs, including disease control and prevention. The **CDC** research program is credited with developing the AIDS vaccine.

Central Intelligence Agency: Created by the National Security Act of 1947 in order to replace the **OSS,** the **CIA** oversees work done by America's other intelligence agencies, as well as having its own particular duties, including the conducting of research in various fields of study, providing counsel for the president and the **NSC** on international affairs, monitoring global electronic communications, and conducting **counterintelligence** operations in foreign countries.

Central Processing Unit: *n.* The component of a digital computer that regulates control of its systems and contains its major computational center.

Cha: *n.* Tibetan for "tea."

Chaos theory: Deals with the seemingly random, chaotic fluctuations found in the natural world. For a much more thorough explanation, read James Gleick's Chaos.

Cheshire: *adj.* Having the characteristics of the Cheshire Cat from Alices's Adventures in Wonderland, namely a wide, ear-to-ear grin.

Chica: *n.* Spanish for "girl."

Chihuly: *n.* A glass sculpture designed by Dale Chihuly.

Chill: *adj.* Very good; cool. *−v.* To relax or take it easy.

Chocolatey: *adj.* Of, or resembling chocolate.

Chorizo: *n.* A spicy, red, flavorful sausage used in many Hispanic and Latino cuisines.

CIA: See **Central Intelligence Agency**.

Clearance: *n.* A requirement for having vocal interaction with others while possessing frequencies that fall outside of the acceptable range of **FE**'s for normal citizens (see **FE Act**).

Clobacco: *n.* A **gengineered** synthesis of clove and tobacco.

Clown: *v.* To ridicule or make fun of. *−n.* A ridiculing statement.

Coherent light: *n.* A light source whose waves are in phase and of the exact, same wavelength.

COINTELPRO: The **FBI**'s acronym for its domestic **counterintelligence** program. Originally named COINTELPRO-CP, USA, the first official COINTELPROs were directed towards American communists in the 1950's, and later were focused on the various radical groups which emerged during the 1960's and '70's (see **Black Panther Party**). The methods used by the COINTELPROs ranged from the expected (surveillance, infiltration, etc.) to the bizzare (attempting to coax Martin Luther King, Jr. into commiting suicide). Due to public scrutiny and criticism, the **FBI** officially ended its COINTELPROs in 1971. However, the programs still live on today in other guises, both official (see **DCC**) and unofficial. To find out more about the exciting exploits of this strange and fascinating program, read The COINTELPRO Papers by Ward Churchill and Jim Vander Wall.

Comemos: *v.* Spanish. A conjugation of the verb, "comer," meaning "to eat."

Compañero: *n.* Spanish for "companion" or "friend."

¿Comprendes?: Spanish for "Do you understand?"

Consciousness uploading: *n.* A process in which an organism's consciousness is uploaded into a new host.

Corpo: See **coporate police**.

Corporate police: *n.* As the corporation's power increased, so did their need for security, leading them to develop their own, internally operated police forces. **Corpos** are officially sanctioned by the U.S. government, wield many of the same powers as the local police, and in many cases, have extralegal capabilities that make them more similar to an intelligence agency (see **FBI, CIA, NSA**).

Counterintelligence: *n.* The division of an intelligence agency that is responsible for gathering and databasing information about potential political and military threats, preventing sabotage and subversion, engaging in sabotage and subversion, and deceiving the enemy (see **snakes**).

CPU: *n.* See **Central Processing Unit**.

Cracker: *n.* One who is adept at breaking into computer systems and networks. Also, a derogatory term for a Caucasian.

Crossbreed: *n.* A **gengineered** synthesis of at least two, different, distinct organisms.

Cuidado: Spanish for "be careful."

Cuidate: Spanish for "take care."

Curb: *n.* An illegal narcotic which is a synthesis of long-acting barbiturates, antihistamines, and **meperidine**.

Curbed: *adj.* To be on **curb** or to be extremely intoxicated.

Cybernetic: *adj.* Of, or relating to **cybernetics**.

Cybernetics: *n.* 21st century bionics. Also, the science of control processes and communication, especially in regards to the similarities and differences found in biological and artificial systems. From the Greek word "kybernetes," meaning "steersman."

Cyborg: *n.* A **cybernetic** organism comprised of both biological and artificial systems.

Dancehall: *n.* A type of music originated in Jamaican dancehalls in the late 1970's, when DJ's started to toast and chant over **dub** versions of popular recordings. Soon after, "dancehall" became something of an umbrella term for Jamaican music of the 1980's and 1990's. Classic dancehall artists include Shabba Ranks and Supercat.

Darwinian theory: A theory of evolution put forth by Charles Darwin which revolves around the concept of **natural selection**.

Data mining: *v.* Using computer records to search and/or find information about someone.

DC: See **digital cash**. Also **DC's**.

DCC: See **Domestic Center for Counterterrorism**.

Deevolution: *n.* Gradually evolving towards something that is simpler and less complex, whether it be a lifestyle or a **lifeform**. Purposefully spelled with two "e's" rather than one (devolution), so the word is pronounced "Dee-evolution" instead of the negative sounding "Devil-lution."

Department of Defense: Founded in 1949 (as a by-product of the National Security Act of 1947), the **DOD** controls the Army, Navy, Air Force, and Marines. The largest of all the federal departments, the DOD is **headquartered** in **The Pentagon** and is chaired by the secretary of defense. Usually receives at least 25% of the entire federal budget.

Diazecalm™: A trademark used for a powerful antianxiety drug which relaxes the user without making them drowsy.

Digital cash: *n.* Paper money's electronic replacement, **DC's** are stored as encrypted digital code and accessed via **biochip**. Digital cash was initially met with much resistance, but was readily accepted after terrorists (see **Terror Years**) found a way to house highly infectious diseases within physical cash's cotton fibers.

Dios: *n.* Spanish for "god."

Dis: *v.* To disrespect or ridicule. –*n.* A statement of disrespect.

DOD: See **Department of Defense**.

Domestic Center for Counterterrorism: Quietly set up in the late 1990's, this secretive branch of the **FBI** specializes in domestic **counterintelligence** programs (see **COINTELPRO**). While very active during the first part of the 21st century (see **Terror Years**), DCC operations have greatly declined in the last few decades, in direct proportion to the instances of terrorism. The DCC is now called upon only to handle cases of the utmost importance to national/world security.

Dominica: Officially named the Commonwealth of Dominica, this small country is located in the Lesser Antilles, and is one of the Caribbean's least developed and most mountainous islands.

Dope: *adj.* Cool, very good; fresh.

Doublespeak: *n.* A euphemistic, linguistic code where what is said is altogether different from what is meant or actually occurring. Used especially by political, corporate, and military leaders. Examples would be: when armies are called "peacekeepers," when "friendly fire" kills, or when Western nations bring "democracy" to Latin America, Africa, or Southeast Asia. –*v.* To engage in doublespeak.

Dreadlocks: *n.* Long hair which has become so clumped or tangled together that it assumes the shape of rope or cord. Associated with **rastas**. –*adj.* Dreadlocked: To have or wear dreadlocks.

Dub: *n.* An instrumental remix of a single, often featuring an increased bassline, snippets and pieces of the original vocals, and/or the use of delay and echo effects on the instruments. Though a creation of reggae, dub is now also used by musicians in other genres as well. Classic dub reggae artists include Prince Far I and Augustus Pablo. –*v.* To make a dub.

Dynamical system: *n.* A system whose behavior changes through time.

Eastside: The east side of the greater Seattle area, separated from the west by

Lake Washington. Includes Redmond, Bellevue, **Mercer Island**, Juanita, Kirkland, Medina, Factoria, Newport Hills, Eastgate, and Newcastle.

Echelon: *n*. The most powerful and far-reaching eavesdropping network in the history of the world. In operation since at least the 1990's, overseen in large part by the **NSA**, Echelon can intercept and translate any kind of electronic communication, regardless of its point of origin. Utilizes **voice-rec, keyword,** and **language translation** technologies. Thus, if the word "terrorist" is input into its systems, all communications–whether phone, fax, e-mail, or **uniview**–containing the word "terrorist" will be recorded and monitored in their entirety.

Electrochromic: *adj*. Of, or relating to materials that change color or opaqueness in response to electrical input.

Electromagnetic: *adj*. Of, or relating to **electromagnetics**.

Electromagnetic field: *n*. The field of energy produced when an object or body emits **electromagnetic radiation**.

Electromagnetic radiation: *n*. Energy which is emitted as waves possessing both magnetic and electric components. X-rays, radio waves, FE's, UV rays, and visible light rays are but a few examples of **electromagnetic** radiation.

Electromagnetic spectrum: *n*. The distribution and range of **electromagnetic radiation** (see the table contained within this appendix for more detail).

Electromagnetics: *n*. The science of **electromagnetic radiation** and its related technologies.

EM: *adj*. See **electromagnetic**.

EMF: See **electromagnetic field**. Also, electromotive force.

Emfield: See **electromagnetic field**.

Emvest: *n*. A vest-like device that projects an **EMF** around its wearer to protect them from **electromagnetic** attacks.

Epigem: *n*. Gems or jewelry which are implanted into the skin for cosmetic purposes.

Esposa: *n*. Spanish for "wife."

Esta bien: Spanish for "It's good" or "It's fine."

Estilo: *n*. Spanish for "style."

Excalibur: In **Arthurian** legend, the sword that Arthur Pendragon drew from a stone to make him the king of England.

Existencia: *n*. Spanish for "existence."

Exoskeleton: *n*. An intelligent device that replaced casts and splints and greatly improved the recovery time for broken bones. Like casts, exoskeletons surround the injured bone and keep it in in place. But, as the injury heals, an exoskeleton can gauge how much pressure and mobility the bone can bear, and then adjust its mechanisms accordingly. This helps to prevent muscular atrophy and allows for a much more natural, gradual recovery to occur.

Extractor: *n*. A device or mechanism which can remove a **freeread**.

Extraño: *adj*. Spanish for "strange" or "odd."

Eyemouse: *n*. A device which allows its user to move an indicator or cursor around a **uniview** screen with only their eyes.

Fag: *n*. An homosexual male. Can be both a derogatory and an affectionate term.

FBI: See **Federal Bureau of Investigation**.

Federal Bureau of Investigation: Founded in 1907 (as the Bureau of Investigation), the **FBI** handles cases involving the violation of federal criminal laws. Also has jurisdiction over domestic **counterintelligence** operations and plays a large role in maintaining national and international security. Both the **DCC** and the **Freemon** are special divisions of the **FBI**.

FE: See **frequency emissions, frees**.

FE Act: See **Frequency Emissions Act**.

FE scanner: See **frequency emissions scanner, B/free scanner**.

Fellatio: *n*. Oral sex administered to a penis.

Finalmente: *adv*. Spanish for "finally."

Firewall: *n*. A protective barrier of code and data which is erected to prevent unwanted users from gaining access to a private online network, or to control the outside access privileges a user has while inside of a private network.

Flaky: *adj.* Prone to breaking plans or arrangements; not reliable.
Flashback: *v.* To vividly remember a previous occurrence. Other tenses include flashbacks, flashbacked, flashbacking.
Focus: *n.* To elementary and **precollege** students what a major is to college students.
Foglets: *n.* A fog-like cluster of **nanomachines** that have grouped together (usually in the air) to create an interconnected network which has total molecular control over its surroundings.
Fractal: *n.* A fragmented, irregular, geometric pattern that repeats itself into infinity and whose parts are often the same as its whole.
Frat: *n.* A fraternity.
Freek: *n.* See **Freeker**. –*v.* To do something that would cause or elicit a **freeky** response (i.e., "He's **freeking** him out."). Also, to approach a concept with a new or unusual twist (i.e., "I'm gonna **freek** this rhyme.").
Freeker: *n.* Originally **Freemon** slang for a **frequency emissions violator**, now also used by the general public to describe someone who has strange or unusual thoughts, especially those of a subversive, revolutionary, or reality-shattering nature.
Freekspeek: *n.* The words, terms, and sayings used by a **freeker**.
Freek sweeps: Nickname given to the mass arrests that occurred following the passage of the **FE Act** of 2012. Now also used when the **Freemon** conduct a raid on a **gathering**.
Freeky: *adj.* Exhibiting the unusual, **trippy**, and often dangerous characteristics associated with a **freeker**. –*adv.* freekily.
Freemen: *n.* The name given to freed slaves or those having citizen's rights. Also refers to the governing body of the early **Pilgrims** at **Plymouth Colony**, and the title adopted by some of the **militia** movements of the late 20th/early 21st century.
Freemon: Or FREquency Emissions MONitor(s). A special division of the **FBI**, officially founded in 2012 (see **Frequency Emissions Act**) in order to monitor, database, and investigate potential **frequency emissions violators**. The Freemon have no dress code or uniform, negotiable hours, and are considered by many the most independent and least restricted branch of the **FBI**. The Freemon recruit not only from within the **Bureau** itself, but also from the local police, corporate police (see **corpos**), other federal agencies, and on rare occasions, colleges and workcamps. Each Freemon is awarded a single, government-provided, **cybernetic** enhancement upon completion of their extensive training, and have the option to receive others as their career progresses. The acronym Freemon was said to be coined by **FBI** special agent Dale Hoover in homage to the **freemen** of **Plymouth Colony**, but others have argued that the abbreviated name is nothing more than a clever exercise in governmental **doublespeak**.
Freeread: See **frequency emissions reader**.
Frees: *n.* **Freemon** slang for **freqency emissions**, now also used by the general public. To frequenies what vibes is to vibrations (i.e., "She's got some **trippy** frees.").
Frequency emissions: *n.* The **electromagnetic radiation** produced and emitted by all living organisms which is capable of being measured with an **FE scanner**. The term **FE**, and its related concepts, were unofficially created by **Dr. Adrian Wellor**, and officially created by **Michael Brennan**.
Frequency Emissions Act: Passed in December 2012 in the face of increased terrorist activity (see **Terror Years**), this act was a direct response to the nation's inability to effectively identify potential terrorists before they became an actual threat. Among other things, the FE Act officially created the **Freemon** and also established an acceptable range of FE's for ordinary citizens as defined by the findings of the **Brennan Commission**. Though many arrests occurred in the years following the passage of this legislation (see **freek sweeps**), the FE Act succeeded in bringing a sense of order back to America. Interestingly, similar legislation was passed in the other **technologized** nations at nearly the exact same time.
Frequency Emissions Monitor: See **Freemon**.

Frequency emissions reader: *n.* A microchip about the size of a **biochip** which is encased inside of a **biocompatible** material and injected underneath the skin of its owner's forehead at birth. Once inside the body, the **freeread** painlessly grafts itself onto the front of its owner's skull, and remains there for the duration of its owner's life. The **freeread**'s primary purpose is for the remote monitoring of its owner's **frequency emissions**, though it also has the capacity to receive certain kinds of information. Along with the **biochip**, sometimes referred to as the **Mark of the Beast** .

Frequency emissions scanner: *n.* A device which is capable of detecting, sensing, and transmitting an image of an organism's **frequency emissions** (see **B/free scanner, freeread**).

Frequency emissions violator: See **Freeker**.

Frequential: *adj.* Of, involving, having the nature of, or relating to frequencies. –*adv.* frequentially.

Fresh: *adj.* Cool, very good; **phat**.

Fusion Reactor: *n.* A device which creates a nuclear fusion reaction and can contain and harness its energy. In essence, fusion reactors create, hold, and command the power of a small star. One of the most important scientific breakthroughs of the 21st century.

Futurist: *n.* An individual, usually noted in the fields of academia or literature, whose opinions on the future are held in high esteem.

Gates, the: See **gated community**.

Gated community: *n.* A community (including its grounds, services, property, and entertainment) that can be accessed only by its residents and their guests, and is surrounded by a partition which is patrolled by private security agencies. Living behind the gates usually requires a sizeable income and an adherence to certain, uniform standards as determined by the community's corporate owner(s).

Gathering: *n.* An event which brings people together to be **freeky**.

Gelaform™: A trademark used for a soft, moldable, gelatinous substance used in a variety of applications, both commerical and personal. Other, similar forms of the substance are used in law enforcement equipment and as a shock absorber for structures built within earthquake-prone areas.

Genetically accelerate: *v.* A process by which living cells are made to develop and mature at an exponentially faster rate than normal. A common process in cloning and transplants.

Gengineer: *v.* To engage in genetic engineering or a related form of gene manipulation.

Geostationary: *adj.* Being, or relating to a sattelite whose orbit remains stationary over one part of the Earth.

Ghost: *v.* Slang term for going or leaving. Used in the present tense, even when referring to something that is already gone.

Glimmeringly: *adv.* To have or possess glimmering qualities.

Global Positioning Sattelites: *n.* A ring of orbiting sattelites which can accurately pinpoint the location of any object carrying a **GPS** transmitter. Personal **GPS** technology became especially popular after a missing children scare which happened just prior to the **Terror Years**.

Goggles: *n.* Compact, lightweight eyewear that houses a **uniview** screen in its lenses.

Gogs: *n.* Goggles.

Gonna: Going to.

Gonpo: *n.* Tibetan for "sorceror" or "protector."

Goth: *adj.* Gothic.

Gotta: Got to; have to.

GPS: See **Global Positioning Sattelites**.

Gravity-bound: *adj.* Not equipped with **gravity-shielding**.

Gravity-shielding: *n.* A technology which allows an object to be freed from the constraints of gravity. Operates off of the principle that gravity is an **electromagnetic** wavelength with a higher frequency than that of even gamma and x-rays, thereby allowing it to penetrate and affect all known matter.

Gravity-shielding is achieved through the use of a superconducting disc(s) which can resonate gravity's frequency to a lower level where it can no longer penetrate normal matter. Thus, an object can be "shielded" from gravity's effects. –*adj.* Gravity-shielded.

Graylien: *n.* The gray, black-eyed aliens whose images appear throughout the world. Often said to be the perpetrators of alien abductions.

Grill: *n.* Mouth or face.

GS: See **gravity-shielding**.

Hambre: *n.* Spanish for "hunger."

Hard-light hologram: *n.* A **hologram** whose light is so coherent (see **coherent light**) that it becomes tangible.

Headfield: *n.* A device which projects a protective **emfield** around its wearer's head.

Headquarter: *v.* To establish, or to be a headquarters.

Hella: *adj.* Very; exceptionally. Also, a large quantity.

Hellhounds: *n.* Demon-possessed canines.

Herb: *n.* Marijuana.

Herbal café: *n.* A café-like establishment in which marijuana can be legally served.

Hermano: *n.* Spanish for "brother."

HID: See **high-intensity discharge lamps**.

High-intensity discharge lamps: *n.* A type of lamp which keeps metal halide or mercury vapor under high pressure in order to produce visible light (usually of a bluish hue). Used for a variety of purposes, including vehicular headlights.

Hija: *n.* Spanish for "daughter."

Hill, the: Seattle Freemon term for their headquarters, located in Beacon Hill.

Holgram: *n.* An exact replica of a **3-D** image which is created through the projection of **coherent light** (usually a laser).

Holistic: *adj.* Involving a broad scope of things or perspectives.

Holographic: *adj.* Of, or relating to a **hologram**.

Holoview: *n.* A **holographic**, three-dimensional **uniview**, or a **2-D** uniview screen which can be projected into the air via laser lens.

Holy Grail: Said to be the cup which was drank from during the **Last Supper**, and which was also used by Joseph to collect the blood from Jesus Christ's wounds.

Hoverbike: *n.* A **GS** motorcycle.

Huedo: *n.* Mexican slang for "white boy."

Hui jian: Chinese for "see you later."

Hunny: *adj.* Pleasing; good; sweet.

Huxton, Mason William: Born 1995. The only child of **Ordosoft™** founder W.A. Huxton, and current president of the company. Responsible for the rebuilding of **Mercer Island**.

Huxton, William Alan: Born 1952. Raised in a wealthy family, educated in the nation's finest private schools, Huxton was declared a genius by the age of eight. After receiving an honors degree from Harvard in computer programming, Huxton single-handedly created the revolutionary **operating system** which would become the founding enterprise for his history-making company, **Ordosoft™**. After building **Ordosoft™** into one of world's most powerful corporations, **Huxton** relinquished control of the company to his son (see **Huxton, Mason**) in 2028, and now lives in a miraculous retreat deep within the mountains of southwest Tibet.

Hypersteroid: *n.* A steroid which bulks up and strenghtens a person to nearly inhuman proportions.

Hypocenter: *n.* The subterranean focus point of an earthquake. The epicenter is at the surface, directly above it.

Hypospray: *n.* A device which painlessly pushes a substance through the skin and into the bloodstream and/or cells of an organism. Replaced the hypodermic needle.

I & D: See **isolation and detention**.

Ice: *n.* An offensive or defensive barrier of code. For the best description of ice, read William Gibson's <u>Neuromancer</u>.

Icewall: *n.* Layers of **ice**.

IM: *n.* See **instant message**. *−v.* To send or receive an **instant message**.

Immersible: *n.* A tank which has been filled with a liquid or a substance(see **intelligent fluid**) in order to allow a **virtually** connected individual to be immersed within it, thus giving the individual a greater range of motion and options.

Immersible suit: *n.* A **neural-netted** suit which is specially designed to interact with, and allow its wearer to survive in an **immersible**.

Immortalist: *n.* One who seeks to live forever.

Infobomb: *n.* An informational attack which is transmitted via **electromagentic radiation** and is directed towards an **intelligent system**. *−v.* To attack with, or be attacked by an infobomb.

Information theory: Deals with the way information is encoded and emitted from a source onto a channel, and the means by which that information is received, decoded, and understood.

Instant message: *n.* A private, personal communication sent to another individual(s) while online or in a **virtual** group or setting.

Intelligent fluid: *n.* A **transmorphous** substance which is linked to a **CPU**, and can form itself into a solid, liquid, gas, or plasma upon command.

Intelligent system: *n.* A system which possesses intelligent qualities, such as a human, an android, or a computer.

Interact: *n.* An interactive movie.

IR: *n.* Infrared.

IS: See **immersible suit**.

Isolation and detention: Freemon term for the routine procedure of isolating a **freeker** from other individuals (in order to prevent **memetic** infection) and then detaining them.

Jack: *v.* To make an unauthorized connection to a computer or network (usually followed by "into"). Also, to steal or to take with force. Also, to interfere or mess with; to cause harm or injury to.

Jackshit: *n.* Nothing; zero; zilch.

Jam: *v.* To go or leave, usually in a hurry; to move quickly. Also, to do something extremely well, as in the playing of an instrument. Also, to force an object into something else.

Jesus freak: *n.* A derogatory term for the individuals on street corners who preach about or disseminate information on Christianity.

Johnny-courier: *n.* Someone outfitted with a cerebal augmentation which allows them to carry compressed information within their brains, and who is paid to carry and deliver that information to a destination. The term's origins are found in the William Gibson short story, "Johnny Mnemonic," which is collected in <u>Burning Chrome</u>.

Joint Chiefs of Staff: Comprised of a sole, head chairman and the Navy's, Army's, and Air Force's chiefs of staff, this group is the foremost military authority in the **DOD**.

Juke: *v.* To make a sudden change of direction while being pursued, chased, or defended (as in a football or basketball game). *−n.* A sudden change of direction that throws off a pursuer or defender.

Kata: *n.* A long, white scarf used in certain Tibetan ceremonies.

Kemp: *n.* Thomas Kemper® root beer. The term is used especially when mixed with rum.

Keyword: *n.* A word, or a series of words which a computer system is programmed to take special notice of.

Kickback: *adj.* Relaxed; easygoing or mellow.

Kinda: *adv.* Somewhat.

Language translation: *n.* A technology which allows a word to be instantly translated into another language.

Laserproof: *adj.* Incapable of being penetrated by lasers.

Last Supper: The night before his crucifixtion, Jesus Christ and his disciples shared one, final meal together, called the Last Supper.

Late: *interj.* Used the same as "goodbye" or "see you later."

Latté: *n.* A drink that combines shots of espresso with heated milk. The official beverage of the city of Seattle.

LED: See **Light Emitting Diode**.

Legit: *n.* Legitimate.

Lex: *n.* A Lexus®.

Licoricey: *adj.* Of, or resembling licorice.

LIFE spectrum: *n.* Or Living Incorporate **Frequency Emission** spectrum. The range of electromagnetic radiation in which the **frequential** emissions of all **lifeforms** are contained. The theory behind it looks at life as one, single, physical phenomena whose components differ only in the frequency and wavelength of their emissions. Unofficially created by **Adrian Wellor**, and officially created by no one.

Lifeform: *n.* A form of life; an organism.

Light-emitting diode: *n.* A semiconductor diode which produces visible light. Used in digital displays and electronic equipment (usually as an indicator).

Liquidous: *adj.* Of, possessing, or relating to the qualities of liquid.

Live-feed: *adj.* Possessing a live feed from a broadcasting source.

Loofa: *noun.* A mildly abrasive, natural body sponge.

Lo siento: Spanish for "I'm sorry."

Lynchian: *adj.* Evoking the strange, surreal, and disturbing qualities which are often found within the works of filmmaker David Lynch.

Magnetic resonance imaging: *n.* A technique which utilizes spectroscopic devices and magnetic fields to create detailed images of molecular structures.

Makah: A Native-American peoples of Western Washington.

Mano: *n.* Spanish for "hand."

Maricón: *n.* Derogatory Spanish term for "homosexual."

Mark of the Beast: For the oldest (and probably best) description, read the Book of Revelations in The Bible.

Martinique: An eastern-Caribbean island which is a department of France.

Mazy: *adj.* Like a maze; confusing or complex.

Meme: *n.* An infectious information pattern which resides in the brain and can be transmitted to others. Sayings, slogans, proverbs, icons, images, scientific and religious beliefs, fashions, school lessons, songs, and job training are but a few examples of memes and **memetic** infection.

Memetic: *adj.* Of, or relating to **memetics**.

Memetics: *n.* The application of **Darwinian theory** to the ways in which knowledge is transmitted and received, the ways in which the mind functions and learns, and the manner in which culture develops and progresses. Looks at the transmission of thoughts, ideas, and culture as a virus which infects a brain and can influence it to varying degrees, both in positive and negative ways. Memetic theory was one of the most important scientific breakthroughs of the late 20th century, playing a large role in the proceedings of the **Brennan Commission** and the development of the **FE** technology. The **Freemon** are required to take a comprehensive course in memetics as part of their training.

Mento: *v.* Spanish. A conjugation of the verb, "mentir," meaning "to lie(not be truthful)."

Meperidine: *n.* A synthetic, analgesic drug whose effects are similar to those of morphine. Also known as Demerol®.

Metahuman: *adj.* More than human; superhuman.

Mercer Island: Located in the center of Lake Washington, this land mass sustained extreme damage during the earthquake of 2022 (see the **Quake**), forcing its wealthy inhabitants to permanently evacuate the island. Its foundation and infrastructure utterly destroyed, Mercer Island was declared a disaster area and made off-limits to the general public. It remained this way until 2039, when it was rebuilt by Ordosoft™ (see **Huxton, Mason William**) as the world's first **skyland**, and has since been repopulated by many of its original residents.

Mic: *n.* Microphone.

Micronize: *v.* To cause to be, or to become disentegrated by a **micronizer**.

Micronizer: *n.* A device that uses continuous sound waves to disintegrate non-metallic materials into a fine powder which can then be separated and recycled as raw, industrial material.

Micropore: *n.* A material that contains thousands of minute openings which replicate the effects and properties of pores. Used in clothing, bandages, and various other applications.

Militia: *n.* An army of citizens, such as those used during the **Amercan Revolution**, or an emergency-reserve military force (see **National Guard**). Also, the name taken up by groups of armed, mostly rural Americans who banded together during the late 20th/early 21st century around the common belief that the United States government (see **American Empire**) had been corrupted.

Mobius strip: *n.* A theoretical, 2-D surface which possesses just one side. To visualize it in **3-D**, cut a 1" wide strip across the length of a piece of regular-sized paper, grasp the strip by both of its ends, twist one of its ends halfway around, then glue or tape the strip together at its ends so that it forms a twisty loop (which should resemble an infinity (∞) symbol when it is squeezed together at its center). Now get a pen, pick any point on the loop, draw a continuous line along it, and...What goes around comes back around again.

Mole: *n.* A Mexican dish with a spicy, **chocolatey** flavor.

Molecular assembler: *n.* See **nanomachines**.

Momentito: *n.* Spanish for "moment(short or brief)."

Morning star: *n.* A mace with many, protruding spikes.

Morph: *v.* To smoothly transform or metamorphosize into something else.

MRI: *n.* See **magnetic resonance imaging**.

MUD: See **multi-user domain**.

Multi-user domain: *n.* A **virtual** domain capable of being occupied by multiple users at a single time.

Muy: *adj.* Spanish for "very."

Nanomachines: *n.* The self-replicating, nano-scale devices which are the cornerstone of **nanotechnology**. Can be programmed directly and/or controlled via remote.

Nanotech: *n.* See **nanotechnology**.

Nanotechnology: *n.* The use of self-replicating, nano–scale machines to precisely rearrange atoms at the molecular level. Operates off of the principle that everything is made of the same atoms, and therefore water can be turned into a banana, air into sand, or people into plasma, simply by rearranging their atoms into the proper configurations (see **nanomachines**).

Nap: *v.* To attack with, or be attacked by a **synaptic disruptor**.

Napper: *n.* **synaptic disruptor**.

Nasty: *adj.* Excellent; outstanding. *–idiom.* get nasty: to do something extremely well or with extra flair.

National Guard: Established in 1903 by the Dick Act, redefined by the National Defense Act of 1916, the National Guard can be mobilized by state governors or the president. Usually called on to handle natural disasters, riots, and rebellions. Used extensively during the **Terror Years**.

National Security Agency: Headquartered in Fort Meade, Maryland, the **NSA** is not only the most clandestine of all U.S. intelligence agencies, but it is also the largest. Responsible for spying on foreign communications (see **Echelon**) and for maintaining the security and integrity of U.S. governmental communications.

National Security Council: Created by the National Security Act of 1947, the **NSC** acts as the president's advisor on matters of national security. Its members include the secretaries of defense and state, the vice-president, and the president. The **NSC** also recieves counsel from the **CIA**'s director and the **Joint Chiefs of Staff**'s chairman.

Natural selection: *n.* The ability of a species to adapt to its environment and produce viable offspring which can themselves successfully reproduce, thus ensuring that the genetic traits which allowed the species to survive and propagate will be selected by nature to be passed on to future generations under the same or similar ecological conditions. ((whew!))

Net: *n* The uninet or internet.

Neural net: *n.* A vast, interconnected system of neuron-like stimulators and receptors which transmit and receive informational impulses through their connecting fibers in a manner similar to the human nervous system. –neural-netted: *adj.* To be covered with or surrounded by a neural net.

Neurochemical: *adj.* Of, or relating to the chemicals produced by the nervous system and/or the brain.

Nicaddiction: *n.* An addiction to nicotine.

Ní-hao: *interj.* Chinese for "hello."

NSC: See **National Security Council**.

NSA: See **National Security Agency**.

Office of Strategic Services: In 1942, the office of Coordinator of Information was terminated and replaced by this agency. The **OSS** was responsible for collecting and analyzing information about wartime enemies and their occupied territories, as well as engaging in missions of subversion and sabotage. Was replaced in 1947 by the CIA.

OFT: *n.* See **organic fluoresence testing**.

OM: See **optic microprocessor**.

Omega point: *n.* The end of the universe; the point at which all matter and energy collapses back into infinity.

Op: *n.* An operation (i.e., a law enforcement operation).

Operating system: *n.* The software which controls the various aspects of a computer's operation.

Optic microprocessor: *n.* Uses light rays instead of electrical currents to carry its information, which allows it to process hundreds of thousands of signals in the same amount of time that it takes an electronic microprocessor to produce just one.

Ordosoft™: Founded in 1984 by **W.A. Huxton** in his hometown of Redmond, Washington, **Ordosoft™** quickly rose from a fledgling startup into one of the most powerful corporations in the history of the United States, fueled by the innovative operating system created by its genius founder. To this day, **Ordosoft™** still controls the majority of the world's operating systems, and is now firmly established in many other sectors of the economy as well.

Organic fluoresence testing: *n.* The use of special lights and filters to detect the fluorescent emissions given off by organic residues (fingerprints, hair, semen, etc.). Used especially by law enforcement at the scene of a crime.

OS: See **operating system**.

OSS: See **Office of Strategic Services**.

Overstand: *v.* To understand something completely and fully; to go beyond, to transcend something. – *n.* overstanding.

Panoptic: *adj.* Of, or relating to a **panopticon**.

Panopticon: *n.* A structure or system in which individuals are isolated into small areas or rooms where they can be watched and monitored at all times from a central location.

Papasan: *n.* A wide, rounded, concave piece of furniture which is mounted atop a circular base, covered with a large cushion, and whose frame is usually comprised of wood or bamboo tied with wicker.

Patrón: *n.* Spanish for "boss" or "captain."

Peace: *interj.* Used to say goodbye or farewell.

Pentagon, The: Built in Arlington, Virginia in 1943, this five-sided, five-story structure is where the **DOD** is **headquartered**.

Pero: *conj.* Spanish for "but."

Perp: *n.* Perpetrator.

Peto: *n.* Mexican slang for "penis."

Pharming: *n.* A process in which farm animals are **gengineered** to produce pharmaceutical drugs within their bodily fluids, organs, and/or tissues that can be extracted and transferred to another recipient. –*v.* pharm: to engage in pharming. –*adj.* Something which has been pharmed.

Phase space: *n.* The multi-dimensional expanse used to study the chaotic behavior of **dynamic systems**.

Phat: *adj.* Cool, very good; **dope**.

Phodâng: *n.* Tibetan for "palace."

Photonic: *n.* Of, or relating to photons. As the 21st century progressed, many forms of electronic technology were supplanted by ones of a photonic nature (i.e., **optic microprocessors**, fiber optics, etc.).

Pilgrims: English Separatist Puritans.

Plasma torch: *n.* A portable device that produces extreme heat by harnessing the energy of plasma.

Plasmoidal: *adj.* Having the form or characteristics of plasma.

Plymouth Colony: Established by the **Pilgrims** in 1620 on the shores of Cape Cod Bay.

Porto: *n.* Port wine.

Posthuman: *n.* An intelligent **lifeform** which has evolved beyond the human state.

Potlikker: *n.* A Jamaican dish of stewed greens in a flavorful broth, or the juices which are left over from this or a similar dish.

POV: Point of view.

Precollege: *n.* A school which contains grades 7-12. As college attendance became increasingly more common, high schools were renamed, reorganized, and required to have students declare a **focus** by grade 10.

Promo: *v.* Spanish. A conjugation of the verb, "prometer," meaning "to promise(pledge)."

Prozac®: A trademark for an antidepressant drug which inhibits the body's natural release of seratonin. Also known as fluoexetine.

Psilobrew™: A trademark for a beverage which synthetically replicates some of the effects of psilocybin.

Quake, the: On August 18, 2022, a magnitude 6.6 earthquake was **hypocentered** six kilometers beneath the Earth's surface, directly on the fault-slip area located beneath the city of **Mercer Island**. The tremor caused extreme damage to the island and its structures, and was also responsible for the deaths of hundreds of its residents. Because the quake was so shallow, the greater Seattle area was not nearly as affected, and suffered relatively minor damage.

¿Que pasa?: Spanish for "What's up?" or "What's the matter?"

Quiero: *v.* Spanish. A conjugation of the verb, "querer," meaning "to want(desire)."

Rasta: *n.* See **rastafarian**.

Ras Tafari: King Haile Selassie I, the former emperor of Ethiopia.

Rastafarian: *n.* One who practices or adheres to the principles of Rastafarianism.

Rastafarianism: A movement which originated in Jamaica in the 1930's and is largely centered around Biblical scriptures and the belief that Ethiopia is actually Zion and **Ras Tafari** is God. **Rastas** often live a life away from regular society (in the hills, the woods, etc.) and frequently use marijuana in their ceremonies. To understand more, read Leonard E. Barret's The Rastafarians, or listen to the music of Bob Marley, Peter Tosh, and/or Bunny Wailer.

RCC: See **remote controlled camera**.

Realtime: *n.* The physical, as opposed to the **virtual**, world.

Reanimate: *v.* To bring back from the dead or from a state of utter inactivity.

Rear-view screen: *n.* A screen connected to **live-feed** cameras mounted on the rear, bottom, or sides of a vehicle in order to increase the driver's field of vision.

Reconnaissance Escort Xi: An android **crossbreed** created by the federal government to assist their agents in the gathering of information and the inspection of potentially hostile areas.

Redeye: *n.* A wide, reddish laser light used by police helicopters to scan the area below them for a specific **biochip**, or for those lacking a **biochip**. Also, a late-night trip on an airplane.

Remote controlled camera: *n.* A maneuverable, usually airborne camera which can be controlled from a distance. Ranges in size from the visible (such as baseball-sized **GS** spheres) to the nearly-microscopic (such as small, insect-like devices).

Remote-view: *v.* To view something from a distance, as with an **RCC**, via **signature pattern,** or while **astral travelling.**

Reprogram: *v.* To alter or change the programming of an **intelligent system.** In humans, this is often achieved through the use of **neurochemical** therapy.

REX: See **Reconnaissance Escort Xi.**

Rollers: *n.* Police cars which are on patrol.

Roman Empire: Read <u>The Decline and Fall of the Roman Empire</u> by Edward Gibbon. Some say the empire never died.

Revolutionary War: See **American Revolution.**

Roots: *n.* A type of reggae music that is a synthesis of **ska** and rock n' roll. Developed in Jamaica in the late 1960's, classic roots reggae artists include The Wailers, Culture, and Dennis Brown.

Sativa: *n.* A powerful strain of cannabis.

Sattelink: *n.* A wireless link to a sattelite, primarily used for transmitting or receiving information. *–v.* To use a **sattelink.**

SeaTac: Seatte-Tacoma airport.

Selective Memory Inhibitors: *n.* A substance or apparatus which can be programmed to block or inhibit a specific portion of an individual's memory.

Sensorium: *n.* The full range of one's senses.

Sexsim: *n .* A sexual simulation (see **sim**).

SEV: *n.* Security escort vehicle.

Shag: *v.* British slang for engaging in sexual intercourse.

Shout out: *n.* To mention or thank someone, either verbally or written, at or near the end of an artistic work. Here's an example: Thanks to the reader for reading this far into the text. One way or another, random or planned, you've read enough of the story to reach this point. Glad you could make it. Hope you're enjoying the show. Now back to the regularly scheduled program.

Shyeah: *interj.* Used to express disbelief or skepticism.

Siege Perilous: In Arthurian legend, the seat that was occupied by the knight who was questing for the **Holy Grail.**

Siempre: *adv.* Spanish for "always."

Signature pattern: *n.* The distinctive pattern of **frequency emissions** which can be used to identify a particular individual. An **SP** is essentially a **frequential** fingerprint.

Sim: *n.* A simulation, usually occurring in a **virtual** environment.*–v.* To engage in a simulation.

Ska: *n.* A type of dance music which blends Jamaican rhythms with American R&B. Created in Jamaica in the early 1960's.

Skully: *n.* A beanie.

Skyland: *n.* An island in the sky, kept aloft through the use of **GS** technology. **Mercer Island** was the first, though Manhattan, Alcatraz, and Hiroshima have now also joined the ranks.

Skyscape: *n.* An expanse of aerial scenery which can be seen in one, single view.

Skyvan: *n.* A **GS** van.

Skyview: *n.* A large skylight.

Sleeper: *n.* An intelligence term for an agent who is sent to enemy territory to assume an ordinary, civilian identity, and who remains that way until they are activated into duty by the proper signal.

Sleepscan: *n.* A device which uses **electromagnetic** pulses to induce sleep.

Sleepshot: *n.* A **hypospray** filled with a sleep-inducing substance.

Smartbar: *n.* A concentrated food bar which contains mind-enhancing **neurochemicals** and/or herbs.

Smartdrink: *n.* A liquid which contains mind-enhancing **neurochemicals** and/or herbs.

SMI: See **Selective Memory Inhibitors.**

Snakes: *n.* Individuals or organizations who knowingly engage in practices of treachery and deception. Some examples would be: when an undercover cop poses as a drug buyer to buy illicit narcotics, when a publication is set up for the purpose of databasing or entrapping its subscribers (i.e., magazines about possessing or growing marijuana, or catalogs that sell books on how to make bombs and poisons), or when an **FBI** informant infiltrates an organization, rises to a level of respectability within the group, and then suggests to the other members that they do something illegal or ill-advised, such as robbing banks or shooting cops (as strange as this seems, it was done to both the **Black Panther Party** in the 1960's and the Viper-**militia** in the 1990's).

Sopa: *n*. Spanish for "soup."

Sorta: *adv*. Somewhat.

Soy: *verb*. Spanish. A conjugation of the verb, "ser," meaning "to be" or "am."

SP: See **signature pattern.**

SPD: Seattle Police Department.

Spliff: *n*. A marijuana cigarette; a **joint.**

SST: See **supersonic transport.**

Sterilization: A medical procedure which became increasingly common in the 21st century as a means of population control. Encouraged worldwide through the payment of credits or the granting of tax breaks, **sterilization** permanently takes away an individual's ability to make babies, both physically and legally.

Strange attractors: *n*. Nonlinear **fractals** existing in **phase space** which describe the path a **dynamical system** takes when it becomes chaotic (see **chaos theory**).

Streetcam: *n*. A street-mounted camera. Streetcams are found on nearly street in the city, and most are publicly-accessible via the **uninet.**

Stun gun: *n*. A type of non-lethal weapon which renders its victim unconscious or incapacitated via electric shock.

Subs: *n*. Subliminal messages or information.

Sup: *n*. An upwards nod used to greet or check someone. –*v*. To raise the head slightly in order to greet or acknowledge someone.

Supersonic transport: *n*. An aircraft which can travel faster than the speed of sound.

Suspended animation: See **biostasis.**

SWAT: Special weapons and tactics. A specialized unit of the police force used for a variety of situations, including raids and riot control.

Synaptic disruptor: *n*. A weapon that emits an **electromagnetic** pulse which affects the normal functioning of an organism's nervous system.

Tambien: *n*. Spanish for "also."

Tashidelek: *interj*. A Tibetan greeting which roughly translates to "good fortune."

Tattoodecal: *n*. An image or design which is permanently synthesized into the skin. Unlike a tattoo, a tattoodecal does not need to be comprised of ink, and can be made from a near-infinite selection of colors, materials, and substances. –*v*. To administer or receive a tattodecal.

Te amo: Spanish for saying "I love you" to a lover.

Technodevils: *n*. Those who use technology to oppress, control, or suppress others.

Technologize: *v*. To develop technology in a society, country, or culture. *adj*. technologized (used exactly in the same context as industrialized).

Technophobic: *adj*. A fear of recent or advanced technology.

Technorganic: *adj*. A technological construct which resembles a biological organism.

Te nada: Spanish for "it's nothing" or "no problem."

Teleport: *v*. To disappear from one point, span space and/or time, and reappear again at another point.

Telepresent: *adj*. Being in attendance in a **virtual** domain or setting.

Tell: *n*. A sign, expression, or gesture which reveals someone's intentions or true nature.

Technocyte: *n*. A nanomachine used to patrol, investigate, or take action within an organism's bloodstream.

Tengo: *v*. Spanish. A conjugation of the verb, "tenir," meaning "to have(possess)."

Terror Years: The period from roughlty 2006 to 2013 in which an unprecedented amount of domestic terrorism occurred, both in America and the other **technologized** nations. These tumultous times led to the passing of the Frequency Emission Act.

Thought Police: *n.* Any organization which seeks to monitor or control people's thoughts. Used especially in regards to the **Freemon**, who literally fit the definition. To understand the term's historical origins, read George Orwell's <u>1984</u>.

3-D: *adj.* Three-dimensional.

Tipsets: *n.* A device which fits over the fingertips and aids in the navigation and control of a **virtual** environment.

Toon: *n.* A cartoon and/or a character in a cartoon.

Tracers: *n.* The visual resonances an object in motion leaves behind it. Intensified when the object emits light, or when its viewer is experiencing the effects of a hallucenogenic substance.

Transhumanism: *n.* The belief that intelligent life should not be limited to human form, and the pursuit of a **posthuman** existence through scientific and technological means. –*n.* Transhumanist: One who subscribes to or pursues the principles of transhumanism.

Transmorphous: *adj.* Able to change shape or form. –*n.* transmorph: An object or body which has transmorphous properties.

Trench: *n.* A trenchcoat.

Triballet: *n.* A term for a style of music and dance that combines African drums (congas, bongos, etc.) and rhythms with classical ballet compositions and moves.

Trippy: *adj.* Having strange, unusual, or **freeky** characteristics.

Turbofan: *n.* Relatively noiseless, solar/electric-powered engines which propel **GS** vehicles.

Twisty-fit: *n.* A ring made of a **transmorphous** material which can adjust itself to fit the finger of its wearer by twisting the control dial located upon its band.

2-D: *adj.* Two-dimensional.

U-dub: See **University of Washington.**

Un: *indefinite article.* Spanish for "a" or "an."

Unie: *n.* Short for **uniview** or **uninet.**

Uninet: *n.* A single, gigantic network of people, organizations, places, and things through which nearly all non-physical communication occurs. Accessed via **uniview**, the **uninet** contains a near-infinite amount of databases, resources, entertainment, and information. Music, videos, games, software, applications, etc. are not physically purchased anymore, but instead are bought online and downloaded into an indidual's personal database, which can be accessed from any **uniview** with the proper password/**biochip**. The internet's successor.

Uninhibitor: *n.* A substance or apparatus which releases a portion of memory that is normally inhibited or irretrievable.

University of Washington: Founded in 1861 and located in Seattle, the **UW** is one of the nation's most respected medical and research institutes. The birthplace of the **FE** technology.

Uniview: *n.* A combination television/computer/telephone/ radio/answering machine with access to the **uninet**. Created in the early 21st century, univiews come in multiple shapes and sizes, everything from rings to **wallscreens.**

UV: *n.* A **uniview.** Also, ultraviolet light.

UW: See **University of Washington.**

Vámanos: Spanish for "We go," or "Let's go."

Vato: *n.* Mexican for "man," "guy," or "dude."

Verdad: *adj.* Spanish for "true(factual)."

Virtual: *n.* The informational, computer world as opposed to the actual, "real" world.

Virtuality: *n.* The quality or fact of being **virtual.**

Virtual reality: *n.* Reality as expressed through a computer- controlled medium.

Vocal confirmation: *n.* A feature used in **voice recognition technology** to inform the user that their command was heard by the computer.

Voice-rec: See **voice recognition technology.**

Voice recognition technology: *n.* A technology which allows a computer to understand a human voice just as it would lines of code, the strokes of a keyboard, or the click of a mouse.

Voicewave: *n.* A vocal fingerprint used mostly for security purposes.

Von Neumann probe: *n.* A device capable of interstellar travel which contains **nanomachines** that have the ability to replicate themselves from their surrounding environment. The concept is credited to mathematician Joseph von Neumann, although author Philip K. Dick predated him on the concept nearly ten years earlier in a short story entitled "Autofac." (Which can be found within The Collected Short Stories of Philip K. Dick, vol. 4)

VTOL: Vertical takeoff and landing.

Vulturic: *adj.* Having the qualities associated with a vulture. *–adv.* vulturically.

VR: See **virtual reality.**

Wallscreen: *n.* A thin, wall-mounted **uniview.**

Wannabe: *n.* One who desires to be something that they are not.

Wellor, Dr. Adrian Malcom: A scientist involved in the **Brennan Commission** who mysteriously disappeared in 1999, and has not been heard from since. Some rumors say that he is alive, others that he is deceased, but nothing has been confirmed. Unofficially the creator of the **FE** technology (see **Brennan, Michael**).

Westside: The west side of the greater Seattle area, separated from the east by Lake Washington. Includes Downtown Seattle, Beacon Hill, Queen Anne, Central District, Capitol Hill, Rainier Valley, University District, Fremont, Wallingford, Montlake, West Seattle, Ballard, Greenwood, Northgate, Sand Point, Lake City, Mt. Baker, and Ravenna.

Wetvac: *n.* A vacuum cleaner which can suck up liquid.

What: *n.* Something. Usually used with "or" (i.e., "He must be **freeking,** or what!").

White noise: *n.* Electric or acoustic sounds whose intensity is uniform across all frequencies inside of a given range.

White noise generator: *n.* A device which can block out sound within or ouside of a specific radius through the use of **white noise.**

Wo dong le: Chinese for "I understand."

Workcamps: *n.* The natural evolution of the prison system within a capitalistic society, wherein inmates are paid far below minimum-wage to perform various types of labor for businesses and corporations. By earning enough credit, inmates can "buy" themselves out of the workcamps.

Wristcom: *n.* A watch-sized **uniview.**

Xanadeux: *n.* The name given to **Mason Huxton's Mercer Island** estate and the artificial intelligence that controls it.

Xandy: *n.* A **Xanadeux** android.

Xiexie: Chinese for "thank you."

Yin-yang: *adj.* Evoking balance and equilibrium, or having visual elements which are reminiscent of the yin-yang symbol.

Yo: *pron.* Spanish for "I."

Zoomcam™: A trademark used for a unique camera design which allows for extremely-high resolution photos to be taken from a great distance.

THE FE SPECTRUM

Δ / δ
Delta(Purple)

Θ / θ
Theta(Blue)

A / α
Alpha(Green)

B / β
Beta(Yellow)

Γ / γ
Gamma(Orange)

Ω / ω
Omega(Red)

THE ELECTROMAGNETIC SPECTRUM

Name	Frequency, Hz*	Wavelength, m*
Direct current (DC)	0	∞
Power (machinery, power lines, etc.)	10-100	$3 \times 10(7) - 3 \times 10(6)$
Induction heating	$10(4)$	$3 \times 10(4)$
Long-wave radio	$10(5)$	3000
AM radio	$10(6)$	300
Short-wave radio	$10(7)$	30
Television, FM radio	$10(8)$	3
Radar	$10(9) - 10(10)$	$3 \times 10(-1) - 3 \times 10(-2)$
Microwaves	$10(10) - 10(11)$	$3 \times 10(-2) - 3 \times 10(-3)$
Infrared (IR)	$10(12) - 10(14)$	$3 \times 10(-4) - 3 \times 10(-6)$
Visible light spectrum	$10(15)$	$3 \times 10(-7)$
Ultraviolet (UV)	$10(16) - 10(18)$	$3 \times 10(-8) - 3 \times 10(-10)$
X-rays	$10(18) - 10(21)$	$3 \times 10(-10) - 3 \times 10(-13)$
Gamma rays	$10(21) - 10(22)$	$3 \times 10(-13) - 3 \times 10(-14)$
Cosmic rays/photons	$10(23)$	$3 \times 10(-15)$
Gravity	$<10(23)$	∞

* Exponents placed in parentheses ( )

FREQUENCY CLASSIFICATION (300 GHz - 30 Hz)

Frequency	Classification
Extremely High Frequencies (EHF)	30 - 300 GHz
Super High Frequencies (SHF)	3 - 30 GHz
Ultra High Frequencies (UHF)	300 - 3000 MHz
Very High Frequencies (VHF)	30 - 300 MHz
High Frequencies (HF)	3 - 30 MHz
Medium Frequencies (MF)	300 - 3000 KHz
Low Frequencies (LF)	30 - 300 KHz
Very Low Frequencies (VLF)	3 - 30 KHz
Voice Frequencies (VF)	300 - 3000 Hz
Extremely Low Frequencies (ELF)	30 - 300 Hz

Hz = Hertz
KHz = Kilohertz
MHz = Megahertz
GHz = Gigahertz

SHOUT OUTS AND THANK YOU'S

~First and foremost, I want to thank the recipients of book #'s 1 and 1,000–my mother, Sherry, and my father, David. It goes without saying, on so many levels, that I wouldn't be here without you two. Thank you both for bringing me into this world and for all of the guidance, wisdom, understanding, overstanding, and love that you provided for me once I was here. I am because of you. Thank you. I love you both.

~My sister, Amber(Thanks for being my buddy through all the years, Ambie!); my brothers, Mason(Does not the Flame of Orion burn like a star? Stay strong and wise, Mase) and Jason(Fellow wild-child, don't ever stop smiling and having fun!); Gramma Kay and Grandma Chela(I love you both very much...and I still have the blankies you guys made me!), Harold(For all of the love, support, and advice–thank you, from the bottom of my heart), Uncle Hondo(Rasta! Stay up, defiant one) and Kay, the Ortega family(Mark, Louie and Yolanda, Sammy and Gloria, Carl and Janis–thanks for always being in my life), the Stoefen family(We love and remember you, Jimmy–thanks for keeping watch on me from above), the Lowe family(Jeff and Emily–thanks for making me a part of your family), Kim and Andre, and the Stone family(Cathy and Dave–thanks for opening me up to the world of art. Hi Rachael, Sev, and Kiki!).

~Kita, you will ∞always∞ have a special place in my heart. Thank you for everything! I wish U heaven, angel–you deserve it.

~Dug(Soulbrothers since 1975. Keep shining your light on the world, Supes!), Stroms(My brother from Sactown to Seatown–good luck in the Sunny Bay Area, GL), and Mighty Mo(See you at Wayne Manor, blud–and don't forget the pizza...).

~Lexi, thank U 4 being U. U're a beautiful soul, and Eye am so thankful that life's vibrations have drawn us 2gether 1nce again. Chaos, love, and ∞4ever∞...want 2 Xplore?

~The Sactown crew–Benji(March, 2051–meet you at Tosh's), S!(Thanks for kickin' it with me all those times at 46th Street, Seth. You're a true friend. Hi Katie!), Swanny(I'm glad you found what you were looking for, E! Keep smiling!), Tim(See you in SoCal soon), Demetrius(Harlow's, anyone?), Mil(Don't forget, Mac–tread the path carefully...), Mobl(Good luck with your new love, Emily!), and Sierra(I told you I'd get you the Blvd.! Hi Kristen!).

~Jasiri Media Group–Jon(Thanks for the friendship and the inspiration, Word. Let's keep the collaboration going. Looking forward to Source of Labor '99...), Erika(What's up, shady lady?), Upendu(Keep the beats comin', Upe!) and Upie(You have been brought forth by two powerful souls, little one!).

~The Knight family–Sunny(I am so glad that you and Mark found one another–you two are truly meant for each other. What that ringing sound? Wedding bells...?), Dave, Robin, and Breezie.

~The Stromberg family–Ed(Plastic Man™), Dorothy, and Dan.

~The Panetto family–Ray, Minnie, Ray Jr.(Get 'em , Reddi!), Jennifer, Lynda, Samantha, and Kylie.

~The Kaplan family–Bonnie(Thanks for all of the encouragement, B), Rachel, and Julian.

~The "Dug" family–Rosellyn, Anthony(Thanks for reading <u>Water and Earth</u>, Ant!), and Aileen.

~The Coronetz family–Kathy, Nick, and Gene.

~The Lee & Associates family–Joe and Penny, Craig and Cathy, Diane, Pug, Chris, and Brian.

~The Viewridge PCC™ customers(Thank you ALL for the support and well-wishes over the past year and a half–I wish I had the room to mention all of you!).

~The Viewridge PCC™ staff(Especially Mitzi Adler, for all of her assistance and hard work in bringing the book to Viewridge. Thanks, Mitzi!).

~Steve Malone at the University of Washington Geophysics Department(For sharing with me his indispensable knowledge of earthquakes and seismology. Much appreciated, Malone.).

~Judith Roche, Lauren Schwartz, and the 1999 Bumbershoot® Bookfair jurors(Thanks for the opportunity!).

~Reggie Watts and Maktub(Whose frequential sounds continue to amaze me–you guys ever considered doing a soundtrack for a book?), Vitamin D and B-Self, and Michael Tomlinson(Keep up the positivity, my friend!).

~The Artist Formerly Known As Prince, Maxwell, Terence Trent D'arby, Tracy Chapman, Peter Tosh, Creedence Clearwater Revival, Outkast, Earth Wind and Fire, Tesla, Stevie Wonder, and Lauryn Hill for the musical inspiration.

~Philip K. Dick, Aldous Huxley, George Orwell, Leslie Marmon Silko, Khalil Gibran, Carlos Castaneda, Alex Haley, El-Hajj Malik El-Shabazz, Lewis Carrol, and William Gibson for the literary inspiration.

~Marshall McLuhan for the multimedia inspiration.

~Grant Morrison, Alan Moore, Stan Lee, JM DeMatteis, Steve Gerber, Kurt Busiek, Neil Gaiman, and Dave McKean for the comic book inspiration.

~George Lucas, Terry Gilliam, Ridley Scott, Paul Verhoven, Spike Lee, Woody Allen, John Carpenter, and Sam Raimi for the cinematic inspiration.

~J.D. and N.C.(The screenplay is on its way...)

~Life/Goddess/God/Gods/The Universe/Everything–thank you for allowing me this opportunity to conceive and create. It's been an amazing experience, and I am truly thankful to you for inspiring me to bring my conceptual baby into this world, and for providing me with the resources to do it independently.

~Oh yeah, and to myself–smile...you did it. :)

PEACE!!!!

Always read the fine print.

ABOUT THE AUTHOR

Joshua Ortega was born and raised in Sacramento, California, and now lives in Seattle, Washington.
He is currently working on the ((FREQUENCIES)) screenplay, comic book adaptation, and its sequel, VIBRATIONS.

ORDERING INFO

To order ((FREQUENCIES)),
please send a check or money order for $19.99 to:

Omega Point Productions
PO Box 85690
Seattle, WA
98145-1690

Please add $4.00 shipping and handling for the first book,
and $2.00 for each additional book.
WA state residents add 8.6% sales tax.
Make all checks payable to: Omega Point Productions

To order ((FREQUENCIES)) t-shirts, posters, and/or
other merchandise, visit the Omega Point Productions
website at:
www.omegapp.com

Coming next millenium:

~VIBRATIONS~

The evolution of the
((FREQUENCIES)) saga.

Still here? I was just about to leave   Well, at least this gives me a chance to say goodbye. Take care, and I'll see ya next century Peace

ομεγα ποιντ
προδυχτιονσ

This is the end.

This is the beginning...

Visualize a void, the alpha point of this universe, then
the big bang from nothing into nothing, creation
exploding forth creating something, time/eons passing
in seconds of relativity, zoom in on a lone comet/baby
solar system shooting out into space, Earth's creation,
spins for a few seconds in front of us and evolves, pull
back so our POV is of the totality of the universe, a long
second passes, it begins to shrink where only a void
surrounds again, it gets smaller, faster, and shrinks into
whence it came, the omega point.

This is the end.

This is the beginning...

ομεγα ποιντ
προδυχτιονσ

∞